P9-EIG-259

THE

SEVENTH

QUEEN

THE SEVENTH QUEEN

A NOVEL

GRETA KELLY

HARPER Voyager

An Imprint of HarperCollins Publishers

Also by Greta Kelly

THE FROZEN CROWN

This is a work of fiction. Names, characters, places, and incidents are products of the author's imagination or are used fictitiously and are not to be construed as real. Any resemblance to actual events, locales, organizations, or persons, living or dead, is entirely coincidental.

THE SEVENTH QUEEN. Copyright © 2021 by Greta Meier. All rights reserved. Printed in the United States of America. No part of this book may be used or reproduced in any manner whatsoever without written permission except in the case of brief quotations embodied in critical articles and reviews. For information, address HarperCollins Publishers, 195 Broadway, New York, NY 10007.

HarperCollins books may be purchased for educational, business, or sales promotional use. For information, please email the Special Markets Department at SPsales@harpercollins.com.

Harper Voyager and design are trademarks of HarperCollins Publishers LLC.

FIRST EDITION

Designed by Angela Boutin
Map design by Nick Springer/Springer Cartographics LLC
Frontispiece © Nate Allred/Shutterstock

Library of Congress Cataloging-in-Publication Data has been applied for.

ISBN 978-0-06-295699-6

21 22 23 24 25   LSC   10 9 8 7 6 5 4 3 2 1

For Lorelei and Nadia,
may you be as wild and brave as the women in these pages,
and may you always have the courage to be yourselves

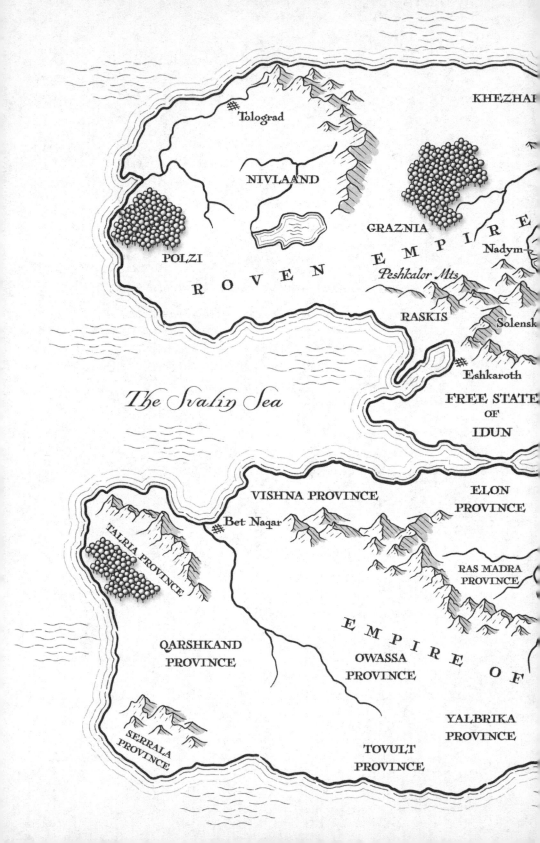

The Lands of Kinvara

SWITZKIA

RAVESH

KIZUOKA
PROVINCE

The
Kinnet
Sea

Khan-e-Fet

SHAZIR
PROVINCE

AVSHIR
PROVINCE

HBRAH
VINCE

NUKUSHBET
PROVINCE

TAMETT
PROVINCE

CALORMAÑA PROVINCE

VISHIR

MINOSSOS
PROVINCE

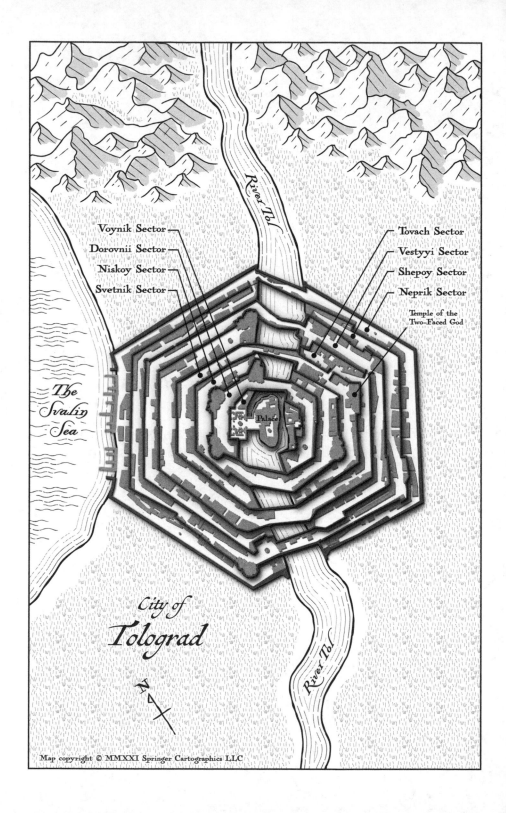

Voynik Sector
Dorovnii Sector
Niskoy Sector
Svetnik Sector

Tovach Sector
Vestyyi Sector
Shepoy Sector
Neprik Sector

Temple of the
Two-Faced God

The
Svalin
Sea

Palace

River Tol

River Tol

City of
Tolograd

N

Map copyright © MMXXI Springer Cartographics LLC

THE LANDS OF KINVARA

SERAVESH

Solenskaya (capital of Seravesh)
Nadym
Kavondy
Peshkalor Mountains

FREE STATE OF IDUN

Eshkaroth

ROVEN EMPIRE

Tolograd (capital city of Roven)
Polzi
Nivlaand
Khezhar
Graznia
Switzkia
Raskis

EMPIRE OF VISHIR

Bet Naqar (capital city of Vishir)
Talria Province
Vishna Province
Qarshkand Province
Serrala Province
Owassa Province

Tovult Province

Yalbrika Province

Ras Madra Province

Elon Province

Kashbrah Province

Avshir Province

Nukushbet Province

Minossos Province

Tamett Province

Shazir Province

Khan-e-Fet (a mountain in Shazir Province)

Kizuokan Province

Calormañan Province

SEAS

The Svalin Sea (body of water to the west of Idun)
The Kinnet Sea (the sea between Kizuoka and mainland Vishir)

1

HELLO, MY LOVE."

All the room's meager heat died at those three words. Even the fire in the hearth seemed to dim. But I didn't need light to recognize the monster responsible for murdering thousands of my people.

My love? He could only mean it as an insult—a way to bait me—but I was no child, and I wouldn't give in to my anger. Not yet. I raised my chin in defiance. "Hello, Radovan."

He smiled, the expression straining his waxen face, as if he were more magic and clay than flesh and blood. Radovan raised both hands, long fingers splayed as if to show the many riches of his stolen empire. "Welcome to Tolograd."

For all the long years of conquest, the decades of Roven pillaging and theft, the room around us told a drab tale of privation and strife. Not at all what I'd expected. It was a simple gray-walled bedroom with narrow, arrow-slat windows and a few dusty bookshelves. The only glimmer of finery in sight was the bed upon which I sat. Its crimson canopy was made of plush Graznian velvet and the sheets were soft and warm against my skin—sheets that I was clutching to my throat like some wooly-brained damsel.

I forced my hands down, pushing past the revolting realization that I had been changed and bathed while unconscious. So despite the fact that I only wore a thin white shift, I stared at Radovan as if I were swathed in silk and glittered with every jewel in my kingdom.

No—empire.

A metal chain—links as thick as a dog's collar—shifted when I moved. I didn't need to look down to know that an emerald the size of a man's fist hung between my breasts. It was Radovan's birthday present to me, this damned necklace. And the fact that I just happened to be wearing it on the very day I was abducted was too suspicious to be coincidence.

Those final moments in Vishir flooded my mind: Armaan's confused, pained expression as he died in my arms; the screams, the wind, the blood soaking my face and souring my tongue; the searing pain in my skull as I was knocked out . . .

No. Not now.

"I was beginning to worry," Radovan said, clasping his hands behind his back when I didn't speak. "I thought you might have been damaged when you didn't wake up this morning."

This morning? My gaze tripped to the night-darkened windows. How long had I been out?

"I'm sure that would have been terrible for you," I replied, the feigned indifference in my voice somewhat spoiled as I searched the room. I needed something—a knife, a club—anything I could use to rid the world of him. But there was nothing. I remembered a ghost-girl promising to help me at one point, but even she had vanished under Radovan's stare.

"It really would have. I've been looking forward to speaking with you for some time." Radovan's head tilted to one side, studying me like I was something strange, something wild.

Truth was, I *am* strange and wild. But I was *more* than that. I was dangerous: a witch, a warrior, a queen. And I didn't need a blade to fight this man.

I shoved the covers back. Rose. And though the floor was

cold beneath my feet, it was nothing compared to the glacial ice surging through me, filling my veins with power and might and the promise of violence. This was going to end. Now.

"Vitaly."

I dove deeper, stretching for the silent storm in my heart where chaos reigned and witchcraft raged. Magic filled my ears with the howl of frigid wind, and the room grayed around me.

Power leapt deep in my chest . . .

And hit a wall. Crashed, rather, and at high speed, it was a brutal collision. My magic crumpled against an internal barrier that shouldn't exist. Because the power that conjured that barrier wasn't my own. It was Radovan's.

The metal chain about my neck twitched, its links writhing across my skin with a warning that was too late to heed. Pain lanced through my skull and burned my chest where the necklace lay. It thundered with the sound of bells that blurred my vision. My knees buckled. I gasped, lurching for the edge of the bed to keep myself from falling.

Radovan's laughter filled my ears. I stared up at him through watery eyes, barely keeping a curse behind my lips.

"Oh dear," he said, closing the distance between us with a few long steps. "You didn't try to use your magic, did you? I'm afraid that won't be allowed."

"What did you do to me?" I gasped.

"I didn't do anything to you, Askia," he replied. "You must know that I don't mean to harm you."

The pain said otherwise. "Then why am I here? Why did you kill Armaan and Ozura to get to me?"

Radovan's face rippled with shock, as if the accusation was insulting. "I didn't kill Queen Ozura."

"Your man killed her." The image of Count Dobor's dagger plunging into Ozura's chest shot through my mind. "She died because of you."

His mouth folded into an understanding frown. "That dagger wasn't meant for her—you know that."

I'd have screamed at his words were it not for the memory of Ozura's ashen face, of her eyes tight with fear as she bled out on the temple floor. Of her promise.

I will serve you better when I see you again.

Radovan reached toward my face, but he brought himself up short when I stiffened. "You must feel her loss very keenly." He sighed. "It was a regrettable end for a truly remarkable woman. And Armaan as well. He was a good man. It's a shame he had to die."

"He didn't *have* to die."

"Of course he did. He married you, Askia. I told him not to, but he did it anyway. The poor fool just couldn't stop himself, I suppose," he said with an almost rueful chuckle as if my skin wasn't still slick with the phantom stain of Armaan's blood and Ozura's dying oath. "Not that I blame him. You are quite lovely."

An animal snarl tore from my throat. My hand moved without my consent, and my balled fist hurtled toward Radovan's jaw.

And collided with nothing. My arm locked, caught by a hand that I couldn't see and couldn't fight. I pulled back on instinct, but the invisible hand only tightened, refusing to release me. It clenched down harder. Harder. Until I felt my tendons snap against muscle and my bones bend. I grit my teeth to contain a scream of pain. Of rage. But I couldn't stop the hurt, and my fury was no match for his power.

Radovan's eyes glittered as they flickered to my fist, frozen a hairsbreadth away from his face. All his stolen magic burrowed through me with a knife-sharp pain that stabbed into my arm. Without moving a muscle, he shoved my hand down and locked my body into statue-like stillness. My mind railed against it—against the helplessness. Lady Night save me, the howling wind outside would topple me.

I'd have taken that frigid wind over the nightmare before me.

"That's better," Radovan said, as I came to an involuntary attention. "I had hoped our first meeting wouldn't be so . . . fraught, but I suppose it is to be expected. You've no doubt heard horror stories about me your whole life. Though I confess it is tiresome to always be seen as the villain." He shook his head with such a put-upon expression that the urge to sneer was overwhelming. Too bad I was still frozen.

"I am not a bad man, Askia. I'm not a monster. And I'll prove it to you," he vowed. "Roven is your home. Tolograd is your home. And if you can't see that yet?" He shrugged. "You will soon enough. Now, I know you must be exhausted, but before I allow you to retire, I do have some guidelines for your new life here.

"As you have discovered, you won't be able to use your magic. The enchanted chain about your neck is preventing that."

I blinked. It was all I could do. Even as the muscles of my neck strained to look down—that much movement was beyond me.

"Surely you can guess what that stone truly is?" Radovan's fingers slid across my shoulder, and the thin fabric of my nightgown was no protection against the revulsion I felt at his touch. Slowly, like he was relishing my reaction, Radovan lifted the chain, holding the necklace high enough for me to see. "My Aellium stone—glamoured, of course. Not that it needs to be anymore."

One of his long thumbs wiped across the gem, and a sticky film of magic shuddered across my face. The brand on my back burned in recognition as the stone's heart turned black, its edges shimmering evergreen in the firelight.

An Aellium stone. The magical amplifiers that were used by Shazir zealots to force a witch into exposing themselves. And used by Radovan to steal magic from his wives. And he'd given it to me. But—

But if the chain was suppressing my magic, then how had I seen that ghost-girl? The one who promised to help me escape. My gaze strained toward the edges of the room, but I couldn't sense the ghost anywhere. Couldn't sense *any* ghosts.

"The chain's enchantment is quite thorough," Radovan continued. "You won't be able to remove it—only I can do that. It will burn you if you try," he said slowly, gravely, as if I were a child playing with fire.

He placed the stone gently onto my chest, a smile playing on his lips as he studied my face. "So many questions. I can see them swimming in your eyes. Even now, alone and terrified, you're soaking up information. Trying to find a way to gain an upper hand. But you can't, my dear. And to ensure you take this lesson to heart, a demonstration."

The stone warmed on my chest a half second before his magic seized my left hand. Each tiny muscle tensed so fast my joints cracked as my hand twitched and rose. My eyes flew wide, but I was powerless against his silent command. Powerless to move, to stop. My fingers closed about the stone . . . and pulled.

Faint blue light crackled down the chain like the molten kiss of lightning. It surrounded the stone, protecting it. Punishing me. Heat seared through skin, through muscle and tendon. I couldn't even scream as the fire kissed my bones with forked tongues of invisible pain. More than pain.

Agony danced through me, pillaging and burning for a second that stretched to eternity. My very marrow boiled. Until, after an age, my fingers opened and the stone fell from my blistered, bleeding palm.

Radovan cupped my hand in his. Magic licked across the wound, and in a blink the pain was gone. The wound now felt days old but was still red and livid. A reminder, I thought, as if the meaty scent of my own burning flesh wasn't enough of one.

Radovan searched my face a moment longer, then chuckled

at whatever he saw. "We are going to have so much fun, my dear."

He angled his face toward the door behind him. "Enter."

The door opened at his command, revealing four armed guards waiting in the hall outside. A strange circular tattoo marred each of their left cheeks. One of them, a captain by the cut of her uniform, stepped forward. She had a round face with high, flat Khezhari cheekbones and smooth terra-cotta skin. She looked me up and down, her dark gaze carefully blank.

All at once his magic evaporated. My muscles went slack, and I stumbled, barely catching myself before I hit the floor. Which was surely the point.

Radovan just smirked. "Captain Qadenzizeg."

The woman in the doorway snapped the gleaming heels of her black boots together with a click that echoed through the room. "Yes, Your Majesty?"

"Please escort Princess Askia—"

"Queen," I snapped, drawing an amused look from Radovan and an outraged one from the captain.

"Really, my dear. I know you consider yourself the queen of Seravesh, but is now really the time to argue semantics?"

"I don't *consider* myself the queen of Seravesh. I *am* the queen of both Seravesh and Vishir. And if I wanted to argue semantics, I'd insist upon you calling me empress, for that is the title Armaan was going to grant me before you murdered him."

Radovan's damned smile didn't even flicker. "Very well. Captain, please escort Her Majesty Queen Askia up to her room."

"Red protocol?" the captain asked.

I wasn't sure what that was supposed to mean, but the disgusted way she was staring at me made my hackles rise.

"Oh no," Radovan crooned. "That won't be necessary. If there is one thing I trust about my dearest queen, it is her will to live."

I felt confusion chase across my face, but pressed my lips

shut. I needed to get to the room he promised. Get some space to regroup. Plan.

His watery green eyes danced as he lifted my still-throbbing hand to his lips, daring me to react, to strike. But I wouldn't give him the satisfaction. I locked my body woodenly in place as he kissed my hand and endured, like I had always endured. Like I *would* always endure until I got the chance to finish this once and for all. "I shall see you soon, my love," Radovan whispered.

I yanked my hand away. "Fuck you, Radovan."

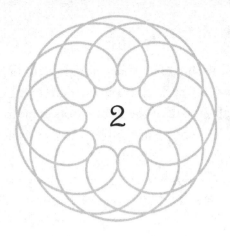

2

RADOVAN'S ANSWERING LAUGH chased me through the door. Fresh waves of hate washed over me, blinding in their intensity. I forced the feeling back. Forced myself to observe, scrabbling at the edges of a half-formed plan as the guards pushed me down the hall.

Given the austerity of the room I'd come from, the corridor was surprisingly grand. My feet slapped against a pristine white marble floor, warm despite the punishing Roveni winter. The walls were swathed with silk tapestries and gilt mirrors. Every corner was lit by witchlight chandeliers dancing in invisible eddies. It spoke of an opulence I wasn't able to appreciate, and not only because it was built on the backs of millions of oppressed people—and the souls of six murdered queens—but because of the undiluted fury rippling off the captain.

She strode beside me, hard face made harder by my parting words to Radovan. One hand clutched the golden hilt of her sword, the other was balled into a fist with the effort of containing herself—an effort I knew she'd abandon after we rounded the first corner.

So I was ready for her fist when it came.

I rolled with the punch, letting Qadenzizeg's rough knuckles trail along my jawline. Her other hand fisted on my collar, slamming my face into a green tapestry whose details I couldn't make out from within the weave. I wriggled against the larger woman's weight, not because I was trying to get free, but because it was expected. And I needed the good captain to get exactly what she expected—needed to lull her into satisfaction so I could move on to more important things.

"Listen to me, *Your Majesty*," she hissed, sending drops of hot spit into my face. "I don't care if you're the crown empress of Vishir or Lady Night Herself, here you are nothing more than a walking corpse. But you *will* keep a civil tongue when speaking to the emperor, or Day Lord save you, I will cut it out."

"All this anger over such a small insult? Such ardor," I sneered, letting Qadenzizeg wrench my left arm behind my back. I struggled against it, trying to leverage my right arm free. "Tell me—is that how you earned your place as captain of the guard—by fighting his battles and kissing his ass like it will make him love you?"

A muscle in Qadenzizeg's jaw tightened, and I almost laughed that my wild jab had landed. Her fingers dug into my shoulders as she spun me around and planted a fist in my gut. I had avoided the worst of the punch to my face, but there was nothing I could do but swallow this blow. I doubled over with a groan and, arms wheeling, I grabbed Qadenzizeg's waist, steadying myself on her belt.

On her knife-filled belt.

She shoved me away. My back crashed into the wall, and I crossed my arms over my stomach.

"You're all the same, you witch-wives. You start out here so brave and filled with bluster."

"It's easy to be brave when you have nothing to lose."

"And that's exactly what you all get wrong. Dying is the easy part, but these next thirty days?" She snorted, shaking her head. "Eventually you'll take a step too far, cross the emperor one too many times. And when you do, I'll be waiting. You'll be begging for death before the end, but I won't be able to give it to you. I won't even want to. Because the truth is, Your Majesty, things can always get worse."

Her proclamation ringing down the corridor, Qadenzizeg turned on her heel and continued on. One of the guards pushed me forward, and we resumed our silent trek through the palace's curving corridors.

The windows we passed were black, and with no servants about, I guessed it was the middle of the night. Or maybe even Radovan's vassals feared going too near his rooms. If they truly were his rooms, I thought, doubt and disgust vying in my mind. Surely a man who lusted after the entire world couldn't be content in that bare cell.

Cell. I winced and wondered, with growing dread, where I was going. The rumors said Radovan kept his wives chained at the top of the Tower of Roshkot, to slowly freeze in the killing cold. Or they said he threw his wives down an oubliette beneath the castle to go slowly mad before he executed them.

I shook my head at the crimson carpet and willed the thought away. Better to focus on the stairs, on the distance between Radovan's room and wherever I was going next. I'd need a solid mental map of this place.

I hoped.

Stepping off the stairs, I followed Qadenzizeg down a long, well-lit corridor studded with sturdy-looking doors all painted in identical cream and gold. It was like being in a terrible dream, where I was running down a never-ending hallway. Only running wasn't an option now, and I knew I'd never have the luxury of waking up.

We stopped at the fifth door, one that had the dubious distinction of being different from all the rest. A long rectangular peephole, complete with brass cover, had been cut in the center of the door.

Qadenzizeg smiled savagely when I raised my eyebrows. "So we can monitor you," she said, crossing her arms. "A guard will be checking in every ten minutes, in case you have any ideas of taking the coward's way out."

"And deprive you the pleasure of my company?" I asked so sweetly my teeth hurt. "I'd never."

The captain's lip curled as she pushed me through the door, slamming it closed on my back. The weight of the lock sliding home jangled up my spine, but Day Lord bless me, at least I was alone.

I leaned against the door, shut my eyes, and took six careful breaths. My gut hurt like sin, but it didn't feel like I'd broken any ribs. Uncrossing my arms, I let my hands hang and tapped the flat of my pilfered blade against my thigh.

Qadenzizeg would be livid when she realized I'd stolen the knife off her belt. And though the thought of her rage was its own kind of wine, I didn't have time to savor it. I needed to hide the knife before she discovered it missing.

The room around me was remarkable for what it lacked. It was beautiful, as sumptuous as the hallways that led to it, but every touch of beauty was marred. A bed sat on the opposite end of the long, rectangular space. Its frame was carved with vines and flowers, and the four posts rising from the mattress looked like the roots of some great tree. But there was no fabric where the canopy should have been. And where a tapestry should have hung behind the bed, there was nothing either. Just a dark-paneled wall and a wicked-looking tapestry hook.

I circled the room and saw that it was the same with the two windows on the wall to my right. They were wide but barred. There were rods for curtains, but the curtains themselves were gone. The fireplace between the windows crackled with flames, but its metal grate was padlocked shut. Same with the long wardrobe on the opposite wall. And the bathroom, whose doorway didn't actually have a door. The tub, made of cream and gray marble was studded with golden fish-shaped taps, but no water came out when I tested them.

I shuddered at the image this room conjured. The comfortable, homey touches; the plush bedcovers and overstuffed armchairs; the wide table set for chess and the vanity covered in makeup—it was all veneer. Designed to lull, to croon a song of comfort and safety. And if I squinted just right, I could almost imagine that this was nothing more than a stateroom fit for a foreign noble.

But I'd never been much of a liar—not to myself. And this room was filled with lies. Lies and the memory of the women who came before me. Women who, if this room was any indication, had done everything they could to get away from Radovan. Even if the only escape was death.

I shook my head and went to the wardrobe. Its stubby little legs offered a sliver of space where I could stow the knife. It wasn't much of a hiding spot, I thought as I wedged the blade between the wood and the thick blue carpet, but it'd have to do.

"Surely you can do better than that, girl."

"Siv," a second ghostly voice chided with well-worn exasperation.

"What?" the first voice demanded. *"If she's canny enough to lift the blade off Qaden, she can certainly do better than this."*

Ice slipped down my back and wound down my limbs. An ice that had nothing to do with fear, but the tether constraining my magic. I smiled, touching the chain hanging against my chest. It was cold—but there was no pain. No fire. *Strange.* Straightening I turned and found the room crowded with women.

Hailing from the whole breadth of the continent, they were young and old, fair and plain, united only in that they were all dead. One stood at the window, back turned away. Another knelt before the fire, warming her hands. Two more sat at the table contemplating me over the chessboard. The last two stood a few feet away, as odd a pair of companions as I'd ever seen.

The one I thought had spoken first was powerfully built, all broad shoulders and thick legs. Her pale hair was set in a long braid that snaked over her shoulder. She wore tight, patchwork trousers and a loose tunic that reminded me of a pirate from a storybook. And though her voice was young, her face was aged. She had skin that crinkled and creased like she'd been out in the sun and wind too long.

The second ghost was a familiar one. I'd seen her fair face leaning over me when I first woke in this hellscape. She was young, my age or slightly older, and held herself with the cool poise that gets beaten into every generation of noblewomen. She clasped her hands in front of her neat-looking gown and watched me like I were an animal she was afraid of spooking.

I grinned, nodding to the woman who'd first spoken. *"The room's bare—you have a better idea where to hide it?"*

Laughter shone in her eyes. *"Voyniks are predators, love. And predators don't look up."*

I followed her gaze to the top of the wardrobe. Sure enough, there was a very dusty shelf made by its top, hidden behind ornate scrollwork on its face.

"You must be Radovan's wives?" I said, transferring the blade to its new spot.

"Got it in one," the rough-looking woman said with a grin. *"Look at you, face-to-face with a room full of ghosts and not a goose pimple on ya."*

"She's a death witch, she must be used to seeing ghosts," one of the women at the table—a priestess judging by her robe—said. *"Though seeing Siv in my bedroom would surely make me scream with fright."*

"You'd be screaming," the rough woman replied with a smirk, *"but it wouldn't be from fright."*

"Siv," the regal-looking woman said with a quelling glance. *"Perhaps a few introductions are in order. I am Princess Eliska of Raskis,"* she said, visibly trying for a smile before gesturing to the woman beside her. *"This is—"*

"I can introduce my damn self, thanks much. I'm Siv of Switzkia, woman of the world and privateer—"

"You mean pirate," the priestess corrected tartly.

Siv grinned. *"Never convicted."*

"You must be Asyl," I said to the priestess before she and Siv could continue what felt like a long-standing argument.

The priestess bent her head in graceful assent. *"High Priestess Asyl of Khezhar at your service."*

"So that would make you . . . Freyda?"

The woman beside Asyl allowed a slight nod. I knew the Graznian fire witch was the oldest—in age—of Radovan's wives. Built like a wire, she surveyed me with what looked like mild disapproval. Though perhaps it was the three ragged scars ripping down the left side of her face that gave me the impression. The stories said that the merchant queen once got into a fight with a black bear. And won.

"And you are?" I asked the plump woman kneeling by the fire.

"Ragata," she said, smiling at me in a dreamy way.

"Ragata," I repeated to myself, memorizing the face of Radovan's second wife before looking finally at the last ghost. Her back was still turned away, and a long veil covered her from crown to waist. It waived with her every diaphanous exhalation. *"Then you must be Katarzhina."*

If Radovan's first wife heard me, she gave no indication. Just stood there. A silent monolith to betrayed trust and broken love. The other wives looked away.

"Don't mind her," Siv said in a whisper that nonetheless carried. *"She's not one for talking."*

I felt my eyebrow arch but didn't comment. Katarzhina and

Radovan had been married for years. They had a child together, too, who for all I knew was still alive, but . . .

I glanced to Siv. *"Is her son still . . ."*

"Aye, Gethen's alive," Siv replied, matching my undertone. *"Simpleminded as he is, poor man still wanders the castle in search of his mother."*

I looked back at Katarzhina, unable to fathom what being trapped here must be like for her. The child that needed her forever out of reach, trapped with the man who murdered her. Had I been in her place, I doubted I'd be up for talking either.

"Radovan said I wouldn't be able to use my magic while wearing the Aellium stone," I began. *"I even tried to summon one of my men, but it didn't work."*

All the queens but Katarzhina glanced at Asyl. The priestess brushed an invisible something from her lap with a secret, knowing look. *"Radovan was misinformed,"* she said, so smug her gossamer body sharpened.

My gaze narrowed. *"In what way?"*

"He has an imperfect understanding of how the stones work."

"But your understanding is perfect?" I pressed.

"The Aellium stones come from Khezhari mines," Asyl replied as if her understanding should therefore be obvious. *"The chain and the stone serve different functions. It was the enchantment on the chain that burned your hand—not the stone,"* she said, eyes dropping to my still-throbbing palm. *"The chain only curbs your power enough to ensure you aren't a threat while the stone does the work of stealing your magic.*

"You'll still be aware of your gift, even if you cannot necessarily use it. It's a narrow distinction, and not one that would be of any use to an elemental witch." Asyl sniffed as if elemental witches were by definition not worth mentioning. *"But for spirit witches like you and I, it makes all the difference. It allowed me to sense Radovan's intentions, even while all my other powers lay fallow."*

I nodded along. *"And it's letting me see all of you. Radovan doesn't suspect?"*

"He's just a sorcerer," she said with a moue of distaste, *"and like all sorcerers, his magic comes from the stone—it doesn't live within him. He can't feel magic inside him the way we do."*

"And you didn't illuminate him," I said, feeling my lips tug upward in an amused smile.

Asyl's brows rose. *"And lose my one advantage? Hardly."*

"I'm glad there's at least some limit to his power," I muttered.

"Of course there is," Eliska replied. *"He isn't all-powerful."*

The *yet* that belonged at the end of that statement echoed so loudly I turned away from it, coming closer to the fire instead.

The tether constraining my magic had begun to rear its head, lapping cold water on my limbs. Even this paltry amount of power was still limited by the dictates of the Two-Faced God. Magic yes, but always at a price. What was constraining Radovan? I wondered. What price did he pay?

"How was he able to use the Aellium stone in the first place?" I asked, my internal voice low, as if weighed down with a fear I couldn't express. I closed my left hand, palm still throbbing. *"He wasn't even touching the jewel, but still he was able to . . ."*

My words petered out, but it didn't matter. Not to these women. Their hard eyes said it all.

"Radovan fractured his stone after Ragata," Asyl said, gaze cutting toward the second queen. Ragata still sat by the fire, eyes lost to the flames. More than lost, I thought. There was something vacant behind her expression. A mind that had receded.

"Fractured?" I asked, still not understanding. *"But how—"*

"The two halves are tied together through Katarzhina and Ragata—through their magic," Asyl explained. *"This way he can use his part of the stone while yours takes your magic. What one stone does, so does the other. A way of ensuring he is never powerless."*

"Great." I raked a hand through my hair, trying to focus on

the positive. I could still see the queens. But what about other spirits, like Vitaly?

Or Ozura.

I thought back to Vishir. I'd gone to see the queen before the burial, beseeched her for guidance. And forgiveness. Forgiveness for the death I caused and the promise she'd made.

I will serve you better when I see you again.

My stomach clenched, sending shooting pains through my core from the memory of Qadenzizeg's fist. *"I don't suppose you've seen the ghosts of a Seraveshi soldier or a Vishiri queen, have you?"*

"I am here, my lady."

Vitaly appeared on my left before I could even finish the sentence. *"Vitaly,"* I cried. *"Thank the Two-Faced God. I thought I'd never see you again."*

"Never fear that," he replied.

"Is Ozura here too?"

A worried look flashed across Vitaly's face, and he nodded to the far window. My attention flew, and I saw her standing beside Katarzhina, more wraith-like than any of the others.

"Ozura?" Her body was as insubstantial as the smoke curling up the chimney. I couldn't read her expression. Didn't want to. *"Why does she look like that? What's wrong with her?"*

One of Asyl's thin eyebrows rose. *"I rather thought ghosts were your domain."* She shrugged. *"How did you bring her here?"*

"I didn't. She made a dying promise to serve me," I replied, ignoring the way my voice quaked. It was harder to ignore the looks of pity the other witches were giving the dead Vishiri queen.

"I see," Asyl managed. *"That was bravely done, but it doesn't always give the best results. Particularly if she feels she has a duty elsewhere. Perhaps she has family in Vishir?"*

I nodded. *"A son."* The anger in Iskander's eyes when I'd seen him last still burned.

"Is he in trouble?"

Trouble? Vishir was at war with Roven. Armaan was dead and Iskander was surely battling his brother, Enver, for the throne. A battle only one of them would survive. *"Yes. Yes, I believe he is."*

"Well that will do it," Asyl said, shaking her head. *"Until she commits to fulfilling her duty to you, she'll be stuck like this. A half death as we say."*

"What if she can't commit to it?"

Asyl shuddered. *"She promised you her soul in defiance of the natural order. Lady Night may have allowed the sacrifice, but that doesn't mean She will forgive an oath-breaker. If Ozura cannot resolve herself to her duty here, her soul will be lost."*

"No. No that can't be right," I said, fighting the urge to cover my ears. "She's already given too much. What if I command it?"

"I don't think you'll be able to command anything," Eliska said, looking to Asyl for confirmation.

"Why not? I can see all of you—and both of them?"

"You can see us because our magic is contained within the stone. You can see your friends because they are soulbound to you. But your ability to see us isn't the same as using your power," Asyl said, as if she were speaking to a particularly dim-witted child. *"Trying to command any of us to do anything will certainly trigger the enchantment in the chain. The chain would stop you."*

Had Asyl been alive, I might have struck her, as much for her condescension as for the suffocating feeling of my own impotence. I resisted, searching for something, anything that I could do to help Ozura. *"Can't I . . . can't I release her?"*

Asyl shook her head. The silent gesture would have driven me to the floor had I allowed it. It was my fault Ozura was dead. Not completely, of course. I hadn't been the one to kill her. Count Dobor was the one who wielded the blade. But there was no escaping the fact that she had died so I could live. She was gone. Armaan was gone. And Vishir?

Day Lord save me, I needed Vishir. The whole damned world needed Vishir, if there was a chance at defeating Roven. But Vishir needed a ruler, which meant the princes were surely vying for the throne. But without Ozura, who was on Iskander's side? Who would—could—protect him from Enver? From the Shazir? I closed my eyes, wishing the ghosts away.

"Eh now," Siv exclaimed softly. *"No sense wasting your tears on a dead woman. She'll come 'round, or she won't—nothing you can do about that. Besides, you've got bigger problems, love."*

I scrubbed my face and nodded. Siv was right. Escape. I needed to escape—I was dead if I didn't. *Focus, Askia.*

Ozura's body sharpened slightly in the firelight, a half smile forming on her lips. She nodded.

I turned to Eliska. *"When I first woke up, you said you would help me escape. What's your plan?"*

It wasn't possible for ghosts to blanch—they lacked the blood required. But Eliska's gray face fell. Siv barked a laugh. Katarzhina disappeared.

Freyda stood, anger scrawled across her ruined face. *"What nonsense is this?"* Her voice was barely audible and scratchy as a cat's tongue, and yet it carried through the room.

"Not nonsense," Eliska said, refusing to quail. Her eyes darted back to mine wide and nervous. *"I don't have a plan—yet,"* she hurried to add. *"But between all of us, we can surely think of something."*

"Something that the six of you haven't already tried?" Even the voice in my mind bit out the words.

"Well, yes. But we were alone, and you aren't. It might take some time, but we can find a way."

The hopeful sound of Eliska's voice grated my skin. *"Time that I don't have."*

"Not necessarily."

I felt my eyebrows rise. *"What do you mean?"*

Eliska licked her lips. *"Radovan didn't always kill us after thirty days."*

"Eliska," Asyl sighed the name like a disappointed mother.

"This is unforgivable," Freyda growled.

Eliska's chin rose in defiance of their reproach. *"Why?"*

"You're offering hope where there is none," the older ghost shook her head slowly, as if she didn't recognize Eliska. *"Hope is Radovan's cruelest form of torture. You know that."*

Freyda turned to me, and though her face was wreathed in phantom flames of anger, her eyes were watery with pity. *"I'm sorry, Askia. But you are going to die here. Best use your remaining time to come to terms with that."*

"She's not going to die," Eliska argued, but Freyda had already disappeared. The princess crossed her arms in frustration. *"I'm right. I know I am. Asyl, how long did he let you live?"*

"Nearly six months," she replied, brushing imaginary wrinkles from her robe as if she were proud of the accomplishment.

"Yeah, we all know he let the original ones live a while," Siv said, throwing her hands in the air, *"but he sure killed me after thirty days. And this one doesn't even have thirty days."*

My head shot up at that. *"What? How long do I have?"*

"You've been here two days already," Asyl said. *"How long were you wearing the necklace before you arrived?"*

"Two days," I said, looking toward the Ozura-shaped spot of darkness. *"A servant gave it to me to wear on my wedding day."*

Four days. Twenty-six left—and today was nearly spent.

"Steady, my lady," Vitaly murmured, as if he could sense the dark roads my mind was crawling down.

He was right. These questions would get me nowhere. More information might. *"How long did you last, Eliska?"*

"Thirty-five days," Eliska said holding up her finger before anyone could interrupt, *"and I think he would have let me live longer had things not taken a turn for the worse in Seravesh. Not that I*

blame you, of course," she said with what I'm sure she thought was a reassuring smile.

"Good. Neither do I" was my sharp reply. *"Why the extra five days?"*

"Simply put, I made sure he liked me."

The room went cold. *"What exactly are you suggesting?"* I asked.

"Radovan has you," she pressed. *"The war against Vishir won't start until spring, so there's really no rush to kill you. If you're smart—if you listen to our advice—we can show you how to endear yourself to Radovan."*

"Endear myself?" The word had edges and corners like the place of rage it sprang from had forged it into weaponry.

"Yes, and the sooner you start the better. At dinner tonight, be nice. Make him like you. The more he does, the longer he'll let you live."

"Nice? You want me to be nice to the man who has brought my country to the brink of destruction—to the man who killed thousands of my people. Who just killed my husband?"

"We've all lost people, Askia," Eliska said softly.

"So I should dishonor their memory by whoring myself out to that monster?"

Eliska recoiled like I'd slapped her. *"That—that's not what I'm suggesting. All I'm saying is that, like everyone else in the world, Radovan wants to be understood. He wants a friend."*

"I don't give a shit what Radovan wants! If he comes too close to me, I will plant that knife in his skull."

"Now that's what I'm talking about," Siv hooted. *"I knew I liked you."*

"You'll never get close enough to hurt him," Eliska argued, but I held up my hand to stop her.

"No. If you really want to help me, you'll help me escape. You'll help me find allies. Ozura once told me there was a resistance movement here and in the other conquered nations. What do you know about it?"

"A tree with rotting roots cannot stand," Ragata said dreamily to the fire.

I rounded on the older queen, hateful words souring my tongue. I swallowed them as I registered the glazed way Ragata's eyes skated across the room.

"Real helpful, Ragata," Siv muttered. *"Nuttier than a carrownut, you are."*

Ragata frowned at some point over Siv's head. *"But carrownuts aren't actually nuts."*

Siv shook her head at the ceiling. *"Point is we don't know anything about a resistance."*

"Nothing?" I looked around at the remaining ghosts. *"What about his court? His councilors and guards? Do you know anything about them I could use?"*

Silence.

I raked a hand through my hair. *"What in the Day Lord's name have you been doing with your time?"* I demanded, the incredulity in my voice echoing. *"Did you never stop to consider that it might be useful to learn something about your enemy?"*

"We're dead, love," Siv replied crossing her arms. *"What would have been the point in spying on these people? There was no one to tell what we might learn."*

I gestured helplessly at myself. *"There's me."*

"Believe it or not, child, we were all rather hoping you'd escape our fate," Asyl said glaring at me from across the room. *"Waste of effort that obviously was, for here you are standing before us venting your spleen. Well, let me tell you, Your Majesty, not one of us asked for this."*

The sound of the door unlocking made me tense. I turned as it opened and a pair of women hurried in. They wore identical gray short-coats and trousers fitted with black piping on the cuffs of their sleeves. The younger of the two bobbed a shallow bow in my general direction before scurrying to the bathroom without a word. The older one, her hair as pure white as fresh snow, approached with silent steps and motioned for me to follow the girl.

"Who are you?" I asked, the coldness in my voice more for Asyl's benefit than the maid's. Too bad the priestess had disappeared along with all the other ghosts save Eliska and Vitaly.

The maid's lips twitched. She bent into another, deeper bow and gestured toward the bathroom, where I could hear a gush of water filling the oversized tub. I felt my eyebrows rise. "Yes, I understand where you want me to go, but what I asked was for your name."

Her eyes tightened, but she didn't reply.

"Have you been ordered to not speak with me?"

A look of confusion flashed across her face, and then cleared with comprehension. She nodded quickly, and then angled her left cheek toward the light. A circular black tattoo was etched onto her cheekbone. The ebony outline was no larger than a coin, but inside it was the image of a broom and a fire iron, their handles crossed.

I frowned, taking in the tattoo. "Qaden had one of those."

The woman nodded again, her left hand rocked back and forth in a way I thought meant "yes, but no."

"Qaden's was the sigil of a royal guard," Eliska supplied from beside the servant. *"Two swords crossed with a crown hovering between them. This woman and the other wear the sigil of a servant."*

"Does everyone in the castle have one of these tattoos?"

The servant nodded.

"Every Roven citizen has one to indicate the class in which they belong," Eliska said, her voice low with distaste. *"Radovan likes everyone to know their place."*

"Interesting."

"That's one word for it," Vitaly said darkly, before he, too, disappeared, giving me some modicum of privacy.

The servant shrugged and once more waived to the bathroom.

"You should go with her. She'll be punished if you don't cooperate."

I turned away from the older woman, so she wouldn't see my expression at Eliska's words. *"They'd really punish her for my behavior? That's despicable."*

"This is Roven."

I couldn't argue with that, so I didn't struggle when the older woman helped me out of my nightdress. *"I can't believe they were ordered not to speak with me,"* I said, tiptoeing to the bath.

I sighed greedily as the almost-scalding water touched my feet. I hadn't realized how cold I'd been, what with the fire roaring in the hearth. I'd have to be more careful in the future. Even if I wasn't using much magic to speak to the queens, over time and in this climate my ice-like tether would eventually snap.

"None of the servants speak," Eliska replied distractedly from somewhere behind me. *"Lady Night have mercy, what happened to your back?"*

I lowered myself into the tub, the heat almost obscenely extravagant to my stress-sore muscles, before looking up. Eliska's face was stricken, and though the older servant was more circumspect in her shock, the younger woman's eyes were wide, albeit glued to the floor like she feared my reaction to *her* reaction.

"I survived," I said to Eliska with a touch of bitterness. *"It's a long story.*

"Don't worry about the scars," I continued aloud for the benefit of the servants. "They don't hurt."

The older one nodded, her expression closing once more. She gave a sharp prod to the younger girl and the two of them set to work, bobbing and weaving around each other in perfect silence. It was like watching a well-practiced dance, only one where neither partner spoke, communicating only with a series of nods and gestures.

"Eliska," I said as a horrid realization dawned in my mind. *"When you say 'none of the servants speak,' you don't mean that they can't speak, do you?"*

Eliska's reply came with a dark laugh. *"Radovan renders all of his servants mute as a part of the terms for their indenture."*

"But what about when they go home or retire or—" My words trailed off when Eliska shook her head.

"They can never speak. They can read and some of the supervisors are allowed to write to convey instructions, but . . ." She shrugged. *"The muting spell is permanent."*

The indignity of the situation washed over me. *"What is he hiding?"*

"Many terrible things, I'm sure," Eliska murmured. *"Whatever will help him maintain control."*

I didn't fight the women as they scrubbed me clean or patted me dry. I let them lead me back into the bedroom and dried my hair by the fire. The wind outside rattled against the windows making me grateful for the heat belching from the hearth. But it did make me wonder. I'd assumed it was the middle of the night when I'd first awoken, but Eliska said I was being prepared for some kind of dinner. *"What time is it?"*

Eliska turned to follow my gaze. *"Only about six in the evening. Roven is mostly darkness and twilight this time of year."*

This and every other.

It was impossible to deny that the gown they wrapped me in was a thing of beauty, though after so many weeks in diaphanous Vishiri dresses, the midnight blue crushed velvet felt heavy to the touch. The gown hung from my shoulders, with sleeves that split at my elbows and fell in a graceful drape to the floor. The neckline, trimmed with two crystal-edged bands, crossed low over my breasts, another band cinched my waist, and yet more glittering white crystals were sewn in perfect vertical lines to the hem. It was like someone had swept all the stars from the sky and rearranged them with furious precision. Beautiful yes, but rigid. At least it fit.

My mind stumbled over itself. The dress *did* fit. Perfectly.

I looked at the wardrobe, taking in the long line of carefully hung dresses and trousers, coats and boots. Each and every one of them was my size.

"Eliska, how is it that this dress fits so perfectly?"

"Someone must have told Radovan—or more likely, told one of his agents."

"Someone in Vishir?" If Radovan still had agents in Vishir, what did that mean for my friends? For Iskander and Nariko? For Illya and my men? Ozura flashed in and out of existence just beyond Eliska's elbow, as if she could hear my thoughts.

"Or Seravesh—Radovan has eyes everywhere," Eliska replied. *"It was the same when I came. Thirty days' worth of beautiful bespoke gowns waiting for me."*

"But why? Why do all this? Why dress us up like dolls, give us this room and the semblance of privacy, of normalcy? Why not just throw us in the dungeon, and let us sit in our filth until the stone has finished its work?"

"You'll find out soon enough for yourself, but . . ." She paused, considering. *"He fancies himself a gentleman, a traditional lord of the old world, all chivalry and duty. Radovan thinks of killing us as a necessity, but he doesn't want us to suffer."*

"He's a monster."

Eliska gave a little shrug. *"No one considers themselves monstrous"* was her quiet reply. *"Not even Radovan. Remember that."*

I was going to say something acidic, but instead I nodded. It was solid advice. Though in a way, it would have been easier if Radovan was the drooling image of evil he'd always been in my mind. But then, when had my life ever been easy?

I surveyed my reflection in the narrow mirror that hung from the inside of my wardrobe. My hair had been brushed out and set with curls. Makeup, applied with a light hand, gave color to my cheeks and mostly hid the faint blue bruise that was rising on my skin from Qaden's fist. The gown suited me, and displayed the green Aellium stone well too—which was probably the point. I looked pretty, in a soft, innocent kind of way.

The jagged scar running across my throat ruined the image, but I was all right with that. More than all right. I'd been proud to display the scar in the Vishiri court. The scar I'd earned the day the Shazir—witch-hating Vishiri zealots—killed my parents. I was proud again to wear it now. It would remind Radovan, and the men and women who propped him up, that I was not a wilting flower, a damsel waiting for rescue. I was a queen. A warrior.

A survivor.

"Who will be at this dinner?" I asked, readying myself for battle.

"Just his newest batch of favored lords." Eliska smiled, an almost savage expression that reminded me so much of Illya, my chest ached. *"You're surprised no one lasts long at Radovan's court? You shouldn't be—you're responsible for much of the recent turnover."*

"Good, but why?"

"He was expecting you to cause war between the Vishiri princes and turmoil in the menagerie. Instead, you married the emperor, rallied the continent, and nearly got yourself named empress."

"Well, I sound damned good when you list it all out like that."

Eliska's laugh was as velvety as my dress. *"Don't get too full of yourself. It's terribly unladylike and you'll never find a husband."*

"Your lips to the Day Lord's ears," I said fervently as my bedroom door flew open.

3

QADEN STOOD ON the threshold, hands planted on her hips. She looked me up and down, jealousy flashing through her eyes before she quashed it.

"Are you going to come quietly, or will I have to drag you out by your hair."

I allowed a slow smile. "Oh, my dear Qadenzizeg," I said, mimicking the way Radovan purred the captain's name. "While I genuinely look forward to the day you and I fight in earnest, that day is not today."

I flicked my fingers in a haughty shooing motion that made Qaden's lip curl. She turned on her heel and stomped out of the room. I didn't try to hide my satisfaction, winking at the older servant before following.

Neither of the door guards accompanied Qaden and me as we swept down the hall and descended the long, curving stairs. She set a brisk pace, no doubt hoping I'd trip on my hem and smash my face into the floor. She severely underestimated me if she thought that was likely. I hadn't spent years training with Arkady and the Wolves to fall now, no matter what I was wearing.

I surveyed my surroundings, marking the people who now milled in the corridors we passed. Nobility by the fine cut of their clothing. Men and women in fur-trimmed coats and dresses admired this crystal vase or that silk-threaded tapestry, but I clearly had their full attention. I could feel them watching me from the corners of their eyes, like getting this fleeting glimpse of me could satisfy their curiosity, their naked desire to be one of Radovan's chosen.

I glanced at Qaden, wondering if she felt that desire too. Or would she be standing behind my chair all night, hand fisted on the hilt of her sword?

Qaden's eyes flicked to me and away again, her mouth curving into a dark smile. "I know what you took," she murmured, too low for anyone we passed to hear.

"I assumed you'd figure it out eventually," I replied. "Is this your way of asking for it back—or is cleaning up after you ransack my room something I can look forward to after dinner?"

"Keep it. I'm sure I'll get it back from you eventually."

I struggled not to react. "Aren't you afraid I might hurt someone?"

"Not even remotely." She smirked. "You have some fire in you, Princess, I'll give you that. Four and Five had fire too—Four even managed to kill one of her guards."

"Four?" My brow creased as I tried to parse her words. "You mean Freyda?"

Qaden gave the tiniest of nods, swallowing down an emotion I couldn't name. "But you know what I've noticed? The ones with fire are always the first to burn out. So you can keep that little knife, if it helps you dream of escaping this place."

"Why?" I asked, my steps slowing as we reached the ground floor.

"Because I know exactly what is going to happen," she replied leading me to a set of dark imposing doors. "Your days will grow shorter. Your dreams will tarnish. Your strength will become brittle. And sooner or later, you'll begin to pin all your hopes on the edge of that blade. Just like Four and Five did. And you know what will happen then?"

She leaned closer to me, whispering in my ear. "I'm going to come looking for that knife. And I'm going to leave you to your misery and despair. Until you crack. And then I'm going to watch you die."

She stepped back, nodding for the guards to open the door. "Enjoy your dinner," she said, flicking her fingers to shoo me away.

Swallowing a swear, I entered the Great Hall on wooden legs, shoulders high. Ready for a fight. The gargantuan space easily matched the Great Hall of Bet Naqar, but size was where all similarities ended. Where the palace of Vishir dazzled and welcomed with glimmering tiles of silver and gold, this space oozed cold menace. Night and day. Summer and winter, I thought, forcing myself to move.

White marble—the same as the rest of the castle—covered the floors and walls of the round room. Thick veins of blue stone ran through the white in a swirling pattern that circled the floor and crept up the rounded walls, higher, higher. Because there was no ceiling to this room that was not a room. Just the tower that lay at the heart of this winding, circular castle.

"The blue stone is Graznian porphyry," Ragata said excitedly, appearing by my side as I crossed the empty space. *"Beautiful."*

It was, I allowed as the tower stretched out above me, dizzyingly high. But that wasn't what made it so terribly amazing. That distinction belonged to the oculus at its center.

A perfect circle of stone was missing from the tower's roof, letting me glimpse a slice of winter sky, where the uncaring stars twinkled far above. There must be some kind of magic sealing it, I thought, otherwise the blue porphyry table in the room's heart would have been covered in a foot of snow and ice.

"Graznian porphyry is exceedingly rare—and terribly suited for

construction on such a scale," Ragata continued. *"Especially considering how unstable the earth is along this part of Roven. A great scar cuts through Roven at the Riven Cliffs, a rift that travels up the length of the coast. Makes the land prone to earthquakes. And here is Radovan, basically constructing the tower from butter."*

I let Ragata natter on without really listening, gathering strength into my chest, girding myself with unseen armor. My steps echoed off the hall's curved walls and I could almost imagine that I wasn't alone. That Seravesh was with me. Letting the thought bolster me, I stalked to the heart of the space, where a table was set and about a dozen men waited.

"Askia, my dear. How good of you to join us." Radovan's voice cut through the light, polluting it. He stood, dragging the other men to their feet, and rounded the table. "You look beautiful."

I swallowed my first response in favor of silence, my shoulders drawing up when he held out his hand for mine. My hands closed into fists, joints locking in place. Radovan simply watched me, an amused smile growing on his face, waiting for me to take his hand. I saw the other men shift in my periphery, wary of the silent battle raging between Radovan and me.

Eliska's diaphanous body appeared between us, her face edged and serious. *"Askia, please. Take his hand."*

"No."

"Just do it," she urged. *"If you don't, he'll only send you away, and what will that gain you? Nothing. So play the game."*

Play the game.

It was the advice Ozura would have given me—that she *had* once given me. I could do it. Just for tonight, I could be what they expected of me. I could endure.

I allowed my anger to vent in one long exhale and slid my hand into Radovan's. His smile grew, eyes glittering as if he knew what bending cost me. I bit down hard on my cheek, repressing a shudder at the too-papery feel of his skin scratching mine. It was like wrinkled parchment that had been smoothed out one too many times.

"Come and join us," he said, the picture of warmth and grace, leading me to the empty seat beside his.

Though turning my back on him felt like exposing my neck to a rabid dog, I allowed him to help me into my chair. I made a show of smoothing my long skirt and placing my napkin in my lap. Shoulders back, spine rigid, I took my time looking at the men around the table through hooded eyes and a studiously bored expression. If I'd learned nothing else in Vishir, it was that good manners could be wielded like a blade. And class was all in the attitude.

Servants oozed out of the darkness at the edge of the hall while I settled myself. They refilled crystal glasses and served the first course of dainty-looking food on golden chargers. The men around the table looked to me. Waiting.

"Traditionally, the highest-ranking woman at the table opens the feast by taking the first bite," Eliska said hurriedly. *"Not even Radovan will eat until you do."*

I smiled internally and waited.

Waited.

Waited.

I took in the men seated with me, studying their faces closely as the silence stretched to an uncomfortable length. It was an eclectic group, I thought, united only by an undercurrent of caution.

The youngest was only a few years older than me. The eldest, an oddly jovial-looking man with pale, glass-like eyes, had to be in his late eighties. His face was so deeply wrinkled it disfigured the class tattoo on his cheek. Most were military men who sat ramrod straight, medals gleaming in the bright witchlight, though two lords were also seated in their finest. I'd expected to see Rovenese features in the faces around me, but they were evenly mixed with men who clearly hailed from other stretches of the continent.

The only man—aside from Radovan—who I recognized was one such traitor. My gaze lingered on Pjeder Tcheshin's face, as Vitaly appeared behind Tcheshin's chair. I'd never seen my old friend look the way he did now. A promise of violence swirling in his gaze. I understood why.

It was Lord Tcheshin who had waltzed into my grandfather's castle a year ago bearing Radovan's proposal of marriage. Lord Tcheshin who had conspired with my cousin, Goran, when it became clear I had no intention of marrying. Tcheshin, who was one of Radovan's most loyal proxies and sympathizers. And for all of that, he wasn't even from Roven.

No matter the dreamed-up name he conjured for himself to sound Rovenese on paper, Tcheshin's face declared the truth: blond hair, pale blue eyes, and lily-white skin—he was a walking Switzkian stereotype. His every breath was a betrayal, not only to his own people but to all the conquered kingdoms lying broken under Roven rule. Complicit bastard.

I looked deliberately away. Sniffed. And with purposeful slowness that almost made my muscles ache, I took my first bite. Beside me Radovan's body shivered with laughter, as if he was aware of what I'd been doing, robbing me of even this small satisfaction.

The men chatted amongst themselves as they ate, filling the hall with light, sparkling banter, but it was impossible to miss how they eyed one another. Each man practically quivered, hoping for their chance to shine, even if it meant stepping on the necks of their brethren. It reminded me of Vishir in the worst way, where words were as deadly as the sharpest blade.

While the men sniped at each other, Eliska stood at my shoulder, feeding me information. Tcheshin, to my immense displeasure, was a perennial favorite of Radovan's, as was the older man, Wenslaus—a Polzi name if there ever was one. And General Kostya Koloii, tall and willowy and in the graying years of life, was one of Radovan's oldest companions.

"What kind of magic does he have?" I asked, eyeing the massive Aellium stone winking at me from a medal-like pin on his chest.

"Koloii is an earth sorcerer," Eliska replied, voice dripping with disgust. *"He used the magic to trigger an avalanche that took out a third of the Raskisi army during the invasion of my homeland. He laughed when he told me how many men he killed."* If voice alone could kill, Eliska would've had Koloii skinned and gutted right here on the table.

"Has Radovan made any of the others sorcerers?" Koloii was the only one obviously wearing an Aellium stone, but since I'd yet to see the stone Radovan wore, a fragment from the one around my neck, I couldn't be sure.

"Wenslaus is one, as the warden of Radovan's prisons," she said with a dark look. *"Radovan's always favored his soldiers, and the Voyniks receive stones almost exclusively."* Eliska paused, her ghostly attention going to Ragata who floated across the table. *"Despite that, there's a rumor Lord Zosha will be receiving one soon."*

I tried not to let my mental confusion rise to my face when I looked at Zosha. He was younger than any of the others by at least a decade. In his twenties, he had long, light brown hair that fell artfully into his eyes. He was handsome, though in that good-for-nothing, layabout kind of way that noblemen tended to be.

"What's so special about him?"

"He's Radovan's stepson."

"My Zoshenko," Ragata whispered in the wake of Eliska's words, an exhalation filled with unmet longing.

Vitaly looked away from Tcheshin for the first time all evening, and I felt his shock echo across the Marchlands. I knew Radovan had a full-blooded son, Gethen, a man who must be in his forties by now. But a stepson? That meant—

"*Ragata was pregnant when Radovan took her*," Eliska whispered. "*Though he never officially adopted Zosha, Radovan raised him as his son.*"

The young lord must have felt my eyes upon him, for he turned and raised a haughty eyebrow at me. "Yes?"

Tcheshin cackled when I didn't immediately reply. "Oh dear, I think you've caught the young queen's eye, Zosha. And here I thought our Askia preferred older men."

"I suspect the list of things you *think* you know could fill several libraries, Tcheshin," I snapped, gaze cutting to Pjeder before returning to the younger lord. A faint blush had crept into Zosha's face at the implication of my attraction. Clearly this was dangerous territory. But should I make things worse for him?

Ragata ran her ghostly fingers through Zosha's hair, her face carved with grief.

"I was simply wondering what your place was. The others I am aware of—their records are notorious. But you seem young to be counted among your distinguished peers."

It wasn't my best shot, but if my aim wasn't completely true, it wasn't far off either. The stupid men at the table smirked, thinking I was belittling Zosha. The clever ones frowned, realizing my words made his youth a success in itself.

"I do my best to be of use to the empire," Zosha said, clever eyes glimmering. "Though you of all people know age isn't a barrier to—how did you put it? Notoriety?"

"The brashness of youth is certainly what's made your story so entertaining," Koloii added, his deep voice echoing through the hall.

"Entertaining?" I let my eyebrows rise in challenge. "Really, General? Was it my youth that allowed me to hold off your army longer than any other leader on the continent?"

"And yet you still failed. Is this really something to boast about?"

"I'm not dead yet, Koloii," I replied. "And I'm not sure defeating armies a quarter the size of yours is anything to brag about. We'll see how you fare against Vishir. Or are you worried that a man your age won't be able to rise to the challenge when faced with an opponent your size?"

Koloii's face went scarlet at the muffled laughter, and doubly so when Radovan's chuckle filled the room.

"I warned you she was a live one, General," Radovan said, gracing me with a warm smile.

"Indeed" was Koloii's cold reply. "But I think she overestimates Vishir, especially now that there is no petulant little girl urging them on to war."

"Little girl?" I smirked, shaking my head. "That's the best insult you could think of? What next, are you going to start in on my feeble female mind?"

"Now, now, Askia. This is Roven, not Vishir. We value our women," Radovan said, taking a congratulatory sip of wine.

"Really?"

"But of course," he said, looking genuinely surprised by my doubt. "I don't hold with any outdated notions of sex, and nor does any man of Roven. Women aren't treated like a second class, like children, the way they are in the rest of the world. What matters here is ability, not gender."

Venom rose in my blood and I smiled, leaning back in my chair. "You sound terribly proud of yourself."

"*Askia.*" My name was sharp on Eliska's lips, willing me to be careful.

"Why shouldn't I be? Under my hand, the north has become truly egalitarian."

"*Askia, don't—*"

"Well of course it has," I said, nearly spraining my voice on sarcasm. "I mean, just look at this table—filled with citizens at the highest echelons of power. And yet," I hissed a breath, like the next words were painful to say, "the only woman here is a prisoner you're forcing into marriage at knife point. Well done."

For the first time, Radovan stopped smiling. His eyes narrowed. The men around me went utterly still, like the act of moving might call down Radovan's anger. *Cowards*, I thought somewhat cynically. If they were smart, they'd come to Radovan's aid and smack me down.

"Be careful, Your Majesty," Zosha said as if he'd read my thoughts. "I'd hate for another of your cities to suffer from your poor choices."

I rounded on Zosha, eyes blazing. "Excuse me?" I said in the echo of Eliska's gasp at this truly terrible low blow. How many thousands of people had died in Kavondy and Nadym when Radovan ordered those cities burned?

"I just mean—"

"I know what you meant," I said, vision going red. Eliska put a staying hand on my arm. Ragata reached out to her son. "I would be very careful with your next words, because if you could see your mother's face right now, *Zoshenko*, you'd know there is no forgiveness for some things."

Radovan's power slammed through me before I was even done speaking. "That's quite enough, my dear. While your journey here was no doubt uncomfortable, that is no excuse to lie to young Zosha. Pay her no mind, my boy, your mother was never anything but proud of you."

My jaw snapped shut on the tip of my tongue, filling my mouth with blood. My spine crashed into the back of the chair so hard I knew it would bruise, but I didn't care. Seeing Zosha go sickly, ghastly pale was worth it. I wanted to laugh at the terror trilling through these big, powerful men. Fear and uncertainty. Because—no matter Radovan's calming words—they didn't entirely believe him.

And while Zoshenko wasn't an uncommon nickname, the

fact that I'd used it in the same breath as his dead mother would make them wonder. Could I see her? Hear her? And if I could, who else was talking? I might not have had the ability to smile, not with Radovan's magic controlling my every twitch, but my eyes howled with laughter.

"We all know very well that you cannot use your magic. You will need to do better if you wish to enjoy company, my love." Radovan sat a little straighter, mentally brushing his hands of me, leaving my body frozen as he turned away. "Now Kostya," he said, addressing the general. "How did your family celebrate the solstice?"

The rest of the dinner passed that way. My body locked in place, muscles shaking with the effort of remaining so still. The others studiously ignored me, to the point where they didn't even look at me for fear. But of me or Radovan? I wasn't sure. Only Zosha glanced at me quickly and away again when he thought no one would notice. He didn't speak for the rest of the night, but I saw the way his shoulders curled in with shame.

Good, I thought, but wasn't able to rejoice in it. Because Ragata was crying into Zosha's arm, desperate to tell him that I'd lied. That she loved him, and nothing would change that. But Zosha was beyond her reach. He couldn't hear her, and never would again.

"Are you proud of yourself?" Eliska asked when I made it back to my room that night.

I shrugged, grimly relieved that my body was free even if I wasn't allowed to speak. *"Not really."*

"Good," Eliska replied, voice colder than snow. *"Lady Night, Askia, Ragata has been nothing but kind to you, and for you to use her like that—hasn't she suffered enough?"*

I winced, knowing she was right, but unwilling to show her how much my mistake hurt. *"I didn't think about how it would affect Ragata. His words just—"*

"They were just words, Askia. If you had stopped for half a second you would have realized that maybe he wasn't trying to hurt you, but trying to warn you?"

"Why would he do that? You said it yourself, he's Radovan's creature."

"That doesn't mean he wants to see your people butchered."

I tried to snort, but even that much sound was beyond me. I settled for yanking a brush through my hair. *"Like he's doing anything to stop it."*

Eliska sat heavily on the edge of my bed, rubbing her neck. *"When are you going to learn that no one is all good or bad? And while the people here may be complicit in Radovan's crimes, that doesn't mean they rejoice in them. If you are going to make any allies, you need to offer them at least the hope of redemption."*

Her words made sense. I knew they did, but all I could see was Nadym going up in smoke and the sound of Misha's screams when Kavondy burned. *"Even if they don't deserve it?"*

"Since when has life ever been about what we deserve?"

I scrubbed my face with my hands. *"Why did he even give me the chance to speak? He can control my every move—probably even shove words in my mouth. So why let me pretend at freedom? I don't understand."*

"For the same reason he gave you those clothes and this room," Eliska replied, gesturing at the chamber. *"He wants to be loved—the more so because he knows he doesn't deserve it. Believe that if he could bend you to his will, make you love him with his magic, he would. But not even his sorcery can accomplish that. And anyway, he has more important things to use his magic on than controlling your every move."*

"You make it sound as if his power has limits."

Something in my voice made Eliska's face soften. *"He has limits, Askia. They are far greater than a witch's would be, but they exist. When he hits them, he hits hard."*

"How so?"

"The stone essentially overheats itself, causing a backlash of immense pain. Radovan knows this all too well—it's why he almost never goes to battle himself anymore. He can't stand looking weak in front of his men."

"What does he use his power on, then?" I asked, chewing on the inside of my cheek as I forced my overtired mind to move.

"Just because he can't control you doesn't mean he doesn't try to control everything else. Roven has expanded under his rule, yes. But the more it expands, the more he feels the need to control it. Tame it. He spends most of his waking hours scrying on his stolen empire, commanding his few closely watched lieutenants."

I swallowed, but it didn't relieve the growing knot in my throat—or the hopelessness, the fear that I could no longer ignore. Because if Radovan knew he couldn't control me . . . *"What if he doesn't let me leave again? What if this was it?"* Lady Night curse me, even the voice in my mind sounded weak. Frightened. But I had to know.

"I think you intrigue him enough that he will give you another chance," she replied slowly. *"But you need to listen to me when you speak with him—and Asyl and Ragata too. There is a reason he let us live beyond the thirty days required to seal our magic in the stone. We can help you win him over and secure the time you need to escape this terrible place. But you're going to have to give him something other than scorn."*

"I don't think I can stomach kindness. Not for him."

"What about respect?"

"That even less."

"Not even for your people?"

Ozura appeared beside Eliska, and for one wild moment I thought I heard her speak—thought I heard her echo Eliska's words. But no. She was beyond me. She could only stand in silence at the end of my bed, waiting for an answer.

I only had one.

"I'll try," I said, refusing to acknowledge the chunk of my soul sloughing off. *"But I need you to get me information while I do."*

"What do you need?"

"You know who Radovan depends on, his senior councilors and military advisers. One of them must know something that can help me. Maybe they have contacts in the rebellion. Maybe they're hiding something I can use against them. Against Qaden too."

Eliska smirked at that. *"Siv will be happy to take that assignment. What else?"*

"I also need to know how the castle is laid out—from the top of the tower to the lowest dungeon. I'll need names of servants and palace guards, shift schedules, delivery drivers—hell, even court etiquette. I don't know what will become useful, so I need to know everything."

"All right," she crooned as panic started to edge into my tone. *"I will speak to the others, and we'll come up with a way to find everything you need to know. In the meantime, you should rest."*

Air chuffed out in a mirthless laugh. Although the bed looked comfortable enough and my body was tired, I doubted I'd get any rest with my mind churning. And my heart? Well, my heart didn't bear looking at.

"I doubt that will be possible."

Eliska nodded, the understanding on her face almost unbearable. *"The first night will be hard,"* she allowed, softly. Hard, but not the hardest—for that night would be my last. Eventually she shrugged. *"Try to sleep."*

She faded; her gray form burned on my eyes like the afterimage of a candle I'd stared at too long.

Alone, my shoulders slumped. My limbs were heavy as I changed into a nightdress. My feet dragged across the floor to the bed. I hauled back the covers and tucked myself in. Waited. Waited for the scrape of metal on wood, for my captors to peer through the peephole and see me in bed. Waited until the little door shut once more—to be sure of my solitude.

Only then did I let myself feel it: the loss, the despair, the bone-deep longing. Not just for freedom. For my friends. For Armaan, cold in the ground. For Nariko and Iskander, left surrounded by enemies. For Misha and Arkady and all my soldiers carrying on the fight without me.

For Illya.

And only when the night darkened, and the moon gilded my chamber in silver light, did I let the tears fall.

4

ILLYA

Interregnum.

The word echoed through the Great Hall, striking the gold and blue ceiling before falling to the foot of the empty throne with a juicy flop. Lord Elon, senior-most member of Vishir's Council of Viziers, was still talking, but the susurrus of worried whispers filling the hall nearly drowned him out.

"How can that possibly work?" Lady Nariko asked from Illya's right side.

He glanced at her, at her unkempt hair and rumpled dress, at her face still lined with horror at Queen Ozura's murder and Askia's abduction, and wasn't sure what to say. So he offered the truth. "It isn't meant to work. Not for long."

"Vishir will be ruled by the Council of Viziers," Elon continued, ignoring the noise, "under the guidance of both Prince Enver and Prince Iskander until such a time as a new emperor . . . emerges."

Nariko gasped. She wasn't alone, but as far as Illya could see, the surprise was contained to the young. The older members of court surely remembered the last time an emperor "emerged."

Because in Vishir, it wasn't the eldest son who claimed the throne.

It was the surviving one.

Illya crossed his arms. Though he and the Seraveshi guard stood on the far eastern edge of the Great Hall, he was tall enough to see over the crowd, past the line of viziers standing before the dais like a human shield, to the two princes.

The brothers stood with their backs to the throne, garbed in head to toe black. Though their resemblance was unmistakable, Enver was slighter and softer than his half brother. Still, he had something Iskander lacked: confidence. The sort of confidence his people would be reaching for in the days ahead.

The loss of their father was a blow for both princes, but Iskander had lost his mother too. For all her faults, Ozura had been a force of nature, the rock on which Iskander's whole life had stood. Without her, the young prince seemed . . . hollow.

Illya only knew Prince Enver well enough to dislike him. Enver had been a constant thorn in Askia's side, belittling her at every turn. And worse, he was a Roven sympathizer. It was Enver's friend Count Dobor who had murdered Queen Ozura, and many more, during Askia's wedding to Emperor Armaan. A fact that the council seemed to have already forgotten. Fools each one. If they were smart, they'd have killed Enver two days before, when Armaan had been found bleeding out on the floor of Ozura's mausoleum.

But it wasn't up to him. And Vishir was not Illya's problem.

Askia was. The thought burned through him with an urgency he couldn't escape.

"Regarding the Empire of Roven . . ." Lord Elon's voice rose, whip-sharp across the hall.

He needn't have bothered. Silence blanketed the space at the merest mention of Roven. Illya straightened, hand falling to the hilt of his sword.

"A portal was found in the rooms of Count Dobor. A portal through which the sorcerer Radovan crossed to kill Emperor Armaan and abduct Queen Askia."

Elon paused, and Illya watched the older man's gaze flick to the corner of the hall where the sun's light couldn't quite reach. Like the very presence of the red-robed Shazir priests polluted the air itself. Illya shifted, battle ready.

"In the course of his questioning, Dobor alluded to the possibility that this wasn't the only portal in the city of Bet Naqar," Elon continued with a deep breath. "Because of this, we are decreeing a mandatory search of every building in the city—a search overseen by Lord Vizier Khaljaq of Shazir Province. We will root out any Roven traitors. We must. I will urge you all to cooperate."

"Lady Night," Nariko whispered. "When was Khaljaq made a lord vizier?"

Illya barely heard anything over the blood pounding in his ears. A *portal*? In Count Dobor's rooms. If he had a portal, if they thought Radovan had used it to take Askia, then . . .

Then what the hell was stopping Illya from using it to save her?

A small hand touched his arm, pulling him back. "What?"

Nariko frowned up at him. "Khaljaq. Did you know he was being made a lord vizier?" she asked, her voice heavy with quiet dread. "Did Captain Nazir say anything to you?"

Illya returned her frown. He and the captain of the late emperor's close guard had struck up a friendship over the weeks Illya's men had spent in Vishir. They had even spoken about the possibility of combining forces once Askia and the emperor were wed. But things change when an emperor dies. Many things, it seemed.

"No," he replied. "No, he did not." Askia would be livid when she found out. "And it's Khaljaq who is in charge of searching the city. For portals."

Nariko only nodded, dark eyes wide with fright. "But . . ." She looked around furtively and leaned closer. "But the Shadow Guild has portals throughout the city too. If the Shazir find them, they'll accuse us of aiding Roven. I have to warn them."

Illya grabbed her arm before she could move. "Don't," he said, quiet and firm. "The Shazir are waiting to see who reacts. If you leave now, they'll know you have something to hide. You can't let them know about your . . . gifts." He held her gaze until he was sure she understood before releasing her. Askia would never forgive him if he let something happen to Nariko.

Which was why Nariko should be coming with him.

"Are you sure you won't join us?" He knew it was a vain question—she'd refused more than once, but he felt compelled to ask it one more time.

Her mouth quirked a mirthless smile. "You think I'll be safer sailing to Tolograd with you, than I will be here?"

Nariko had gone so far as to buy passage north on a Calormañan merchant ship for Illya and his men, a ship that—Day Lord willing—would leave today. If Iskander reopened the port for them. And yes, taking Nariko—a healer—into Roven was dangerous. Witches had long been hunted by Emperor Radovan. But leaving her here? "Look around Nariko. Can't you sense the fear?"

Illya let his gaze float across the enormous space. He could almost taste the tension in the air. It was building, like the metallic tang of electricity before a storm. "Things are going to become . . . difficult here. For someone like you."

She didn't flinch at his words, or bridle in unfound denial. Something in her face softened, acknowledging. "I know," she murmured, her gaze moving past the gathered lords and ladies. To Iskander. "But Ozura would want me to stay. For him."

Illya wanted to argue but knew better. For all her delicate manners, Nariko had an iron, intractable will. She would become a formidable woman, he thought suddenly. If she survived.

"The announcement is done. Come."

Nariko wove through the crowd of milling nobles, toward the dais on which Iskander still stood. Alone.

It unsettled Illya for a reason he couldn't quite name. Until a small man appeared, planting himself in their way.

Nariko jumped back, stepping on Illya's foot as she recoiled from the Shazir priest. "Excuse me, Brother," she said, sinking into a curtsy that even a week ago wouldn't have been required. *Even two days ago,* Illya thought, the ticking of a clock scratching at the back of his mind.

"How can we help you, Lady Nariko?"

If it was possible for a person to wilt, Nariko did. "I've arranged for a ship for Captain Illya and his men . . . we were hoping to speak with Prince Iskander regarding passage through the blockade."

The priest looked Nariko up and down, eyes full of greed and desire before turning a speculative gaze toward Illya and his men. He sniffed at whatever he saw and stepped away. But he didn't go to Iskander.

But to Khaljaq.

The men exchanged a few quick words before Khaljaq beckoned them all forward and led them to Iskander.

"Prince Iskander," Khaljaq said, his voice a dry rasp. "Lady Nariko and Captain Illya to see you."

The prince seemed to shake himself at Khaljaq's words. He blinked. "Nariko. Illya," he said slowly, like it took him a second to place their faces. "Did you hear about the portal?"

Nariko shot Illya a very worried look. "We did."

"Any indication as to where it leads?" Illya asked, trying not to let the words become too saturated with hope.

"No," Iskander said, the admission making his shoulders droop.

"We, of course, have no way of knowing," Khaljaq added. "Only a witch—or sorcerer—can cross a portal."

"And Dobor didn't say?"

Khaljaq's eyes narrowed on Illya, as if he expected Illya to bend. Illya held his gaze unafraid and waited.

"The traitor claims that it leads to other portals, a whole network of waystations that spans all of Vishir and Idun, penetrating deep into the northern continent."

"All the way to Roven?" Illya asked, aware of the eagerness in his voice, but unable to curb it.

"It must," Iskander said, rousing himself enough that something like light began to spark in his eyes. "You think we could use it, don't you? To get her back."

"I think we have to try," Illya pressed, as if his fervor could force Iskander back to the land of the living. Back to action.

"Alas, that we cannot do." Khaljaq's words seemed to rake across Iskander's face, leaving him smaller. Leaving him less. "As I've said, only a sorcerer can cross that portal, and we simply cannot allow Count Dobor to leave our care."

Illya felt his lip curl. "Not even if it means saving Askia? What about the Shadow Guild? Why not ask the witches of Vishir to help?"

A slow smile lifted the corners of Khaljaq's lips like the rictus grin of a naked skull. "Your devotion to Her Majesty Queen Askia is . . . admirable," he said, wielding Askia's title like a blade, skewering Illya with his own exposed emotion. His love. For Askia.

"But," Khaljaq continued, "we have yet to ascertain whether or not the witches of Vishir are in league with Radovan. Should they be found innocent, then we can entertain the idea of using the portal roads. But only then."

As if you'll allow any of them to be found innocent. Illya wanted to snarl the words, hurl them at Khaljaq's feet and shove his sword through the old man's heartless chest.

He swallowed the urge. Forced himself to nod in agreement. Because any further protest would only waste time—time Askia didn't have.

And anyway, Illya didn't really need Khaljaq's permission.

Khaljaq's smile deepened, no doubt feeling as if he'd won something. "I'm told you wish to inquire about leaving Bet Naqar."

"Yes," Illya replied, tightly. "We've chartered a ship and are ready to sail to Tolograd. To rescue Her Majesty Queen Askia. However, we need Prince Iskander's permission to pass the blockade."

"And you have it," Khaljaq smiled, incandescent as he answered for Iskander, who now gazed at his feet like a child lost in the crowd. The Shazir priest held out his hand, into which a waiting Brother slid a scroll. "Your permission, Captain Illya. May the Day Lord shine upon your journey. It is truly the God's work you do."

He held out the scroll, but when Illya grasped it, Khaljaq didn't let go. "The tide turns within the hour, Captain Illya. Do be sure you don't miss it."

Illya yanked the scroll out of Khaljaq's claw-like grip, refusing to react to the tacit threat and the very real knowledge that the Shazir were doing their level best to ensure Iskander's isolation.

Well damn them all, he thought, brushing past Khaljaq and sweeping Iskander into a tight embrace. "I know what it is to lose everything—everyone—you've ever cared for," he murmured, too low for Khaljaq to hear. "It is a grief that will never leave you, but Iskander, you must not let it consume you."

He felt a tremor shake down Iskander's spine and wondered

if anyone had even thought to comfort the poor boy—for that's what Iskander was in his heart. A boy whose parents had just been murdered. But he needed to be more if he wanted to become emperor of Vishir.

He had to become more.

Iskander sniffed. "I hear you," he whispered.

Illya pounded his back once, drew back. "Take care of Lady Nariko. For Askia."

The prince nodded silently, swallowing down emotion before pulling his head up to meet Illya's eyes. "Save her?"

Illya's smile was filled with edges and the shards of broken dreams. "Of that, I can promise you."

Illya forged a path through the still-milling nobles, heading for the doors. Only when he stepped into the hall did he take a breath savoring the feeling of release. Of escape from the hall that had become saturated with fear and brimming with the blunt edges of panic. A pot ready to boil.

Not your problem, he thought, dragging a hand through his hair. His duty was to Askia. To saving her.

He squared his shoulders and faced his men having made a decision. "Take this," he said, handing Misha the scroll, and with it his command of the close guard. "Get out of Vishir as fast as you can."

Misha's face furrowed with confusion. His wasn't the only one. Only Nariko, who was still in Illya's shadow, seemed to understand. Though how, Illya wasn't sure.

"Captain, no," Nariko said, a new worry settling atop her thin shoulders among all the others. "It's too dangerous."

"Stay to the plan," he continued to Misha. "Head to Idun. Pick up Arkady and as many of the Wolves as you can and get your asses to Tolograd."

"What about you, Cap?" Misha asked, deep voice dipping low like the first rumble of thunder.

Illya summoned a smile. "I'll meet you there."

"How—" Misha's eyes went round with understanding. "The portal. You can use it?"

Illya nodded.

"But it won't take you directly to Tolograd," Nariko said in a hurried whisper. "A hundred miles at most; you'll be jumping through dozens of portals, and—"

"Will it get me to Tolograd faster than the ship?" he asked, not allowing so much as a hint of fear into his voice.

Nariko looked up at him, dark gaze hard and appraising. "It could."

"Then the danger is worth it."

He turned to Misha. Held out his arm.

Misha grabbed it, crushing Illya's forearm with the strength of his grip. "May the Day Lord bless you. Lady Night keep you."

"And you," Illya said, the oddest feeling of loss worming through him as he watched the men leave. When he joined the Wolves, almost a year ago now, he hadn't expected to find a home. But he had, Illya realized. Not just soldiers-in-arms. Brothers.

Only when the men were gone did he turn back to Lady Nariko, wondering. "How long have you known," he asked, "that I'm a—that I'm like you?"

Her gaze floated up toward the ceiling where an orb of fiery witchlight bobbed, silently calling to him. She smiled. "The fires always burned just a little brighter whenever you saw her."

Nariko shook her head and wrapped her arms around him in a firm embrace. "She always burned brighter too," Nariko whispered. "When you were in the room."

Nariko turned away before Illya could reply and disappeared into the Great Hall. Leaving Illya alone, to savor her words. To cherish them for one sparkling moment.

Before he put them away.

Because now was not the time for soft emotions, not even for love. No. Now was the time for vengeance. For fury.

For magic.

He stalked through the empty halls, shouldering through the doors to Dobor's apartment without meeting a soul. He barely saw the detritus of a broken man's life scattered about the floor. The overturned furniture. The shredded clothes, no. His eyes were for the portal. For the two Shazir priests standing guard.

"Captain Illya," the one on the left said when Illya approached. "How can we help you?"

Illya ignored him, eyes on the wall behind them. On the doorway, outlined in black lacquer, standing in the shadow where a wardrobe once sat.

"Captain?" the man asked again.

Illya watched both men as their eyes narrowed. As their bodies tensed. As their muscles coiled, ready to strike.

Too late.

He burst into action, a fluid dance of death. The only art at which he'd ever excelled. He cut both men down before they could so much as scream. Their corpses smoldered, clothing singed where his blade ran them through. A blade that was still alight with flames. *His* flames.

Fire magic roaring through his veins, Illya stepped through the portal.

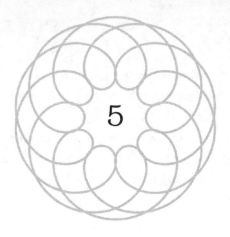

5

GOOD MORNING, *Princess.* How are you today?"

Qaden's unusually cheerful voice made my jaw ache with the memory of her fist. I wouldn't rise to the bate. Knowing the non-reaction would annoy her, I simply raised an eyebrow and waited for Qaden to move on from gloating about my still-unusable voice and tell me what she wanted. What Radovan wanted.

Somehow my entire day had become consumed by all the things Radovan desired. The thought made me frown. I'd spent all morning pacing through my room while Eliska filled my ears with lists of things Radovan liked and disliked. Asyl appeared for a few moments to add her thoughts only to disappear when Siv arrived and declared the whole plan useless.

"Just kill the bastard and be done!" she cried, like Radovan couldn't seize control of my body at a moment's notice. But even as she spoke my mind kept returning to the wardrobe and all those carefully crafted clothes—and to what Eliska said just the night before: that Radovan wanted to be loved. There had to be a way to use it.

The two maids appeared before I could formulate any sort of plan. They'd laid out leather trousers, a dark tunic, and a very warm, fitted evergreen coat lined with gleaming silver fox fur. My heart stuttered. The outfit practically shone with the possibility of freedom.

The prospect of getting out of the castle, of getting a feel for the lay of the land, filled me with grim excitement. Only the realization that Radovan wanted me to feel this way tempered my mood. It was surely the carrot meant to ensure my good behavior when I met with him.

When I met and played nice.

I was more than willing to do exactly that, but any confidence I had in my ability evaporated as Qaden sauntered around my room. She sifted her way through the contents of my vanity, rifled through the gowns hanging in the wardrobe, even peered under the bed.

The casual invasion of my privacy made my mind flash to Nariko—to the way she'd searched my rooms in Bet Naqar. Thinking of Nariko sent a pang of longing through me. It was almost homesickness, that feeling of missing her. I swallowed it down, unwilling to expose any weakness.

"*Oh. That one,*" Asyl said, the look of curiosity on her face disappearing as she looked at Qaden. Freyda, as if summoned by Asyl's unhappiness, emerged from the wall on the left.

"*Did you know her from Khezhar?*"

"*No, but she was brought here not long after I was, given a position on the guard.*" Asyl tossed her long hair over her shoulder, oblivious to the way her tresses hit Freyda in the face. Not that Freyda noticed. Her silver eyes were heavy on Qaden's face. Watching. Studying.

"*My people had the good sense to imprison rabid-dogs like Qaden-zizeg,*" Asyl continued, an ugly look crossing her face.

"*Imprison? What for?*"

She waived my question away like the reason made no difference. "*Hardly matters—unpowered animals like her were always whining about something. But she was there right through the Khezhari-Roven war.*"

I blinked, caught off guard by the blatant prejudice in Asyl's voice—not just about Qaden, but about unpowered people in general. Then I remembered the many years of bloody oppression normal humans had faced at the hands of Khezhari witches . . . witches like Asyl.

"Perhaps Qaden wouldn't have become so brutal had she not been treated so brutally by your government."

Asyl snorted. *"Are you defending her now? Radovan's loyal pup."*

"Wouldn't you be loyal to the man who freed you?" It was Freyda who replied this time. Her voice was soft, filled with all the dark deeds done during midnight hours.

I nodded, watching Freyda, mind humming with curiosity. How had she managed to kill the former guard captain?

Qaden stepped in front of me, demanding my full attention. Her rather unruly black hair was tied back, pulling the delicate skin around her dark eyes smooth. Faint wrinkles creased her forehead like a list of grievances she was carefully curating. Her full lips twisted into a smirk. "You know, I have to say, this is an improvement. Silence suits you, Princess. In fact, I think I'll suggest we make this a permanent change."

I rolled my eyes, making it as clear as silently possible that I didn't give a shit what she suggested to Radovan. She wouldn't get under my skin. She wouldn't trick me, anger me into losing my last chance at . . .

"Remember Seravesh, Askia," Eliska murmured as if she, too, were disgusted by the well-mannered deception I was preparing to dive into. *"Do this for Seravesh."*

Vitaly appeared by Eliska's side, his mere presence echoing her sentiment.

Seravesh. I thought of it—of the red-roofed cities that by now would be covered in snow. The sky would be filled with the warm haze of chimney smoke, the streets tinged with the sweet scent of cinnamon *karons*. Children would be playing in the snow, their parents watching over them with hot cider in their hands, resting through these short winter days.

Yes. I could do this for them. It might tear my soul to bits, but I could do it. For Seravesh, I would.

I nodded toward the door, and Qaden, still smiling, led the way.

I counted our steps, adding approximate distance to my mental map of the castle. Thirty steps down my corridor. Twelve steps down one flight of stairs, and then down the next hall. Twenty-eight. Twenty-nine. Thirty.

Qaden's closed fist hammered into the door, one precise floor beneath my own prison-chamber. I barely had time to feel the full impact of how imaginary my boundaries were in this place before Radovan's muffled voice beckoned us inside.

A wide battered desk took up much of the study, its scuffed wooden surface was stained and discolored with the patina of use and age. Bookcases stretched up to the ceiling and were outfitted with a tarnished brass ladder on wheels. The cases overflowed with careworn copies of books in every language I knew and more. A pair of rather threadbare chairs sat before the fire, with a half-finished game of chess laid out on the table between them.

All in all, it was not the kind of space in which I expected to find the Monster of the North. This was a humble room, one not designed for show and intimidation, but for the grinding and somewhat banal work of leadership.

Radovan looked up from his papers, gaze flashing between Qaden and me, and smiled his snake-like smile. "Hello ladies," he said, leaning back in his chair. "Are we having a good morning?"

"Very good, sir," Qaden said, her gaze sliding toward me. "I do enjoy the silence."

"Qadenzizeg, you are wicked." Radovan chuckled, clasping

his hands over his narrow waist. "How about you, Askia. Are you enjoying the silence?"

Anger that I couldn't quite control flooded through me. My skin burned with it, more powerful than the tether permanently stiffening my joints with cold.

"*Look contrite,*" Eliska whispered, materializing in front of the bookcase on my left.

I took a breath. Scraped my teeth along the inside of my cheek, letting the pain center me. I looked at Radovan, shook my head no.

One of his dark brows rose. "No, I didn't think you would." He stood with a sigh and circled the desk. His footsteps echoed through my head like a challenge. Closer. Closer. Daring me to flinch. He raised a hand, then paused, as if to see whether I'd slap it away.

I let my eyes drop, focusing on the black fabric of his collar, on the gold-piped edging that fell open, exposing the dip of his collarbones. The dead, fish-like skin stretched tight revealing the slow leap of his pulse thrumming beneath his flesh.

The Aellium stone grew hot as I imagined the feeling of his blood on my hands. If he could see the thoughts on my face, he said nothing, just brushed his fingers up the column of my throat. A reminder of my own impotence.

Something popped beneath my skin. Heat seared up my throat, restoring my voice in a wave of pain. I forced myself to stay silent. Stay still. Waited for Radovan to step away. But he didn't. His fingertips dragged upward, lifting my chin to the light, tracing the edge of my jawline. The bruise from Qaden's fist had surfaced overnight, staining my skin purple and blue.

"What happened here?" Radovan's voice was almost ragged with anger, dragging my gaze up to meet his watery green eyes. Outrage blazed in those otherworldly depths.

Eliska was right, I thought, weighing my options. Radovan

really must see himself as a knight from the old tales. Why else would he care about me getting knocked around by one of his guards? He was going to kill me anyway. It shouldn't have mattered. But it obviously did, I realized, feeling fear shiver through Qaden's body.

"Say something, Askia," Eliska urged.

"Tell him it was Qaden," Siv added, appearing on the captain's other side, her voice brimming with savage pleasure.

As attractive as the thought of getting Qaden into trouble was, I couldn't bring myself to do it. Her devotion to Radovan had been apparent from the first moment I met her, but here in this cozy little office, her fear was exposed too. I wasn't the only one in danger. Whatever the private battles we waged were, they were between Qaden and me, and I didn't need Radovan to take care of her for me.

Ozura appeared in the space past Radovan's shoulder. Her body was still half smoke, but her face was set. Her starlit eyes glittered as she looked at me, read my face. Nodded.

"Tell me what happened, Askia," Radovan purred. "I want to protect you."

I dragged my attention back to him. Let one shoulder rise and fall in a languid, boredom-filled shrug. "Nothing important."

Radovan frowned. "Someone has struck you, my dear. It most certainly is important."

"It was me, sire. I did it. I didn't like how she was speaking to you." The confession bubbled out of Qaden like it simply couldn't be contained.

Radovan turned slowly. "Captain." The exclamation was soft but filled with a kind of growing menace that made the small hairs on my arms rise.

"Please. She barely made contact," I said with a scathing snort—enough to jerk Radovan's attention back to me.

"My Voyniks do not strike unarmed women."

The sheer number of retorts I could have flung at him nearly struck me dumb. I stifled them. Let my brows rise. "I was a soldier first, Radovan. I know how to take a punch."

Radovan blinked, his eyes danced across my face with surprise. "Very well, Qadenzizeg. Since Her Majesty does not seem to harbor any ill will toward you, I will forgive you. This time."

Qaden folded in two, she bowed so deeply. "Thank you, sire."

Radovan nodded once, surveying his guard through hooded eyes. "Now apologize to Her Majesty."

Qaden straightened slowly. The blood fled from her face, casting her skin with a sickly green tinge. She rotated toward me, her body so rigid she looked like she was on hinges. She opened her mouth, only to close it again. Swallowed. "I apologize for striking you, Your Majesty."

"And you promise to never do so again," Radovan prompted.

She winced as if the words hurt. "I promise to never hurt you again."

"Very good, Qadenzizeg," Radovan said, squeezing the captain's shoulder. "You are excused."

With a hurried bow to her liege, Qaden all but fled the room. The door slammed behind her, the sound echoing in the narrow space between Radovan and me. Every nerve in my body screamed to fling myself on him, to wrap my hands around his neck and . . .

I forced a humorless smile. "Well, I feel terribly safe now."

Radovan laughed in a way that was surely meant to convey delight. The sound did nothing to warm me. "Qadenzizeg has always been zealous in her loyalty. I normally wouldn't complain, but she does occasionally rise above her station."

"As if you don't go out of your way to make sure she feels like your most intimate companion."

Radovan just smiled. "But you surprise me, Askia," he said,

ignoring the comment as he tilted his head. "Why did you come to her defense?"

"Yeah, why did you defend her?" Siv echoed, drawing an impatient shush from Eliska.

I did my best to stay focused on Radovan rather than the ghosts crowded around us. The weight of his full attention clung uncomfortably to my skin, like my every twitch was an answer he could judge. It felt like being interviewed by Ozura.

I glanced over and saw Ozura's lips move. A sound I couldn't quite hear hissed across empty space.

"Yes, what?" Siv asked, catching the words I couldn't hear.

"Did Asyl have truth witch abilities?" I asked, mentally aiming the question at Eliska, only to have Asyl appear beside her.

"I did. And Radovan surely does too." Asyl crossed her arms like it could stop Radovan from using her magic. *"Be very careful how you answer him, Askia. No truth witch enjoys being lied to."*

I stretched my lips into a smug smile. "Probably for the same reason you insist on calling Qaden by her full name," I replied, and shrugged when he looked confused. "Because it will annoy her."

Radovan inhaled my words in the half second after I spoke them, but I wasn't afraid. They were true—if not the whole truth. He shook his head. "You're as wicked as the captain, Askia. Although, for the record, I don't call her Qadenzizeg to annoy her."

"Oh?"

"No. It's a beautiful name—the name of a rare flower, you know. She should wear it with pride." His hand shot out before I could blink, fingers digging into my bruised jaw. Pain seared through my face while his magic slithered beneath my skin. Healing me. But he wasn't done.

His hand dropped to the base of my neck, sliding beneath my tunic. I moved, latching onto his wrist. "Don't."

He froze. Frowned. "Don't you want me to heal it? To heal them all?"

I swallowed. Of course he'd seen the scar on my neck, but the fact that he knew about the other ones—the ones on my back . . .

A shiver I couldn't contain worked down my spine, shattering once more all illusions of privacy. "No," I said, slow and clear. "I am what I am, Radovan. These scars are what made me."

The sharp feeling of appraisal peppered my skin. He hadn't moved. Neither had I. "But after what you've been through. The trauma. Most people would want to forget."

"I'm not most people," I shot back. "I don't want to forget, because if I did—" I snapped my jaw shut on the rest of the words, on what they exposed.

Understanding softened his gaze. "Because if you forgot you might not get your vengeance."

The empathy—Radovan's empathy—made a small piece of my soul go black with shame. "Wouldn't you?"

"Why, yes, Askia. I really would." His gaze dropped to my lips, filling my body with ice and panic. But he stepped away. Clasped his hands behind his back with a slight bow. "Very well. All will be as you wish." He paused, shaking his head almost in wonder. "I've heard a lot about you, and yet you're not what I expected."

"Good." I flashed a smile when he shot me a pointed look. "You've lived a long time, Radovan. I'd hate for it to get boring."

"Oh, no," he said with a chuckle. "Boredom is for the unimaginative. And I have never lacked for vision. In fact, that's why I asked you down here today. Let me show you."

He beckoned me to one of the windows, passing obliviously through the ghosts of three of his wives and one Vishiri queen.

I followed, feeling their approval and caution and doubt as I passed, not tarrying to analyze their reactions. They'd no doubt tell me what I was doing right and wrong later. Right now I needed to be on my guard and on my game.

I peered through the narrow window, the glass amazingly smooth in the neat, gilded frame. The sky was clear over Tolograd, as if the sun wished to shine its brightest for the few hours it had before ceding to the ever-grasping darkness. Made me long for Vishir, that sunlight. But unlike Vishir, where light and heat traveled hand in hand, I knew from experience that the full winter sun meant it must be freezing outside.

"Tolograd was a broken city when I came into power. Dirt streets crowded with buildings made of mud and straw. People and animals everywhere—all of them lice-ridden and starving. The air choked with smoke from fires that never went out. And the *smell*. Day Lord save me, not even the winter wind could shift that stench."

I watched Radovan speak from the corner of my eye. Watched the shadow crossing his face as the memory of his city rose in his mind. Memory. Because that place was no more.

"Look at it now," he murmured. "Scoured clean. Made anew."

I obeyed the command, looking intently out the window, past the castle walls and the raging blue-black waters of the River Tol, which surrounded the castle grounds, and took in the land beyond.

Tolograd was a city of walls. Splayed out on both sides of the river, it spread like a set of descending stairs. Homes and businesses of the inner city clung close to the river and the castle at its heart. They rose to a uniform height, identical white granite walls the same stone as the castle but tiled with indigo shingles.

Past the inner city, beyond a circular wall, was another tier of homes and buildings, a level shorter. Then another wall, another tier. Another. Another. Eight in all stretching from the castle to the sea, the port a gleaming speck in the distance.

"What do you think?"

What did I think? I thought the sectors were like the tattoos—just another way for Radovan to demarcate his people. Separate them. Control them. From the Neprik toiling in near slavery all the way up to his Voynik soldiers and noble Dorovnii.

"It's very . . ." I shook my head, struggling to find the right word. "Orderly."

"Yes," he said, seizing on it like the greatest compliment. "It is orderly by design. This city is my garden, and I've grown it, pruned it, tended and cared for it. There is no more poverty here. No hunger. No chaos. It's wonderful, isn't it?"

"It is." And it was. But it was also sterile. Stifling. And wholly unsustainable. People weren't plants. You couldn't sow them in rows and expect them to grow in place. People were unpredictable. Ever-changing. Chaotic.

Human.

"This is what I want for the north. For the world. Is that really so bad?"

I looked at him hard, brow furrowing. "Do you really want an answer to that?"

He held my gaze for a long moment. I could feel the gears of his mind moving. He opened his mouth—and there was a knock at the door.

Radovan smiled. "Enter."

Zosha pushed through the door. Froze when he saw me. Bowed. "You asked to see me?"

"Yes, Zosha. Come."

Zosha came as he was called. His face was neutral, but there was something almost strained in the way he was not looking at me. "How can I serve?"

"I was hoping you would show Her Majesty around the castle grounds."

Zosha stiffened slightly. "If you wish it, my lord."

"If I wish it," Radovan murmured, frowning with clear dissatisfaction. He glanced from me to Zosha and back again. "I see. Askia, I think things might go smoother if you apologized to Zosha for your unkind words last night."

I crossed my arms slowly. "No."

"Askia." Eliska gasped. *"No—you must apologize."*

"Come now, Askia. I had the captain apologize to you, it's only fair you do the same for Zosha."

Zosha, for his part, was looking at his feet, clearly wanting nothing from me.

"Do it, Askia," Eliska insisted. Even Siv and Asyl murmured their encouragement.

But I had another idea. Risky. But all the best ones were.

"No. You commanded an apology from the captain, which is your prerogative; she is your subject. I am not. And I will not apologize for something I don't regret."

Radovan's eyebrows drew together, and for the first time he began to betray a growing displeasure with me. That genial mask began to slip. "Zosha is like a son to me, and it would please me if the two of you were on friendly terms. Especially if he is to be your daily guide around the castle. But if you're not interested in leaving your rooms . . ."

He let his words trail off, evaporating into the air like a choked scream in the middle of the night. I refused to so much as blink. "If Zosha wishes to earn my respect, he is welcome to try." *You both are*, my words implied. "But I am not going to waste my time lying to either of you."

Radovan's jaw set. The vein in his temple leapt against his pale flesh. "Do you not understand the opportunity you are squandering here? I am trying to start a relationship, but if you are not willing to—"

"No, Radovan, it is you who is missing an opportunity."

"Askia, please. Be careful," Eliska begged.

Vitaly shushed her. *"Give her a second to think."*

But I didn't need to think—I already knew what to do. Curiosity swirled in the air around Radovan. A curiosity I needed to nurture.

"What opportunity?" Radovan asked slowly, like that could keep his anger in check.

"The rarest of commodities that all rulers both need and fear." I smiled as his curiosity bloomed enough to shade his anger. "The truth."

Radovan cocked his head to the side like a cat spotting a mouse. "The truth?"

Zosha rocked back on his heels. Slid his hands into his pockets. Edged away.

"Lady Night save us, she's done for," Siv moaned.

"It's not too late to apologize," Eliska said quickly.

"Yes," Asyl agreed. *"Perhaps if you—"*

Ozura stepped forward, silencing the other ghosts with the force of her presence. My lips tugged up into a tight smile, sensing her approval.

I nodded. "I cannot offer you kindness, or promise my respect, but I will give you what no one else in your life will: honesty."

"Tell me, Askia, do you think my people are lying to me? Or that I'm too much of an imbecile to know fact from fiction?"

His words were delivered with no small amount of annoyance, but I could hear an undercurrent of interest beneath them.

"I'm not saying either of those things. But I know what it's like to rule. I know how it feels to have people crowding around you, fawning over your every exhalation in the hopes they will rise in your esteem." All right, it wasn't *that* common an experience for me, but it had happened once or twice, and I'd hated it every time. "It's exhausting. Don't you find it exhausting?"

I sensed him struggling not to react, but the slight twitch of his lips betrayed him. The fact that he'd given me—and all the wives—a room of our own and perfectly fitted clothes, that he hovered over us, pulling out chairs and coming to our defense, betrayed him. He was a monster. Of that I had no doubt. But one with a deadly insecurity for what people thought.

I met his gaze, willing him to feel my sincerity, compelling him to feel the worth of my offer. "Again, I cannot say that I will always be courteous. But my lack of sugary words to lull you, or manners to charm you, will be to your benefit—you'll always know what I truly think. Honest and impolite as I might be, I am offering you the very center of who I am. Scars and all."

I felt the weight of his considerable attention fall onto my shoulders, tasting my words, savoring my meaning. Considering. I held his gaze, drawing him in. When his eyes fell to the base of my neck, I knew I had him.

"You continue to surprise me, Askia," he murmured. He flashed me a crooked smile. "Enjoy the day, my dear."

6

THE STUDY DOOR closed, echoing in the space between Zosha and me. His eyes were wide, still not quite meeting my face. He opened his mouth, only to close it again—as if it was an act of will to remain silent. Zosha jerked his head toward the stairs and walked away.

I smiled at his back, following him through the white and gold halls and down the stairs. Since he didn't seem interested in speaking to me, and none of my ghosts had joined us, I used this as my chance to look around properly for the first time.

Like my descent into the Great Hall last night, we took the curving stairs down—curving, I realized, because they hugged the edge of the central tower–turned–Great Hall. Corridors sprouted off every landing with people everywhere. Stony soldiers and silent servants, giggling young noblewomen and haughty-faced mothers and fathers. Many of them nodded to Zosha, a few even going so far as to bow as he passed. He nodded to his admirers but didn't stop to speak with any of them— much to the pained heartbreak of a few teenage girls who sighed after him with overly perfumed longing.

Fewer people took the time to appraise me. I supposed that since I was dressed plainly, they assumed I was one of Zosha's servants. Only a few sharp-eyed people saw my face, saw my tattoo-less cheeks, and realized who I was. I winked at one such woman, a Dorovnii noblewoman judging by her class sigil, who was shepherding her doughy husband up the stairs. She gasped with recognition, stumbling backward into an ornamental table inlaid with Kizuokan jade.

Zosha looked over his shoulder, finally meeting my eyes. I smiled, knowing it didn't warm my expression. With a frown, he picked up the pace. In a few minutes we were off the stairs, through the castle, and out a pair of ebony doors set with golden vines and wicked-looking thorns.

The cold that greeted us took my breath away. Literally. In seconds, all the moisture in my face was sucked out. Air burned in my lungs. My fingers went numb. It was worse than trying to bring a spirit out of death, I thought, instinctively pushing the few dregs of my magic away. I drew up my hood and clumsily buttoned my collar. I thought a Seraveshi winter was cold, but Day Lord save me, was the sun only an ornament here?

Zosha cocked a dark eyebrow at me, jamming a fur-lined hat over his head, before yanking on a pair of thick gloves. How I longed for a pair of gloves. I'd have to request them from the maids, I thought, stuffing my aching hands into my pockets.

Once we were buttoned up, Zosha and I were back to staring at one another. The silence between us stretched thin. It was like a test, seeing which one of us would break first. But I'd been through worse than this.

Zosha looked down, shoved his hands into his pockets. "There has been a castle on this island since Roven's beginning, though it wasn't originally the capital," he said, turning on his heel and setting off across the snow-covered courtyard. "The old capital—the city of Volgorod—was further south along the River Tol. However, a cataclysm struck in the year 1046, destroying the city and creating the Riven Cliffs."

I thought of the maps I'd seen, of the scar that cut Roven in two, and savagely wished for another cataclysm.

"The capital was moved here to Tolograd after the disaster, but it was never much more than a provincial backwater. That is until the emperor rebuilt the old castle in his first decade of rule. The castle is oriented around the central tower. Two tiered walls encase the tower with their own watchtowers set at the cardinal points. And the curtainwall surrounds everything."

He continued as we crossed the courtyard to where the curtainwall rose from the ground, further separating the castle from the city beyond, as if the raging of the river weren't impediment enough. We scaled a narrow and icy set of stairs, reaching an equally slippery battlement, where guards bearing pikes and crossbows stood watch beside braziers that burned so hot the fires within them had to be magically fed.

Zosha went on and on—and on and on—about the castle's construction, about the source of the white granite and the blue porphyry. Ragata appeared while he spoke, dragging magic out of me involuntarily. The cold yank of the tether was almost unbearable, but I didn't have the heart to banish her. I watched her while Zosha continued, watched her nodding along with his words, beaming with pride. She even mouthed along with his speech—though I wasn't sure how she knew what he was going to say, unless—

"How many times have you done this?"

"Done what?" Zosha asked, clearly annoyed by my interruption.

"Given this tour to Radovan's wives."

"Three."

I frowned. "Only three?"

One of Zosha's shoulders twitched. "Queen Siv was never well-behaved enough," he said, before reverting to his tour-speech.

After that, I only half listened to his explanation for why the castle was built hugging the island's northern bank rather than in its center (unstable bedrock), and mostly tuned out his grand speech about the watchtowers. While he gestured to the nearest one, I turned away to look across the river, the eight-tiered city beyond—nine if you included the island. From this distance it looked like a toy. All rigid lines and clean-looking streets. Doll-sized people darting here and there, dark specks against a white backdrop.

"The domes themselves aren't truly copper—"

"Yeah, yeah, I know," I said, having already heard Ragata give this part of the speech. "They're red brass. Copper, zinc, iron, and lead. Which is *so* fascinating, but what I really want to know about are the people. Tell me about all the little tattoos." I knew about them from Eliska, of course. But I wanted to know what Zosha thought, wondering if the son of a murdered queen might be my first ally here.

Zosha's eyes narrowed, crinkling his own tattoo, as he dragged his attention from the tower to my face. "How do you know the chemical makeup of red brass?"

I waived the question away. "I read a lot."

"You can hardly be widely read if you know about the castle's architecture, but nothing about this mainstay of Roven culture."

"Not a mainstay, surely." I grinned, goading him enough to keep him talking. An annoyed Zosha I could use—mine for information. Scared and angry Zosha was only good for sullen silence and mind-numbing architectural details.

"What is that supposed to mean?"

"Well, Radovan's only been in power for what? Eighty years? That's barely a blink in the grand history of Roven. Things can always change back, don't you think?"

Zosha hissed out a breath, like he was trying to silence me. He looked down the battlement, as if judging how far away the guards were and if they could have overheard. "I don't know if you're brave for saying such things in defiance of possible consequences, or a fool for not considering that there might be any."

I kept smiling. "What can I say? The contradiction is part of my charm. Are you going to answer my question?"

"What charm?" He glowered. "And which question?"

"About the tattoos, of course," I replied, my voice too innocent. The question about changing Roven would keep.

"The tattoos indicate social status," he said after a long pause, turning away from the tower to look across the city—glower at, really. "It's more complicated than that of course—everything here is."

"I have time," I said, keeping my voice mild. The stone around my neck seemed to twitch in laughing defiance of my words. Time? Five days gone, twenty-five remained.

Twenty-five days before I escape . . . or am murdered.

"Roven is a . . . rigid place," he said, pulling my attention away from the cliff of my impending doom. "Tolograd even more so. The class you're born into—nine in all—is the class you live in until you die. It predicts the way your life and the lives of your family will pass, what you will do, who you will marry—even what parts of the city you have access to."

"So if you're born in poverty, you'll die in poverty," I said, not bothering to hide my disdain.

"There's no real poverty here," he said, not quite responding to my jab. "You can imagine how deadly homelessness would be here during our winters. Any Neprik who can't afford housing is given a home in exchange for working in public service."

"It's slavery, Zosha. Hiding it behind the name Neprik doesn't change that," I said, my voice flat. "Tell me, are they allowed to speak or are voices only desirable in the higher classes?"

"Only castle servants are rendered mute. And they belong to

the Shepoy class—servants and laborers. Anyway, the muting is as much for their protection as the nobility's."

"Do explain."

"Surely I don't need to," he said, giving me a hard look. "You just came from Vishir. You know firsthand how palace conspiracies can trap everyone in webs of intrigue and lies. Politics is politics, no matter where you are. Here, though, the servants aren't at risk of being drawn into games of power, and because of that, no too-cunning noble can use them as scapegoats for their bad behavior."

"But to never be able to speak—"

"They don't mind. Of everyone in the Shepoy class, the servants here are the lucky ones. They are compensated handsomely for their work. Their lives are nothing to despair of."

"Only a man would think that taking a maid's voice would protect her." I spat the words, letting them freeze in midair before striking Zosha's face with dark shards of darker meaning. He blanched.

"I'm sure that nothing untoward happens—"

"Because of course no nobleman would press his advantage with a servant?" I shook my head. Arguing this point with Zosha wouldn't change anything—might only alienate him, and he was only just becoming useful. *You want to change things? Kill Radovan*, I thought trying to vent my anger.

"So the Neprik and the Shepoy are the lower classes," I said, forcing myself to move on. "I assume there are some kind of special names for skilled workers and merchants?"

Zosha swallowed, looking guilty enough to make me feel slightly less angry with him. "The Vestyyi are our skilled workers. And what you would call a merchant class we call the Tovach. Most of the Roven citizens you would have encountered in Vishir would have been Tovachii traders."

I felt my brows twitch. Count Dobor was no merchant. "I'm

sure they were, but no Roven citizen I've ever met had tattoos on their faces."

"The tattoos only appear when we're on Roven soil. The emperor doesn't like the idea of our people being persecuted for the way they look."

"Yes, that must be the reason," I said, my voice loaded with doubt. "And I'm sure the fact that the lack of tattoos makes it easier to spy has nothing to do with it."

Zosha's shoulders skimmed his ears, but again, he refrained from commenting. "The middle class is also composed of the Svetniks, priests and scholars, as well as the Niskoy—lower nobility." He paused, eyes flicking toward the nearest guard. "The Voyniks are their own class."

The phantom scent of burning timber and charred flesh tickled my nose as the wind screamed a dirge for the two cities burned at Voynik hands. "Your soldiers have their own social class?"

He nodded. "The largest in Roven."

"And it's above the lower nobility?"

I shouldn't have been so surprised. Roven was nothing if not a war machine. Yet it was surprising that Radovan valued his soldiers more than any of his nobles. Or maybe not surprising.

Telling.

Zosha was back to looking carefully away from me, and I was getting the sense that saying any more about the Voyniks might be dangerous. "That would leave the upper nobility."

He nodded. "The Dorovnii," he supplied.

"That's only eight classes. You said nine."

He flashed a smile. "You're forgetting the emperor."

Radovan in a class of his own. Typical.

"So where do witches fit in in this ice-covered utopia of yours?"

Zosha looked at me—really looked at me. His eyes filled with such frank appraisal that I had to wonder if his hesitance and fear up to this point was nothing more than an elaborate act. "Witches have no place in Roven," he said, his voice low—too low to carry.

Something dark rumbled in my chest. "What about Branko?" I demanded, speaking the name of the fire witch who had burned my cities with such vehemence the snow on the battlement wall should have melted.

Zosha bit the inside of his cheek, considering. "There are a few powerful witches in the empire, of course. Men and women willing to work for the emperor. They're overseen by the Voyniks, but they don't belong to the warrior class, not really. And the emperor will never allow them entrance into Tolograd."

I smiled. "He fears them."

"Who wouldn't fear a man like Branko?"

"And yet your emperor set that monster loose on my country. On my people. What happens when there are no more cities to burn?"

"The same thing that happens to all the other witches in the north."

The Aellium stone was suddenly heavy beneath my clothes. I could almost feel it ticking against my flesh, a phantom heartbeat running counter to my own. "You murder them. You murder them for their magic."

He winced at the emotion in my voice. "Magic is a resource that only a small percentage of the population can naturally use. The emperor has decided it should be redistributed." He spoke the words automatically, like a lesson learned by rote.

"Redistributed?" I sneered. "Don't hide behind sterile phrases. The more distance you put between yourself and the truth won't make you any less responsible for it." From the corner of my eye, I saw Ragata quail at my outrage. "Lady Night curse you. Between Radovan and the Shazir, there will be no more witches this time next year."

"We're not like the Shazir," Zosha said quickly. "The emperor doesn't think magic is evil, he just believes more people should be able to use it. Only one percent of the population are born witches. Now almost ten percent are sorcerers."

"Yes, but you still had to kill that original one percent to do it," I pressed. "And even if you discount those deaths, as you so clearly do, exactly how is the magic redistributed? How many Nepriks working as 'public servants' have magic?"

A flush that had nothing to do with the cold started in Zosha's cheeks, creeping into his crowned, crossed-key Dorovnii tattoo. "The magic must go where it is needed the most."

"You mean it goes to the powerful. To the never-ending war—to blood and death," I said. Ragata put a staying hand on my shoulder, but I was already so cold, I hardly noticed. "Tell me, Zosha. Will you look them in the eye—the witch you'll kill for magic?"

"I will never have magic."

Zosha spoke the words slowly. Carefully. It made me pause long enough to drag myself away from anger. Consider what he was trying to say.

"Please listen," Ragata begged. *"He's a good boy—he's my good boy."*

Zosha cocked his hip against the battlement wall, angling his head closer to mine. "I think you will find—if you're smart enough to look—that none of the Dorovnii have magic. Every sorcerer in Roven either is, or was, a Voynik."

I felt my eyes narrow. Why would Radovan only make soldiers into sorcerers? If it was Vishir, every member of the Council of Viziers would have a stone—they'd demand one. Didn't Radovan want to keep his nobles happy? Unless . . . unless what he really wanted was to keep his nobles in line.

I thought back to Vishir, to the always grasping and scheming court. To power-lusting men like Enver and Ishaq. How many times had I wished for a way to shut them all up?

"So there are Voynik sorcerers all over the north. How many in the city?"

He shrugged. "Very few wear the power openly."

"Like General Koloii," I said, thinking back to dinner and wondering. "Who else? Qaden?"

"I can honestly say I have no idea. But that's the thing about Roven you need to understand. It's the soldiers who have the power here."

Something hard flashed in Zosha's eyes. It made me pause to consider my next words and wonder. The rebellion Ozura had mentioned . . . I'd always assumed it would begin with the weak, with the downtrodden rising up and demanding more, as they had in every other land. But Roven was nothing if not a contradiction.

Perhaps this rumored rebellion had begun among the highest echelons of society—not that I'd seen any evidence of it thus far. My gaze cut to Zosha. He was looking over the battlement, giving one of the guards an easy smile like he didn't have anything to worry about. Maybe he didn't. Maybe he was playing both sides.

"Don't." Ragata appeared before me. Nose to nose, eyes blazing, which only made me colder. Gone was the flighty woman whose mind wandered through architectural avenues that only she could see. *"I will help you fight Radovan. I will help you escape. But you leave my son out of it."*

"My lady?" Zosha's voice came from far away.

Ragata's form almost seemed to solidify, demanding a promise. But it was a promise I couldn't give. I had to survive this place—had to escape before Radovan killed me for my magic. My people needed me to survive. And so, ironically, did the

Roven people. Because if I—crippled though I was by the chain around my neck—still had ghosts combing the castle, what would Radovan do with the full breadth of my magic? There was no door he wouldn't open. No secret he wouldn't uncover.

And Zosha knew it. Feared it.

Which meant I could use him.

I made myself look at Ragata, see how her face ached with longing. Guilt echoed through my heart. Guilt and empathy, for I knew what it was to long for a lost mother.

But I needed Zosha's help. At least for now.

"I lied to you last night," I said, softly. "Your mother never said she was disappointed. I'm sure she loves you very much."

"What?" Something shuttered behind his eyes. "Why are you telling me this?"

I cocked an eyebrow. "Was this not why you were so forthcoming with your information?" I smiled at his suspicion and shrugged. "We orphans have to stick together."

"I'm not an orphan," he hurried to say. "I still have the—I still have Radovan."

Back to toeing the line, I thought, feeling my smile slide into a smirk. "Of course, you do. He is *like* a father to you, after all."

7

SIX DAYS HAD passed since my meeting with Radovan in his study, and my days had fallen into a predictable rhythm. I'd walk with Zosha in the morning, join the court for luncheon and supper, and spend the long evening hours shadow-sparring with Vitaly. The training wasn't doing much to improve my technique, but as the hours and days passed, sloughing off my flesh like so much dead skin, the physical exertion was the only thing keeping me sane. Or letting me sleep. For only in utter exhaustion could I find the solace of oblivion.

Because there was an ever-present itch between my shoulders, like the weight of eyes on my back. Radovan's eyes. His attention haunted my waking hours. His attention . . . but not his presence. For I hadn't seen him—not even once—since our meeting, and even the ever-optimistic Eliska had to admit his absence was unusual. She said it was a good sign, her voice too hopeful for me to agree with.

Not when I noticed that the Aellium stone had begun to glow.

The change in the stone was so small, at first I thought I was imagining it—for the cursed gem always sparkled. But when I saw it shining against the bathwater, I knew this was more than my own imagining.

Eliska's face fell when I asked her about it. *"No, you aren't imagining it. The stone is glowing brighter for every day you spend here."*

I didn't bother voicing my despair; Eliska's tone was miserable enough for the both of us. *"Does Radovan plan to keep me locked up here with nothing to do but watch this damned stone glow?"*

"I don't think so. He's considering your offer," Eliska said, bracingly. *"If he's not sure he wants to hear the truth, it's only because he knows he needs to. Wait. Be patient. And when your chance comes, seize it with both hands."*

Even though she initially opposed this plan, it was good advice. But I was still waiting for the opportunity as Zosha and I walked once more along the battlement wall. Something of a warm front had descended upon Tolograd, making our daily walks *almost* bearable.

Of course there was snow everywhere, and the ornamental pond in the center of the courtyard was still frozen, but the thick cloud cover above made the ground warm enough to entice the castle's Dorovnii outside. The way they laughed and played painted the courtyard in rosy shades of happiness. The people who made this frigid wasteland home simply couldn't ignore the merriment of midwinter and the accompanying promise of a far-off spring.

Not even Zosha was immune to it. Though caution and suspicion still struck him, normally making him a dour companion, he was smiling and laughing today.

Well, not with me. I was sure that wouldn't have looked good to the rest of the court. No, he was leaning up against the curtainwall, heating his hands over one of the braziers and trading bawdy jokes with a particularly good-looking Voynik. In fact, Zosha quite often liked to tarry around that particular guard, who even I had to admit filled out his soldier's kit admirably.

I smiled, nuzzling my cold nose into the fur lining of my

hood, and wandered along to give Zosha a bit of privacy. A pack of girls were huddled arm in arm below my part of the wall, exchanging frilly secrets in whispers that their excitement made carry. A few older couples walked languid circles around the courtyard, like the white stone walls and muddy snow underfoot were the finest of Vishiri gardens. A group of young mothers crowded around the pond, hawkishly watching their children skate across the ice. It all looked so . . . normal. As though these few warm days let them forget they were all forced to live in this castle like sheep in an opulent pen.

On the far side of the courtyard, where the garrison jutted away from the curtainwall, a group of Voyniks were sparring. Qaden watched them, arms crossed, her expression riddled with dissatisfaction. I could see why. The pair currently suffering her scrutiny were getting sloppy. Poor grip, loose form, and feet planted too far apart on the slippery ground.

Vitaly's diaphanous form hovered among them, watching—*studying*—the training with a scowl I understood too well. If Illya had been their captain, the pair would be doing laps right now. I wondered why Qaden was letting the fight continue. Their incompetence was likely to get them both injured. Maybe that was exactly the reason—she simply didn't care if her people got hurt.

A sound caught my ear. Just beyond the circle of soldiers, I spied a group of boys. They were huddled in the eave between the garrison and the curtainwall. I squinted, making out a rickety-looking staircase, but that was not what the boys were looking at.

Jeering at, I amended with a frown. The boys had clumped snow and ice into balls, hurling them at whatever poor creature was trapped beneath the stairs. I looked around, eyes wide, waiting for someone to see the mischief and call it off. As I thought it, one of the Voyniks watching the spar with Qaden turned. Saw the boys. And looked away.

I felt my face harden. What had I expected? That a Roven Voynik would show mercy to a tortured creature? They couldn't even summon mercy for humans. Why should they care about an animal?

Weaving past the on-duty guards, I stalked toward the boys. I was halfway down the wall when Qaden looked up, marking me so casually it was obvious she'd been aware of my presence the whole time. She smiled. Rose.

Leaving her guards behind, she marched straight past the boys and their helpless prey without so much as a blink. My steps didn't falter as the distance closed, but I kept my movements loose in case she decided to try something.

She saw that, too, judging by her smile. "Well, well, look at this. A Seraveshi princess all alone."

"Hardly alone," I said, matching her tone, ice for ice. "I'm perfectly surrounded, but then you Voyniks always need numbers to feel brave."

A splotchy flush worked into Qaden's cheeks. "Are you feeling brave, Princess? How many days do you have left, now?" She shot a smug look toward the stone on my chest, clearly knowing full well what the ever-growing glow meant.

"Enough to know that I can die easy," I replied, gesturing to the fumbling soldiers below us. "If that's how you train your soldiers, my people have nothing to worry about." I shook my head with a smirk. "I trained with the Khazan Guard, you know. You're going to be obliterated."

"You should learn to hold your tongue."

"And you should learn to lead," I shot back. "Why are you letting them continue the spar? They're only going to hurt themselves."

"Then they'll get hurt," she replied, as if my argument were utterly beneath her. "And they'll learn more for the injury than any words."

I felt my mouth twist into a frown. "That's no way to teach—"

"Why not?" Qaden demanded. "It's how I learned, and I guarantee I could best any Vishiri swordmaster you put in front of me."

I looked her up and down slowly, taking in her corded muscle and easy grace even on the slick, icy stone. "Now that I'd like to see."

Her answering smile was a slow, feral thing. "I'm sure you would. Who knows, maybe Radovan will use your magic to part the mist and let you watch from beyond the grave. Now where's your minder? You shouldn't be wandering alone."

"Lord Zosha is otherwise engaged."

Qaden looked past me. Snorted. "Are you just now realizing Lord Zosha won't be seduced by your meager charms?" She smirked as if she expected me to fall back and faint. "Poor little princess. Yours isn't the first heart Lord Zosha has broken."

"Of the two of us, I'm not the one pining over an uninterested man," I said, flashing a knowing smile. "Where is your dear unrequited love? Does he know there's a mob of boys torturing an animal beneath your nose?"

Qaden glanced over her shoulder. An expression I couldn't identify flashed across her face. Pity? Fear? It was gone before I could name it. She hitched up her shoulders. "I'm no one's mother." She pushed past me, no doubt to give Zosha an earful about letting me wander.

I shook my head. Least I could do was teach those evil little warts a lesson before Zosha dragged me back to my rooms. I stalked the length of the wall, circling the boys from above. Listening to their taunts with a slowly growing anger boiling in my gut.

There were six of them in all, and though I was terrible at judging age in children, I guessed they were all between eleven and thirteen. Old enough to know better than to pick on defenseless animals. They hurled fistfuls of snow, packed with ice and small rocks. Pained yips and howls whined out from beneath the stairs. They'd trapped a dog, I thought, though I still couldn't see the creature from my vantage point.

I drew my shoulders back and walked down the stairs, pausing halfway down with the kind of poise I'd seen Ozura use more than once to silence whole rooms. "What do you think you are doing?"

The boys started. A few of the younger ones took a step back uncertainly. Dropped their snowballs. But the older ones glared up at me, finding comfort in numbers. Typical Rovenese bullshit.

The biggest one stepped forward, jutting his chin at me—no doubt to make sure I saw the crossed key and crown sigil tattooed on his cheek. *How wonderful*, I thought, as he licked his lips, drumming up his courage. *A little Dorovnii monster in the making.*

"None of your business," the boy said, spitting to one side. "We don't answer to Niskoy bitches like you."

I laughed, the sound high and cold in my ears as he flushed. Even as my mirth echoed, my muscles tensed, as I let myself sink into a crouch . . . and vaulted over the railing, landing silently between the poor, whining dog and the boys. Rose slowly.

"Oh, my dear little Dorovnichki," I whispered, watching him flinch at the diminutive he'd certainly outgrown several years ago. My gaze seared into his. I smiled, pulling off my hood, felt my wild hair tumble loose and let the weak sunlight shine on my face. My perfectly smooth, tattoo-less face.

"Don't you know a witch when you see one?" I crooned the words, walking slowly, languidly forward. I felt like the villain from a fairy tale—and loved every second of it. "You know we eat wicked little Dorovnii boys in Seravesh."

My smile fell away as the boy paled enough to blend in with

the snow around him. My muscles coiled, and like a desert snake, I lunged forward half an inch as if I were about to pounce.

He squealed at the tiny movement. And they all sprinted away. I laughed at the sight: the future of Roven running back to Mommy and Daddy because of little old me.

Still laughing, I turned back to the staircase. Crouching, I squinted into the darkness. All my laughter dried up. Blood drained from my face.

It wasn't a dog they'd been torturing. It was a man—a middle-aged man in a filthy coat and threadbare trousers. He'd wedged himself into a tiny ball at the smallest corner of the staircase. He turned toward me, pale eyes filled with pain and confusion. His hair was perfectly white, wispy, and terribly uneven, like he'd tried to cut it himself. There was an angry gash above his right eyebrow, spilling blood into his still-terrified face.

"It's all right," I said slowly, holding up my empty hands. "They're gone. You can come out now."

I reached out, but the movement made him cry a high keening whine of fear. "Shh, shh. It's all right. I won't hurt you," I said, drawing back. "My name is Askia," I continued, trying a different track. "What's your name?"

The keening stopped as I spoke, and he went very still. I could see he was listening to my words, but he didn't reply—or couldn't. Instead he began to hum a strange chorus of unintelligible, almost self-soothing, off-key notes.

And if he couldn't speak then that meant this poor, broken man could only be . . .

"Gethen?" I asked, shock echoing through my voice.

As soon as I said it, I knew I was right. The resemblance was almost uncanny—long, lanky frame, eyes like sea glass and a slightly hooked nose. The sole prince of Roven was huddled before me, face bruised and bloody as if he belonged to no one.

Radovan, the man who'd conquered half the world, let his own helpless son—the only child that carried his blood—wander alone without anyone to care for him. He let his own captain of the guard simply walk away while his only child was being hurt. Because this wasn't an isolated incident, of that I was sure. Those boys had tortured Gethen before. And how many before them had done the same? No consequences. No punishments. What the hell?

"What is that? Is it a song?" I asked, softly, scrabbling for something to say. But he was no longer paying attention. He'd wrapped his arms around his waist, started rocking slowly back and forth, oblivious to my presence.

I railed against my own helplessness, mind racing, searching for what to do next. I couldn't just leave him here. It was brutally cold outside, and his coat didn't look anywhere near thick enough to keep him warm, especially not with a head wound. It might not have looked deep, but eyebrow cuts always bled something terrible.

"What can I do?" I asked, not sure if I was speaking to the man or the universe.

Magic rustled through me, prickling my skin as it tiptoed into my limbs. I shivered, senses expanding.

"*Sing.*" The command came from the ghost beside me. The ghost I'd only seen once and never heard speak. Katarzhina.

"*Sing,*" she urged once more, her voice desperate behind the veil that still hung over her face, shrouding her. When I didn't act, she went to her knees, and began singing a familiar set of notes. The same notes Gethen was singing, only from Katarzhina the music was pure and beautiful, clear and angelic.

My own voice was far too weak to match Katarzhina's, but the song pouring out of her was simple, and after a few moments, I knew I could copy it well enough to join her. I licked my lips, felt my heart beating fast in my throat. Took a breath. And sang.

It was a slow, rolling song. The melody repeated in a clear four-beat cadence. It was a lullaby in every sense of the word, low and soothing. It filled even my cold heart with comfort, though a kind that was tinged with longing for my own mother.

I kept singing, even as silence spread out around me. Even as I sensed the courtyard go still, felt the men and women turn slowly with muted horror.

I ignored them. They were inconsequential, these people who stood by and did nothing. Better their horror than their lack of honor. And if I thought I hated them for watching the north crumble and burn from the far-flung safety of their white city, I hated them twice over for being too weak-spined to stand up for one of their own.

So I sang. I sang as Gethen went still. As his body slowly uncoiled. I sang as he crawled out of his hiding place and stumbled to where I knelt.

When the song ended, Gethen's lips twitched in what I thought was meant to be a smile. His attention peppered across my skin, as he studied every inch of my face. His lips twitched again, and with one papery finger, he poked me in the cheek.

I laughed. And he copied me, the melody of our frail, temporary joy filling the cool winter air.

A shadow fell over us.

I shivered, knowing to whom it belonged. I looked up, and found Radovan staring down at us, his expression almost unreadable. Almost. Because what I saw in the corners of his pale eyes was concern. Gethen must have seen me tense, as he clasped my arm with one surprisingly strong hand.

I made myself smile. Made myself pretend Radovan wasn't standing at my back. I reached out, dabbing at his cut forehead with the edge of my sleeve. He blinked, leaning away with obvious pain. "It's all right, Gethen. We just need to get that cut looked at."

As I said it, an old woman appeared—the older of my two maids—and took Gethen's hands. She smiled in a reassuring kind of way, coaxing him to his feet.

"Go with your minder, Gethen," Radovan said, his words soft, tired even.

Gethen's head bobbed up and down, but he didn't rise. Instead he pointed his finger at me, almost in question.

"Askia can come and play with you later," Radovan said. "Go on, son."

Simple as that, Gethen let the maid lead him past me, walking stiffly toward the castle. Though I was relieved he was safe, I was very aware of the frigid, immeasurable threat created by his absence. It was a tang of danger that soured my tongue. My heartbeat leapt, as Radovan's attention bored down upon me.

I pushed to my feet. Turned slowly, hating that I had to lift my chin and expose my neck to look up at him.

Radovan's brow creased, he was looking at me so intently. His face was only a few inches from mine. Heat rose from his body, steaming the air between us. But was he nervous? Or enraged?

And did the difference matter? Either could lead me to a locked cell in a dark dungeon.

"How do you know that song?" he said finally, his voice haggard. And though I knew he was old—nearly a hundred now—this was the first time I'd seen that age in his eyes.

Reality around us seemed to sharpen. I'd told Radovan I wouldn't lie, but the urge to hide, to obfuscate burned through me. Still, there was no other explanation for how I could know that lullaby except for the dead queen who'd knelt beside me in the snow.

I willed my heartbeat to slow. Willed myself to meet Radovan's eyes. "You know how."

Radovan's face fell, and like a door slamming shut, his expression closed. He stepped back, snow crunching too loud beneath his feet. He drew himself up to his full height, eyes hooding.

Gone was the false warmth, the feigned geniality that he'd heaped upon me from my first moments under his thumb. What remained was a husk of a man who should have been cold in the ground two decades ago.

"Come."

8

IT WAS MY time in the Vishiri court that allowed me to keep my emotions from my face. To contain my fear, my panic, and lock them away. Far away.

I followed as Radovan turned on his heel, cutting a swath through the watching Voyniks and quailing Dorovnii. I didn't need to see the warning—the fear—in Zosha's eyes to know that everything now hung in the balance. Not only my life but his now, too, for he was surely meant to prevent such scenes from occurring.

You never said you would answer all his questions—just that you would be truthful in the answers you did offer. The words ran frantically through my mind, a too-frail shield that I knew wouldn't protect me. Not from this man.

I half expected Radovan to drag me back to the castle, leaving me to rot in some forgotten corner of his dungeon. Or to lock me in my room with only the ghosts for comfort. So when he headed for the castle gates, I exhaled sharply through my nose.

With no words, and only Qaden shadowing us from a few yards away, Radovan led me through the portcullis. He paused, like he was struggling to make up his mind.

I shifted my weight, scanning the world around us for some clue of what was coming next. The bridge over the River Tol was cobbled with perfectly cut bricks of some black stone that had gone slightly gray with snow and frost. Statues rose from the railing every ten feet or so; the kings and queens of Roven's past stood sentinel on the bridge, each one bearing an orb of witch-light in one outstretched hand.

It was beautiful, in an imposing kind of way. The kind of place that would usually see young couples strolling arm in arm, but there was none of that here—and not, I thought, because of the cold. Not that it was empty. Traders and artisans, servants and scholars crawled along the bridge to and from the castle, all under the careful eyes of the ever-watching Voyniks. But there was nothing companionable in their interactions. They were doing the business of Roven, and that's all.

A brutal breeze off the river had me pulling up the hood of my cloak. And that's when I saw it. Saw him.

The long, ash-blond braid. The flash of green ink on pale skin.

My heart flew into my throat.

Illya?

The thought trilled wildly through me, hope springing into the sky. The man turned.

All that hope fell straight to the ground with an echoing crunch.

Not Illya. A stranger with dirty gray hair and a green scarf. I tugged my hood lower, hoping Radovan was too preoccupied with his own internal struggle to have noticed mine.

Focus, Askia, I snarled at myself. *Now is not the time to fall to pieces, not with Radovan beside you and Qaden at your back. Illya isn't coming. No one is—it would be suicide. And even if he was,* I thought, savagely stabbing the tiny spark of hope straight through the heart, *there's no way he'd have gotten here already. You're on your own. Save your own damned self.*

As I thought it, Radovan shook himself like he'd come to a decision. "This way," he said, voice soft.

He angled left, cutting through the crowd to a slip of stone where the curtainwall met the bridge. The necklace grew hot against my chest and before I could ask what he was doing, the bare patch of stone flickered out of existence, leaving an archway fitted with a wrought-iron door in its place. A door without a keyhole, I realized as the still-warm Aellium stone burned bright once more. Radovan placed his hand against the metal and with a weak rattle, like the last sighing breath of a dying man, the door opened. A tickle of impossibly warm air caressed my cheeks.

I frowned as I followed Radovan down a set of stone steps, steps that weren't icy, nor even wet with melted snow. This impossible stairway hugged the edge of the island without even a railing to protect us from the churning black water below.

I watched the river's current with greedy eyes and wondered. Was this it? My chance for escape? Could I take the leap before Radovan had time to stop me?

The thought burned within me. My legs begged me to do it, to jump. *Do it. Do it now.*

A single droplet of water splashed onto my cheek, born of the river crashing against the island's stone walls some thirty feet below and carried upward on a wind I couldn't feel. One drop. That was all it took to shatter my hope of escape. Because even within this bubble of magical warmth, that droplet was cold enough to make me shiver to my core.

I didn't give my disappointment time to fester, for we'd arrived.

My eyes widened as stone transitioned—incredibly—to grass. Green grass preserved in a magical spring blanketed a little plateau that sat perhaps twenty feet below the castle walls. It jutted from the base of the island, too circular, too flat to be made of anything but magic.

Perhaps fifteen feet in diameter, it was empty save for a soli-

tary bench of bone-white alabaster and a handful of statues—
statues that were so detailed, so horribly lifelike I almost thought
they were ghosts. Especially when I recognized two of them:
Katarzhina and Ragata. Yet they didn't move, and my magic's
tether didn't blanket my body in a chilly gust of air.

Radovan eased down on the bench, arms braced almost
tiredly on his knees. "Will you sit with me?"

That request made me cold. But now wasn't the time to argue over something seemingly trivial, no matter how distasteful. Tearing my eyes away from Ragata's statue, I sat as Qaden
stepped away, posting herself on the path, just out of earshot.

"I must admit, I've been curious about you for a long time.
Even before I sent Lord Tcheshin to your grandfather with the
proposal."

"I'm shocked," I replied, voice heavy with sarcasm. Had he
really brought me down here, to this . . . this place, just to tell
me this?

"And then Tcheshin told me of how you fixed that fallen
bridge," he continued, all but ignoring me.

I smiled humorlessly as the memory washed over me. It had
been a cool spring day, that day everything changed. I'd returned
to the castle covered in mud, and with more than one stick in
my hair from repairing a bridge that had washed out on the out-
skirts of Solenskaya. Tcheshin had flung open the doors of my
grandfather's hall and laid Radovan's proposal at the dainty feet
of my cousin's latest conquest, mistaking her for me. He'd been
only too amused to learn the truth.

"I can't say he was impressed by the revelation."

"Ah, Tcheshin is a useful servant, but limited as such men
usually are. It impressed me, which—in my humble opinion—is
what mattered."

I didn't bother to hide my grimace, but that only made
Radovan laugh.

"I'm allowed to be impressed by you, Askia. You've proven yourself a woman of action. A person who sees a problem and fixes it. These are admirable traits, and ones I think we share. Just look at my city. I've told you what it was like when I came into power. And now?"

I sniffed. "I suppose it does look very clean."

Radovan chuckled at my bland answer. "Come now, you said you'd tell the truth. Be frank with me, please. I want to know what you think."

I lifted my chin. "Why? Why do you care what I think?"

Radovan blinked, eyes going wide first with surprise then with a kind of beseeching need for understanding. "I suppose I want you to see what I'm fighting for. I want you to see it's worth it, to attain a better future for all of us."

"I will never see it that way," I said, my voice dropping under the weight of the vow.

Radovan tilted one hand to the sky. "And yet I live in hope. Can you honestly tell me you don't wish the same for your people?"

I felt my mouth become a thin gash across my face. "No," I answered. "I do see the allure of this place. The people here prosper. They're safe and fed and warm, and I know that can't be an easy thing to accomplish in the coldest place in the world, but—"

"But?" he prompted when my words failed.

I shook my head at the ground. "Things are so organized here, so rigid—I don't know how your people survive it."

"They survive it because Roven has always been keen on structure."

"But to this extent? You've branded your people with their lot in life. You regulate, not only who belongs where throughout your city of gates, but who can *be* what. And all of it is based on where they were born and who they were born to."

"You make it sound like this isn't something that happens

everywhere. Even in your beloved Vishir, there is only one emperor, one heir, nobles and peasants, rich and poor. All I've done is ensure everyone knows their place."

"But that isn't all you've done." I looked at him, willing him to understand what I was trying to say. "It must be maddening to wake up every day knowing you will never achieve more, that you can never strive for better. People aren't meant to live in narrow little boxes."

"You really think so?" he asked, sounding genuinely curious. "I think it must be freeing, not having to worry over choice."

"Easy for you to say when you're the only one able to choose," I said with no small hint of bitterness. "Choice is what makes us. Didn't the Two-Faced God make us with free will, so we could forge our way in the world, and live lives of our own making?"

Radovan shook his head. "You have all the idealism of youth. Believe me, I've lived long enough to know free will is an illusion. When given the choice, people will always take the easiest path. They want what their parents had, what they know. Safety, home, family. My way provides this. All I've done is lit a lamp to show them their way."

"You haven't illuminated the darkness, Radovan, just given them a candle and one tiny path to cling to. Don't you see that the world you created excludes the possibility of someone like you?" Maybe that was the whole point, I thought as the words left my lips. Free will must have been terrifying to a man who needed control the way he did.

Radovan shook his head, like a tired parent who knew better than his overwrought child. "No, Askia. People like me—like you—we always find a way to rise." He grinned at my incredulity. "You don't believe me? Just look at my history and tell me I wouldn't have found a way."

"I know very little of your history."

"Really?" Something I couldn't identify crossed his face. "I suppose there isn't anyone else left to remember those days."

"Do you really think that's why I'm uninformed?" I clenched my hands at the false wistfulness in his voice. He looked at me with a curious expression. "I didn't think you wanted people to know how you came to power," I explained.

He shrugged. "Well, you aren't *people* now, are you?" He smiled at his private joke. I did not—not that my lack of reaction bothered him.

"I was about to turn eighteen when I was crowned king, though I confess it had nothing to do with my own striving. My uncle was on the Council of Nine—the ruling order of nobles who ran the country. Fools each one. Their insatiable grasping and petty infighting led Roven to the brink of destruction. And my uncle was the worst."

Radovan's mouth twisted with the memory of a man I suspected he feared even now. "He was an evil man, my uncle. Took my brother and me from our family when we were just boys. To groom us for power, he said." An ugly look ghosted across Radovan's face, filled with darkness and terror. I almost felt sorry for him, until I remembered he'd taken me from my family—my people. That he had become the same monster he'd once destroyed.

Keeping my voice neutral, I said, "I didn't know you had a brother."

He smiled, softly, sinking deeper into the past. "I did. Gethen."

My eyebrows rose. "Gethen?"

"Yes, I named my son for him." He sighed deeply, like doing so could blow away the cobwebs of memory. "Two purer souls have never lived. But in the end, I couldn't protect my baby brother."

His pale eyes rose, locking on to one of the statues: one of a man who, if I squinted just right, looked like Radovan might have in his distant youth. Could this be the original Gethen? I wondered, gaze poring over the other statues—the faces of an older couple, mother and father? And a young woman, beautiful even in stone. A sister? Was this his family? All of them kept here frozen in time beside the two wives he'd loved the most. As if he feared that the passage of years might make him forget their faces.

Before he killed them. Never forget that, Askia, I thought before I could do anything so foolish as pity this monster.

"But you *can* protect your son," I said, guiding the conversation away from Radovan's brother. In truth I didn't want to know what terrible mistreatment they'd suffered to set Radovan on his blood-soaked path. Knowing might only make it harder to destroy him.

"You're right," Radovan said slowly, as if the idea had never occurred to him. "I can still protect him."

"Then why haven't you?"

"I thought I was," he said. "I thought if I kept him out of the way, sheltered from the cut-throat dogs in my court, he could live his life as happily and normally as possible."

And out of sight. The words rose unbidden in my mind, instinctual but truthful. "You're ashamed of him, aren't you—to have a son unworthy of your legacy."

"No. It's not Gethen's fault he's this way," he exclaimed, the words rushing out of him too quickly to be true. "If anything it's a failing of the Two-Faced God and magic itself. It isn't fair, that I have all this power and no ability to cure him."

"Gethen doesn't need a cure," I said, the words curdling in my mouth. "He needs you to accept him. To love him. He is *your* child. And he is vulnerable. Day Lord save him, he can't even speak. By ignoring him and shunting him aside, you only leave him open to attack."

Radovan's gaze went sharp, like a raptor sizing up new prey. "You think Gethen was targeted? That those boys were tormenting him to get to me?"

"Don't be ridiculous," I scoffed. "Those boys were behaving exactly as any pampered and spoiled child does when they have too much time on their hands and no supervision. I think Gethen was an easy target, and he has been for many, many boys before them."

He nodded slowly, like he was tallying up his options. "Entitlement is the most pernicious and wicked of evils."

I rubbed a temple. "You'll hear no argument from me."

A slow smile spread across his face. "Why, Askia, are you agreeing with me?"

"Don't make this worse" was my flat reply, though Radovan simply laughed.

"What do you think I should do?" he asked.

I shrugged. "I'm not a mother, but you can't be the first one in this position. Speak with the boys' parents, let them know what happened."

"Make sure there are consequences," he murmured.

I shrugged again. "If those boys are punished for picking on Gethen, others will surely think twice about doing the same," I said, holding out no hope of there being any real consequences. Noble children were almost always insufferable little weasels.

"It's good advice," he said finally.

But he didn't move. Didn't rise. Just sat there, staring at his brother's face. His sister's. Katarzhina's.

I stilled my mind, reaching for that calm space of peace I'd always felt before I took my place in the ring to fight. Because Radovan hadn't brought me here to discuss Gethen. Not really.

Radovan turned to me, his expression intense with warring desires. "Can you see them, the ghosts of the other queens?"

The answer was obvious. There was only one way I could

have known how to calm Gethen. That he was asking the question either meant he was testing my honesty or wasn't sure he wanted to know.

Maybe both.

"Yes."

Radovan went very still, but I could feel emotion rippling through him. Like a late-fall storm that couldn't decide between rain and snow, the conflict within him grew. I could see it in the rueful tilt to his lips and the angry flash in his eyes.

"I didn't think you'd be able to see them," he said at long last. "Why do you think you can? None of the elemental queens could wield their magic against me. And Asyl, who was a mind witch, said she couldn't either."

The way he asked the question, innocent and curious, like the answer wasn't the stuff of life and death . . .

"Why do you think Asyl owed you the truth?"

His shoulders seemed to drop with self-pity. "I suppose she didn't. But I saw you try to summon a spirit. It was beyond you. Yet you can see the queens? Why is that?"

I looked away, trying to navigate the rocky shore between truth and honesty. "What you would call 'using magic' is beyond me, but you fail to understand what it is to be a witch. Magic isn't a tap we can twist on and off, it's in our blood and in our bones. We're always aware of it—even muzzled and bound."

He nodded. "So the queens of Roven surround us even now."

"Please, you're not that interesting."

"Really?" he asked, with the audacity to laugh.

"You took their lives, not their personalities," I replied, coldly satisfied to see the smile slide off his face. "They come and go as they please."

"They must truly despise me."

I shifted, looking at him full in the face so he couldn't miss the incredulity seeping out of my every pore. "You murdered them, Radovan. How do you expect them to feel?"

"Even Katarzhina? Even Ragata?" His voice was low, meek almost, but if he thought it would make me pity him, he was terribly wrong. There was nothing soft in my feelings toward Radovan, no. I was filled with sharp, jagged edges writhing, pleading to be loosed and tear the skin from his bones.

"You betrayed them worst of all. You made them think you cared about them. Loved them. But they were disposable to you. And even that, they might have forgiven. But you took them from their sons, Radovan. And that they will never forgive."

"It was necessary," he replied, matching me for intensity. "My people needed a leader and my body was betraying me."

"And that's why you *killed* Katarzhina," I snapped, utterly devoid of fear or sympathy. "What about Ragata?" I said, stabbing my finger at the older woman's statue. "Seven years, Radovan. Why let her live if you were just going to tear her away from her son?"

"She took him first." He nearly shouted the words, eyes flashing ancient and insane. "Didn't she tell you? She sent him away, smuggled him out of Tolograd in the middle of winter. Alone. A boy of six who I had raised like a son. Didn't she tell you that?"

"She's not really in a fit state to tell anyone much of anything," I said slowly, like his anger and insanity were entirely beneath me. So as to calm the beast within.

It worked, for he flinched with something that could have almost been described as guilt. "It was the coldest winter on record. Zosha would have died out there. Measures were taken."

"Measures." I shook my head. "I'm sure the fact that the war with Khezhar was going poorly didn't factor into it at all. That your desire for her magic didn't make the decision for you. So you tortured her to find Zosha and you killed her out of greed. Just like all the rest of us."

"No," he said, the anger in the word propelling him to his feet.

I refused to so much as flinch. "No?"

He dropped to his knees, seizing my hand with a fervent kind of desire. Not anger or even pride, but the desperate need to be understood. The act was so sudden, so shocking, I couldn't disguise the surprise running across my face even as he continued, "That's not why I did it. Not at all. I regret their deaths—all of them—but it *had* to be done.

"Don't you see? All around us, the world was falling to ash. Polzi and Nivlaand were at war. Khezhar was ruled by a circle of witch-priests who used holy dictates to enslave their non-magical population. Graznia was overrun with plague. And the monarchies in Switzkia, Raskis, and even your Seravesh were beginning to fray—if not from corruption, than from uncertainty in succession."

Images shuddered through my mind. Sounds and sights, memories that didn't belong, ran rampant through my body. Things I had never experienced, never seen—no, these were Radovan's memories. As if by invading my mind he could force me to agree with him.

Terror shuddered through me as I struggled to break free. But how? How could I fight this battle when my mind was locked in battles of the past—soaking up blood and gore and death and the frail justifications of a man who always wanted more?

"The north was crumbling. But I could stop it. I could bring order to the chaos."

His voice echoed through me. A light in the darkness. A fresh wind that chased away the acrid scent of smoke, the reek of burning flesh.

"But to do so, I couldn't simply be strong. The emperor who unites us all has to be the strongest, the best. And I wasn't—not with thousands of witches crawling through the country, blessed by Lady Night. And why? Why you?" he cried, like the injustice of it still chaffed. "When I was the one who needed the magic. When I was the one who should have been blessed. It wasn't fair. But to every problem there is a solution, and if the methods were distasteful . . . well, I am strong enough to live with that guilt too.

"And I do feel guilty, Askia. I'm not some monster who can kill without remorse. I loved them, and their deaths nearly destroyed me."

The urgency in his voice, the desperate need to prove himself, colored everything. Polluted it. As if seizing control of my mind could convince me he was right to steal us. Conquer us. Kill us. The fool.

I yanked my hand away, severing the connection. The twin stones we wore on our chests flashed, bathing this mausoleum of memory in a sickly green light. Radovan fell back, cheeks flushed, eyes shining, like the effort of forcing his memories into my head was exhausting . . . and invigorating.

"You think you brought order?" I whispered the word, so great was my disgust. "No, Radovan. You can't just burn the world down and say you made it better simply because there's nothing left to catch fire. You didn't conquer the north to save the people. You did it because you wanted to, like a child who steals toys out of jealousy. Because you can play with them *better*. That's the reason you steal magic.

"You loved them? You don't know the meaning of the word," I said, filled with such scathing hate that it brought me to my feet. "I'd like to go back to my cell now."

9

THE MAIDS WERE late in coming to my rooms. For the past seven days, they'd appeared in the ringing echoes of the ninth bell. But the ninth bell had come and gone hours ago. No maids. No Zosha. No freedom.

No surprise.

At the tenth bell, Eliska and Siv, my near-constant companions, had disappeared to see if they could learn anything about this new exile. They hadn't returned by the eleventh bell. Or the twelfth. I had begun gnawing on my fingernails, a habit I thought I'd left behind in childhood, by the time the second bell of the afternoon came and went.

I paced the length of my room, wearing trenches into the stone. The fire blazed in the hearth, but I couldn't feel its warmth. Not with my silhouette outlined in the green glow of the Aellium stone, mocking my helplessness.

I could've cut my tongue out. Radovan was angry with me. Sure, he said he wanted my opinion, but why had I thought it was a good idea to be *so* honest with him?

I hadn't thought. That was the problem. That was—if I was being honest—always my problem. This time, I'd been angry and appalled by his pathetic justifications, and I'd let him know it. What had Eliska said? No one sees themselves as a monster.

Well, I'd done my best to shatter Radovan's illusions of decency, and here was my reward.

I was eyeing the door, wondering if Qaden's knife could be used to pry it open when the maids finally arrived. Food was served. Water was drawn. Clothes were sorted.

"Lady Night, thank you," I said, weak-kneed with relief as the women headed for the bathroom. "What took you so long?" I asked, not expecting a response, at least not with words, but . . .

But neither woman would look at me. There was something studied and nervous about their silence, a creeping anxiety that lined both their faces.

Was I to be punished further? I wondered, eyeing the gown as I dressed. It was sewn from night-black silk, the split sleeves a light gossamer fabric that swayed in the heat from the fireplace. Gold embroidery covered the bodice, accentuating the low heart-shaped neckline and narrow waist before blooming out in the skirts.

It took my preoccupied eyes a long moment to see the shape of the embroidery: wings and talons and flames. It was a dress made of Roven's banner, the golden falcon. I'd have stepped into the hearth and burned alive if the grate wasn't locked.

This was no simple dinner dress. No, this gown was meant to be displayed.

"Askia, something is happening in the Great Hall." Eliska appeared between me and the mirror, Freyda, Asyl, and Siv at her back.

The sight of so many queens made the ground beneath my feet feel unsteady. *"What is it?"*

"Not sure, but the whole court is gathering," Siv said, striding to the windows, watching.

"Is that unusual?" I asked, trying to keep my confusion from my face. *"Couldn't it just be an audience day?"*

Eliska shook her head, tightly. *"Radovan doesn't hold audiences."*

"*And it isn't just the lords gathering,*" Asyl said. "*Whole families are waiting in the Great Hall. As if there is to be an announcement.*"

"*And not a good one,*" Siv added. "*Like a funeral, down there.*"

"*This is bad,*" Freyda agreed. "*Radovan has always hated his Dorovnii.*" With that grim pronouncement, she slid through the door.

A little line furrowed between Eliska's eyes. "*Did you say anything to him yesterday that might have made him gather the court?*"

My eyes widened. "*The court? No.*"

"*But you did lose your temper?*" Eliska pressed.

"*Well, yeah. You would've too. He was claiming to love us and that stealing our magic is necessary to save the world. It was complete crap.*"

"*I miss all the good stuff,*" Siv muttered with a petulant sigh. "*Maybe he's decided to kill you sooner.*"

I rolled my eyes. "*Thanks for that, Siv, always a pleasure.*"

"*He won't,*" Asyl said, sitting with a flounce. "*The stone hasn't had time to burrow into your soul.*"

Another cheery thought, but I took it to heart. Radovan wouldn't kill me tonight. "*So what is happening?*"

"*You've got incoming,*" Vitaly said, shooting through the door with a whoosh of frigid air that only I could feel.

"*Qaden's on her way,*" Freyda added, reappearing beside Vitaly.

"*Lady Night protect you,*" Asyl murmured.

"*I realize it's pointless to say this to you,*" Eliska began, setting a hand on my arm, "*but be careful. Guard your expression and for the love of the Two-Faced God, hold your tongue.*"

My bedroom door opened, not with a bang but with a whisper. Qaden stood in the hallway, hands fisted at her sides. She jerked her head, a silent command to come. I frowned. Why wouldn't she look at me?

Siv whistled, low and long. "*What's eating Qaden? She looks about to toss it.*"

Asyl appeared in the hallway, circling the oblivious soldier. *"I haven't seen her look this terrible since Freyda killed her sister."*

My foot caught the edge of my hem, and I stumbled against the doorway. *"What?"* I demanded but the ghosts were gone. I cursed the chain around my neck. Cursed the queens for sliding away. I knew Freyda had killed one of her guards—heard as much from Qaden herself. But Qaden's *sister?*

When Qaden told me, she made it sound like nothing. Like the dead guard was no more than a rival, someone she hated and was glad to see in the ground. But knowing what I did now? It explained why she disliked me with such a fervent passion, even if I wasn't the one who committed the act. I represented Freyda, and that I could understand.

What it did not explain, however, was her current look of dread.

Because Asyl and Siv weren't wrong. Qaden's skin was tinged green. Her lips were twisted into a resolute frown, like if she allowed herself to feel she might scream. Or cry. *Lady Night, what is happening?* I wondered, but there was no one to ask.

Well, that wasn't entirely true, I thought, following Qaden down the stairs. I could ask the captain herself—if I could withstand her reply. But her anger didn't bother me. Not really. No, what bothered me was the emptiness around us, the deserted corridors and hollow silence, like a sharp intake of breath before a scream.

"Qaden," I said, speaking her name slowly, carefully. "What is going on?"

"Nothing." She growled the word, every inch of her shouting in contradiction.

I wet my lips. "Please, Qaden. I know something is happening."

"You know, do you?"

"Yes," I said, hurrying to match her pace as she sped up. "It's obvious isn't it—I mean the castle is deserted and you look—"

Qaden whirled with a blur of speed. She pinned me against the wall with one arm, knife to my throat. "Please, Princess. Tell me how you think I look." Though she snarled the words, her voice was soft.

My pulse leapt in my neck, beating so hard it scraped against Qaden's blade. I made my body still. Forced my heart to slow. "I was going to say you looked worried, Qaden. Nervous."

"I'm far past worried. Worried doesn't even begin to cover it."

"Tell me why." I pressed forward far enough that Qaden had to draw back the knife or kill me. She drew back. I pushed the advantage. "Tell me what's happening. Perhaps I can help."

She barked out a mirthless laugh. "I think you've helped quite enough."

"What's that supposed to mean?"

"What exactly did you say to the emperor yesterday?" she asked, accusation sharpening her voice.

I frowned my confusion. Why was everyone so worried about that conversation? "We spoke about many things, the city, the other queens—"

"The prince?"

"Yes" was my slow reply. Qaden pushed away from me, shaking her head like she'd never been so disgusted with anyone in her life. "Why? What's happening with Gethen?"

Her jaw quivered like she was trying to contain a steady flow of thought that didn't want to be bottled up. "The worst part is that you claim to be a warrior," she said, her words bursting free in the middle of a thought that didn't make any sense.

"So?"

"So any decent warrior would know to study her opponent. And the one thing you should have realized by now," she began, shaking the tip of her blade at me, "is that Radovan never reacts in exactly the way you expect."

My brow furrowed. "What's that supposed to mean?"

She looked down, jammed her knife into its sheath. When she looked up again, the heat had left her eyes, the anger and fear were carefully smothered. Even the green tinge had washed out of her face. Her mask was so set, it made me shudder. The fear and anger I could take, but the emptiness? In a soldier, emptiness only meant one thing.

"It means that what happens now is on your hands."

Qaden continued down the stairs, dragging all hope of conversation with her as she went. I followed with heavy steps. My mind raced backward, combing over every word I'd spoken to Radovan, analyzing his every reply and reaction.

What I kept coming up against was Gethen. Qaden had acknowledged his part in this, and the clue must lay with him. I'd chastised Radovan for letting his son be bullied. Told him to speak with the boys' parents. Was that what this was? A public shaming?

Was I so wrong in my assessment of how noble children got away with everything?

I squared my shoulders, as I stepped off the final stair. Well, it definitely wouldn't win me any allies among the Dorovnii. And it would certainly be uncomfortable to sit through for everyone involved. But they'd all think twice now about picking on Gethen. Wasn't that a good thing?

Yes, I thought. It was. *They* should be nervous. But me?

No. Anxiety would do nothing to help me. I rejected it, because if Qaden and the nobles were afraid, then I needed to be calm—to show them what it meant to be a queen. I lifted my chin, arms loose at my side, eyes hooded. If Qaden could wear a mask, so could I.

The Great Hall's double doors opened. I entered, three steps behind Qaden. And though the captain set a brisk pace down the black-carpet aisle, I walked slowly, sedately, refusing to let her drag me along in her wake.

The Great Hall, with its swirling white and blue stripes expanding out around me, was filled with people all straining to get a good look. The aisle seemed created just for that purpose. It meandered in a slow spiral, so I would do a full turn around the hall before reaching Radovan.

Let them look, I thought, surveying the nobles of Roven as boldly as they watched me. Whole families stood crowded together. Bloodlines from the ancient Roven houses, yes, but also men and women whose faces bore clear traces of foreign birth. Nobles from all the conquered nations who'd thrown in their lot with Radovan when the going got tough, when it became easier to give up and join the winning side.

To say I hated them would have been an understatement. Their shortsightedness and cowardice only made it easier for Radovan to conquer us. I'd have gladly thrown them into the freezing waters of the River Tol, letting the current bear their bodies back to the homelands they'd betrayed.

But then I saw the children. They peeked out at me from between the skirts of sumptuous gowns and decadent coats. Round-faced and wide-eyed, watching me, watching the haughty woman I pretended to be, with fear and awe and wonder. If my steps didn't falter, my heart certainly did. Because it was easy to hate an adult for their decisions, but much harder to come face to face with the children they'd made those decisions to protect.

I pushed the thoughts away, softhearted as they were, for Radovan waited. The massive blue porphyry table at which we'd dined when I first arrived was still there, but it couldn't be called a table anymore. No, now it was a dais, complete with a hulking porphyry throne.

Silver steps encircled the table-turned-platform where Radovan sat alone. His blue throne lay in a perfect shaft of sunlight from the oculus high above. The throne glittered with diamonds and sapphires and emeralds and a hundred other gems I couldn't even name. But it wasn't the only throne. A second, smaller chair waited . . . for me? I eyed it with more suspicion than a bear would a trap.

Radovan's hair, more brown than red and several shades darker than my own, was tied back from his face. He wore no crown upon his brow. He didn't need to, the aura of his power was unmistakable. So complete it held the gathered nobles in the same silence as the soldiers at his back.

And it was only Voyniks who stood behind him. Two rings of stone-faced soldiers in full regalia separated the Dorovnii and local Niskoy from their emperor. Strange that Radovan would trust two dozen men and women with swords to stand behind him over unarmed civilians. It only heightened my awareness of the tension in the room, the muted anger and muffled fear that clouded the nobles like a thick perfume.

Radovan stood as I made it to the stairs. He held out a hand in an invitation I knew I had to accept. Carefully ascending the steps, I knuckled through the chaste brush of his lips on my hand and took my place on the second throne, wondering what fresh hell the next minutes would bring.

Radovan sat, leaning back in the throne, one foot cocked carelessly over the other knee. He watched his court in a silence that stretched. And stretched. And stretched. Until the complete absence of noise became a scream.

He smiled. "Thank you for coming. It's been too long since we've all gathered together, though that will surely change in the coming weeks," he said, throwing me an affectionate look. "I must confess I invited you all here, not to share any urgent news or discuss matters of state. No. This is a personal matter. One that is long overdue.

"Regarding Gethen."

Radovan's left forefinger twitched. Twelve guards detached from the wall of soldiers and waded into the crowd. No—not waded, I thought, watching them go. *Waded* implied they were searching for something, someone. No, these guards knew exactly who they were looking for, marked them more completely than an arrow in flight.

The nobles jostled against each other, shrinking back and away from the throne in an outgoing tide of silk and fur. But no one spoke. That was the strange thing. There were no outbursts of wounded pride as the soldiers trod on this man's foot or that woman's hem. There were no outraged cries, as six families were plucked from the crowd and pushed to the dais. No words at all.

My eyes widened, and then widened some more as six sets of parents were lined up before the throne. The parents, I didn't recognize.

But I knew the children.

The six boys who had been throwing rocks at Gethen stood white-faced with their parents. Not even white. Gray, almost corpse-like. Their entire bodies trembled—a fear so palpable I had to lock my body in place to keep myself from moving.

And then I saw the soldiers. The Voyniks still stood with each family—stood *behind* each family.

One for each person quaking at Radovan's feet.

The air practically boiled with tension as I watched—as we all watched. My hands curled around the arms of my chair as the youngest of them shifted from one foot to the other. As they darted glances at the Voyniks behind them—at the Voyniks who wouldn't meet their eyes.

If the boys fidgeted in their fear, their parents were better at keeping their faces neutral. But only just. Their waxen skin and downcast eyes betrayed them. Betrayed the growing terror of knowing there were wolves all around them. Closing in.

I sent a silent call across the void, but my voice could contain no command—not with the chain about my neck. Without the touch of compulsion, it was just a cry, a silent internal prayer that brought goose bumps to my flesh.

"I'm sorry to say that your boys were caught throwing rocks at my son yesterday." Radovan broke the silence, sounding almost chagrined, like he was embarrassed to have this confrontation. It was an act I almost believed. I *would* have believed it if not for the presence of the court. The guards. The soldiers waiting, with hands poised on their swords.

The father of the oldest boy took a few steps forward. Steps that faltered when Qaden dropped down from her perch on Radovan's right side, planting herself in his path. His eyes flashed with indignation though he tried to hide it by bowing low.

"We did hear about the incident, my lord," he began, his voice smooth and confident. "Utterly shameful. A disgrace. I apologize for my son's behavior. We all do," he said, gesturing to the group for whom he now spoke. "The boys will apologize to Prince Gethen."

"Gethen is no longer in the city," Radovan cut in. His voice was still calm. Studiously so.

The other man stilled. "I see," he stammered. "Well, in any event, rest assured the boys will be punished."

"'The boys will be punished.'" Radovan murmured the words in a quiet echo, like he was tasting them. "Tell me, Lord Volvukov, were you ever punished?"

The lord—Volvukov—blinked; his expression of regret became stilted. Pained. "Excuse me, my lord?"

I sensed rather than saw the queens appear at my back. Even Katarzhina was there, body taut with rising worry. But I didn't need their worry, I realized with growing alarm. I needed help.

"Ozura," I called. She'd spent over twenty years at the side of an emperor. Guiding him. She would know what to do. To say. *"Please."*

"Were you punished, Lord Volvukov, when *you* bullied

Gethen?" Radovan asked, as if he was only curious. But the stone was warming against my skin, telling a different tale. One of a power that was slowly building to something terrible.

"You and Gethen are about the same age, are you not?"

"We are, my lord."

"Yes. I remember you as a boy, Volvukov. You were spirited and oh, so clever. Good attributes in a boy, the kind any father would be proud of. I'm told your son is much the same."

Volvukov blanched. I would have, too, if I had just learned that Radovan was asking questions about my son. "Yes, my lord. Caslan is very bright. All his tutors say so. He will grow to serve you honorably. Of that I am certain."

"Honor?" Radovan huffed a faint laugh, the kind that starts in irony and ends in cruelty. "Funny that you should bring up honor to me."

Ozura. I cried her name across the Marchlands, willing her into existence. I needed her. Needed her whole. Not the half wraith she'd been since her death, but all of her. Complete and cohesive. I let the command marshal beneath my skin, flinging it out with everything I had.

The chain bridled against the magic gathering within me, sending shooting, sizzling pain across my flesh. If Radovan noticed, he didn't glance in my direction. No one did. The whole hall was locked on to the man beside me. The monster whose whisper was more terrifying than any snarl.

Volvukov glanced back at his fellows, but there was no aid to be found there. He wet his lips, looked up at Radovan, eyes wide. Pleading. "Is it, my lord?"

Radovan nodded. "It was clear to me very early on that Gethen's life would be filled with struggle. He isn't bright or energetic or clever like you and your son. His is a simple mind. He will never grow up to serve his empire, marry a fine woman like your wife there, or have a son. But he does have one advantage.

"*Me.*"

Radovan's voice lowered as he spoke, losing any pretense of kindness, of geniality. Dropping the illusion that this was but a discussion between two fathers.

"Queen Askia has reminded me of my duties toward Gethen." Radovan's back straightened bone by bone, as if his body could barely contain his growing rage. "She pointed out—quite rightly—that I, too, am responsible for Gethen's consistent and decades-long mistreatment at the hands of your children."

"Askia, what have you done?" Eliska whispered.

But I had no words for her—no words to the parents looking at me with wide-eyed horror. No words for the Voyniks watching me with growing hate for what I had put into motion.

I railed against the chain. Even as my skin grew red and blistered, I pushed. Pushed past the well-deserved agony, forcing my power to slither across it, link by link. Hunting. Searching.

"*Ozura.*" I screamed her name across the void, across the dying promise that forged my soul to hers. Chain be damned, I *needed* her. I willed my body to remain still, my face unreadable despite the pain—because the court was turning to me. Their expression sliding from hate to confusion at the sight of the chain, silently burning my flesh.

"I thought leaving Gethen to his minders was a kindness, that excluding him from the court would shelter him. That it would spare him the never-ending cruelty I suffered at the *honorable* hands of noblemen. But my clever Dorovnii have bested me again. Bested me for the last time."

Lady Night save us. Was this even about his son at all? Or was this all just vengeance—vengeance for whatever horror Radovan and his brother suffered at their uncle's hands?

Radovan rose, malice swirling around him more terrible than a blood-soaked cloak. "From this moment forward, Gethen is off-limits. He may never rise to rule, but he is still your prince and my son. No harm or harassment will be tolerated or go un-punished."

Radovan curled his hand into a fist and Volvukov crumpled. All the parents did as the smallest whiff of power exhaled from the stone. But it was only a fragment, this compulsion to kneel. More was coming.

"No," I whispered, willing my limbs to move.

"*No!*" Eliska clamped her hand over mine, as the other queens crowded around me, holding me back.

"*But this isn't what I meant,*" I cried, Qaden's warning about Radovan's unpredictability rushing through my mind.

"*It's too late,*" Eliska said. Her lips, as insubstantial as a spi-der's web, brushed my ear. "*Whatever you said or didn't say, Ra-dovan is doing this for you. He sees you as an ally now. Whatever happens next, you must not react.*"

"*No!*" I shoved against the chain's magic, blisters popping on my chest as I commanded Ozura to come. Now. I shoved through the ghostly hands of the women around me, muscles tensing as I prepared to move, to throw myself onto Radovan and make him stop—

"*Wait.*" Ozura's order rippled across the void, slipping through a tiny crack in the chain's enchantment. I froze, watching as her body followed a moment later, hovering in the space between me and the line of boys.

She was here. The command worked. I could hear her, speak with her. But whatever relief I felt couldn't last, not with so many children hiding their faces, weeping now. Knowing without knowing that an end was coming.

"*I have to do something.*"

"*No, my lady,*" Vitaly said, body shimmering into existence beside Ozura's. "*There's nothing you can do for them now.*" His face was filled with grief and mourning, but his eyes were something else, lost to a Marchland vista I could not quite grasp. Like death was pouring forth from his ghostly gaze, reaching for the men and women before him.

"No, please, my lord. They're just boys. I—we were all just boys once."

Volvukov's pleas bounced off Radovan like hail on stone. He smiled. "You never answered my question, Volvukov. Were. You. Punished?"

Blood drained from Volvukov's face. His eyes widened, until they were all pupils and panic. He looked up at Radovan, then at Qaden who was slowly circling him. At me. Wild. Beseeching. But I was frozen, locked in place by the hands of six dead queens. Their touch hummed through the stone, filling me with their thoughts, their voices, their terror.

Don't do it.

Lady Night, curse you.

Radovan, stop this, you fucking monster.

Enough, Rada. Please.

Volvukov turned back to Radovan, squared his shoulders, pulling himself together from his knees. "No."

"No," Radovan repeated, voice grave. "Of course you weren't punished. And because you weren't, neither will you punish your son. The cycle will just continue, and Gethen's suffering will never end. And that, I will not allow."

"Captain."

Qaden moved before Radovan even finished speaking. The sound of her sword scraping against the scabbard filled the air. Steel flashed through the sunlight like a shooting star. And took Volvukov through the chest.

The other Voyniks followed suit, skewering the kneeling men and women in an instant. But it wasn't enough. Not for Radovan. Not for the madness gripping his mind.

His face twisted into a wordless snarl. He flung out one hand

and magic poured forth. It was a twisted perversion of healing magic, befouled for murderous rage.

There was a wet crack. A sloppy thud.

Volvukov's head bounced onto the bottom step, rolled back. It watched with unseeing eyes as Radovan beheaded them. One by one, like a child popping the tops off dandelions. Their bodies fell, twelve men and women, mothers and fathers hitting the floor, soaking their sons in blood.

Six voices screamed in my mind—no, seven, for I was screaming too. Screaming so loudly I was momentarily deaf. But I could see. I saw the other nobles flinch away and cover their children's eyes. I saw the boys fall at their parents' feet, mouths wide with uncomprehending horror.

Beside me Radovan laughed. A breathless chuckle, like he was marveling at his own power, drunk on it. I recognized the glassy look in his eyes, for I'd seen it before, when he'd forced his memories into me—only now it was so much more. So much worse. It was the look of a man drunk on blood and lusting for more.

Qaden's hand fell on the shoulder of Volvukov's son. Pushing him to the ground. Into the blood pouring from his mother's gaping neck. He stared at his father's head, eyes wild and uncomprehending.

Qaden's face was carved with lines of barely suppressed horror. Tears welled in her eyes, but I knew she wouldn't stop. She was a soldier, and she'd received her commands.

She clasped her sword in both hands. Tensed.

"Stop."

My voice rang across the open space, cutting off screams and freezing soldiers and restraining ghosts. Qaden's sword stuttered to a stop in midair. It was like I'd suddenly gained the ability to seize control of living flesh. She looked at me, expression pleading.

Radovan turned. His eyes seared into mine, but I held his gaze. Willed my mind to find the right words. Failed.

"Hurry, Askia," Ozura barked. *"You have seconds."*

I forced all the pity and horror and revulsion out of my voice and rose. "This is enough, Radovan."

Confusion rippled across his face chased by a shadow of betrayal. "But you told me to see them punished. You said it was my duty to protect Gethen. And you were right. This is the only way to keep Gethen safe."

"But you have punished them," I said, keeping my tone calm, reasonable, unaffected even as guilt burned through my chest at what a few of my words, spoken in anger, had wrought. "Believe me, there is no greater loss a child can suffer than the death of their parents. These children know that you had to do this—it was for their own good. We all know that. And you have taught them a very powerful lesson."

I smiled, each and every muscle in my face shattering as I did so. "These boys will learn from this. They will become better men because of it. The kind of men who will stand up for the weak and the powerless. The kind of men any emperor would be proud to have serving them."

Radovan's eyes were hot on my face, inhaling my words, but I couldn't tell if they were sinking in. I didn't know if they would be strong enough to slake his thirst for blood. To override the cruelty that had ingrained itself into his bones over this last century.

"Katarzhina, help me," I demanded of the woman who knew and loved him best.

Katarzhina grabbed the stone in one pale fist, her grip so strong it made my heart go still. Her essence crackled along the chain and found the chink in its enchantment—the tiny fissure that allowed me to command Ozura into cohesion. Without hesitation, Katarzhina shoved through it, into the stone. Into me.

My lungs turned to lead, barely able to expand for the frigid presence of a dead woman shouldering her way into my living skin. But it was necessary as her words filled me, nearly seizing control of my body. She was inside my mind, my bones, binding us together in flesh that was not quite big enough for the two of us, and couldn't last forever.

"Please, Rada," I said, softly, not recognizing the sound of my own voice as my hand slid into his. "Gethen is safe. Enough now."

Radovan went utterly still, as if he could see Katarzhina in my eyes, hear her in my voice. His gaze softened, and he smiled. It was a frail, fragile thing. Like he was a lost child who finally had found his place in the world.

It was monstrous.

It was terrifying.

It was the only chance of salvation these boys had.

"Very well, my dear." His hand tightened around mine, and that same healing magic he'd just used for murder was turned on me, wiping my blistered skin clean. The stain on my soul, I knew, would never lift.

"Captain," he said, still smiling, "please have these boys taken away. Perhaps the Svetniks can organize some sort of re-education for them in the lower city."

Qaden's blade fell to her side so quickly I thought she might be about to fling it away, only stopping herself at the last moment. "As you wish." With no more than a shallow nod, guards half bolted from the line behind Radovan's throne. They grabbed the blood-covered and broken boys and practically ran from the hall like they feared Radovan might change his mind.

But he had already turned back to me, that wide almost innocent smile on his face. "I would dine with you, my dear, but I'm afraid I have business to attend to with General Koloii."

"That's all right," I said slowly, a wave of nausea washing over me as Katarzhina's presence seeped out of my body. The urge to vomit only amplified as Radovan bent, pecking my cheek in a kiss as light as the brush of a moth's dirty wings.

"I'm glad you were here with me—to see that I do know what it means to love."

With one last hideous grin, Radovan turned. He cut a path through the still-cowering nobles, his general and half the guards on his heels. I barely saw him go. Was still reeling from the death, from Katarzhina's presence. From Radovan's parting words. This was his idea of love? Twelve dead men and women. Six dead children.

No. The children weren't dead. I'd stopped him in time. But only just. And Lady Night curse me, it was all my fault. I—

"Askia. Do. Not. React. Not now. Not when the court is watching." Ozura appeared mere inches from my face, her gaze burning me with the lick of cold flames. *"There is an opportunity here. Don't squander it to satisfy your own guilt."*

She was right.

I took three slow breaths. Straightened my spine and forced my eyes past the bodies. Past the gore. Past the bloody trail of child-sized footprints staining the floor.

"Captain," I said in a steady voice. "Please make sure these people are buried properly."

Qaden wiped her blade on the edge of her coat, sheathing it slowly, reverently. I'd seen such actions before, such careful movements done to withdraw, to flee from the horror of war and the terrible consequences of living with yourself once the battle was done. When she looked at me, there was no emotion left in her face, except perhaps for the sliver of guilt shining in her dark eyes. "I am not sure the emperor will wish for—"

"Then he may take the matter up with me," I said, my voice patient, yet firm. With the eyes of the whole court upon me, I could not get into a shouting match with Qaden. I could not break down and cry or beg forgiveness. "And I will tell him that Queen Katarzhina requests these men and women receive at least that much respect. And Queen Asyl demands it."

Though neither woman had said as much, I could feel the desire in my mind, as if we were still linked. Not that the lie mattered. Nor did it matter if Radovan overruled me. What mattered was that I tried, here in front of the court, to give voice to the Dorovnii the emperor hated so much.

The crowd around me recoiled as my words fell to the blood-soaked floor. Men and women looked about themselves, still too scared to speak. The revelation that, despite the magic imbued in the chain, I could see and hear the dead queens of Roven was but one more fear atop a day filled with fear. But it was what those queens might say, that had them quivering once more.

For her part, Qaden looked unsurprised by my words. She simply nodded. "As you wish," she replied, her voice far softer than it had ever been with me before. She dipped her chin a fraction of an inch, in acknowledgment. And thanks.

Her gratitude almost broke something in me. For I deserved her hate and her rage for all the blood that lay quite literally at my feet.

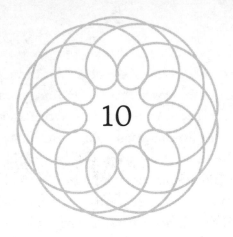

10

I MADE IT across the Great Hall, up the stairs, and through the door to my room before I let myself feel it, the shock and guilt that made my joints want to shatter. I sat carefully, rigidly in the chair by the fire. A sob rose in my throat, burning like broken glass.

I refused to let it loose. Refused to let myself express it, to offer the slightest chance at release. Because if I did, I might never stop. Or worse.

I might begin to feel better.

"Askia?" Eliska touched my shoulder with light fingertips. *"Are you all right?"*

"Are you?" I shot back, my eyes tearing through the room, taking in the sight of Eliska beside me and Ozura in the chair opposite. Ragata was curled up in the middle of my bed, Asyl and Freyda perched on the end of the mattress, each sitting so still it was like they feared to move. Siv leaned against the far wall, one hand covering her eyes. Vitaly was beside her, face unbearable to behold. And Katarzhina.

It was to her that I looked now. To the only true queen of Roven. Katarzhina stood beside her window, studying me. I could just make out the lines of her face through the veil, ravaged with anger and mourning. *"Was this my fault? Did my words convince Radovan to kill those people?"*

"*No*," Katarzhina replied. "*The blame lies with him alone.*" She shook her head. "*He wasn't always like this. He was good once. Decent. But somehow, time has changed him.*"

Asyl made a sound of agreement. "*I don't think people were meant to live so long.*"

Katarzhina wasn't wrong. Ultimately the blame lay with Radovan. But there was no way to escape my part in that blame. "*If I had just kept my damned mouth shut.*"

Eliska knelt at my feet, taking my hand. "*You couldn't have known.*"

"*But I did know—*"

"*Oh, shut up.*"

I flinched at the ice in Ozura's voice. She watched me over steepled fingers, her face hard and unyielding as stone.

"*I didn't forsake my rest to listen to you give in to self-pity,*" she said.

"*This isn't self-pity,*" I retorted. "*Don't you understand what I did? What I caused?*"

"*I know exactly what you did. You saved those boys.*"

"*I didn't save them.*" I shook my head. "*I should know—I had to watch my parents murdered. That terror will chase them forever. And I caused it.*"

"*You caused nothing. Do you really think Radovan would have let Gethen be bullied forever? That he didn't know about it? Do you think it was a coincidence that he just happened to be there when you saw it?*"

"*You weren't there. You didn't see his face.*"

"*I have no doubt he was surprised to hear you sing Katarzhina's lullaby,*" Ozura said, flicking my words away. "*But he knows enough about you to know you'd never stand by while an innocent person is tormented.*"

I drew back further, brow furrowing. "*You're saying that—*"

"*I'm saying Radovan will use any excuse he can to grind down his Dorovnii. Now, what else have you learned from today?*"

"*What?*"

"*Besides realizing you cannot control a monster like Radovan, what did you learn?*"

I forced my mind to move. To think. To turn away from doubt and pain. I could confront them later, but only if I lived.

"*Radovan likes you,*" Eliska ventured. "*I doubt he would have spared the children had anyone else intervened. And like it or not, he listens to you. You could use that.*"

More than one of the ghosts winced at the idea. "*No,*" I said flatly. "*Today proves that Qaden was right. Radovan never reacts in the way you expect.*"

"*But—*"

"*No,*" I said, one hand cutting through the air. "*You might have been able to sweet-talk him. But I never say the right thing. I need another option.*"

The queens looked around at each other, eyes bright with thought. A brightness that soon faded when no one came to any conclusions.

"*What about other ghosts in the castle?*" I ventured. "*Surely they would know something I could use. If I could just speak to them—*"

"*I doubt you'll be able to,*" Asyl said, smoothing an imaginary wrinkle from her robe.

I frowned at that. "*Why not? I can hear Ozura now.*"

"*Yes,*" Asyl allowed, "*but it's clear to me that whoever designed the chain's enchantment had as limited a grasp on magic as Radovan does. They didn't suspect that with our magic trapped in the stone, you would be able to see us. I would guess that the same principle applies to Ozura. She is soulbound to you—an oath she made not only to you but to Lady Night Herself. Whatever enchantment keeps you from using your magic, it wasn't strong enough to prevent you from reaching her in your time of need.*"

"*I've defeated the chain before,*" I replied, coldly proud of the burns on my chest. Even with Radovan's healing touch, they still smarted, but it was a pain drenched in victory.

"What you endured to bring Ozura to you is but the smallest brush of the chain's power. Test it more if you wish—though if you ask me, you have better things to do than to waste your precious time in screaming agony."

Asyl and I locked eyes, a silent battle waging between us. And even though I wanted to push the chain's bounds, I knew part of the urge was only to spite the other woman. She was right. I hated it—but she was right.

"Fine. I can't speak with the other ghosts, but you can. Now, what else?" I dragged a hand through my hair when no one spoke. *"Come on, there has to be someone I can use. Some ally we haven't thought of."*

"I doubt you'll be making any friends here, love," Siv said, tiredly. *"Didn't you see the court today? They're shitting themselves. Not just because of your influence on Radovan, but your ability to see us."*

"Siv's right," Eliska said with a bitter smile. *"There's nothing they fear more than someone exposing all their sins."*

Great. The Voyniks were too loyal, the servants too helpless, and the Dorovnii were too scared. And if Radovan stole my magic? I shook my head at the floor. They'd really have someone to fear then.

I straightened, an idea filling me. *"That's it. Fear."*

"I'm not following," Siv said, looking from me to Eliska and back again.

"The fear of exposure. The fear that someone might actually learn all their little secrets," I replied, something like purpose burning within me.

"You want us to spy?" Freyda said, her voice filled with doubt.

"But we already are—on Radovan and his generals," Asyl whined.

"*Let Vitaly and Ozura take over those duties,*" I said, glancing at the ghosts for confirmation before continuing. "*But the six of you, you know this court. You know the players here. So I need your eyes on the Dorovnii. We need to find out what they're hiding, all their weaknesses.*"

"*And then do what?*" Siv asked, coming closer to the fire.

"*And then, I'm going to make the Dorovnii see what they should truly fear.*" I smiled at their uncomprehending faces and pointed at the closed door behind me. "*If I can uncover all their secrets from behind a locked door with only a fraction of my power, then—*"

"*Then imagine all the things Radovan will learn in a few weeks' time,*" Ozura said, nodding along with a small laugh. "*Brilliant. They'll be tripping over themselves to befriend you.*"

"*Or lining up to kill you,*" Freyda muttered.

I waved the words away. "*I can defend myself. Besides, with Qaden and the guard following me around, no one will get close enough. Though, speaking of Qaden,*" I said, remembering Asyl's earlier comment. "*Freyda, what happened between you and Qaden's sister?*"

"*What are you talking about?*" Ozura asked, craning her neck toward the fire witch, but Freyda wasn't looking at her—wasn't looking at anyone. The whole of her attention was on her hands, clasped together as if protecting something small and fragile.

"*Freyda killed Qaden's older sister, Jai,*" Asyl said slowly, when it became clear that Freyda wasn't going to reply. "*Jai was captain of the guard at the time. Qaden went mad with grief. Took a six-month leave to take Jai's body back to Khezhar for burial.*"

"*Yes, but why did you kill Jai?*" I pressed. In what little time I'd spent with Freyda, I knew she wasn't the sort of woman to let her anger get away from her. Siv I could see trying to kill one of her captors out of spite—or for sport—but Freyda?

Qaden's taunt about Freyda trying to kill herself echoed through my head. Did I know enough about Freyda to judge what she would do? Did I know enough about any of the queens to predict how they reacted to this terrible, cruel, extended death sentence?

"What happened is between Jai and me," Freyda said slowly.

Siv gaped at Freyda like she was mad. *"Jai isn't here. I doubt she'll mind."*

"That's where you're wrong," Freyda argued, before looking at me and shaking her head. *"I'm sorry. I can't tell you more. I promised not to."*

"You promised?" I shook my head, her words jangling through my mind until they finally hit. *"Wait. Promised who? Qaden? Or Jai?"*

Freyda only shook her head again, saying nothing more. Whatever the secret was, it was safe with Freyda and Jai, wherever her spirit was. Except . . .

Except something about the situation was still off. Something in the way Qaden spoke of it didn't sit quite right. Had she been in on the plan? My eyes went to Siv. She hadn't found anything yet, but if she looked deeper? Siv gave me the slightest of smiles, understanding what I was asking without words.

"Ozura," I said, turning to the Vishiri queen. *"I need to find the rebellion you were in contact with. Do you have any names?"*

"I do, but I doubt anyone was foolish enough to give me their true ones."

I grimaced. Of course, it wouldn't be that easy. *"Still. Tell the others what you know, maybe something will ring a bell. The way things are here, I think we'll find the rebels right under this very roof."*

Eliska bit her lip. *"I'm not sure we'll be able to follow all these people and find a way for you to escape."*

"I know." It was the worst part of my plan, but there was nothing for it. *"I've had plenty of time to study the security around the gate. The fact is, I'm not going to be able to get out without help. So I need you to expose the skeletons. Every hidden affair and deal gone wrong. Every dirty secret. These things build. What we learn about*

one lord will lead us to another one, and another. Until eventually, we'll find someone with so much to lose, they'll beg me to flee with them.

"*We can do it,*" I said.

Because really, there wasn't another choice.

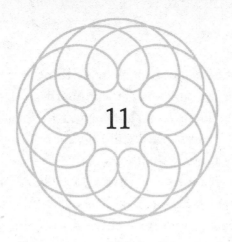

11

WHAT WILL IT take to keep you quiet? Money? Information?"

A lazy smile spread across my face at the sudden pallor in Countess Arikatova's face. I hooked my arm through hers as we passed a pair of bored-looking guards who barely glanced at us as we ambled by.

"Depends on the information," I replied in a careful undertone, dragging the countess along on my circuit of the Great Hall.

The day after the execution brought with it a cold front so frigid it drove even the hardiest of Roven men indoors. So I was more than happy to take our daily walk inside when Zosha suggested it. At a certain point, it was simply too cold outside for thought. And with the Great Hall brimming over with bored Dorovnii, I could put my spy game in motion without delay.

With the queens, Vitaly, and Ozura scouring the castle, I'd accumulated several books' worth of naughty deeds in less than twenty-four hours. And all it took was a gentle word here or a significant look there to convey what I knew to the always-watching Dorovnii.

It was so easy, I began to wonder why they hadn't started avoiding me. Then again, watching me blackmail their peers was probably better entertainment than anything else they could expect to see over the dark and frozen months.

"I'll tell you about Anya Parimatova Roshka," the countess said in a rush. "The youngest child of Count Oleg Parimatov."

"What about her?"

"She was the emperor's mistress," the older woman said, her heavily powdered face alight with cruelty. "About two months ago, she left court to go on sabbatical to the Vozen temple of Lady Night. At least that's where her mother claims she is. Conveniently close to the Kirskov Summer Palace, don't you think?"

A smile that didn't belong to me rose on my lips. "She went to Kirskov to bear a child?"

The countess snorted. "To be *rid* of a child. The emperor has no desire—or need—for heirs. Not that dear Prince Gethen will ever inherit the throne."

"Does Radovan know?" I asked, mind spinning for a way to use the information.

"Of course," she replied, as if this should be obvious. "One doesn't leave court without the emperor's permission, least of all the woman warming his bed."

I frowned, hating myself for being disappointed, for wishing more hardship upon a young woman who had done nothing wrong. But the cold, practical corner of my mind knew that poor Anya's situation would have been more valuable had her family secreted her away under Radovan's nose. Having a count in my pocket would have been useful.

I feigned a yawn. "And why should I care about any of this?"

"Because, while the emperor knows the true reason for Anya's departure, her husband does not."

"Who is her husband?" I asked, brows rising.

The countess bared her teeth, smiling like she knew she had something good. "A Lieutenant Bora Roshko. He is one of the emperor's most trusted soldiers. He personally guards the emperor's most valuable treasures, you know. He apparently has no idea what's been going on behind his back, poor soul."

"Poor indeed," I muttered. "I guess he didn't know that one of Radovan's greatest treasures was his own wife."

The countess gave another cruel smile at that, and I patted her withered hand before releasing her back into the wilds of Radovan's court.

"What do you hope to gain from this web your spinning?" Zosha asked. He'd peeled back while I spoke with the countess, but now that I was alone and prowling, he'd returned to my side.

I smiled. To his credit, he'd already caught on to my game. Though I suppose it was obvious from the way I made a point to seek out certain people. From the way they universally blanched as I spoke. Still, it was fun watching Zosha chew on his words, see his thoughts shift from reporting me to Radovan to protecting his fellow Dorovnii—and himself—from the web I was spinning.

"What do you think I'm hoping to gain?"

"A knife in the back."

I laughed. "Not a chance. I have eyes everywhere, after all." He grimaced at that, but I just kept walking, all too aware of the men and women who shrank as I passed, only to lean forward again, ears straining to hear what I might be saying. "Not that I would blame anyone for trying," I muttered with an ennui-filled shrug. "No one wants to imagine *him* with my power."

Zosha sucked in a sharp breath. "Be careful, Askia. Someone will eventually tell him what you're doing."

"To what end?" I asked, completely uncaring. "I'm dead anyway. Only then, all my secrets will come tumbling out. There's not enough soap in Tolograd to scrub away the blood that will stain these floors."

Zosha shook his head, unimpressed, but unable to argue. "You really think you'll find someone desperate enough to help you escape?"

"Who said anything about escape?" I said, my voice too innocent. "I'm just hoping to stay alive long enough to stir up a little trouble for my dear, sweet betrothed. Who knows, perhaps I'll discover something useful enough to stay my execution by a day or two. I don't suppose you know anything worthwhile?"

Zosha's only reply was a slight narrowing of his eyes, clearly wondering, the way everyone was wondering, whether I had anything on him. I smiled sweetly, letting the thought weigh down on his shoulders. I was sure he was hiding something, but in solidarity with Ragata, none of the queens were saying anything. Good thing I still had Vitaly's loyalty, though my onetime soldier hadn't found anything.

Yet.

"This is reckless, Askia."

"Because I have so much to lose."

"The emperor will punish you if he finds out."

I leveled a hard look at him. "Punishment is a frail kind of threat when the axe already hangs over your head—or hangs around your neck," I said, holding up my chain. "Besides, there are worse things than pain, Zosha."

"Like what?"

"Like Radovan ruling the world."

Zosha flinched, glancing around to see who might have heard, but I knew no one was close enough. No one living anyway.

The crowd parted ahead of me, and I spotted a streak of pale blond hair. Perfect. I sped up, prowling through the crowd, hunting down my prey. He almost eluded me. Almost.

Because as much as the Dorovnii feared being on the receiving end of my blackmail, they loved watching others suffer. A balding man from the lower nobility—judging by the lack of crown on his cheek tattoo—got in the way of my target, dancing back and forth with a gleeful smile. Giving me just enough time to pounce.

"Pjeder, is that you?" I called, in an airy voice that belied the vicious laughter brimming in my eyes. "It's been ages. Won't you walk with me?"

Tcheshin's back stiffened as my voice slid beneath his ribs like the point of a knife. He turned slowly, a smile fixed on his face. "Queen Askia, how are you today?"

I wanted to laugh at the way he hurled out the greeting like a gauntlet thrown. "I'm wonderful. Shall we?"

His smile almost became a snarl as he said in a low voice, "As if I truly have a choice in the matter."

I let one of my brows rise. "Pouting now, Tcheshin? Really."

Air seethed out from between his pursed lips. He clasped his hands behind his back and fell into step. We walked a few long feet in silence before he looked over his shoulder and grimaced. "I'm not saying anything with your dog following me."

I glanced at Zosha, who shook his head and dropped back, pausing at one of the long tables to chat up a strapping young man playing cards with some equally pretty peers.

"Is that better?"

He grunted.

"I'm surprised you're saying anything, Tcheshin. Don't you want to know what I have?" It was a wonderful little piece of embezzlement that Freyda had uncovered. I'd shaken my head in wonder when she told me.

I'd suspected that Ozura, Eliska, and Katarzhina might have a flair for espionage—they were raised in noble courts after all. But Freyda had a particular skill for uncovering what she called "creative accounting." Then again, she'd run one of the wealthiest merchant clans in the north. Maybe it wasn't so surprising she knew how people hid their dirty money.

People like Tcheshin, who was secretly stealing a percentage of Switzkia's annual tithe to Radovan.

"I can guess," Tcheshin bit back.

I almost shouldn't have bothered spying at all. With the reputation I was building it was hardly necessary. "You have something to exchange?"

"Of course."

"I'm listening."

"No. It's not something you should hear. It's something you should see." My gaze cut to his, and it was his turn to raise his eyebrows and smile. "Has dear Zosha not told you what lies beneath this very hall?"

I looked away, scanning the crowd of fine-clothed nobles and sharply dressed guards. They all walked in small groups, or huddled over long dining tables, playing cards or dice. There was even a group of guards sparring near the throne, where Radovan sat looking on.

Doors peppered the edges of the hall, but none of them seemed to get any special attention from either the Dorovnii or the Voyniks. What could be beneath us? Treasure? I thought back to the countess's tale of young Anya and her poor cuckolded husband. But why would Tcheshin think I was interested in money? Unless what he was really leading me to was a way to escape? My heart sped up. "Tell me."

"No," he replied, holding up a hand when I turned to him. "But I will draw you a map and arrange for the space to be made . . . available to you."

"Tonight," I ordered. "Leave instructions on your bedside table when you go to sleep. You may burn them in the morning."

My lip twitched with a bare smile as his already pale skin went even paler. It wasn't strictly necessary for him to keep the map all night, but the thought of him tossing and turning for fear of the ghosts in my employ amused me when nothing else here did.

"Tcheshin," I called, before he could melt into the crowd. He froze, half turned back to me. "Is there any news of the Black Wolves?"

A delicate sneer twisted his face. "Still crouching along the Idunese border, last I heard. As if the Free State will keep them safe."

"I want you to get General Arkady a message."

Tcheshin's eyes bulged. "You jest."

Again, I let one of my eyebrows rise. The gesture alone was enough to make him sweat.

"It's . . . it's not possible."

"Make it possible," I said, my voice softer than death's own kiss. "Don't forget what I have on you, Pjeder. If Radovan ever finds out, he won't just kill you. He'll kill everyone you've ever known."

"You wouldn't."

My answering laugh curdled in my ears. "Two weeks ago, you'd have been right. Now? You belong to me. Find a way."

He gave me a tight nod and slipped away. Zosha stepped into the place Tcheshin left and we continued on, but I wasn't really seeing anything. My mind was too full of thoughts of Arkady and the Wolves. Had Illya and my close guard returned yet? What would Arkady do once he found out about my plight? Send help?

No. No he wasn't foolish enough to do that. He would probably try to fold the Wolves into the Idunese defense forces. The Free States of Idun had a sizable navy. They had to, seeing as they controlled the only strait through which ships could pass from east to west. But their land army had never been large. Though that must be changing with Roven on the horizon. I hoped it was.

Or maybe Arkady would take the Wolves into Vishir. I tried to imagine the always grim and stalwart General Arkady wading through the rocky shoals of the Vishir court. The image it conjured almost made me laugh. Between Arkady and Illya, the court of Bet Naqar wouldn't stand a chance.

A carefully ignored corner of my heart ached at the thought of Illya in Vishir—at the memory of our time there. At what could have been. *No, Askia. Don't torment yourself.*

Focusing, I thought that it wouldn't be a terrible idea for Arkady to go to Vishir. He and Illya could help Iskander shore up his claim to the throne. Illya seemed to like Iskander well enough, and we all knew Enver was too easily persuaded by sweet-talking Roven words.

But it wasn't as if Iskander hadn't made some inadvisable alliances. Barely two weeks ago he'd gone behind my back and aligned with the Shazir. So, did I really want Arkady and Illya to throw in their lot with him?

No. Neither prince truly deserved the throne. Still, of the two men, Iskander was the better option, though the thought of placing the lesser of two evils on the throne of the largest nation in the world was . . . well, it was absolute shit to be honest.

I realized my head was starting to hang and forced my neck back up. How did Ozura feel, I wondered, trapped so far from home? She surely never imagined she'd be stuck in Roven with me when she swore her soul into my service. Not knowing what was happening must be slowly destroying her. Lady Night knew I wasn't exactly coping with it well.

The crowd shifted, rolling back and forth in waves before me, and I saw Radovan sitting alone. But not completely isolated. About three dozen Voyniks stood in a loose knot around the dais. They'd been taking turns sparring in pairs for Radovan's amusement. Though he sat on his throne, he'd leaned forward to speak with the men and women of the guard, seeming to enjoy the casual atmosphere, the camaraderie.

Radovan's sea-green eyes cut up to mine, like he could feel my gaze upon him. With the twin stones connecting us, maybe he could. He raised an eyebrow, gesturing to the empty seat beside him in silent invitation. No, command.

Disquiet rippled through me like a pebble through still water. I allowed my chin to dip with a tiny nod, and wove my way through the Voyniks, skirting along the makeshift edges of their training ring to the dais.

Sliding into the throne, I eased back, crossing my legs and hoping I looked calm. Radovan leaned back as well, hands clasped loosely as his head angled toward me. "I've been watching you."

"Oh?" It was a weak reply, but as my other reaction involved a shudder, I made do with what I could.

It was agony to comb through my every response before speaking, trying to parse out all the ways my words could be misconstrued. And somehow I needed to guard what I said while still speaking the truth. It was excruciating, but I knew from last night that this was the stuff of life and death.

"My court seems fascinated with you," he said, his voice too soft for the guards around us to hear. "Terrified. But fascinated."

"I suppose I should be satisfied, but knowing how long winters can be, I'd guess that any distraction is a welcome one."

He breathed an almost-laugh, all but ignoring the sparring match now. And how his Voyniks disliked that. I spotted Qaden over Radovan's shoulder, watching me with suspicion simmering in her dark eyes.

No. Not quite suspicion. Warning, perhaps? I'd hoped she might soften to me after the executions—after I'd stopped Radovan from killing the children. Or rather, stopped him from making Qaden kill them.

Apparently this fraction of a thaw was as good as it was going to get.

"You were speaking to Tcheshin."

I nodded, reaching for how to answer the implicit question in a way that was both truthful and wise. "Just looking for information."

He hummed, a sound that flirted with the edge of displeasure. "Information on what?"

"Everything. But right now, I want to know what's happening in Vishir." Since it was true, I didn't fear the touch of Radovan's magic rustling across my skin.

He studied me for a moment longer, like he was trying to guess my thoughts from my expression. "You're worried about your Prince Iskander."

Something in the way he said it made me bridle. "He's hardly *my* anything."

"Really?" One of those red-brown brows rose again. "Count Dobor was quite convinced that the young prince was in love with you."

I gritted my teeth, cursing Dobor in my mind and wishing it was possible to refute the claim entirely. Unfortunately, Iskander had pretty well spelled out his feelings for me. Though I didn't reciprocate them, the last thing I wanted to do was expose Iskander to Radovan. Not like this.

Because I couldn't help but feel the possessive undercurrent that ran through our every interaction. That the reason Zosha was my companion was because he would never be in danger of feeling for me the way Iskander did. The way, I thought, Radovan wanted me to feel for him.

I managed a shrug. "I am not so easy to love."

This made Radovan smile. "Those of us in power never are."

I allowed a nod, noticing with silent amusement that Radovan didn't ask whether I loved Iskander. Was he afraid of the answer?

The thought fled when he turned back to the fighting and grinned at his glowering captain. "Ah Qadenzizeg, I was just thinking of you. Perhaps you will take the ring next?"

Had I been eating anything, I'd have choked. He was just thinking of her? In the context of our conversation? I watched

Qaden closely when she bowed to Radovan. Nothing in her face betrayed any emotion. Not pride or satisfaction for being on her liege's mind. Certainly nothing that implied affection that went beyond the bounds of duty, much less love.

My mind went immediately to Freyda. To Qaden's sister. And to my encounter earlier with the countess.

The pieces began to fall into place, coalescing into a terrible picture that I couldn't bring myself to examine closely. Because while Radovan might pantomime emotions, might play at flirting, there was something utterly reptilian about him. The thought of him acting on those games was more revolting than the memory of twelve severed heads rolling across the floor.

"I'm sad to say that I don't think I can help you," Radovan said, as Qaden began going through a quick warm up.

"How so?" I replied, trying not to sound as confused as I felt.

"My contacts in Vishir have become rather diminished as of late. As you well know," he said, gracing me with an indulgent smile.

"Is this where I'm supposed to apologize?"

He laughed and from the corner of my eye I saw the ever-watching court wince. "Not at all, my dear. You quite effectively locked Vishir down before your departure. I'd be annoyed if it wasn't so impressive. Though I do regret having to sacrifice Dobor."

"I can see why," I said, voice dripping with enough sarcasm to hide the unease worming through me. "He was so very adept at making friends." Ozura appeared beside me, her presence a warning.

Radovan laughed again, a velvety sound that left me feeling like slime had slid underneath my collar. "That he was. But to your real question, Vishir still stands. My sources tell me the princes are deadlocked, neither is strong enough to wrest control from the other, so they are ruling Vishir jointly."

Ozura closed her eyes against the news.

"Iskander is alive," I said, bracingly. She just shook her head, her lips no more than a gash across her face, body practically humming with dread. I understood why. Iskander must be further entrenched with the Shazir. How else would he be holding his own against Enver?

"This displeases you?"

"Of course." The admission was slow and unwilling, and I was glad to see Qaden squaring off against her opponents—both of them. Watching her fight would give me somewhere to look rather than at Radovan. "It hardly seems tenable."

"It most certainly is not," Radovan agreed amiably. "But it does make me wonder if you would be willing to speak with me about some aspects of Vishir's court."

I leveled a hard look at him. "Which aspects?"

"The Shazir?"

I jerked back. I'd have told him to go to hell—politely—had he said anything else. "What about them?"

"Everything," he replied, intensity sharpening his expression. "You have to know a thing to destroy it. Don't you agree?"

Did I? I didn't used to think so, but my short time here was teaching me otherwise. Every hour spent had made me realize I was in no way ready to meet Radovan on the battlefield. That—if I survived it—this experience would be the key to tearing him down. "Yes. Yes, I do."

"Askia. Be. Careful," Ozura whispered with so much urgency it sent a puff of cold air down my spine.

He nodded, cocking his head to one side. "So, will you do it? Will you help me destroy the Shazir?"

That was quite the question. Would I feed one enemy to another? If anyone could destroy the Shazir it was the monster beside me. But if I gave him the information he was looking for, would I be betraying Vishir? Would I weaken them? Warring duties scrabbled within me, and I had to look away.

And I saw Qaden move.

It was an understatement to say I wasn't impressed by her training methods, by how she'd let her new recruits fumble through sparring in dangerous conditions. And learning lessons through injury was something I would never agree with—something no swordmaster I'd ever trained under would have condoned.

But I'd never seen anyone move quite like Qaden did now.

Her opponents—both men—attacked her from different sides. The taller of them was a giant of a man with an arm span as wide as Qaden was tall. That alone should have given him all the advantage he needed. The second man was stockier with biceps as big as my thighs. He threw all his considerable weight into every swing.

But if Qaden was shorter and slighter than her opponents, she was also faster. She moved like smoke, there one moment and gone again. It was a dance, a whirling, blurring dance of speed that my eyes could barely track.

I was distantly aware that my hands had curled around the arms of my chair. My eyes were wide with awe . . . and longing. Though I doubted I'd ever *like* Qaden, Lady Night curse me, I wanted to learn from her. Learn how to move like that, because no one—not Illya nor Captain Nazir of the Khazan Guard—moved like that. And she was as good as either of them. Twice as good as the men she was fighting.

Make that *fought*, I corrected as she closed in for both killpoints, felling one man and then the next in a single fluid, spinning move. The movement brought her full circle. She stopped instantly, bending into a deeply graceful bow to Radovan. Rose. Her cheeks were flushed, but she was barely out of breath at all.

Her dark eyes met mine as she rose and a slight smile worked its way onto her lips, like she could read the eagerness in my face. The look vanished as her gaze flickered to Radovan and back, her body stiffening. Trying to contain worry? I wondered.

"Care to spar, Queen Askia?"

I braced myself for Radovan to object, but he only laughed. "Please do, my dear. That is exactly the kind of spectacle I live for."

His words were nearly enough to make me refuse. Nearly. But fighting Qaden just might, *might* make him forget that he asked me to sell out Vishir.

And anyway, it could be my last chance to hold a sword. I rose and stepped into the ring.

As if she'd heard my last thought, Qaden handed off her blade and called for two practice swords. Pity. But the chance to take a swipe at Radovan during the spar would have been too much for me to deny—though I probably wouldn't have gotten within three feet of him before his magic took me down.

Qaden tossed me a sword, bringing her wooden blade up to her face in salute. "Watching your words today, I hope?" she said, voice hardly audible over the quiet din of the hall.

"Yes," I replied, copying the gesture. "Believe me when I say that I will not be so careless again."

A hint of a smile sparkled in her eyes. "Good," she said, and punched me in the face.

It shouldn't have been possible, but she lunged so fast, closing the distance with her off hand, that I barely had time to register her fist before it connected with my cheek. I rolled with it as best I could. Stumbling back a few steps, I blinked quickly, trying to clear the pain from my eyes in time to see her coming again.

She brought down her sword twice so hard my wooden blade groaned. The shockwave of force shuddered up my hand and arm as I parried. It was worse than fighting Captain Nazir to join the Vishiri guard. I'd been outmatched then, too, but Nazir had been trying to take my measure. Qaden was trying to send a message. With every adder-fast swipe and crushing blow she was reminding me the cost of my careless words—of the pain I had caused.

But I didn't need her to help me remember.

"Vitaly. Help."

The ghost's response was immediate. I barely discerned a whisp of gray vapor before he was clasping the stone. As Katarzhina had done the day before, so Vitaly did now. He shoved his soul into my body, plunging me into a cold so intense it made my muscles seize, and for a second I couldn't move. It was a second too long.

Qaden brought her sword down on my forearm and I felt my bones bend. Quake.

I cried out, hobbling backward, sword dangling from my hand by the simple fact that I couldn't open it.

She paused. And while her master laughed in glee, there was no joy in Qaden's eyes. No satisfaction. Just a question. *Had enough?*

No. No, I hadn't.

I made myself small. Let Vitaly grow, his presence washing over me with a phantom cinnamon scent that lingered in my nose, reminding me of home. It gave me strength. Made me brave. And so I wasn't afraid when Vitaly took control.

We rose. Passed the sword into my left hand. And smiled; it was Vitaly's strong hand anyway. We attacked.

Surprise flashed across Qaden's face as we fought her. Attacks that had been overwhelming a moment ago were met. And returned. Together, Vitaly and I forced her on her back foot. We bore down hard, desperate to take advantage and keep her on defense, but Qaden was too quick to be trapped for long. She readjusted. And rather than getting sloppy, she only got more precise.

It was damned impressive, I thought, even as Vitaly growled in my mind, frustrated by my lack of reach and lesser strength.

"We up your training tonight," he swore in such a vehement voice it reminded me painfully of Illya putting new recruits through their paces.

Qaden lowered her shoulder, and our blades met in another bone-crunching blow. There was no bracing for such a hit. For a split second my feet left the ground. I flew back and hit the floor so hard that for a moment I couldn't breathe.

Vitaly's presence seeped out of my skin as I struggled to reassert control over my lungs. Blinking back tears from my eyes, I found Qaden standing over me, wooden sword hovering at my throat.

"Match," she murmured, expression guarded as if unsure of my response.

I cracked a smile, surprised there wasn't blood on my face, and accepted her hand when she offered it. Sure, she'd kicked my ass—but that was the way with soldiers. You took your lumps and if you didn't bitch at the end, you just might earn some respect.

"Well done," Radovan exclaimed, his voice souring the moment of understanding that passed between Qaden and me.

I dropped her hand as Radovan swept between us. "Well done indeed," he crowed, planting a kiss on Qaden's forehead like she were a child taking her first steps. "And you as well, my dear," he said turning to me. "I thought she had you for a moment there early on. I had no idea you could fight left-handed."

"I live to surprise," I replied dryly before turning back to Qaden. "Thank you for the fight, Captain. It was a wonderful education. I hope we can continue it."

A curious look passed over Radovan's face. "It's been a long time since I've seen the captain impress someone so thoroughly. You truly enjoyed the fight? Even though you lost?"

Enjoyed? I shook my head, eyes going to Qaden—for it was she who needed to see my sincerity. "I've never seen or fought anyone who moves like her. It's brutal. And beautiful."

"Really?" He sounded taken aback, but I barely more than glanced at him as I nodded.

"Really. And I think you'd better give her a promotion before I poach her."

Radovan laughed at that, a deep sound that came from his belly. Qaden's dark eyes widened slightly, only to school her expression.

"A promotion," Radovan mused. His body shifted, cutting between Qaden and me, too casual to be coincidence. "Perhaps that can be arranged. For the right trade." I felt my brow furrow and he smiled a reptilian smile. "Will you tell me about the Shazir?"

Clever bastard. I could do this for Qaden—secure a possible ally—but it would be at the cost of my allies in Vishir. Not that the Shazir were my allies. And if it were only they who would suffer for my words, it would be an easy decision to make. But—

But I might need Qaden to escape. And if Qaden didn't appreciate me doing this, the other guards might. The Voyniks might have seemed like one great hive mind, but I knew better. Surely there was someone among them who didn't quite agree with everything Radovan was doing. Everything they had done in his name. Qaden certainly hadn't. Not when he ordered her to start killing children. Doing this for Qaden could show them I was on their side. But none of it would happen if I didn't tell Radovan everything I knew about the Shazir.

Ozura appeared on Radovan's left. *"Askia, say nothing."*

But why? I thought. Why protect the Shazir? Vitaly appeared on Radovan's right. *"Do it, Askia. It isn't your duty to protect the*

Shazir. Tell him and maybe—just maybe—you'll make an ally of Qaden. She's the kind of ally that could get you out of here."

"*Qaden will never betray Radovan,*" Ozura snapped, looking at Vitaly like she'd never seen him before. *"Like it or not, the Shazir are part of Vishir. You have a duty to protect Vishir."*

Vitaly just shook his head. Ozura stepped forward, and I felt her marshaling her arguments. But it was too late. I knew what I had to do.

I threw the dice.

"All right."

"All right?"

"I will tell you about the Shazir."

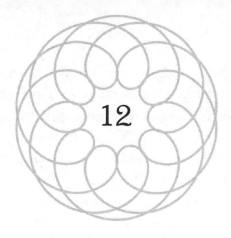

12

RADOVAN WASTED NO time taking me up on my promise. After a curt gesture and a few whispered words to a waiting servant, I was whisked out of the Great Hall, bundled in a warm sapphire cloak, and ushered outside. I wasn't exactly thrilled by going into the cold, but by the time we stepped into the courtyard, a black and gold troika pulled by a team of three ebon-coated horses was waiting.

I slid into the troika's well-cushioned seat, glad for the heavy bear skin blanket that covered my lap—even if I did have to share it with Radovan—because Lady Night save me, it was *freezing* outside. The kind of cold that my body was quickly losing the ability to sense. If I wasn't careful, I could get frostbite within a matter of moments. The danger high in my mind, I pushed my magic away—and the still-arguing Vitaly and Ozura with it—eager to preserve what little warmth I had left.

Even so, a shiver worked its way down my spine, drawing an amused smile from Radovan. "Allow me, my dear," he said, in his typical approximation of gentlemanly care, only to ruin the image a second later when the Aellium stone warmed beneath my clothes.

I didn't need to guess at the magic he was pulling, because before I could blink, a ring of fire erupted on the troika's edges.

Blue-white flames danced above the lacquered paint, all the more impressive for that it didn't actually touch the wood.

Any fire witch could summon flame, but this level of mastery, this ability to harness the magic and sustain it without any help from nature was . . . well, breathtaking. Horrifying but breathtaking. In moments, I was encased in a little bubble of warmth. Not even the cruel winter wind, which began to howl as we started across the bridge, could cut through the heat.

I glanced at Radovan and found him watching me from the corner of his eye. Swallowing down the sour taste at the back of my throat, I managed a very wooden thank you.

He smiled, dark amusement glittering in his gaze. "You're very welcome."

"Where are we going?" I asked, as we passed beneath the towering garrison leading into the city.

"Somewhere we can speak privately."

I settled back in the seat when he failed to get more specific. If he wanted to keep me in suspense, then fine. I'd been running on adrenaline from the moment I'd awoken in Tolograd. A sleigh ride wasn't going to scare me.

I gritted my teeth at that last thought, wishing it was true. But wishes were pointless. So even though I wanted nothing more than to see Ozura appear beside me, to whisper instructions in my ear, even though I was terrified of what my words might shake loose in this man's twisted mind, I willed my body to relax. Wait. Observe.

If the Dorovnii were all crowded in the Great Hall with nothing useful to do, the rest of the city clearly didn't have that luxury. Soldiers and citizens moved quickly this way and that throughout the Voynik sector. Cartloads of weapons and provisions were being dragged from massive storehouses along the River Tol and loaded onto huge sleighs pulled by teams of wooly-coated horses. I memorized everything, as if my eyes alone could tell me where the battle supplies were being taken. Seravesh? Idun? Or had war with Vishir finally arrived?

Before long we passed into the Niskoy sector. Unlike the Dorovnii, fewer members of the lower nobility could afford the indulgence of whiling away their days at fun and games. No, these people had actual work to do facilitating the running of Radovan's empire. Though few were outdoors, I glimpsed many through the wide windows of the white buildings we passed. Bent over desks with quills in hand, their air of studied work colored the snow-covered streets.

When we passed beneath the gate to the Svetnik sector, we turned off the main road, taking a curving boulevard north. It was the first clue I had to our destination. Scholars and priests hurried along the sidewalks, bundled up against the cold. High-pitched laughter rang from schoolyards and I looked, half hoping to see the faces of the boys I'd orphaned a few days ago, but of course not. A pair of girls chased each other across the frozen yard. Their teacher rushed after them, knocking into a passerby so hard the hood fell from the figure's face.

For a second, that stumbling stranger was Illya. Illya who scowled at the teacher and the girls. Illya who turned to shout only to catch sight of Radovan in the passing sleigh and bow.

I didn't bother doing a double take, cursing my twisting heart for playing these games with me. Twice now my subconscious had conjured Illya's face. And for what? Hope of rescue? What was it that Freyda had said? Hope was the cruelest torture of all. Well, she was right.

I put away the hope, folding it up tight and tucking it away like my favorite dress, and focused on what was coming. Focused on the road, which ran in a circle all the way back across the River Tol to where a temple rose in the castle's long shadow.

Built in the same uniform white stone as the rest of the city, it would have been unremarkable but for the three domes capping its roof. The domes, like cloves of garlic, twisted in tight spirals shot through with stripes of blue porphyry. It was like the castle's Great Hall had been pulled inside out.

I wondered what the likeness was meant to convey. That Radovan was honoring the Two-Faced God by building his hall in the image of the temple? I doubted it. Not only because I knew the castle had been built first, but by how hard it was to reach the temple. Rather than on the main road leading from the castle's bridge, the temple was clear on the other side of the city. We'd had to cross the River Tol on a much plainer, narrower bridge to reach it. It spoke volumes of Radovan's opinion about both religion and the Two-Faced God.

Radovan did not share power. Ever.

Then why are we here?

With that question echoing through my head, we halted before the temple's hammered copper doors. I left the troika's protective bubble of warmth, snow crunching beneath my boots like broken bones.

The air inside the temple was almost damp, as if the spacious interior and studied finery was only veneer atop a rotting skeleton. The impression intensified as I took in the sea of blue-black kneelers, the dozen theater-like balcony boxes, and the altar that dripped in silver and gold. It was the emptiness, I thought. The crypt-like sense of abandon.

Not a single person waited for us in the temple's heart. Not a single worshiper, priest, or priestess knelt, looking to the Two-Faced God for guidance. The only sound in the cavernous space was our footsteps, Radovan's and mine.

We cut a diagonal path across the vast room. Brushing through a narrow door, Radovan led me up a tight staircase lit not by witchlights, but by tallow candles that burned sweetly in the darkness.

When I stepped off the stairs, I found myself in one of the

balcony boxes. They'd seemed out of place to me from below but standing within one felt downright perverse. Two winged armchairs sat at the edge of the balcony, a table set with tea and cakes perched between them. It was profane, treating this place like it was meant for entertainment, not worship.

He held out a chair, watching me closely. "I hope it's not too hard for you to be here."

I frowned, not quite following. "What do you mean?"

"Well, the last time you were at a temple was the day of your wedding—the day you lost Ozura. I hope this place doesn't bring up bad memories, though if I may be so bold, you did look beautiful."

The air in the room seemed to evaporate. "You were there?"

"Not physically," he said, ignoring the accusation in my tone. "But I saw you in reflection," he continued, nodding toward the stone glowing on my chest. "Green really does suit you— Armaan obviously agreed. You know, I've often wondered what he said to you as he took your hand that day, but sadly the stone is only good for sight, not sound. I don't suppose you'd care to tell me? No? Ah, well. No matter.

"Though now that I think of it, perhaps your evident displeasure has less to do with bad memories than it does with our little picnic here."

He'd just casually admitted that he could spy on me through the stone, only to wonder if I was offended by the *food*? The urge to rip off the necklace was so overwhelming, my fist clenched. I felt the rugged edges of my own burned palm, still calloused from my first night here. My first lesson—but apparently not the last I'd learn from this monster.

This is a power play, Askia, I thought furiously to myself. *He wants you off-kilter, or too angry to think. Don't rise to the bait. Play the game.*

I counted to three before answering with as much nonchalance as I could muster. "Where I come from, eating in temple is disrespectful."

He gestured to the chair. "Then it's a good thing you're in Roven now."

I sat, feeling like my joints were wrought of steel rather than flesh. Waited in silence as Radovan settled across from me and began serving the tea.

The sudden thought of Armaan serving me this way rose ruthlessly in my mind, so fierce my throat closed. I shut my eyes, willing away the emotion that came with it. The regret and the fragile edges of heartache for all the things that could have been.

When the worst of it passed, I opened my eyes again and found Radovan studying my face, a teacup balanced in his skeletal fingers. "You surprise me, Askia," he said, taking a slow drink. "I didn't take you for a religious woman."

I shrugged, squaring my shoulders to face him. "I am, in my way." One of my brows rose when he kept looking at me, face expectant. "I'm hardly alone in finding peace in prayer."

"Or strength in submission?" His smile deepened when I scowled. "Just something my Asyl used to say."

"To the God, perhaps."

He made a soft noise of musing agreement. "Have you spoken to Asyl at all?"

"Some."

"And? How do you like her?"

I swallowed my first response. Though she'd agreed to help, some of the things she said about normal humans, her superiority, it left a bad taste in my mouth. "Well enough."

"Hardly a glowing opinion," he said dryly. "Though not surprising. Asyl, like all the witches of Khezhar, was convinced of her holy mandate—of her God-given right to rule. I suppose the Khezhari theocracy is the flip side of the Shaziri coin. One worshiping Lady Night, the other the Day Lord."

A grimace pulled at my lips. I'd been only a child when Khezhar fell, but everything that I'd read about the place, everything I'd been taught . . . well, if there was any good that came from Radovan's power-lust, it might, *might* have been the fall of that ruthlessly theocratic state.

"I've found zealots usually miss the point in a god with two faces. Balance in everything."

"My thoughts exactly," Radovan agreed. "I have nothing against religion. Though I admit I am something of an ambivalent believer, I understand why it is comforting to . . . simpler minds. But those are the same minds that are so easily swayed to extremes. It's why I and my Svetniks keep such a wary eye on faith here in Roven. All in moderation, I think. The last thing I want is to see another Shazir rise in the north. Don't you agree?"

"You know I do," I replied woodenly. And then, unable to contain the questions, I asked, "What are we doing here? In the temple? Why not discuss these things in the castle?"

"Can you think of a better place to discuss zealous men than in the space their words defile?" He grinned as if he expected me to follow suit and shrugged when I declined. "Perhaps I just wanted you to myself—away from the distractions of my court and guards. This place is good for seclusion."

I nodded, trying to parse the meaning behind his seemingly benign words. Away from distractions? Perhaps he didn't need Zosha to tell him what I was up to with his Dorovnii. Had his apparent ability to see me through the stone told him all he needed to know? Or did his ever-fragile self-conscious streak make him worry that his guard and his court might prefer me to him?

I motioned for him to speak, knowing that the only possibility of answering these questions would be to face his.

"It must have been hard for you to see them again when you returned to Vishir."

All my determination to meet his questions head on evaporated. There was no reply that I could make—that I was willing to make—to that.

"Come now, Askia," he chided, reading my thoughts from my face. "You said you would speak to me of them. Are you going back on your word?"

The question left his lips almost gently, but the tiny hairs on my arm rose in warning. This was not the time to break my promise. Not for the Shazir.

I reached for the tea, took a long steadying drink. "No. I am not going back on my word. Of course it was hard to see them again. They murdered my family."

"And brutalized you."

My gaze flew to his face at the way he said the words, at the anger and outrage in his voice. As if he didn't intend to do the same. To do worse. The contradiction solidified something in my spine. "They subjected me to their test, yes."

"And yet the test failed," he said, like I was such a clever little girl for fooling them. "Why do you think that is?"

"Simple," I replied, leaning back in my chair the way Ozura had so often done. Not to cede ground, but to indicate control. "Aside from healing, the spirit magics are hard to detect. You can't see someone reading your dreams any more than you can see ghosts judging your every action."

"Do you think many spirit witches escaped their wrath?"

I scoffed. "No. More likely a lot of nonpowered men and women died for nothing."

"And yet the Shazir were never punished?" Radovan shook his head, disdain souring his features. "That more than anything else makes me unspeakably angry. I might not have known Armaan personally, but he always struck me as a fair man. But to allow the Shazir to continue without any consequences is incomprehensible."

He sipped his tea like he had any right to claim the moral high ground—like killing witches for greed rather than faith was somehow better. "Did you never demand an answer from him? I can hardly imagine the frank and righteous woman sitting before me was willing to let the Shazir survive as they always had."

Was that a hint of jealousy I detected in Radovan's voice? My eyebrows rose. "I did ask him why they weren't punished."

"And the answer?"

This was harder, because how much of Vishir's weaknesses could I expose to this man? Then again, how much did he not already know?

Count Dobor had been pulling Prince Enver's strings for months, if not years. Dobor knew about the drought in central Vishir and that Shazir province now provided much of the desperately needed crops. About the Shazir presence in the Khazan Guard. And if Dobor knew, then surely Radovan knew as well.

I held the little teacup in my hands, letting the frail heat from its porcelain sides slide into my skin. "Armaan may have found their beliefs barbaric, but he didn't punish the Shazir because he needed them."

"In what way?"

"Shazir province produces two things," I said, something in me sinking as I parroted Armaan's words to this man. "The first is grain. Because of the drought, the Shazir are feeding a huge swath of Vishir's population."

Radovan nodded. "That would put Armaan in a tough situation," he said, like this was all new information to him. "Clever of the Shazir."

That made me frown. "What makes you say that?"

"Well, you must ask yourself who gains from all this?" Radovan leaned forward to make his point. "Only the Shazir. They get to swoop in and save desperate people—people they will inevitably convert to their cause—all while pinning the very disaster on their enemies: the witches they hate."

His argument made sense, but it also betrayed the fact that he already knew all about the Shazir. And if he already knew about them, then what was the point of this conversation? Was it just a test, to see how far my promise to him stretched?

"It's beautiful really," he continued. "Almost makes me wonder if the whole thing was engineered."

"How could the Shazir create a drought?" I asked, seeing not beauty, but the memory of riding past dull-eyed children with distended, empty bellies. "The Shazir abhor magic."

"I'm sure they do," Radovan said. "But I was always told the problem with punishing the Shazir was that there wasn't nearly enough evidence of their crimes. Sure, the witches of Shazir province certainly disappeared," he said, holding up a hand when I opened my mouth to argue. "But your esteemed parents aside, was there ever any evidence that they were outright killing witches?"

I swallowed. "No."

"Then doesn't it stand to reason that the Shazir might have found a different use for those witches?"

My fingers tightened around the teacup. It was an act of will not to break it. "No witch is that powerful." The words came out slowly, but my mind was racing ahead of me, twisting down terrifying avenues.

I knew the Shadow Guild would never condone such an act—if it was even possible for witches to create, let alone sustain, something as vast as a drought. But sorcerers? I stared across the table wondering. Was Radovan working with the Shazir? Was he behind the drought?

And then I remembered how Radovan had first appeared to me, not as the spectral figure sitting by the fire in the castle south of here. But as a red-robed Shazir priest emerging from the darkness of a Vishiri cemetery, blade in hand to kill Armaan.

"Not alone, certainly. But working in concert? With the aid of a certain kind of stone?" His eyes flicked to the Aellium stone on my chest and back up to my face, one eyebrow cocked.

"It would be suicide. The effort would surely kill them," I said, knowing I was grasping at straws.

"Which would only make the idea more attractive to the Shazir." He smirked. "Would you really put it past them?"

Something rose in my throat. Something knotted and scaled that made the air taste like blood and fire. "I would put nothing past any of my enemies," I said, because he was right. I could see the Shazir resorting to such measures. But I could also see Radovan moving such pieces into place. Magic leapt through me in answer to my growing anger. Vitaly and Ozura appeared once again, but this time there was no argument be-tween them, just twin looks of shock and horror.

"Is this your way of claiming responsibility?" I asked. "Of admitting you've been working with the Shazir the whole time."

"Hardly. I've already said I am not myself an avid supporter of religious endeavors . . . However, I may have ensured certain ideas reached certain people at the right time," he said, leaning back with a smug smile on his face, no doubt feeling like he'd won something.

And he had.

My mind whirled, outrage painting the edges of my vision red. He hadn't brought me here to learn about the Shazir. Nor simply to test my promise. No. It was vanity. He wanted me to know just how clever he was—engineering the Shazir threat from a world away. That he might allow me to play games with his court, but he was the true master, here and everywhere.

"Which people?" The demand was cold on my lips, echoing throughout the temple.

Radovan's smile deepened. "Why Khaljaq and the other twelve leading members of the Shazir. I have copies of all our correspondence in the palace. I do wonder what would happen if those letters ever got out."

I didn't have to. Because with the blood of Armaan and Ozura already at Radovan's feet, the knowledge that the Shazir had been working with this man all along . . .

It was the key to destroying them. Once and for all.

And he was what, just handing it to me?

"What do you want for that information?" The words tasted like ash, but I had to ask the question. Not only for Vishir, but for my parents. For myself.

"I'm sure I'll think of something," he replied, eyes twinkling as he took a long draught of tea. "You know, I never truly imagined that Armaan would give the Shazir such latitude—even with the drought. It's never something *I* would allow."

Ah. There it was. The second reason he was telling me all this. It wasn't simply to show me how much better he was than me at political games. It was to show me how much better he was than *Armaan*. For if I had given my affections to Armaan—a man unworthy in Radovan's eyes—then knowing all about his meddling with the Shazir must make him far greater by comparison. He had everything I needed to destroy the Shazir after all and must therefore be far more worthy of my affections.

It was disgusting, the way this man's mind moved. And monstrous. What was the point in earning my affections when he planned to kill me? It didn't make sense. But could I expect to find sense in a man who would have killed six children for bullying his son? Who had already killed six wives? Who took power like a storybook dragon did gold all because he knew he wasn't worthy of the power that comes from loyalty freely given?

And now what? If I was good and obedient, he would just release the information? No. It was just another carrot, like my wardrobe and fake-freedom to walk around the castle—a way to make me docile. It was a game.

And if it was a game, I could win.

Moves and countermoves, Askia. Victories and sacrifices.

"But you said Armaan had a second reason to stay his hand?" Radovan asked, setting his cup down, his expression smug. "What was it?"

I smiled, vindictive pleasure filling me with shards of glass. "The second reason? Soldiers."

"Soldiers? I don't think I understand."

"Well, you know how many soldiers it takes to secure an empire. Armaan did too. But many of his soldiered were, if not from Shazir province, then converts to the Shazir faith. If Armaan were seen to punish the Shazir . . . well."

"Well?"

"You can imagine how upset his soldiers would become."

Radovan's eyes narrowed as he considered my words. "It would have surely caused discontent."

"It would," I agreed. "And among soldiers, discontent spreads quicker than plague."

"Among nobility too," Radovan said, and I could see him beginning to apply Armaan's lesson to himself. Good.

For it was my turn to lean forward. "But the difference between soldiers and nobles is that soldiers are used to doing things about their discontent. They have the tools and training to change the world. I daresay they even have the strength to topple an empire. Luckily, Armaan was clever enough to keep only a manageable force in Bet Naqar."

Unlike the number of Voyniks you keep here. My unspoken words coated the table between us. "And yes, that choice might have made his nobles rather bolder in their scheming than your court is, but—"

I shrugged, letting my words trail off with a conspiratorial smile. "Armaan was wise enough to know that, while letting his nobles play politics might have been inconvenient, politicians don't actually accomplish anything. But soldiers? Well. Men of action don't usually waste time on debate, do they? If they see a problem. They'll fix it."

The beginnings of disquiet rippled across Radovan's features. The realization that he might be holding the wrong class in suspicion made the air around us go cold, yet somehow warmed my insides.

I took a sip of tea to hide my smile and nibbled on one of the pretty little cakes while he thought.

After a moment he seemed to shake himself free of his stupor, studying me with fresh eyes. "I—" He shook his head, chuckling at whatever he was about to say.

"What?" I asked, not sure I wanted to know.

"Well, I doubt you'll appreciate what I truly mean as a compliment. But I was thinking that I can see why your cousin was so desperate to ally himself with me. You remind me of myself at your age. Half soldier, half politician. We even look something alike. You're my very own Lady Night."

The idea that we could be anything alike made the tea and cake rise up in my throat begging for freedom. My eyes went to the altar, a prayer for the strength to temper my words. "I suppose Goran was always a politician in the most classic sense: forever grasping for power with no idea what to do with it once attained."

Radovan laughed, though it was short-lived. He shook his head, his face folding into a mask of regret. "I always try to keep a native representative in the territories I acquire, but I will confess that Goran has been a disappointment."

Radovan sighed long and deep, looking up at me with wide eyes. "I regret what happened in Kavondy. It should never have come to such extremes. Had Goran been able to smooth the transition, that tragedy could have been avoided."

"Could it?" I asked, my voice hard. Could it have been

avoided? Or was it certain from the moment Vitaly failed to kill me in Idun? I just managed to keep the torrent of words locked behind my lips. Because even though I wanted to hurl them at his feet, I knew they wouldn't find their mark. I knew that this man, in his twisted mind, would never feel true regret for any of his actions. He would always find a way to justify them. As he did now.

"Yes. I believe that you could have ensured a peaceful transition. Not that I in any way blame you. No, it was all Goran's fault."

But it really wasn't. The blame lay with us as well. With Radovan. But, perhaps more so, with myself. I shook my head, willing the thought—the guilt—away. I would analyze it later, when I was alone and could mourn in peace. But Radovan was watching me, an expectant gleam in his eyes. I reached for something, for anything to say. Grasped my rage and held tight until I was able to ask, "Was he ever punished?"

Radovan's head cocked to one side. "Do you want him to be?"

"Those deaths will not go unanswered," I replied. Not the ones my cousin caused to our people. Nor the ones Radovan had caused, not just in the north, but those dead by the hands of the Shazir too. My words a promise. A promise to myself. To Radovan. To the Two-Faced God Itself.

I couldn't bring them back.

But I would give them the revenge they deserved.

13

ILLYA

THE FLOORBOARDS BENEATH Illya's feet creaked in ancient agony as he crossed the office. Arkady had claimed the space when they'd burst through the garrison's portal and overtaken the two dozen Voyniks stationed at this remote outpost in the Polzi hinterlands. The older man now sat behind the scarred desk, toying with a cylindrical slip of parchment, a message from Misha, no doubt.

Illya sniffed, waiting for the general to rouse himself from whatever internal musing had him looking so grim. The office, which had once belonged to the garrison's commander, was a cramped cave-like space made of the same ill-joined timber and stone as the rest of the outpost. And though the fireplace cut through some of the cold, it was so clogged with soot, almost as much smoke filled the office as the chimney.

"What did the prisoner say?" Arkady's voice was low, laden with worry.

No. *Worry* was the wrong word, Illya thought. This was something else.

Illya frowned, dropping his gloves onto the desk with the wet plop of fresh blood. "Same as the others," he replied. "Of the four portals in the subbasement, one leads to Raskis, two lead further into Polzi. The fourth leads to Roven."

"The stronghold at Kirskov?"

Illya nodded. "Kirskov."

Arkady grunted. The other Voyniks had confirmed this information, so it wasn't a surprise. It had been much the same since Illya first crossed that portal in Dobor's study ten days ago. Ten days of crossings . . . and blood. And though he'd felt something like happiness to reunite with Arkady and the Wolves in Idun, the feeling had been short-lived. They were running out of time.

Askia was running out of time.

He knew Radovan was after Askia's death magic—had learned as much from Ozura before she was murdered. It was Nariko who'd told him that the theft would take time. But how much time?

The queens from Graznia and Switzkia had lasted only thirty days before Radovan killed them. And the queen from Raskis . . .

Illya turned away from the thought—the pain and worry—before dark waters could drag him under.

"Are you ready to cross the Roven portal?" Arkady asked, eyes still lost to the flames.

Of course he was, Illya thought. He'd been ready since he'd first heard of the portals. It wasn't as if he had wanted to make a home in any of these waystations. None of the men did.

It was sheer luck that Illya had even crossed the portal in Idun. As Nariko had suspected, the portals only traversed hundred-mile spans. He had found himself fighting through Voynik guards in waystations across northern Vishir. When he caught a blade to the side—more a result of exhaustion than any skill on his opponent's part—it made sense to seek out Arkady in Idun.

Lucky he did, too, for he found that he wasn't the only witch hidden in the Black Wolves. Arkady had quietly kept twenty others—allowing Illya to expand his rescue from a one-man team to a crew of forty-two, with the witches able to carry one normal soldier through the portals with them.

"Just say the word—we're ready to take you and the rest of the Wolves through."

Illya watched the general take a long, labored breath. Watched Arkady turn and that cool blue gaze rise. "Not just yet."

Illya raised his chin, waiting. But nothing came. It was as if the older man's words had gotten caught in his chest and festered there, for Illya could feel hostility roiling between them. "What do you need to say, Arkady?"

The general's eyes flashed at being called out. "Something I shouldn't have to say, *Olexan*."

Illya flinched. It'd been almost a year since anyone had used that name. Hearing it now felt like spitting on the grave of a man long since dead. Illya forced his shoulders down, gripping the back of the chair in front of Arkady. "What is that supposed to mean?"

Arkady tossed the scroll across the desk, letting it fall like a gauntlet thrown. "You tell me."

Illya reached for it, but the moment he picked it up, he knew what it was. He didn't need to unroll it, to see his own writing, scrawled in haste and heartbreak, to know what it was. A request for reassignment, sent the day of Askia's wedding to Armaan.

He'd been strong enough to let her go. Strong enough to endure her wedding. But watching her become Armaan's wife? Watch her bear his children?

No.

He hadn't been strong enough for that. So he'd written

to Arkady asking to return to Idun. A request just received, it seemed.

"One of the runners brought it through the portal this morning. Care to explain why you wanted to abandon your queen to Vishir?"

"No."

"*No?* Then let me ask you, what about the situation were you unable to handle? Speak. Don't pretend it was simple cowardice."

Illya ground his teeth together. "Not cowardice. Honor."

"What in the name of the Day Lord is that supposed to mean?"

"There is honor in putting your people before yourself. Honor in stepping aside if it's what was best for her—if it made it easier."

"Easier for *her*?" Arkady's eyes bulged. "You aren't telling me that—that *this*—is something she feels too?"

Illya had no response. Not to that. Not for Arkady. And not when every time Illya closed his eyes he saw her, standing bathed in moonlight, burgundy hair loose and wild. Not when he'd memorized her face from that night, daring him to lay a claim and take her right there. Like she didn't care how far apart their stations were. She'd seen him and wanted him anyway.

"Well?"

"Nothing happened," Illya replied, all too aware of the bitterness in his voice.

"And nothing ever will," Arkady growled. "Do you hear me? When King Fredek took you in, it was with the understanding that there would never be anything between you and her. Ever. You have nothing to offer her. Nothing but loyalty."

A low grumble began in Illya's chest. "I will always be loyal to Askia."

"Will you?" Arkady asked, a challenge bright in his eyes. "Will you always? Or will you someday find honor in putting *your* people before yourself? Before Askia?"

It was like being kicked in the teeth and Arkady knew it. The general blew out a long breath, rubbing his eyes. "It's not that you aren't a good man, Olexan. Illya. But Askia is the closest thing I have to a daughter. I don't want to see her hurt."

"I won't ever hurt her."

Arkady snorted at that, more exhausted than enraged now. "I don't think that's a promise you can make."

"Yet I'm making it anyway. And don't even think of taking me off the rescue mission. I'm going. So are we ready to move out now, sir?"

Arkady crossed his arms, giving Illya a long look. "Only you and the witches are crossing to Kirskov."

Illya widened his stance. "And where will you be?"

"I'll be taking the other men overland to the coast. We'll rendezvous with Misha and the ship."

"And from there you'll head north?"

"North to Tolograd," Arkady confirmed. "If something should happen in Kirskov that compromises your mission, head east instead. Here." Arkady angled a weather-beaten map toward Illya, stabbing it with one thick finger. "There's a hidden inlet the locals call Old Baba's Cove. Get there before the tide turns on the full moon and we'll take you all on to Tolograd."

"Get delayed, or captured, and—"

"And we're on our own. I know." Something dark and writhing coiled in Illya's gut. A sense of something left unsaid. His eyes rose, almost unbidden, to the window. Just beyond the garrison's curtainwall, a far more impenetrable and ancient wall of forest stood sentinel against the steady encroachment of humanity. It was forbidding, that green and black abyss which spanned from here all the way up the Roveni coast to the very edge of Tolograd.

He shook his head to free himself of the unease. He'd never been completely at home in the woods. How could he be, raised as he was on the great grass steppe of his homeland? But if they were smart—and fast—they could make it out of Kirskov without incident, same as they had the other portals. The Voyniks had grown complacent over the years of occupation. All their attention was turned outward toward the people they oppressed. They spared no thought to the enemy attacking from within.

Except.

Except there was that feeling, a suspicion niggling the back of Illya's neck. If it was all so simple, why wasn't Arkady coming with them?

"You think we're walking into a trap." He spoke the question like a statement, but Arkady nodded anyway.

"All the prisoners claimed that Kirskov was nothing more than the emperor's Summer Palace. A favorite vacation spot. But look at this place."

Arkady thrust the tip of his blade into the map, right atop the tiny black dot nestled in the lee of the River Tol's two branching arms.

"Protected not only by two rivers, but by the Riven Cliffs," he said, glaring at the huge expanse of cliffs, a great tear in the fabric of Roven. "Nearly impossible to invade a place like that. Not only impregnable, but a mere five-day journey to Tolograd?"

Arkady shook his head, a bitter laugh chuffing out of his chest. Illya watched him, marking the new hollows in the general's cheeks, the deep circles beneath his eyes. "Think about it. Radovan must know his portals have been compromised, but he's let us come this far anyway. Why? Why let us get so close, if not to snare us—snare all of you, the witches he covets so dearly?"

"If you're so sure it's a trap, why send us?"

"Because if it works, you'll reach Tolograd well before we will. You'll have time to ferret out this supposed rebellion Queen Ozura once knew about and make contact with them. We'll need all the time—and all the allies—we can get if we have any hope of saving the queen."

His words rang true. Almost. Because that sense of hostility hadn't lessened. Not even an inch.

Illya crossed his arms. "Be straight with me Arkady: Are you sending me to Kirskov to save Askia? Or to die?"

Arkady's answering smile was a grim dance of death. "Why can't it be both?

"Dismissed."

Illya turned on his heel, taking his anger at Arkady—at the world that put him in this position—and stalked into the hall. He left the bloodied gloves on Arkady's desk where they belonged.

He'd do anything to get Askia. Anything to save her. But the man who'd agreed to torture information from enemies on Arkady's behalf, that broken soul with nothing to lose? That man was gone.

Because Illya did have something to lose. Someone.

Askia.

Arkady had been partially right. Letting her walk away without telling her how he felt? Actually stating the words, plainly? That was cowardly. Duty and station be damned. If he found her, saved her, he wouldn't turn away again. He'd stake a claim, be worthy. And finally, *finally* kiss her. Even if only once.

General Arkady be damned.

THE PORTAL ROOM LAY IN THE GARRISON'S BASEMENT UNDERBELLY. Illya guessed it was once a kitchen storage room, for the walls were stained with outlines of long discarded shelves and the air smelled of flour and sage. But all that perished once Roven came.

What remained now were four painted doorways—outlines

marked in bold black lacquer, nearly identical to the one he'd first seen in Count Dobor's rooms all those days ago.

A man standing near the last portal wove through the crowd of milling soldiers and snapped Illya a quick salute. "We have the order to go, Cap?"

"We do," Illya replied, but something in his voice made the other man's brows rise. Fyedik was a smart man—you couldn't be dense if you were a scout, but Fyedik had a special kind of canny that had kept him alive a lot longer than many of the Wolves. Let alone a witch.

"We expecting trouble?"

"We're going into enemy territory, so it's likely," Illya said. "Break out your map. Gather round," he added, louder this time. He crouched beside Fyedik and the proffered map, sketching out the plan and its contingencies for the men.

He was grimly happy that none of them seemed scared by the news that they were likely heading into a trap. But he wasn't surprised by their stoicism either. Fear was one of the first casualties of this never-ending war. Right after hope.

"The first step is getting out of Kirskov. We engage only enough to secure an exit—little impact as possible, we don't want to be caught now. Understood?" Illya waited for the men to nod their assent, but most of his attention was on Fyedik and the other earth witches. If a creative exit was needed, it'd be up to them to provide it.

"All right. Weapons drawn, and magic at the ready. Move out."

Illya clapped Fyedik on the back, waiting beside the portal as the scouts went through first. After a slow ten-count that set his teeth on edge, Illya sent the next group through. Then the next. Until it was his turn.

His sword was clenched in one hand, while the other went to his breast pocket where a slender circlet and a lock of burgundy hair lay folded beside his heart.

He stepped into the portal . . .

And knew instantly that something was wrong.

Portals usually had a kind of gelatinous liquidity like swimming through a dense pool. Not now. The stone parted reluctantly around his body. His muscles strained against it, thighs burning as if he were moving through a pit of gravel. Through a nonworld whose every fiber reached out to catch him.

And he was running out of air.

Illya shoved forward, pulse pounding in his ears. The knowledge that the rest of his men must surely have pushed through was cold comfort. Not when his mind screamed, go back. But he couldn't. Not when he was so close to finding her. So even as his vision narrowed and grayed, he fought. One step and the next.

Ice-cold air filled his lungs as he breached the surface. But he couldn't rejoice in it. Because as his back foot left the portal, it clipped the hard edge of stone. The wall behind him let out a great scrape, like a mason sliding bricks together. The boom echoed through the room.

He didn't need to look to know the portal was gone.

They hadn't walked into a trap. They'd walked *through* it.

His men were spread out before him, weapons drawn, staring down the length of a ballroom with palpable surprise. Because why would Radovan keep a portal in a ballroom of all places? One that glimmered with bright gilding and whose walls were covered in frescoes of dancing maidens and gallant knights. Though the sun shone bright and clear through the windows on the long eastern wall, the golden chandeliers hung with twinkling witchlights. Like a party was about to begin. Like the doors were moments from being thrown open for a grand fete the likes of which would make even the great court of Vishir sigh in longing.

Except that the door on the other end of the room was less a door than a complete tear in reality.

There, on the opposite end of the room where a set of double doors should have been, the ballroom simply ceased. What lay in its stead was an expanse of corridor so white the word almost lost all meaning. For if black was the absence of color, this pale emptiness was the absence of life.

Or it would have been, were it not for the old man seated behind a tidy-looking desk. He watched them, pale eyes dancing. As if the sight of twenty-one hostile witches was exactly what he was hoping for. Like Illya and his fellows were on a stage with a show about to begin.

Illya wrapped his fingers tighter around the hilt of his sword, hardly acknowledging the instinctual unease worming through his core. He wove through his men, coming forward, closer to what could only be a second portal. Fyedik stood at the fore, his eyes widening as they met Illya's.

"Dima," the older man said, the word little more than a puff of smoke in a strong wind.

Understanding settled something inside Illya. Not because it was good news. It wasn't, for Dima was the name of one of Illya's mind witches. His gaze cut to his right, where Dima stood, brow drenched in sweat from a battle that Illya couldn't see. Couldn't see because there was another mind witch—or sorcerer with mind witch powers—fucking with their perceptions. Not good news. But knowing was always better.

"Windows," Illya murmured back to Fyedik, stepping forward.

The old man grinned. "You must be Captain Illya. Welcome to Roven."

Illya tried not to flinch at that. Tried. "How do you know my name?"

"My dear boy," the old man began with a warm laugh, "you'll soon find that knowing things is rather the point of me."

"Will I?"

"Of course. You didn't really think we were unaware of your use of the portal roads, did you?"

Illya shrugged, feeling his men shifting at his back. If they could just get to the windows . . . "I suppose your master was bound to notice eventually."

"You don't give us enough credit, Illya. We knew of your journey the moment you stepped through that portal in Bet Naqar."

Illya's mind tripped over that. Because if they'd known that long, it meant there was someone in Vishir who'd tipped his hand. But who? And was any of this even the truth? "So you just let me take out waystation after waystation? Kill all those devoted Voyniks?"

"Necessary sacrifices, I assure you."

"Why?"

"Why, because of you. Because of all of you. Twenty-one witches, battled-tested and brimming with magic. My emperor would go through very great lengths to secure the lot of you. Luckily, patience was the best course, for here you are. It really was remarkably thoughtful of Queen Askia, to provide a dowry to the emperor with such flare."

"Don't say her name," Illya snarled, taking a step forward. Flames flashed along the edge of his blade as if he couldn't contain his anger.

It was an easy ruse to conjure. He was angry. But not so angry he couldn't also create a diversion for the others, giving Dima a chance to break the illusion. To give Fyedik a chance to get the others to the windows.

But the old man simply tilted his head to one side, studying Illya with mild amusement. "You are a strong one, aren't you Captain Illya. I can feel your power from here, boiling beneath your flesh. Not quite as strong as dear Branko, of course, but then I'm guessing you've had to suppress your magic for a long,

long time now. Still. Your power will be a great boon to Roven. The emperor will be pleased."

"But you'll never see your emperor again," Illya said, diving deep for the magic within him. Sweat beaded down his face and chest as his tether twitched its fevered reins. He let it come, glorying in the added heat.

The man shook his head in false sorrow. "No, my dear boy. It's you who will never see your queen again. A shame, I'm sure, to come all this way only to be dragged to Tolograd like a pig for slaughter. I'm afraid you'll spend the rest of your days chained right beneath your queen's very feet.

"And the worst part, I think, is that she'll never know it. She'll spend her remaining days believing you forsook her. *Abandoned* her.

"It's tragic, don't you think?"

"You shut your—"

"Oh, I wasn't speaking to you, Illya. I was speaking to my friend, Kostya. What do you think, General Koloii?"

Illya blinked and in that half second of darkness, the illusion shattered. Not that of the ballroom or the strange portal door, but the illusion that they were alone.

Voyniks ringed the room, swords and bows drawn and raised. Worse than Voyniks. Sorcerers. For green Aellium stones were pinned neatly to their collars like fell war-medals, gleaming in the unforgiving light.

It was exactly as Arkady had predicted. A perfect trap springing shut. Outnumbered two to one. No way to escape.

Unless . . .

Unless Illya made one hell of a diversion.

The old man's words still rang in Illya's mind, a summoning that drew all of his desperation, all his rage, all his endless hate. Endless, like the magic burning inside him. Almost as strong as Branko, was he? Well, they were about to find out.

Without warning, Illya bound forward. One step.

He heard the thwack of a bowstring.

Two steps.

He felt the concussive slap of sorcerous magic unleashed.

Three steps.

He lunged.

And let his magic explode.

14

THE GREAT HALL was as full it had been for the past two days.
The only difference was that I wasn't looking to blackmail anyone today. No. That wasn't the only difference, I thought, skirting the edges of the vast space.

There were half the usual number of guards on duty. I'd
have laughed, but I knew better. Radovan might have taken
my words about the danger of too many soldiers. But how that
advice might become snarled and twisted as he considered it, I
had no way to anticipate. And though I was glad there were less
Voyniks, I didn't want to be the cause of any more deaths. Even
Roveni ones.

I shook my head, trying to banish the memory of those dead
nobles and their forever scarred children, forcing myself back to
the present. I had work to do. I was looking for a moment, that
fleeting beat of time I might seize to slip away from Zosha. Because, true to his word, Tcheshin had left me instructions on his
bedside table. Instructions and a map that Ozura had described
to me this morning.

As far as maps went, this one was sadly lacking. It indicated an out-of-the-way door within the Great Hall itself. Why
Tcheshin wanted me to see this door was beyond me. Unless he
was trying to get me in trouble, but that seemed petty even for

him. Especially when he knew I'd take him down with me if I got caught. Still.

You must never underestimate your enemies, Askia.

Asyl had been the only queen around when I returned from my outing with Radovan. She'd been unsure about the door when I asked, and scoffed at the plan, saying it probably led to a guardroom and that I should avoid it unless I wanted to be locked in a cage for my remaining days.

Something about the way she said it, the way her mouth tightened with a hint of panic, made my hackles rise. An impression which only intensified when none of the other queens appeared that night. Whatever was beyond that door, it wasn't nothing.

Zosha strolled beside me. He looked like he hadn't a care in the world, but I knew it was all facade. He'd practically shoved me toward the wall in an effort to keep his body between me and the rest of the court. He might have been too cautious to tell Radovan what I was up to, but that didn't mean that Zosha was willing to help.

I studied him from the corner of my eyes. Smiled as we came around to the eastern edge of the hall, where a certain guard was on duty. Zosha straightened incrementally, then shot me a look when I laughed.

I pressed my lips together to stifle the sound, thanking Lady Night for this bit of good luck. "What's his name?"

"Who?"

"That sweet-looking young man you're straightening your coat for."

"I'm not—" Embarrassment brought a crimson stain to his pale cheeks. "Dimitri."

That made me snort with unqueenly glee. "Dimitri? Like the fairy tale? As in the valiant knight who fights the ice-drake?"

"Yes," he replied tightly, but I could hear the laughter building inside him.

"Dimitri, Dimitri, save me from the frozen monster," I cried in a tiny, taunting voice.

"Frozen queen is more like it," he said, nudging me with his shoulder. "Please do shut up."

I shook my head, still smiling. "You should talk to him," I suggested, trying not to sound too eager, or too interested.

He shrugged in a way that told me he very much wanted to. "Can I trust you to behave?"

"Of course not," I replied with a grin. "But isn't that part of my charm?"

We were too near to the guard in question for Zosha to reply. No matter. It wasn't really up to him anyway, I thought, smiling at young Dimitri. The guard returned the smile, nodding to me with a kind of solidarity that hadn't existed yesterday. I supposed that securing Qaden's promotion earned me a bit of goodwill from the Voyniks—even if it hadn't seemed to make all that much of an impact on Qaden herself.

"Lord Zosha, weren't you just saying you had a question for Dimitri?"

"Um." Zosha looked so dumbstruck he reminded me suddenly, painfully, of Nariko when faced with the prospect of speaking to Iskander.

"Don't mind me," I said, nodding like Zosha's response was something comprehensible. "I'll just be over here."

With a game wink at the guard, I strolled onward, hands clasped loosely behind my back. Looking at nothing in particular, I tried to remain inconspicuous on the edges of the crowd, forcing my expression into one of boredom.

The door on Tcheshin's map was ahead. But there was nothing remarkable about it. The door was made of the same stone as the rest of the hall, striped through with massive streaks of blue and white. A small handle gleamed in the wood, beckoning.

My lady, I need to speak with you.

"Vitaly, perfect," I said as the ghost appeared. *"I need your eyes. Is anyone watching me?"*

"Only Lord Zosha."

"Damn. Let me know as soon as he looks away." I bit my lip, scanning the crowd, all the other nobles and guards looked busy at their games. And Radovan wasn't in the hall at the moment, closeted with his military advisers according to the whispers at court. Tcheshin's instructions only allotted this one hour to investigate. This was it. If only Zosha would look the other damn way.

The door was only a few steps away.

Five.

Four.

Three.

"Now."

I lunged for the handle. It turned silently in my hand, pushing open into a blackened staircase beyond. I slid through as fast as I could, shut the door behind me. Paused. Waited for my eyes to adjust. Waited for my heartbeat to ease.

"Vitaly, are you there?" I thought the words slowly, hating the way they sounded worried. Hating that I was afraid even here in the inside of my mind. Hating the way the ever-growing glow of the Aellium stone lit the stairwell in green shades of foreboding. And though I'd never seen them, these steps felt familiar. Because if there was one thing I knew about castles, it was that only enemies were kept below.

"I'm here."

"Do you know what is at the bottom of these stairs?"

"No, my lady. I haven't ever seen anyone come in here before." His words fell away with the feeling of bated breath. *"How is it that the door is unlocked?"*

"Tcheshin arranged it," I said, goose bumps prickling my arms from the constant pull of magic.

"But why?" he asked. *"Why would Tcheshin tell you about this place over some other piece of information? If this place is out of bounds, why? And what is the cost of trespassing?"*

I didn't have an answer. But having seen firsthand the cost of bullying Prince Gethen, I could guess.

"I would proceed with caution."

"Don't I always?" I frowned when Vitaly failed to comment and started slowly down the steps, straining to hear what might await me at the bottom. *"You wanted to talk to me?"* I asked, trying to bank my growing nervousness.

"Yes," Vitaly replied, floating beside me. *"Have you ever heard of the Council of Nine?"*

I drew up short, angling my head toward Vitaly. *"I have,"* I replied, surprise echoing through my head. *"Radovan said the Council of Nine was the body that ruled Roven in the decades prior to his reign."*

Vitaly nodded. *"The council apparently still exists. Only instead of representing the nine provinces of the old Kingdom of Roven, it represents the nine kingdoms that will and have fallen if Radovan continues unopposed."*

"The nine kingdoms," I thought slowly. *"That's the seven northern kingdoms Radovan has already conquered, as well as Idun and Vishir?"*

"Idun, yes, but not Vishir. Roven itself is the ninth," Vitaly said heavily. *"You were right to assume not everyone here is content under Radovan's rule. There are people at court who see him as the destruction of Roven. They think the war he's brewing with Vishir is going to get everyone killed."*

"They're right," I said, hope making me smile. A hope that immediately soured. Yes, there were people here who wanted to see Radovan fall. But why hadn't they come to me? Wouldn't they want to help me escape before Radovan's thirty-day clock expired? Unless—

I swallowed hard. Unless it was simply easier for them to kill me. It wouldn't stop Radovan from finding another death witch eventually, but it would buy them time to grow in strength and numbers. In which case, staying hidden was the perfect ploy. Hidden and close and—

Something hard plummeted through me.

"Is Zosha a member of the Nine?"

Vitaly's starlit eyes filled with a heavy sort of sadness. He nodded.

But before I could process the news, the dark air before me swirled and shimmered, coalescing in the diaphanous form of Asyl.

"What in the name of Lady Night are you doing down here?" she demanded in a half whisper like she was afraid someone might hear her.

I frowned at her appearance. Gone was the ever-peaceful priestess, erased by the wide-eyed woman before me, wringing her hands together in distress. *"Tcheshin told me I need to see what's down here, so I'm going to investigate. Why? Is someone looking for me?"*

"Of course someone is looking for you. You're the last damned queen of Roven. You can't just disappear without people noticing."

I felt my brows rise. *"Well there's no point in turning back now. I may as well keep going and see what's down there. It might be my only chance."*

Asyl swooped down in front of me, trying to block my way. *"No, Askia. Go back. Please."*

I'd thought she looked nervous before, but now, now she looked outright guilty. *"What's down there?"* I asked, drawing myself up straight and looking down on her from the higher step.

"Nothing."

"Nothing?" I mentally combed through every detail of the castle the queens had ever given me. And came up empty. *"If it*

was nothing, then why wasn't I told this place existed when you all were giving me the layout of the castle? Why did you tell me this was a guardroom last night?"

Asyl winced as I caught her in the lie. Her gray eyes went to the sky like she was asking the other queens or Lady Night Herself for backup. When none came, she heaved a great sigh. *"You wanted to escape. We all need you to escape—if not because we've grown fond of you, then also because you're the best hope we have at defeating Radovan. Ozura told us how you united Vishir, and we need Vishir. The world needs Vishir to stop Radovan."*

"And what does that have to do with this place?" I demanded, my voice colder than the Marchlands I could feel unspooling just beyond my reach.

Asyl lifted her chin in clear defiance. *"We didn't want you to get distracted."*

A sound of outrage hissed out of Vitaly and I felt my expression harden.

"That is not your call to make."

I pushed through Asyl, descending quickly. The steps bottomed out, not in a corridor, but in what looked like some sort of workroom. It was a close, windowless space about half the size of my bedroom and lit with an orb of witchlight that floated near the ceiling.

A small desk was shoved in one corner, covered with scrolls and maps and bits of silver chain. The walls were papered with more maps and diagrams, only interrupted by a narrow door across the room. My gaze leapt past the papers, landing with a thud on the workbench before me.

There, on the dented and scarred wooden tabletop, lay a small pyramid of open boxes. Silver pendants sat within them, each one set with coin-sized Aellium stones. The stones glittered with malice, invisibly coated in the blood of the witches who'd died in their forging.

If I was frozen in the doorway, overcome with the terrible urge to destroy those stones, Vitaly and Asyl weren't. Asyl crossed the room, standing opposite me with her arms wrapped around her middle like she was trying to guard her vital organs. Vitaly went to the desk, leaning over in concentration as he read the various letters and missives strewn over its top.

"So this is where he does it—makes the Aellium stones? Creates his sorcerers?"

Asyl nodded, the movement tight and unwilling.

"Come see this, my lady," Vitaly beckoned. *"There's a letter here about the Aellium mines."*

I went to the desk, shifting some of the paperwork to get at the letter that had caught Vitaly's eye. A letter countersigned just two weeks ago by a very familiar name: Lieutenant Bora Roshko, the cuckolded soldier who guarded Radovan's most precious treasures. My lips twitched with the shadow of a smile and filed the information away for later use.

It confirmed Ozura's—and Asyl's—information about an Aellium mine in Khezhar. The skin on the back of my neck prickled. Was this why Asyl, the Khezhari queen, was here trying to stop me? I turned the page.

"'The emperor has decided that the Heart must be moved to Kirskov where it can be secured under His Eminence's eye. The unrest in Khezhar and other acquired provinces poses too much of a threat to the Heart and, with it, the future of the empire. The Heart will be moved within the week,'" I said, reading the letter "aloud" for Asyl and Vitaly.

I looked at the priestess and saw the complete unsurprise on her face. Tossing the letter onto the desk, I crossed my arms. *"Care to explain what this is all about?"*

Asyl shifted from foot to foot. *"The letter is speaking of the Heart of Khezhar."*

My gaze narrowed. *"And what is that?"*

The priestess rubbed her face. *"What do you know about how the stones work?"*

"I know what you told me," I snapped. *"How much of that was a lie?"*

"It's not that I lied—that any of us lied, but . . ." Her words faltered and she paused for a moment like she was gathering her thoughts. *"The Aellium stones function, on one level, as a syphon. They attune themselves to a witch's magic. They store the power that goes unused when a witch is at rest. And they tunnel a path from that witch to the source from which all magic comes.*

"In the old days, witches used the stones as an extra power source, a temporary way to wield more magic while mitigating the effects of the tether. But we always knew better than to wear the stones for too long, and we understood the risks of using the stones in battle. The risk of dying while bearing a stone."

"Why?"

"Because magic is a matter of the soul. The stones, they pull magic out of us, and after too long, our souls are pulled out too. The reason you see us so clearly, we six queens of Roven, isn't simply because our magic is trapped here. It's because our souls are trapped here too."

"In the stone," I said, coldness creeping over my skin—a feeling that had nothing to do with the tether's ever-leeching chill. On some level I knew there had to be a reason I could see the other queens so clearly when Vitaly and Ozura came and went like smoke.

"Yes," she replied. *"And also no. There is only one place in the north where Aellium can be mined. The vein of stone runs deep in the mountains of my homeland, and it all leads back to one great stone. We call it the Heart of Khezhar, and it is the stone from which all other shards have come,"* she said, gesturing to the stones on the bench between us.

"Stones, like the one which you now bear, create pathways, not only to a witch's magic, but to the Heart itself. When we die—when

I died, my magic may have been captured within that stone, but my soul was captured in the Heart."

"No," I said, not quite believing her. Not wanting to believe her. Because if she was speaking the truth, then it meant— *"How could you possibly know any of this?"*

Asyl's answering smile was soft and filled with understanding. *"The Khezhari priesthood ruled my country for centuries, our records are vast. Our libraries without equal. You are not the first death witch, Askia. Though you are rare, there were some who came before you, including those who have seen the Heart, seen the souls trapped within it."*

"How many?" I asked, my body shaking. *"How many are trapped?"*

"Before Radovan began his campaign to redistribute magic? Hundreds. But now?" Her shoulders rose in a terrible, helpless gesture. *"Thousands."*

"But, but why? Why hasn't anyone ever freed them? Surely if you destroy the stone—"

"You can't," Asyl said quickly, almost too quickly, like she was afraid of even entertaining the thought. *"No one can destroy the Heart—it's the only physical relic of Lady Night in existence. It could be deactivated, maybe, if you freed the trapped souls, but not destroyed. It's not possible."*

Vitaly shifted, catching my eye with a knowing expression. One which begged me to wait. For now. *"You said the Heart contains both the souls of the sacrificed witches as well as their magic?"* The way he said it brewed with possibility. Asyl agreed slowly, suspiciously even, but Vitaly was already looking at me.

"You think we could use the Heart as a weapon?"

"Don't you?" Vitaly asked. *"Kirskov is only a week's journey from here. If you could escape, and reach it . . ."* He shook his head like he was dumbfounded. *"All that magic pent up in one place. If you took it—"*

"No," Asyl said quickly. *"You can't use the Heart. It isn't meant to be wielded."*

"I don't care what it was meant for," I said, flatly. *"If it can help me destroy Radovan, then I will grab it with both hands."*

"That much power will kill you," Asyl cried. *"Haven't you ever wondered why Radovan doesn't wear the whole Aellium stone? Why he saddled you with the larger piece? Or why the rock around your neck is so much bigger than all the other stones here? Why you never see Radovan hold his half of the stone?"*

Yes, of course I did. Despite being here for more days than I wanted to count, despite being on the receiving end of his power on more than one occasion, I'd never actually seen the shard of stone he'd cleaved from this one. Never seen the source of his terrible, stolen power. The most I'd seen were flashes of green, glowing from the necklace he must wear beneath his shirt.

"The larger the stone, the greater the magic, but there is such a thing as too much power."

"What do you mean?"

Asyl shook her head, reaching for words. *"When it was only Katarzhina's healing magic inside the stone, Radovan was fine and there was no backlash. When he added Ragata's earth magic, he thought it would be the same. And in the beginning, it was. Until he turned his sights on Khezhar.*

"My people fought him. Fought hard. We had secret passes through the mountains, whole underground networks we used to smuggle supplies to our warriors. They allowed us to withstand the invasion. That was until Radovan lost his patience and decided he'd had enough. And you know what he did then?"

I nodded, my lips numb. Of course I knew. Everyone did. It was the moment that shifted the entire axis of the world and transformed Radovan from some northern despot to a true and terrifying power. *"He took down a mountain."*

"Yes," Asyl said, and even from where I stood, I could see that

her eyes were brimming with tears. *"He took down a mountain. The tunnels collapsed and hundreds—thousands—of Khezhari men, women, and children were trapped beneath the crumbling earth. It was the end of Khezhar. But that's not all that happened."*

Vitaly shifted, looking slightly ill as if hopelessness were starting to creep in.

"What happened?" I asked.

"Can't you guess?" Her voice was filled with bitterness. *"Haven't you ever wondered why Radovan hasn't set foot on a battlefield since? Why he didn't bring down the Peshkalor Mountains and ride triumphantly into Raskis and Seravesh?"*

"I thought—" My words died on my tongue, because the truth was that I hadn't thought. Hadn't wanted to consider it, because it was the nightmare we all feared.

But Radovan wasn't the sort of man to hold back. Which meant—

"What happened to him?"

"He was wounded," Asyl replied. *"He brought the mountain down, yes, but unleashing that much magic—even while wearing an Aellium stone—has consequences. It would have killed him had he not already had healing magic flowing through him, sustaining his life. As it was, he was unconscious for almost three months, and in screaming pain for another two. The stone he claimed was fused with his breastbone. His healers had to cut away the rest of the stone, the one you now bear, hoping they could eventually pry the smaller shard free. They never could. To this day the stone is still embedded in his skin."*

And just like that any hope of using the Heart against Radovan shattered. But as the hope faded, another realization rose. My eyes cut to Asyl, skin hot. *"He was unconscious for three months? Bedridden for two more?"*

Asyl shook her head at the sky, lips twisting. *"There you have it,"* she said with a half sob. *"The great secret as to why I lived as* long as I did; he was too weak to kill me. Eventually, though, his hatred outgrew his pain."

"For your magic."

"Yes, but also because he simply hates witches. He may not admit it, but he does. And he hated Khezhari witches with a particular fervor."

"What made the witches of Khezhar so special?"

She scoffed. "Because we didn't cower and hide. We took our rightful place in society and we ruled. We perfected it. An entire theocratic kingdom ruled by a priestly caste of witches, with the unpowered living in service. You can see why Radovan would hate us, unpowered swine that he is."

Her words danced through my skull, leaving me feeling like something sour was coating my tongue and sliding slowly down my throat. It was the fervor, I realized. The fervor of zealotry I'd only seen in men like Khaljaq.

Qaden was from Khezhar, I remembered. She'd been in prison during the invasion. A prison Radovan freed her from. Even now she hated witches with an undimmed ferocity, the same ferocity with which I hated the Shazir. "Why was Qaden in prison?"

Asyl tutted, tossing her long hair back over her shoulders. "A woman like that, there could only be one reason. Part of the underground rebellion probably, one of the rabble-rousers who started the bread riots that autumn."

"Bread riots?" I exclaimed. "She was imprisoned because she wanted to eat? Asyl, don't you hear yourself? Don't you hear what you sound like? You're no better than Radovan."

"How dare you?" she demanded, her voice high. "You wouldn't understand, you were raised to fear your power, to be ashamed of it. But we knew better in Khezhar—we guided our people into an age of enlightenment."

"No, Asyl." I slapped my hand on the flat of the worktable,

feeling nothing but grim joy at the pain echoing up my palm. Better pain than this . . . this feeling of disgust. *"Magic doesn't give you the right to starve your people, any more than might gives Radovan the right to terrorize his."*

"Askia—"

"Don't." I turned away, trying to swallow my disappointment with her, and with a history I had no power to change. But why? Had I really thought the other queens were like lost princesses from a fairy story? Had I thought they would all be paragons of good, images of righteousness? Was I really that naive to assume they wouldn't be—people? Good and bad? Strong and weak? Moral and . . .

And was I really in a position to judge? Hadn't I considered using the Shazir? Considered pointing them toward Roven in the hope my two enemies destroyed each other? I turned back to Asyl and looked at her. Really looked at her, at the self-righteous line of her jaw and the bridled way she held her shoulders, and wondered . . . was I looking in the mirror?

And then I saw it. The door she planted herself in front of as if to keep me away.

"Don't ever—not for one moment—think you can decide what I should or shouldn't know," I said, voice soft but firm. *"Tell the others. And get away from that door."*

Asyl vanished in a puff of vapor that coated my skin in anger and regret as I headed for the door. I tried to ignore it, tried to shrug it off, but the idea that I'd just learned the truth of her, and about myself, clung to me like ill-fitting shoes.

I shook my head, trying to regain a sense of equilibrium, to recall my goal in sneaking down here. Part of me knew I'd stayed too long. That any hope I had of returning to the Great Hall with no one the wiser had vanished as completely as Asyl had. But I couldn't go back now. Not after seeing Asyl standing in front of this door, guarding yet another secret.

I had to know.

The handle turned easily, and I stepped onto a narrow balcony. A single flight of stairs lay before me, leading down to a massive room. And—

Lady Night . . .

Shock electrified my body, freezing me in place.

The alabaster space before me was almost cave-like in its grandeur. The room, which was easily the size of the Great Hall, was lit by series of unadorned witchlights floating in rigid lines all the way down its length. And what that light illuminated . . .

Tables. Workbenches, like the one in the office at my back, stood in straight rows, nearly a hundred of them, I thought. Perhaps fifty of them in use. But what lay on their tops was not boxes of Aellium stones. It was far, far worse . . .

People.

Witches.

Men and women, young and old, lay chained to the tables with Aellium stones set into the straps over their chests. The stones glittered menacingly in the light, winking at me from my perch. Mocking my helplessness.

Every nerve trembled and shuddered, as I walked down the stairs. How long had I been here? How many days had I wasted playing games with the court while all these people lay here dying for Radovan's greed?

And they were dying, I knew. Because as I drifted, numb and horrified, my eyes cut mercilessly to the near wall, to the metal hatch and the cloth beneath. The cloth that covered something lumpy. Many somethings. But it did not quite cover the pale foot poking out. A small foot, I thought. A child's.

It beckoned me, singing a song of damnation. Compelling, demanding that I peel back the cloth and witness the true extent of Radovan's evil. I was halfway across the room when a muffled cry slammed into my back.

"Lady Night, no."

The horror in Vitaly's voice made my knees lock. Foreboding played a dirge on my ribs. I turned slowly, eyes wide with a horror that had no name.

The man on the nearest table was awake. Gagged, but awake. His pale, blue-gray eyes seared my skin, anchoring me to the spot. A lesser man would be weeping with fear and hope—that desperate killing hope that ground me down day by day. But not him. Here was a man that despair could not bend.

Illya.

I ran, hands slamming onto his table as panic crawled up my throat. "I'm getting you out of here."

But how could he be here? *Why* was he here? He couldn't be a witch. He always seemed to hate that I was a witch, hated that I'd turned to the Shadow Guild for training. It was like he didn't trust them. Of course, neither had I, but necessity had forced me out of hiding.

I shook the thoughts away. They could wait. Illya couldn't.

I fumbled at the straps across his chest, my fingers numb and bloodless. No matter how I scratched and pulled, the straps remained fixed. My knees hit the floor, searching frantically until I found the lock holding him in place, immovable even as Illya strained, muscles corded with effort. Wordless screams that the gag couldn't muffle filled my ears.

A key, I thought, willing my mind to move. I needed to find a key.

I whirled in a full circle, ignoring the way my heart hammered against my sternum. Sprinted to a workbench near the stairs. My hands raked across the top, sending papers flying as I searched desperately for the key. But nothing. It wasn't here. Whoever ran this room of horror must have it. My vision flashed red with the urge to skin that faceless man alive for what he'd done to Illya and the hundreds, thousands who had come before.

"Think. *Think*, Askia." There was no key, but that didn't mean there wasn't something else. Some other way to free him. The lock securing the straps wasn't that big. Could I break it? I had to try. But to do it I needed . . .

I launched up the stairs, taking the steps three at a time, flinging myself into the office. The office where the stones were set in their metal casings. Where I'd seen tools, thick bars of steel and—

A file.

I snatched it up, ignoring the way the file's teeth bit into my palm. Running back down the stairs, I leapt the last four to the ground. I stumbled, knees skidding against the floor, but shot back up and sprinted to Illya, who still struggled. Still screamed. But he wasn't the only one. The others were watching too. Straining. Shouting. A symphony of broken men and women begging me to hurry, to set them free.

I wedged the file between the loops of the lock. Pulled. And pulled. Sweat beaded on my brow. My muscles screamed. My jaw ached from gritting it so hard. Something buckled. But it wasn't the lock breaking. It was the file.

"No, no, no," I said, something between a breath and a sob. "Please. Lady Night—Day Lord. Help me."

I snatched up the file. Raked it across the lock, sawing with all my strength. My vision narrowed, blocking out everything but this worktable, this man, this lock. Sound bombarded my ears, but to my mind it was a distant, pointless thing.

So even though my ears registered a change in the way the prisoners screamed, my mind didn't.

Until a hand fisted my hair. It yanked me back so hard, the file fell and the muscles in my neck and shoulders screamed in agony. Zosha towered over me, a dagger clutched in his white-knuckled hand. His face scarlet with anger.

"Get up," he commanded, pushing me away from him. He

brandished the dagger, entire body tense like he was afraid I would attack him. "Don't you know what will happen if Radovan finds you here? Get up, Askia."

I rose slowly, turned, like I could protect Illya with my body. Hands balled into fists. Ready to fight. "Zosha, no. I can't—I know this man and I am *not* just going to leave him down here."

Something flickered in his eyes. Something terribly close to guilt. "Askia—" Zosha said, slowly, like he was trying to reason with a madwoman. He lunged. But Zosha was no fighter, and I was ready for him this time.

I grabbed his wrist as he moved. Using his own momentum against him, I spun his body around. In a blink his arm was behind his back, blade clattering uselessly to the ground.

"Askia, stop!" Vitaly's command rang out through the room, cutting through the fog of panic and desperation. I froze and turned to the ghost, saw the miserable conflicted expression on his face. *"Illya has time—you have time—to help him escape. But you have no exit strategy here. What is the point of freeing him now if you both get captured upstairs?"* Vitaly spoke slowly, as if willing me to understand.

He didn't need to. I understood. That terrible realization was what brought tears to my eyes. Zosha wrenched out of my grip, eyes wild as if he'd expected me to already have the knife at his throat. Quickly, as if he feared I'd change my mind, he crouched down, grabbed the blade, and slid away.

Away from Illya, who watched me now, face hard, demanding an answer.

I strained against the storm of emotions whipping through me. Against the way my heart reached toward Illya. "I'm so sorry, Illya—I had no idea you were down here. I don't have a way for us to escape. Not yet." My voice broke, small and pitiful as it was. I pressed a quick kiss to his brow. "I will come back for you," I promised, hurling the words like a threat at the feet of the

Two-Faced God.

"Let's go," I said, nodding to Zosha. We marched in lockstep back up the stairs. Back into the office.

And ran straight into Qaden.

All the blood rushed out of her face in a gush of shock and . . . and terror. She looked back and, as if the gesture set my senses free, I heard the shuffling of footsteps on the stairs behind her. The murmur of conversation. She wasn't alone.

And Lady Night defend me, I knew that voice.

Radovan.

"Go," Qaden hissed, her gaze locking on to Zosha. "Get her out of here. Now."

15

I FELT MY jaw drop in surprise at the warning, but Zosha was already moving. He grabbed my hand, pulling us back out of the office. We ran side by side down the stairs and across the workroom. Tears welled in my eyes as I passed the prisoners, my fellow witches.

Hold on, I begged them silently. *I am coming for you.*

A door waited for us in the shadowy reaches of the hall, narrow and rusting from little use. Its hinges squealed as Zosha pulled it open and dragged me into the darkness of this false, shame-filled salvation.

Zosha moved ahead, his footing sure enough to tell me that he'd crept through this place before. That did nothing to help me, though, and I stumbled after him, banging my foot on something hard enough to fall forward. My arms wind-milled, hands scraping against narrow stone walls, bracing in time to stop me from falling face-first onto a staircase.

I gritted my teeth, following Zosha up what must have been a seldom-used servant's stair. Adrenaline burned in my veins, unslaked and unabated by the long trek upward. Every scrape of my boots on the stone seared through my senses, heightening my outrage and my anger.

The appearance of a window, a narrow slash-like gap in

the gray stone wall, was all that indicated our arrival out of the earth. The light streaming through illuminated the rigid muscles in Zosha's back. His hands were fisted, ready for a fight.

Good. Because he had a lot to answer for . . . as did the ghost queens.

We had traveled up almost five levels by the time Zosha stepped off the spiraling stairs and flung open a door. He barely paused to check if the way was clear before he stomped out. I followed, realizing we were only a few floors below my room.

We stalked down the hall, united only in our anger and silence. I watched him from the corner of my eye, tense, ready for him to make his move. Because Vitaly's words were echoing through my head:

Zosha *was* in the rebellion—the Nine. And if he wasn't working with me, then it only meant he was supposed to kill me in a desperate ploy to gain time against Radovan's unstoppable hunt for power. Death witches were a rarity after all, and only Lady Night knew when he might find another.

My days were growing short either way.

We made it to my room on a cloud of mutual outrage, but the unspoken accord of silence shattered as my door slammed shut.

Zosha rounded on me. "What the hell were you thinking?" he demanded, his voice carefully low as if to make sure the guards outside my door wouldn't hear anything.

I shouldered past him, stalking past the scared and guarded faces of the dead queens, of Ozura, watching with a careful closed expression, and Vitaly, whose eyes brimmed with undimmed anger.

I cast a baleful glare at the gathered queens before turning it on Zosha. "What was I thinking?" I asked, matching his tone. "What are *you* thinking? How can you sit in that hall—how can you dance and flirt and play cards—knowing what's happening below? I thought you were different, that being Ragata's son would make you care. Clearly I was wrong."

I shook my head, unable to convey the depth of my disgust. "Don't you have any decency? Any sense of honor? Or has living here turned you into a heartless bastard?"

"Don't you *dare* judge me. I am doing what I have to, to survive. We all are. Did it never occur to you that we're all so well-behaved because we know exactly what's happening below? Because no one wants to risk Radovan's wrath?"

"People are dying, Zosha. Why didn't you try to stop it?"

"What, like you were going to do?" he sneered. "What was your grand plan, Askia? After you freed all those witches—what then? Did you even stop to think about how you were going to escape before I stepped in and stopped you?"

I swallowed, knowing I'd thought no such thing. But . . .

"There were at least fifty witches down there, Zosha. And my friend—the man you have trussed up in chains—is the deadliest swordmaster I have ever seen. We would have gotten out."

"How?" Zosha pressed. "Where would you get a weapon for your vaunted swordmaster? Those people have been starved, their magic is being sucked out of them, and they're weak. And even assuming they could muster enough magic to put up a fight, do you really think they could've escaped into the freezing cold? Past the hundred sorcerers in the city? Past the two thousand Voyniks stationed along the river? Past Radovan?"

It was his turn to shake his head, to plant his hands on his hips and glare at me with disdain. "Don't tell me that's the best plan you have. Because if it is, then I just did you a favor. Do you know what Radovan would do to you if he knew you were down there? He'd lock you up. He'd put you in chains for the rest of your very short life and have the Voyniks outside watch you around the clock."

"And that would be so inconvenient for you, wouldn't it, Zosha?" I said, my voice dripping with venom. "Because then, how would you kill me? That was your plan all along, wasn't it—yours and your dear Nines?"

Zosha's body stilled as the heat fled his face. His mouth worked, but no words came out.

"What are you talking about?" Ragata asked, coming to her son's side, eyes wide. Scared.

"What are you talking about?"

I scoffed at his careful answer, at the way he unwittingly parroted his dead mother. "You know exactly what I'm talking about," I replied, my voice going soft. "You both do."

Confusion chased across Zosha's face, followed quickly by comprehension. His gaze darted around the room, as if he'd suddenly see the ghost he was looking for.

"What, did you think you were special?" I asked, with a mocking laugh. I stalked forward, pushing my face into his, until we were nose to nose. "You've watched me blackmailing the court with their secrets. Did you really think I wouldn't have someone tailing you? That I wouldn't find out about the Nines?"

Zosha staggered back, looking like I'd slapped him. His face went ghostly white. Funny, I'd always thought that expression was stupid. But seeing him now, with his dead mother looking at him, I thought it was apt.

He licked his lips. Ran a hand over his whiskers. And went for the door.

"Don't," I snapped, stepping in his path. "You owe me an explanation. You owe us both explanations."

"About what?" he asked, his voice weak, frightened even as he tried to look everywhere but at me, only to fail because he knew somewhere in this room, his mother was watching. Waiting.

"About everything. About your supposed rebellion. Who else at court is part of it? Qaden? Is that why she helped us escape?"

He shook his head tightly. "No. She isn't. And I don't know

why she helped us." He frowned at me. "What do you have on her?"

I sidestepped the question. "What about Illya, my friend downstairs? Did he come to you—you and your supposed rebellion? Did he ask you for help?" I came closer, staring up into his weak, traitorous face. "Did you betray him?"

"Oh, my child," Ragata breathed.

He raised his chin. "I had nothing to do with your friend. Neither did the Nines."

Out of the corner of my eye, I saw Vitaly shake his head, the gesture filled with the same disappointment now coursing through me.

"Why not work with me? We could escape this place together—and you will need to escape, Zosha, because if I can find out about the Nines, so will Radovan once he has a thousand dead eyes at his disposal. It's not too late to escape."

Zosha's shoulders dropped, but even in my anger, I could see his face cracking with regret. I seized his hand. "We could take the Nines with us. We can rally my army and go to Vishir. We can defeat Radovan once and for all."

"It wouldn't work."

"Why not?"

Zosha pulled away, shifting from one foot to the other like a child struggling beneath the weight of guilt. He was nothing more than a lost little boy in desperate need of his mother. But he wouldn't ever see her again. Not unless he was discovered. Captured. Killed.

"You've seen the city," he said, his voice a low rasp of suppressed tears. "But you still don't understand. It's not just the Voyniks standing guard, or the gates that keep us all penned in. It's the people. The men and women you see on the streets and pity are the very same who would sell you out before you could so much as speak.

"And even if we could fool them all, or bribe them into compliance, then what? You think the port isn't watched, that the ships aren't searched when they arrive and when they leave? I suppose we could try to escape over land, but spring is still two months away. We'd die of exposure within the first two nights. Don't you see? The risk of failure is simply too high."

I drew back at the pleading sound in his voice. Because that's what it was. He wasn't trying to convince me of my folly. He was pleading, begging me to let him end it.

I sneered. "So what's the plan, Zosha? To have you wait and watch and when the time is right, plant that knife in my back?"

Zosha swallowed hard but didn't deny it. "There's no telling how long it would take Radovan to find another death witch. Could be years. Decades even. Time enough for Vishir to choose an emperor and stop Radovan."

"You really think Radovan isn't cunning enough to exploit the divisions in Vishir? That he hasn't already? Radovan will sow enough chaos in Vishir to hobble them as long as necessary. *So why not help me?*"

Zosha's eyes shone, betraying the conflict brewing within him. Because deep down part of him agreed with me. "It's safer this way."

"Safer? For who? Because Radovan will kill you for this. Or do you think he'll be lenient on you because—after all—you are *like* a son to him."

"No," Zosha said, exhaling a mirthless laugh. "I know he'll kill me. But better I die robbing him of your power than to let him have you in a certain-to-fail escape attempt—one that could expose all the Nines. I'm sorry."

"You're *sorry?* Listen to yourself. You sound just like him—trying to convince me of the necessity of my death like it will somehow absolve you. As if my permission will make it easier."

I looked him slowly up and down, a reckless rage funneling

through my body. "But it won't, Zosha—you would know that if you'd ever taken a life. I have. I've killed evil men before. And I've killed good ones too," I continued, feeling Vitaly at my back. "I had all the justification in the world, but it doesn't help. I will carry their deaths with me until my last breath—a weight that will never shift."

I took a careful predatory step toward Zosha, watching his every exhalation, preparing for him to move, to go for the knife. "I don't think you have the stomach to kill me, Zosha. Not with your mother watching."

He winced, curling in on himself as my words slashed across his face. "I don't have a choice," he whispered.

Even in my fury, I pitied him. "Then what are you waiting for?" I asked, holding up my hands, making myself a good target. Calling his bluff. "Take your shot. We'll see who wins this fight."

Zosha's hands moved, but not for the knife. He raked his fingers through his hair, looking like he'd aged ten years in the space of this conversation. "Maybe that's what I'm waiting for," he said tiredly. "For you to give up fighting."

"Never gonna happen," I vowed.

"Then Radovan wins."

Zosha shook his head, and this time, when he went for the door, I didn't stop him. He reached for the handle. Turned. He looked back at me, eyes hard on my face for a moment that stretched out between us. "If you're going to make your escape attempt, do it soon. Because no matter how much Radovan pretends to like you, he isn't going to let you live a second longer than he has to. Just . . ."

He swallowed hard, eyes shining. "Just don't fail. For me."

The door snapped shut behind him, echoing into a stillness that was anything but empty.

"*Askia—*"

I whirled on Eliska so fast her already halting voice went silent. She took a faltering step forward. The other queens, damn them, stayed well back.

"Did you know?"

"About your friend? No, I—"

"Not about him. About the other witches trapped in that chamber?"

Eliska didn't reply. She didn't have to. Her silence was answer enough.

"We told you everything you needed to know."

I saw Vitaly's head shoot up, entire body electrified with shock. Because it wasn't one of the wives who spoke. It was Ozura.

Dark energy crackled across my flesh as I stepped up to her. *"You knew Illya was down there? You knew this whole time?"*

One of Ozura's finely plucked brows rose, as if my anger were both unjustified and entirely beneath her. *"Of course I did."*

A low ringing began in my ears. *"What was the point in swearing your soul in service to mine if you were just going to betray me like this?"*

"I've done nothing but act in your best interest," she replied, completely uncowed.

I slashed my hand through the air, as if the gesture could erase her words. It was bad enough that she'd done this to me in Vishir. At least she'd been alive then, maneuvering as I was toward her own goals. But she wasn't alive to play politics now.

And she was supposed to be on my side. *"Enough. You don't get to decide what's best for me. Not anymore."*

"I wouldn't have to make these decisions if you were capable of making them yourself," she replied, voice frigid. *"Your priority needs to be escaping this place and returning to Vishir—your home. Not saving people who are as good as dead already."*

An anger that went beyond rage, beyond betrayal funneled

through me. My magic answered, or tried to. Power flailed against the enchanted necklace, so fierce the chain grew warm. Hot. Chain and stone seared through the room like a second sickly sun. So hot my skin sizzled, but the pain was nothing.

"You need to leave."

"Askia, please—" Eliska tried again, but I cut her off with a look blacker than the deepest hell.

"Lady Night curse you. Leave!"

16

IMPOSSIBLY, I SLEPT, though my dreams were filled with the twisting corridors of a vast hedge maze and the ever-silent avenues of a graveyard all bathed in green light. But not just any graveyard, the graveyard of emperors in Vishir. Its mausoleums filled with the restless, unspeaking dead. My parents. My grandfather. Armaan. Illya.

The next day dawned differently than all the others, and not only because of the dried tears on my cheeks. My body was heavy with a bone-deep exhaustion that threatened to drag me to the floor. I punched my pillow, trying to take comfort in the knowledge that Illya certainly had longer to live than I did. But how? How had he even gotten here so fast? And was he alone? Was Arkady here, too, or were he and the Wolves even now roaming the wilds, searching for a way in?

I gave up on sleep, glaring across my room as if that could fend off the screaming sense of foreboding. Was it because I was alone? Vitaly had gone to watch over Illya. And Ozura and the queens? Well, I'd screamed at all of them to leave—leave before I figured out how to kill someone who was already dead, stone be damned.

So Siv wasn't pacing the length of the room railing about how bored she was following Qaden. Ragata wasn't waxing poetic about the structure of each stone in the wall. Eliska wasn't trying to cram my head full of etiquette. I was alone. But that wasn't the problem.

The maids were helping me dress when the realization hit, making me stumble backward. My hip hit the edge of the bed, but I barely noticed the small pain. The older maid reached out a hesitant hand and touched my arm, a silent question in her eyes.

"Fifteen," I whispered, numb fingers brushing across the face of the Aellium stone—the stone which now glowed hungrily enough that only tucking it beneath my heavy winter coat could hide the shine. "I only have fifteen days left."

Pity flashed through her eyes. She nodded. I laughed, all too conscious of the hysterical bent to my voice. Funny. How could it not be funny? That the only person in this cursed city who never lied to me was a woman who couldn't speak.

"Askia? Are you all right?"

Eliska. Of course it was Eliska. She was the only one of them who would have the nerve to face me right now. She appeared over the old woman's shoulder, keen understanding in her face. My laughter dried up all at once. "Yes," I said, not bothering to speak the word in my head. "I'm all right."

The old maid took my hand and led me to the vanity, sitting me down like I was a child. There was something comforting in the way she shook my hair loose of its braid and began brushing it out in long careful strokes. If I closed my eyes, I could almost imagine I was home, my mother brushing my hair while my father read aloud in the background.

Longing rose up within me, sharper than any knife. My eyes opened as I purposely shattered the dream. I sniffed. It wouldn't do to lose myself to such visions.

I wasn't one for fantasy anyway.

"It's all right to be scared," Eliska murmured, kneeling at my feet. She tutted when I didn't respond, when my gaze slid to her

and away again. I watched her shake her head from the corner of my eye. Watched her frown. *"I know you're mad, but please, Askia. Let me be here for you. Who else could understand this?"*

I looked up to the ceiling, blinking back tears. Tears because in truth, I wasn't mad. Not really. My anger, usually such a dependable source of strength, had utterly failed. Yes, in the moment I'd been angry that they hadn't told me about the witches. Mad at Aysl and her prejudice. Mad at Zosha and his unwillingness to help me—and determination to kill me. At Ozura for always thinking she knew best, damn whatever anyone else thought or said. I'd even been mad at Illya for having come to Roven in the first place. But the sun had fallen and risen again. The realization had come, a harbinger of death, and I felt . . . somehow . . . less.

"You can't keep things from me," I said, the voice in my head soft.

She nodded. *"I know. I'm sorry."*

"Are you, though?" I demanded, flesh puckering from my magic's tether, the heat from the hearth little balm against the chill. *"Because you don't seem nearly sorry enough. When was the last time you were down there, Eliska? When was the last time you faced any of those poor trapped people?"*

Her face tightened with guilt, and I knew the truth before she even spoke. *"I've never gone down there,"* she admitted softly. *"It's too hard to see our people like that when there's nothing we can do to help them. That's why we didn't tell you. And Ozura agreed. She thought—"* Her words trailed off and she shook her head.

"Thought what?"

She seemed to hesitate. *"In the short time I've known you, it's become clear to me that you aren't the kind of person to let an injustice slide."*

"And that's a bad thing?"

"No, of course not. It's just . . . Sometimes you lose sight of the big-

ger picture. Because whatever else Zosha said yesterday, he was right about one thing. If you could've freed your friend and all the others, you would have without hesitation. And you would have gotten them all killed. Ozura knew that—though she could have expressed that concern better yesterday."

I shoved away her justification for Ozura's actions, not yet ready to forgive the Vishiri queen. *"They're going to die down their anyway, Eliska. Isn't it better to die free?"*

"Perhaps," she replied. *"But you must understand, you wouldn't have died with them. You'd have been dragged back up here in chains, and any hope of escape would be utterly lost. Your magic would be Radovan's, our secrets his.*

"You'd have sacrificed the world, all to save fifty people, only so they could die 'free.'"

"You're right," I murmured. *"I would have risked everything to save them. But Eliska? I still will."*

She shook her head. *"That's not possible."*

"Nevertheless. I have to try."

Eliska rose, rubbing her face with a hand as a frustrated laugh shook out of her chest.

"What?"

"You," she said, facing me, looking suddenly ancient. *"You and my brother would have made quite the pair."*

"Really?" I asked, with a soft smile. Strange that in all the time spent with Eliska, I hadn't once thought about her brother—the man I had been promised to as part of a treaty to stand against Roven. It seemed like a whole other life, a whole other woman.

"Yes. Olexan was every bit as upright as you. Too serious sometimes, but he had a good heart. I think he'd have insisted on saving those people too. You'd have made a good match."

I closed my eyes at her words. At the endless desire for a life that would always be out of reach.

I turned away from the pain. Smiled. *"Well, you'd have hated my cousin."*

She laughed, like she in turn had forgotten the second half of the treaty, which would have sent Goran over the Peshkalor Mountains into Raskis to marry her, a woman he could never have hoped to match.

"I'm sure I could have found a way to be rid of him," she said, smiling a slow wolfish grin. *"We are not so civilized in Raskis."*

A surprised chuckle bubbled out of me and I knew I must look insane to the servant. Oh well. She probably knew I could see the other queens—everyone else did. But my smile stuck, as I looked up at Eliska. Upright and tall and willing to do any-thing, sacrifice anything to keep me alive. I didn't always agree with her methods, but—I exhaled long and hard.

"I'd have liked to have you for a sister."

Her breath caught, and silvery tears gathered in her gray eyes. *"I'd have liked that too."*

Thankfully the maids were gathering their things, giving me a place to look. Last thing I needed was to break down cry-ing. Soon they were gone, leaving me with my thoughts and my ghosts and the uneasy trepidation of knowing that Zosha was coming soon. No doubt he was still furious. Furious enough to take his shot? I shrugged internally. At least watching his every move would make our little walks more diverting.

"I don't think he's come to that yet," Eliska said, hearing the thoughts. *"Ragata was with him last night, and when I went to check on her, he looked quite poorly. I doubt he's in any condition to . . . well, you know."*

I did know, which was why I knew that no amount of lost sleep could stop a person from taking a life if they were con-vinced it was the only way forward. I didn't reply to Eliska, but I did stretch my hand over the lip of the wardrobe and retrieve the knife. It was its own kind of answer. I'd just finished tucking it in my boot when a knock came at the door.

I braced myself before opening it, but it wasn't Zosha waiting on the other side. It was Qaden. A smile twitched her lips at whatever she saw in my face. "Lord Zosha is otherwise occupied," she said in a voice so bland it was almost possible to believe she hadn't caught me in Radovan's dungeon—and helped me escape. "Shall we go for a walk?"

I followed Qaden into the hall, gritting my teeth, waiting for her to lash out with words and fists, but the explosion never came. Her face, though guarded, didn't appear angry or even perturbed. If anything, she looked almost content.

When we hit the stairs, I began heading down only for Qaden to place a staying hand on my shoulder. "I thought we'd go up today."

"Up?" I asked, brow furrowing.

She shrugged. "To the northern watchtower. It's not so cold, and the watchfire will keep us warm enough."

Though I had plenty of secrets to peddle in the Great Hall, I was intrigued enough to agree. Intrigued . . . and wary. It certainly wasn't every day Qaden wanted my company. The change was so drastic I had to wonder. Because no matter how grateful she might be for her promotion, Qaden wasn't the sort to show kindness to her enemies.

There were four watchtowers facing north. One rose from the curtainwall, and three more that branched out from the castle at varying heights. The ache in my legs was enough to tell me we were headed for the highest one.

This tower, like the others, was capped in a great pointed copper dome—that much I'd seen from the courtyard. But what hadn't been visible was that the dome wasn't solid, but a series of interlocking metal strips. The woven copper was just enough to cut some of the truly ferocious wind while providing a good lookout to the four Voyniks on guard.

A giant brazier filled with fire burned in the tower's center—though perhaps burned was the wrong word. The fire didn't seem to have any fuel, nor did it belch out any smoke. It shouldn't have been possible. But one look at the nearest guard told the tale. An Aellium stone pendant hung on her lapel, letting her feed the fire while she stood watch.

I turned away from her, wondering how many of the witches beneath our feet had fire magic. The thought left an acrid taste on my tongue. I crossed the breadth of the tower and looked through the barred ropes of metal, past the sprawling circular city, gazing north. There was a point in the far distance, where the gray, clouded sky met the white snow-covered horizon and became one. It looked like freedom to me.

Qaden came up beside me, and by some unspoken command, the other guards fell back, positioning themselves behind us. With the wind blowing at my back, I knew our words would be lost to the sky, unheard and unknown. Private, or as private as anything here was.

But still Qaden didn't speak.

Though the silence unfurling between us could almost be called companionable, I knew it couldn't last. There must have been a reason she brought me here, and the reason was probably to do with the workshop, with the witches who were dying below.

Did it make her sick, the knowledge of those innocent people being murdered? Or did she think it was a well-deserved end for people who were so like those that ruled the onetime theocracy of Khezhar?

Asyl's words and zealotry rose up in my mind, leaving me unclean in some indefinable way. Like if I didn't say anything, I was somehow agreeing with her. Like my silence made me complicit. So even though Qaden was my enemy, even though she was playing her part in other unspeakable crimes, I forced my lips to move.

"I spoke with Asyl yesterday," I began, hating the hesitance in my voice. "She had some truly terrible things to say about how the world should work."

A dark laugh tumbled from her lips. "I bet she did."

I nodded, contemplating my next words carefully. "Look, for whatever it's worth, I wanted to say I'm sorry for what the witches of Khezhar did. But I hope you know that we're not all like that. We don't all see nonpowered people like they're—"

"Animals?" Anger flashed across Qaden's face, a spasm she controlled swiftly from what felt like years of practice. She shook her head at the sky before looking at me in a hard, appraising kind of way. "How old are you?"

"Twenty-two."

"Twenty-two," she murmured, repeating my words in quiet disbelief. "Then you're too young to know what life was like in old Khezhar. But you're old enough to know better than to say that not all witches are like Asyl, expecting it to make me feel better. I know not all of you are like that, but it doesn't invalidate my experience or soothe the torment my people suffered at the hands of witches like Asyl."

I felt my face flush—at the well-deserved shame worming through me. I hadn't intended to offend her with my own ill-considered words. But I knew by now that even good intentions could cause pain. Qaden nodded at my silent reaction, looking so, so tired.

"Do you have any idea what it was like to live in Khezhar as a *mere* human? They treated us like cattle," she said when I shook my head no. "Worse than that even, because cattle don't have the ability to think, to see the life they can never have. We were nothing but the lowest of servants.

"They said it was their divine duty to care for us, but that was their excuse to take away our freedom. They enslaved us and said it was for our own good. That we wouldn't know how to handle money if they paid us. And couldn't possibly make our own choices. We couldn't even read—well, who kept us from learning if not them?

"We weren't even allowed to marry. They bred us like farmers who pick and choose advantageous stock. And when we dared to speak out, to beg for more—not even demand, for we couldn't imagine demanding anything of them—we were imprisoned. Tortured. Killed as a lesson to the rest.

"That was supposed to be my fate," she said, eyes shining in the weak daylight. "Before Radovan's invasion, I was set to be executed."

"I know," I murmured.

She nodded, tearing her eyes away to look at that distant horizon. "There were days—whole years even—when I'd have gladly thrown in my lot with those Vishiri madmen and let all you witches burn."

Though it made something inside me break, I couldn't honestly blame her. "And now?" I asked, my mind and heart racing in opposite directions. "Is it all vengeance to you, what Radovan is doing?"

"It was once," she admitted, her voice bitter. "But time and age have cooled something inside me." She shrugged. "Hate is simple, but life—especially in Roven—is complex. I've lost my hate somewhere along the way. I don't rejoice in what's being done to you—to any of you. But I will endure it, the guilt and the shame. Even if it damns me in the end."

"Why?" I asked. "Why go through all of this and do nothing?"

"Because Radovan saved me," she replied, her gaze returning to mine. "He saved me, and whatever else he is, I know he will never allow Khezhar to rise again."

I frowned, but when I looked at the city below, her words didn't ring true. "Qaden, look around you. Look in the mirror and see the tattoo on your face—can you honestly say Roven is so different than Khezhar?"

"Yes," she said, softly, sincerely. "It may not seem that way to you, but to someone who has survived true enslavement, this is a whole new world."

"But it doesn't have to be like this either. There's better out there."

"Perhaps," she replied, frowning like she didn't believe me, like she was afraid to. "But this is enough—knowing that no one will grow up the way I did. It's enough. And that's what I brought you up here to say.

"You may have gotten me this promotion—though why you did, I still don't understand. And I may have covered for you yesterday, but in the end, none of that matters. You helped me. I helped you. That's as far as this can go. I will not cover for you again, nor aid you in whatever plan you're no doubt brewing."

She looked me square in the eye, as if willing me to take her next words to heart. "You need to understand that I made my choice a long time ago. I am with Radovan. Until the end."

Her shoulders fell and her words faltered. Like the weight of this oath were bearing down on her, crushing her, and even considering breaking it was beyond her strength. Finally, she seemed to shake herself, meeting my gaze.

"I can't go back to the way things were."

For one glimmering second, I thought I'd found my key, my way to escape this place. "But don't you see? I don't want things to go back to the way they were. There wasn't a place for women like us in that world. It's gone, and nothing can bring it back. But I do believe that there is a way forward. For all of us. Together."

She looked at me, considering my words. I could feel it in the way her eyes peppered my face, in the way her body leaned toward mine, desperate for more, for better. This woman, who had endured all the darkness of the world and found light here in the ever-twilight of Roven, she deserved more than this pale, sterile kingdom and the half-mad emperor who'd built it.

Overhead a bell clanged twelve mournful tolls. The air between us reverberated, and Qaden stepped back—no, stepped *away*.

"We should go," she said, expression closing. "He wants to see you."

17

I FOLLOWED QADEN out of the tower, the specter of what could have been haunting my steps. There was a certain respect in the edges of the silence between us now, the respect of enemies who understood one another, maybe even empathized. But we could have been more. We could have been allies. *Should* have been on the same side.

Should have been friends.

But that wasn't to be. As we walked, side by side, down the tower, I was sure in the knowledge that if I tried to escape, Qaden would try to stop me. What would happen next, only Lady Night knew.

It wasn't a happy realization. But it wasn't a surprise either.

"Where are we going?" I asked, as we passed the hall leading to Radovan's study. "The Great Hall?" I prompted when Qaden didn't reply.

She shook her head, though the gesture was half-shrug. "He said it's a surprise."

I nodded, knowing I wasn't getting more from her. Qaden had thrown in her lot with Radovan, after all. If she wouldn't betray his trust even as far as exposing our destination, then truly was no hope of convincing her to help me escape. Unless she was hiding something truly shocking. *And hiding it well*, I thought with a frown. Siv had yet to uncover even a whisper of impropriety or slip of judgment—aside from letting me go from the dungeon.

I smoothed away my frown, as the stairs made their final turn. Radovan waited on the ground floor, bouncing on his toes in boyish excitement. "Askia." He beamed my name, gracing me with a slight bow. "I have a surprise for you, my dear."

"Really?" I replied, not able to keep the suspicion out of my voice. "Am I going to like it?"

He laughed, like my question was a good joke, and held out his hand. "I'm certain of it. Shall we?"

Arm in arm and with only Qaden as an escort, we walked past the Great Hall and the many curious Dorovnii within it. Rather than making for the courtyard, we headed deeper into the castle. Even though I'd never set foot in these halls, Radovan's love of uniformity made itself known.

Until, that is, we reached a bare stretch of stone wall right where a door should have been. I felt the Aellium stone heat through my tunic. My skin smarted, still blistered from the chain's punishing burn, as Radovan pressed the flat of his palm against the wall. The stone rippled away, as repelled by the touch of his bare flesh as I was. A staircase remained.

A warning tiptoed across my back, as we started down. Was this another entrance to the workroom-prison of the witches beneath the Great Hall?

My gaze clawed at the walls, scrabbling for purchase, for some kind of clue, but there was nothing. Truly nothing. The walls and floor and ceiling were the same uniform white stone as the rest of the castle, only not. The white stone above us was veined in swirling waves of gray and silver. It glimmered in a way that even I had to admit was pretty. But this stone was just . . . blank. It had no dimension, no depth. I couldn't even see where the masons had joined it.

The same as the stone in the workshop beneath the Great Hall. Lady Night, give me strength. Did he mean to reveal Illya to me like some kind of terrible gift? As if he was a house cat presenting its owners a rat it's killed? I took a careful breath, stealing myself. For if Radovan ever realized what Illya meant to me . . .

Two Voyniks sat behind a desk at the bottom. The younger of the two sprang to attention before Radovan. The older— Wenslaus, the man from my first ill-fated dinner—didn't. His pale gaze flicked from Radovan to me, glittering with amusement before he turned fully to Radovan. I only half listened to the inane exchange of pleasantries, gazing past the men, studying.

If this place was connected to the workshop, I couldn't yet see how. All that lay before me now was a single corridor that seemed to run the entire length of the island.

For a reason I couldn't quite explain, it reminded me of the hospital in the Shadow Guild. Although this wide hallway didn't contain even the impression of windows, it was lit by a series of white-burning witchlights. The orbs sat suspended near the ceiling in rigid intervals down such a vast length it made my eyes water just trying to behold.

Then I saw the reflection of the light against glass. The dark pockmark of an iron drain. I shivered. It was sterile, this place, that's why it recalled the hospital in my mind. But this was no place for healing.

A hospital was built like this to battle infection, but this place was built to cultivate fear. To glory in a blank canvas and revel in the splash of blood against white stone. Ordered against the chaos of torture. This was a dungeon only Radovan could devise.

A cold wind that only I could feel washed across my skin, leaving a terrible numbness in its wake. I'd miscalculated. I'd made my last mistake. Pushed Zosha and Qaden too far. This was it. Fifteen days of freedom. But the rest?

Radovan's teeth glittered in the harsh light. "Shall we?"

No.

No, this wasn't the end of anything. Not yet. *Snap the hell out of it*, I thought fiercely, willing my fear back and locking it down.

I met Radovan's eyes. Squared my shoulders. Nodded.

With that amused smile set, Radovan and I walked alone down the prison's main corridor—"main" because I was sure there had to be many of them, a whole network of cages riddling the island's bedrock. But as we passed one cell and the next, I began to wonder.

They were small, perhaps eight feet square, but completely sparse. No beds. No worktables. No iron hooks or chains hanging expectantly from the walls and ceilings. It was uniformity at its most terrifying, but it also presented a puzzle. Because as much as this place glowed with the promise of violence it was, to a cell, completely empty.

Our footsteps echoed down the hall, and Lady Night save me, I had an image of living in fear of such a sound. Growing dread narrowed my vision as we walked that unending corridor. So much that I stumbled when Radovan finally stopped.

I looked up, saw his smile widen. Saw his cold eyes flick to the left. I raised my chin. And looked.

And found a man looking back at me.

"Tada," Radovan murmured in my ear, one hand fanning out as if offering me the sweetest of delicacies.

An eternity of confusion hummed in my mind. Followed by recognition. Then shock. "Goran?"

I'd often fantasized about what I would do if I ever saw my cousin again. I'd delighted in daydreams of torture and punishment for the traitor who sold Seravesh for a crown, who orchestrated the murder of our grandfather and welcomed Roveni armies with open arms. This was the man who allowed the burning of Nadym and Kavondy and who had the deaths of thousands on his hands.

But not once did I imagine finding him in a Roveni prison. Never did I think that my second-greatest enemy would be served to me on the proverbial platter by the first.

I stepped closer, looking past my own reflection in the cell's glass door. Prison life was not agreeing with Goran. He was a tall man, my cousin, but he was so folded into the corner of the room, long arms wrapped around longer legs, it was hard to tell. He'd grown gaunt. His eyes and cheeks were sunken, skin stretched painfully thin over his skull. A full and scraggily beard covered half his face—he must be dying to shave it, my poor vain cousin. A smile almost cracked the ice covering my face.

Then I saw his wrists. They poked out of his white tunic, brittle as stuffed hay in a scarecrow. His skin, pale as the walls around him, was mottled blue-black with a ring of bruises that made my heart still. More bruises gathered in the gap of his collar and danced a faint trail all the way up the left side of his face.

I met his blazing blue eyes, and knew that despite injury and fear, he recognized me too. I saw the hopelessness in that gaze, the despair, and found to my surprise that I could not rejoice in it.

"What is this?" I asked, turning to Radovan.

He'd come to my side, watching me watch Goran with a satisfied tilt to his smile. "I suppose you could call it an engagement present," he replied, his voice so merry it coated the walls in an invisible layer of filth.

I managed not to frown, but it was a very near thing. "You're giving me Goran?"

"I'm giving you his death," he clarified, his brow furrowing when I didn't reply. "Don't you like it? Don't you want his death—for all he's done to Seravesh?"

The tiny hairs on the back of my neck writhed, as I tried to respond both truthfully and in a way that wouldn't shatter the tattered remnants of my soul. "Yes. The penalty for his betrayal was always death," I replied, trying—and failing—to not look at Goran as I spoke.

Radovan beamed. "And I'm going to see it done, Askia. For you." One of his skeletal hands found my shoulder and I struggled not to recoil.

"When?" I asked, hating the weakness in my voice.

"The new year's feast is in five days' time," he replied. "I thought it would be the perfect time to begin making amends to you, my love. We will put Seravesh to rights. Together."

"What do you mean, put Seravesh right?"

Ozura shimmered into existence just over Radovan's shoulder. She must have heard my fear echo through the Marchlands and come.

"Stay calm, Askia."

It was always so easy for ghosts to say this to me in the most horrible moments. But despite the inane words of comfort, and the anger I still felt toward her, I was glad she was here. Glad I wasn't alone.

"We must begin to rebuild," Radovan replied, like the idea was a novel one—one that only he could have ever thought of. "And come spring, we will."

We. The word hung between us, a promise dangling from a tree. If Radovan was going to keep to his thirty-day schedule, I'd be cold in the ground long before the first month of the new year ended. But the way he was speaking now, made it sound like . . .

"Would you like that?"

"Of course, I would," I murmured, and damn me to Lady Night's darkest hell, I wanted to believe him—I wanted to live.

"Askia." Ozura barked my name, panic lancing through her voice.

"*I know,*" I snapped back.

Because it was a lie. Of course it was a lie. All Radovan's promises were lies. But what made them so convincing was that *he* believed them. It was how he'd turned Goran, and how Dobor turned Enver. It was what made Radovan so dangerous. He believed everything he said, until the moment he changed his mind. And then, all bets were off.

"I thought you would."

He smiled, leaning against the glass door to Goran's cell. A lock of reddish-brown hair, like dried and crusted blood, fell into his eyes. How many times had I seen Iskander lean toward me in just that way, drawing me in with flattery and flirting? And at least I had brotherly affection for Iskander.

My gut rolled over on itself.

"We're going to do wonderful things, you know. First in Seravesh, and then in Vishir."

Ozura took a stuttering step forward. I tried not to notice her, or the way her face tightened. Instead, I smiled.

"I noticed you skipped over Idun, there. Cocky, aren't you?"

He laughed. "Idun is a foregone conclusion. You know that. Especially with what I have planned for Vishir."

"What plans?"

My chest constricted at the way Ozura's ghostly visage flickered. I wanted to go to my knees and beg for information or bat my eyes with false flattery for more. To plead for why he was skipping over Idun—and Arkady and my Black Wolves—like their defeat was already complete. But that wouldn't work.

Radovan wasn't interested in my weakness. I forced my eyebrows to rise with doubt, let my smile turn condescending. "You have plans for Vishir? Please, it's the middle of winter. Even if it wasn't, you just said you weren't going to march on Idun yet. And in case your grasp of geography is rusty, I'll remind you that you can only reach Vishir through Idun."

"My love, your doubt, it wounds me." He pressed a hand to his chest, his voice velvety with mirth. "I can't have you thinking so little of me, so I'll let you in on a secret: I know how to ensure Vishir is too busy with its own troubles to aid poor Idun at all."

"And that is?"

"Civil war."

My smile almost flickered, would have flickered had I not forced the muscles in my face to freeze. "Civil war? There hasn't been more than an uprising in Vishir in what—fifty years? That kind of unrest takes a long time to brew, and you're going to do it in a matter of months? It's not possible, not unless . . ."

Not unless things between Iskander and Enver had taken a turn for the worse. Unless their animosity had bloomed and their opposing allies were pulling them further and further apart. Unless the war for the Lion Throne was pulling *Vishir* apart.

Black and gray splotches appeared in Ozura's body, as if her despair were interfering with her cohesion. *"What is happening to my son!"*

"What have the princes done?" I asked, injecting my voice with all the ice currently flowing through my blood from the tether's bite.

"Nothing . . . *yet*. But their impasse cannot last forever, and their willingness to rule jointly is wearing thin. With what you've told me about the Shazir, and Prince Iskander's reckless alliance with them—I know I can push Vishir over the edge. All it will take is just a little bit of pressure. A touch here, a nudge there, and Vishir will fall."

I blocked out Ozura's terrified gasp, bending my focus entirely on Radovan. "You make it sound so easy. Yes, the princes are young, but there are older and wiser people around them who will council restraint. Civil war won't come so easily," I said, no longer sure if I was speaking to Radovan or Ozura.

Radovan just laughed. "You're forgetting how wonderfully

ambitious young men can be. Still," he said, a wolfish gleam in his eye as he bent closer to me. "Want to bet?"

There was only one answer. I felt my mouth twitch a smile. "Yes."

His eyes burned across my face, lingering for a long and terrifying moment on my lips. "I thought you might." He stepped back, grinning. "It's almost midday. Dine with me?"

I nodded, ignoring the ocean of acid in my gut. "But Goran—" I looked toward my cousin, forcing an unforgiving coldness into my eyes. "May I have a moment to speak with him?"

One of his eyebrows rose. "Have some things you need to say?"

"Didn't you, when you finally bested your treacherous uncle?"

"Yes, yes I did." He smirked, clearly happy to understand and be understood. Radovan reached forward and slid back a small window in the door. "Take as long as you need."

You did well," Ozura murmured as Radovan walked away. Her voice was hollow and spent. She looked terrible, I thought. Afraid.

"*You should be in Vishir right now. With Iskander. Not here haunting me. Day Lord protect us, what if Radovan was telling the truth? What if he has a way to push Vishir into war? Is it possible?*"

"*Without someone to lead them? Without Armaan, or me—or you. Yes.*"

"*Me?*" I shook my head. "*Maybe with Armaan alive I could have helped, but now?*"

"*Now you are the last queen of Vishir. You are the empress that should have been, and Iskander and Enver aren't the only ones who know it. You can unite Vishir. But—*"

"*But only if I get out of here. Now.*"

Ozura nodded. "*Your time is up, Askia. I'm sorry about your friend, and I'll do anything you ask of me. But you have to get to Vishir.*"

"Who are you talking to?"

I flinched and turned in one haphazard motion, not sure if I was more surprised to hear an apology leaving Ozura's lips, or my cousin's voice. Goran stood, breath a faint fog on the glass, looking down at me with unveiled distaste.

"What do you mean?"

"You have that look in your eyes," he said, his voice barely more than a rasp, raw from disuse. Or screaming.

I shuddered. "What look?"

"That distant, thousand-yard stare you get when you're seeing something no one else can see." He huffed a laugh. Shook his head. "I used to think you were mad, you know. It made perfect sense when Radovan told me you were a death witch."

My eyes narrowed. "What else did Radovan tell you, Goran. To make you betray your people and your family."

"You're not my family," he hissed. "You're just the bitch who usurped my throne."

"It was never your throne."

"But it should have been," he cried, a blotchy flush staining his gray-white cheeks. "I was groomed my whole life to be king after Grandfather. The Frozen Crown was mine. Until you came along, delivered out of nowhere broken and mute, and suddenly nothing else mattered to the old man."

I snorted. "Our grandfather wasn't some sentimental fool. He barely took one look at me that first year."

"Perhaps. Or perhaps you were simply too young to realize the truth of it. That seeing you was painful. He looked at you and all he saw was his daughter. And suddenly I was nothing."

"That's your excuse?" I said, my voice so cold it should have shattered the glass.

"That's what you wanted, wasn't it?" he replied, looking so tired. "When you asked to speak with me?"

It wasn't. What I really wanted was a moment to think, a

moment to indulge in panic before stuffing it away where Radovan wouldn't see it. But now that we were here, face to face, I realized Goran was right. I did want to understand why he had so thoroughly betrayed us.

"Maybe it is," I admitted. "Maybe that explains why you listened to Tcheshin when he came to Solenskaya that spring. But it doesn't explain the rest. It doesn't explain Grandfather's murder. Or Nadym. Or Kavondy."

Goran flinched, like my words were the pelting of rocks hitting his flesh. "Grandfather wasn't supposed to die," he whispered, almost too soft to hear. "Tcheshin's men were supposed to take you, secure the throne for me, and go. Grandfather would have been imprisoned, but he would live."

The naivete was almost breathtaking. Our grandfather? Going quietly into prison? Never. "You didn't know him at all if you thought he'd allow that while he still lived."

Goran wilted in on himself, but any pity I'd felt at seeing him like this was long gone. "What about Nadym?" I asked. "Kavondy?"

He shook his head, trying to fend off my words. "As soon as you and the Wolves began fighting back, my reign was over. Branko put himself in charge. He was the one who orchestrated all that destruction. There was nothing I could do."

"There is always something."

"No," he cried. "No there isn't. Look at me now—five days from death and tell me there's something I can do. Look at yourself, standing there at Radovan's side and tell me you're any better."

"I am fighting," I snarled. "To my last breath, I will fight. Will you?"

The question just slipped out of me. I didn't even know where it had come from. Except once spoken, I knew it was right. I knew it as surely as I saw Goran's head perk up.

And oh, it was cruel, the idea that took root in my mind. Cruel and deceitful and might slowly kill everything good inside me. But . . .

But I was needed in Idun and Vishir.

"What are you saying? Will I fight? What does that—"

I shook my head, eyes cutting to a blank patch of empty air to my left. "No. He's not strong enough to do it. He'll just betray us again."

"No, I won't," Goran said, pressing his hands up to the glass. "Who are you talking to?"

"To Grandfather, of course," I replied, barely glancing at him before turning my gaze back to empty air. "It's a bad idea." I shook my head. "I doubt *I* could do it, much less this traitor."

"Don't tell me what I can or can't do," Goran said, desperate now. "What are you planning."

"What am I planning?" I asked, cold and incredulous. "I'm planning to kill Radovan."

He drew back, eyes bright with hope and desire. "You are?"

"Yes, but for some reason Grandfather thinks you're the man to wield the knife. Like we could ever trust you to go through with it."

"Me? What do you mean? When?"

"At the execution. Radovan likes to be close to his kills, doesn't he? You'll be in the perfect position." I let my face fold into lines of doubt, as I watched fear creep into his features.

"But I'd be killed."

That made me laugh. "You're already dead, Goran. The question is: When you face Grandfather in five days' time, will he see a coward? Or a patriot?"

My words seemed to rattle around Goran's skull, but I knew I'd found my mark. The hope for redemption, desperate and suicidal though it was, was too good to pass up. Because even though he wasn't a good man, my cousin, he wanted to be.

"He'll never succeed," Ozura whispered in my ear.

"He's not meant to," I replied, hating how cold I sounded.

"Then why?"

I refused to acknowledge the accusation in her words. *"Because I'll need a distraction to escape."*

"I'll do it," Goran said, glowing with the manic shine of a man who had only one purpose left. "But how?"

I glanced down the corridor, but neither the guards nor Radovan was paying attention to me. Bending over like I had an itch, I pulled Qaden's dagger out of my boot, slid it through the little window and into Goran's hungry hands.

"Are you sure you can do this?" I asked, my voice softening despite my undimmed anger and ever-growing guilt.

"Yes," he murmured, looking at the blade like it was the hand of the Day Lord's salvation. "I can do it."

I nodded. "Grandfather thinks so too. I have my doubts, but maybe you'll prove me wrong." I swallowed hard, afraid to imagine the hell Grandfather would someday give me for this deception. "Good luck, cousin. And good-bye."

18

I LEANED AGAINST the crenelated top of the castle's curtainwall and looked out at the city of Tolograd. The cold air scoured my lungs, and for the first time in two days, I made myself stop. I'd had two days of adrenaline pouring through my veins, of spending every moment clawing toward an escape plan. But I could feel my body giving way to exhaustion, whether or not I had time for it.

My spy ring of dead queens was running nonstop, locating the people who had access to the workshop, who had keys to chains, to doors and provisions. The pieces were coming together, all starting with Radovan's mistress, Anya.

One of the first secrets culled had become the most valuable, for where did her jilted husband work but in the workshop, guarding the witches and the Aellium stones for the man romancing his wife. I was getting closer, so close. And yet everything was still out of reach.

Because it was getting harder to find time to wield the information I'd so carefully, ruthlessly collected. With each day that passed, Radovan kept me closer and closer, like the ever-growing light of the Aellium stone on my chest were a beacon pulling him in. Not because he suspected me—he didn't seem to have any clue about my plans. It was because his perverse attachment to me was growing. He wanted my thoughts on everything from the important to the inane.

It felt like I'd spent the last forty-eight hours having two conversations at once. What I needed, desperately needed, was help. Living help. But my only two options had made it very clear they couldn't or wouldn't help.

Eliska appeared on the wall beside me, brow creased with open concern. *"Are you all right?"*

A gust of frigid air that only I could feel smacked me in the face. I embraced it, letting the tether take its dues as the price of speaking with Eliska. But Lady Night, was I freezing. *"Yeah,"* I replied, rubbing my eyes. *"Just a bit of a headache. How are the preparations going?"*

"You know how," she said with a disapproving sigh. *"Slowly. Possibly too slowly for the insanely tight schedule you've put us on."*

"Muster up the courage to look those witches in the face and then tell me to wait," I said, unwilling to bend. *"I don't have a choice, Eliska. Illya came here to rescue me. I can't leave him."* The memory of Illya's face flashed into my mind, the way his gray eyes filled with hope. And terror. I wouldn't leave him, wouldn't let him go. Not again. No matter what the queens said.

Each of them had tried to convince me I was rushing into things. That I didn't have time to organize an escape for myself, let alone fifty weak and starving witches. But there was no time for anything else. And I'd rather act than passively wait for Radovan to choose my fate.

At least I had Ozura on my side. Though Ozura's desire to go back to Vishir, to reach Iskander, was both palpable and painful. The strength of her panic . . . part of me wondered if her judgment was becoming questionable.

Vitaly appeared, as if summoned by my unease. He shared a heavy glance with Eliska. *"You still want to push through with the escape, don't you?"*

I drew back a half step. *"What do you mean? Don't you want me to? I can save Illya and myself, get back to Vishir—"*

"That's Ozura talking. You're gambling your one chance at escape with a plan you know is reckless at best, and Ozura is pushing you into it."

I scoffed. *"She is not pushing me into anything. Yes, she's eager to return to Vishir, but so am I. Vishir is in trouble, and I can't let it fall into civil war."*

"Vishir isn't your responsibility," Vitaly said, voice brimming with impatience.

"But it is. I was meant to be empress—"

"What was meant to be ceased to be anything when Armaan died. Think about what kind of claim you really have—unconsummated wife to a dead emperor does not make you a queen, let alone an empress. Not when two full-blooded heirs are there to succeed the throne." He raked a hand through his hair as if frustrated by my own lack of sight. *"Yes, Vishir is important, but it was only ever supposed to be a means to an end. And escaping here without a plan so you can rush into yet another conflict with no information is a bad move."*

My face was numb from the onslaught of Vitaly's words, from the truth in them. Whatever claim I had to the Lion Throne was rickety at best. And while I truly believed I could help Vishir . . . did Ozura? Did she really think I could help? Or would she just say anything to get me—to get *us*—closer to Iskander again?

"Why, whatever is happening here?" Ozura's body seemed to boil from the ground like fog rising off a lake—too abrupt to be coincidence. I frowned at the hard look in her eyes. At the way Vitaly subtly shifted his weight, widening his stance. Had she been waiting for Vitaly to come to me?

Eliska took a step closer, bridging the gap between all of us. *"Vitaly was just voicing his concerns about the haste of this plan. And truth be told, I think he might be right. This is reckless."* She turned to me. *"Radovan as good as said he wants to keep you at his side, perhaps even to rule with him. You have all the time you need to plan a proper escape with real, living allies."*

Ozura's attention flew to me, smiling smugly when I shook my head.

Impossible, and not only because each day at Radovan's side made me feel increasingly complicit in his crimes. There was danger in the affection of a man like Radovan. *"That's not an option, Eliska, and you know it isn't. Eventually Radovan will ask for something I can't—I won't—give. It may be madness to go through with the escape, but I still think it's my only chance to get out of Roven alive."*

Eliska's diaphanous face twisted, and if it were possible for ghosts to be sick, I would have taken a step back. She swallowed. *"You're right. I'm sorry,"* she said, bowing her head. *"What can I do?"*

"What you've been doing. And, well . . . you can pray."

I turned around, the sight of the city lying just out of reach suddenly too much to bear. I cast my gaze across the courtyard. Everything seemed so normal, so calm. Just like in my first few days in Tolograd, the yard was filled with nobles, young and old, walking along shoveled paths or playing in the snow. Soldiers sparred near the barracks and servants hurried to and fro decorating the castle with evergreen wreaths and streamers and lights.

Radovan was closeted with his generals, the only time he ever let me out of his sight, it seemed. Though I needed the reprieve from his company, it was those very meetings I desperately wanted to be at.

Even having one of the queens there to listen in was a pale substitute for being there in person. Not when Radovan's every fleeting expression might offer some further clue as to the dark roads down which his twisting mind traveled. *No point in getting sidetracked on it*, I thought. I needed to keep moving.

The castle doors swung open and a familiar figure exited. Zosha paused on the steps, scanning the crowd. Then his gaze found mine. He frowned and cut across the yard, hurrying up the curtainwall's slippery steps.

He looked haggard, I thought. His normally pale skin was washed out and dark purplish circles bruised his eyes.

"He hasn't been sleeping," Ragata said, appearing at his side, wringing her hands together.

"Yeah well, planning a murder can be hell on the conscience," I shot back without an ounce of mercy.

"Hello, Zosha."

He nodded. "Askia." Zosha pressed his lips together, eyes dancing past me across the battlements, but more words didn't come.

His hands clenched and unclenched, almost like he was trying to work himself up for something. In someone else I might have thought he was getting ready to take his shot, but I didn't think he had the backbone to try and kill me when we were alone, much less in front of half the court and three-dozen highly trained Voyniks.

"What do you want, Zosha?"

"I want to help." The words spilled out of him in a softly spoken rush.

My eyes narrowed. "With what?"

"With your escape."

It was not what I was expecting at all.

He whispered the last word, stepping closer. His gaze was so intense, it was like a physical weight. There was fear there, but there was also resolve.

"Please, Askia, give him a chance," Ragata said, her voice weak, pleading.

"Why?" I asked, aiming the question at them both.

"I know you don't trust him," Ragata said, leaping into an

answer while Zosha's face worked, sifting through words. *"But I promise this isn't some kind of elaborate trap. Listen to him, I beg you. Listen, and . . . and take him with you. Don't let him stay imprisoned here."*

Ragata's words thawed something inside of me. Not only because she was a mother desperately struggling against the veil of death to help her child, but because it was Ragata. Poor, half-mad Ragata, who could barely string more than two sentences together unless it was to do with architecture. Yet here she was, forcing herself into a lucidity that made her ghostly body flicker.

But it wasn't enough. It wasn't enough to hear this man's mother make his case for him. I needed to hear it, hear why, in his own words. "Why, Zosha? Why should I trust you?"

"Maybe you shouldn't," he said, speaking through bloodless lips. "But Askia, I've been watching you, we all have, for weeks now. With barely any magic, and without a single friend, you've managed to take control of the entire court. The Dorovnii answer to you now—you see that, don't you? Even the Voyniks are sympathetic. I mean, do you know how rare it is for Qaden to befriend anyone? Let alone one of the witch queens? And Radovan listens to every word you say like it's been handed down from Lady Night Herself."

"And yet you're here, wanting to help me leave. Not stay?"

"No," he said, shaking his head quickly. "You *have* to leave. Because if you can do all of this alone, in less than a month—and with your death hanging over you—imagine what you could do with Vishir behind you."

Or with Vishir's help, I mentally amended, mouth quirking from the memory of Vitaly's words. Still, Zosha made a very good case, I had to admit it. If only to myself. But . . .

"What about Illya?"

Zosha's shoulders dropped a half inch. "He was caught five days ago coming through a portal in Kirskov. There were twenty witches with him, but . . . but Radovan's men were waiting for them. They were outnumbered two to one. Your man nearly destroyed the palace creating a diversion. And was caught. The Voyniks are still hunting the rest."

Twenty witches? Where did they come from? Vishir? I shook the thoughts away, useless that they were in this moment. Only one question mattered now.

"Does Radovan know who he is? To me?"

Understanding settled heavily in Zosha's gaze. "I don't know. But you'd be the last person he'd tell."

"Why?"

He gave a halfhearted shrug. "He wants your affection. Your love."

"At least until he needs something from me." There was a terrible, bitter taste on my tongue. "Five days," I murmured. "Five days ago, you let my friend be imprisoned without telling me. Four days ago, you were ready to die killing me for your Nines. Now you want to help me? It's a quick turnaround, Zosha. You really expect me to believe that you and the other Nines aren't going to kill me the first chance they get?"

"I know my motivations look suspicious," he said, grabbing my arm, willing me to listen, to believe. "But I've already gone to the other Nines. Convinced them it's worth a chance."

"It's true, Askia," Ragata added, looking as desperate as her son. *"I was there when he went to them. They agreed to give him this chance."*

"But why?" I demanded, my chest filling with doubt. *"Why would they agree now, when they wouldn't before? What if they only agreed to ease Zosha's mind—because they knew he wasn't strong enough to do the deed? What if they're sending someone else to finish me off?"*

"They didn't. I was watching them after Zosha left," Ragata said, pleading now. *"They're giving you a chance, both of you. They even*

gave him poison in case he gets caught. Please, Askia. Please. Don't make him stay in a place where his only allies see him as expendable."

I looked away from the pain in Ragata's voice. "*It still feels like it could be a trap.*"

"*Does that matter if it is?*" Eliska asked, watching me from between Ozura and Vitaly. "*You need help—living help. If Zosha is willing to give it to you . . .*" Her words trailed off and she shrugged. "*Can you afford not to take it?*"

"Please, Askia, I can help. I'm guessing you have a way out of the castle, but what about a way out of Roven?"

My ears perked up, and Zosha smiled, like he knew he'd said the magic words. "You don't have anything on that yet do you? Well, you're in luck. The portal your friend used to reach you— the one in the Kirskov Summer Palace—there are more of them there. They will be guarded, but Radovan has a whole network of portals. They lead all the way from here to the southern tip of Vishir."

Kirskov . . . The word sparkled in my mind. "*If I could get to Kirskov, I could get to the Heart. And if I reached it, I could destroy it. Without stolen magic at his disposal Radovan and his whole sorcerous army would be nothing—or nothing more than any other foe.*"

"*Now this is a plan,*" Vitaly said, body crackling with excitement.

Eliska's response was more cautious. "*But Radovan will still be able to find you through the stone,*" she said, eyes dipping to where the stone lay beneath my coat.

"*That was always going to be the case,*" I replied. I'd taken to hiding the necklace beneath my clothing ever since Radovan revealed he could see me through it. Still, I couldn't help but grimace at the thought of all the times he could have been watching me, spying on me. "*If I'm careful to keep the stone covered, though, he won't be able to see my exact location, just a general sense of where I am.*"

"*It's not much,*" Vitaly allowed. "*You'll have to be fast.*"

"*No.*" Ozura pushed between us, cutting so close to my body that the feeling of frozen spiderwebs lingered on my skin.

"*No?*" I asked, refusing to step back. "*What do you mean, 'no'?*"

"*I mean you can't bother with the Heart. Not now. It's too much of a risk. You must get to the portals and get to Vishir. You're needed there.*"

The sheer desperation in her voice . . . I almost didn't recognize her. "*Ozura, I know you're worried that I might get caught,*" I began, willing her to calm down. "*But don't you see? If I could release the souls trapped in the Heart, Radovan would be powerless. Hell, his entire army would be powerless. Think about what that could mean—not just here either, but in Vishir too. The Shazir have been using the stones and captured witches to manufacture the drought. Without the stones, the drought is over. We could expose them for what they really are.*"

"*You must not expose the Shazir.*"

This time I did step back. "*What did you just say to me?*"

Ozura's eyes widened, as if realizing her misstep. She wet her lips nervously, this once-fearsome queen of Vishir. "*You can't expose the Shazir. Not yet. Who else is supporting Iskander's claim to the throne? Without the Shazir behind him, Iskander will be vulnerable. Enver will kill him.*"

"*So will Khaljaq,*" I replied, coldly. "*Yes, Khaljaq will support Iskander's bid for the throne, but once he gets it? Iskander will be disposable. Don't think for a moment Khaljaq wouldn't have Iskander killed at the first sign of disobedience. Or me.*"

"*You're strong, Askia. If you return to Vishir, claim your right as queen, you could marry Iskander. Between the two of you, it would be enough to take the throne. After that, if things calm down, then you could expose the Shazir, but—*"

"*After what?*" I asked, my mirthless laugh drawing a confused look from Zosha. I held up a hand to wait and looked at Ozura.

Really looked at her. *"You're honestly willing to feed Iskander to Khaljaq? And if that wasn't soul-crushing enough, you want me to what, seduce him? Lie to him? Say that I loved him all along and was only confused? We can put aside how shitty your opinion of me must be to think I'd agree to that—what I want to know is how could you do that to Iskander? Your son."*

"He is my son—that's how. And I will not lose another son!" she cried. *"I will do whatever it takes to keep him alive. Why do you think I swore my soul to yours? Because you'd earned it? No. How else was I to reach Iskander if not through you?"*

"And now you're here, half a world away. Trapped while I try to outmaneuver a monster to save my life and stop him before Roven and Vishir tear the world apart. You're right. I'm simply not doing enough."

Ozura's shoulders slumped. She scrubbed her face with her hands, and when they fell away, all her armor fell with it. I'd never seen her more tired. Or scared. *"You've weathered loss before, Askia. I know you have—and I don't mean to minimize it. But for all the horror you've witnessed, you cannot possibly understand what it is to lose a child. When Tarek died, I swore I would do anything—* anything—*to keep Iskander safe. It's not that what you're doing here isn't important. But please, Askia. I'm begging you. Put Iskander first."*

I closed my eyes as if it could guard me from the begging of so great a woman brought low. From the promise I could not give.

When I opened my eyes again, I was a queen—the queen *Ozura* had made me.

"You once told me that Seravesh wasn't more important than the rest of the world. I'm sorry, Ozura, but neither is Iskander. What Radovan is doing, the power he has—it has to end. It has to end now."

Ozura's face crumpled. She fell to her knees, disappearing into the gray sunlight.

"Please," Zosha said, oblivious to the second conversation swirling around him. "I know you must think I'm a coward. But please, Askia, let me have a chance to be different. Better."

I tutted, pushing the memory of Ozura's cries away. "I don't think you're a coward Zosha. Believe me, there's nothing cowardly in not taking a life."

Could I afford to reject his help? Honestly? No. Not with Radovan hovering over me like a dark cloud and the days slipping by faster than the river below. I needed help, told Eliska to pray. And the Two-Faced God had answered with a two-faced ally.

I turned back to him, crossing my arms. "Fine. You want in, you're in."

Zosha's shoulders fell two inches in height. "Thank you, Askia."

"Don't thank me yet. You start now."

He frowned. "With what?"

"I need a distraction."

Zosha raised a hand as we made our way to where the northernmost watchtower rose from the curtainwall. There was a narrow door just ahead whose stairs led to the top of the tower. I could just make out a fire burning from within the interlocking strands of the copper dome. I saw a flash of white teeth from the man on duty, before he ducked away.

I glanced back at Zosha, who flushed in the echo of the soldier's boots on stone stairs. He shrugged, somehow looking both chagrined and self-satisfied. The watchtower door opened before I could comment, and young private Dimitri hurried out.

"Lord Zosha. Your Majesty," he said, eyes bright as he snapped a bow. "How can I be of service?"

"We were just going for a stroll," Zosha replied, rubbing a hand over his mouth to hide his smile.

"And are you having a pleasant walk?"

"I was, only—" I shook my head in false embarrassment. "I've been here for how many days, yet somehow I keep underestimating how cold it is. Any chance I could warm up by your watchfire?"

"Oh." Dimitri glanced quickly back at the tower. "I'm not on duty alone today. Lieutenant Roshko is on watch with me."

My smile deepened, and I blinked rapidly in feigned confusion. As if I wasn't well aware of Roshko's presence here—of how he'd been picking up extra shifts since his wife's disappearance, even ones well beneath his station, like a man desperate to keep busy. "I don't think I've ever met him."

"He's . . . not one for conversation," Dimitri confessed in what I was sure was his best approximation of discretion.

"I see. Well, if you let me go up, I promise not to disturb him. Please, Private?"

Zosha nudged the younger man. "Come on, Dimitri, have a heart. I'll keep you company here while Her Majesty warms herself."

Zosha's company was all the incentive Dimitri needed. He grinned, pulling the door open for me with a flourish. I smiled as I passed, pausing only to glance at Zosha with a hint of warning in my eyes. *Keep Dimitri out of the way,* I said silently. Zosha's answering smile was a tight one, but it was there.

I suppressed a fatalistic urge to laugh as I started up the stairs. With Zosha's lukewarm help at my back, what was there to worry about? Only a betrayed husband who all my sources said was fraying at the seams.

Reaching the top of the guard tower, I had to admit the description was an apt one. Lieutenant Roshko stood with his back to me, hands tight on the railing. He was looking north, face unreadable from where I stood, but even from this angle, there wasn't an unrumpled inch of uniform on him. The hem was falling out of his left trouser leg, his boots were scuffed, and soot stained the back of his coat.

I cleared my throat. He whirled, hands dropping instinctively to his sword as I forced a vacant smile. His eyes widened as he took me in from across the great brazier in the center of the tower. The flames leapt in their grate, painting twisting portraits on the inside of the copper dome.

Between their light and the weak winter sun, I could see the heavy bags beneath Roshko's eyes. Tight lines bracketed his mouth. And I saw the glittering Aellium stone pinned crookedly to his uniform.

"Your Majesty," he said, his back spasming in a slight bow. "Forgive me, I didn't hear you come in."

I forced myself to look away from the stone. To smile. "I apologize if I've startled you. I was just hoping to borrow some of your warmth," I continued, holding my hands up to the flames. "You don't mind, do you?"

His lips twitched a grimace, screaming that he very much did mind. "Not at all, my lady."

"Thank you, that's very kind, Lieutenant Roshko."

He almost turned away. "You know my name?"

"I do," I replied, the very agreeableness of my tone a kind of swipe. "I've made it something of a habit since coming here, learning about the members of Radovan's court."

"But I am not a member of court, my lady."

The reply almost made me laugh. I knew that tone, that depthless disdain for the nobility. I'd used the same one more than once. "And yet yours is a name I've heard before."

"No doubt because of my wife. Her father is Count Parimatov."

I made a noncommittal noise. "And how is Anya?"

His hands curled at his sides. His nostrils flared. I widened my stance incrementally. Here was a man who teetered on the edge of control. One who just needed a little push.

"She is well."

I cocked my head to one side. "Of course you don't really know that, do you?" I asked, hating myself for the blade that was on my tongue.

"I don't know what you mean."

"Yes, you do" was my flat reply.

"I send letters every week."

"Letters that go unanswered. Don't you wonder why?"

Anger rolled across Roshko's face. He took a single step forward, ready for a fight. "What business is it of yours?" he spat, skin splotchy and red. "She's at a religious retreat. She's busy in prayer and—"

"You can't be that gullible," I said without a trace of mercy. "You might not know where she is, but you know she's not at the temple in Vozen. But you're in luck. Because I do."

His expression twisted. "Where?"

"That information will cost you."

Blood drained from his face. He rounded the brazier, stalking forward, daring me to back down. "What do you want?"

It was impossible to hide from the disgust in his words. To fend off the accusation that I was no better than the enemies I so hated. I resisted the urge to apologize, to tell him everything and offer sympathy, but I couldn't afford softness. Not if I wanted to save Illya.

Of all the reasons I had to put Roshko through all this pain, saving Illya was the most selfish. I refused to flinch from that truth. But if my . . . love for Illya drove me to this, it was Roshko's love for his wife that could free us from the shadow of Radovan's rule. If I could convince Roshko to help me.

"I want access," I said, holding his blazing gaze with one of my own. "I want you to leave your keys to the witches and their collars unsecured in your desk for the rest of this week."

His right hand shot out, grabbing my jaw so hard his fingers would leave bruises. "You go too far," he whispered, shoving me into the edge of the brazier with enough force my spine cracked.

The stone on his chest flashed green and the flames arched out around me, licking my spine and neck. They snapped at the end of my braid, filling the air between us with the stench of burning hair.

"Why would I betray my emperor?"

"Because he betrayed you first," I replied, refusing to show an inch of the fear that swarmed through me with each rolling drop of sweat. "Think, Bora," I continued, willing him to listen. "No one leaves this city without Radovan's leave. And yet your wife is allowed to waltz out the front gates?"

"I am a loyal servant."

"So loyal, you weren't even allowed to say good-bye?" I shot back, throwing the heartbreaking detail I'd gleaned from Anya's mother into his face. "That she wasn't even allowed to pack a bag before she left?"

"The temple will provide for her needs."

"No. Radovan is providing for her needs. Open your eyes, Bora. After the years you spent serving him faithfully, why is it that you've been pulling night shifts these past few months?"

"I serve when I'm called."

"A lieutenant standing guard alone? All night? Every night? Strange way to reward your loyalty. Or were you only needed to do a private's job after you married your pretty young wife?"

Something shattered behind Bora's dark eyes, something vital but so, so delicate.

"You know I'm right," I said, softer now, feeling the flames gutter at my back. "You've seen the hunger in his eyes when he watches her. The desire. The possession."

"No."

"Twelve years of service. Ten years on front lines, and you return home not only to a grateful nation, but to an emperor who calls you a friend. He arranged for your marriage when Anya's parents objected. He even gave you that stone.

"All it cost was your wife."

"No." He fell back a few steps, releasing me to claw at his ears like he could unhear my words. But he'd had enough of lies. Cruel as it was, it was time for the truth.

"Yes, Bora. You know I'm right," I said again. "You know she's not at the temple."

I waited, letting the silence stretch, letting him take the next step. The step away from Radovan. Toward me.

"Where is she?" It was practically a whisper.

"The Kirskov Summer Palace."

He closed his eyes as if my words were a blow. No. Not as if. They were a blow, because he knew what happened at Kirskov—why young women were sent there year in and year out. He knew. But the knowing wouldn't lessen the pain.

Guilt rose up my throat. It seeped out of my pores, coating me in a sticky sheen of shame. I had tried to play politics in Vishir, straining against the game in a place where I was ostensibly welcome. I wasn't this person, this hard woman who traded in secrets and pain. Who scarified other people for gain.

But if it helped Illya and me escape? If it got us to Kirskov so we could destroy the Heart? Then Lady Night save me, this slow destruction of who I thought I was would be worth it.

Bora's eyes opened slowly, but I could tell from his expression that this wasn't a world he recognized. It was a new one. A lesser one. He said nothing for a long moment. Taking my measure, I thought. So I let him see.

I pried down the walls of ice and the mask of steel. I let him see past the fear that lay beside my heart to the despair that lined my shadow. The guilt. The resolve.

He nodded once, hand sliding into his pocket. "Take them," he said, voice a ragged wreck of what it once was. "I have spares."

The keys were warm in my palm. But it wasn't enough. "You'll make sure it's empty."

He took a long breath. Nodded.

"Thank you."

"Curse you. Don't thank me. Punish him."

I let the key's teeth bite into my skin, leaving a bloody trail across my palm. "I will. Of that I can promise you."

19

THE DRESS WAS going to be a problem.

I peered into the wardrobe's narrow mirror at the confection of black fabric. Lace clung to the bodice, skimming the tips of my shoulders and down the tight sleeves. The lace continued on the full skirts and train, only now joined by plumes of black feathers that danced with my every exhalation.

It was a beautiful gown, undeniably so. But equally undeniable was its impracticality. For if everything went according to plan, I'd be fleeing the castle tonight, plunging into Tolograd's killing cold wearing nothing but these few yards of lace and silk.

No, not if. When.

I ran a hand over the skirts, as if smoothing imaginary wrinkles would soothe my anxiety too. A pang of longing echoed through me at the sight of those feathers, at the way they reminded me of Nariko. Only she had glowed in her white swan-like masquerade gown with all the poise and beauty of an untarnished soul. And me?

My hair was pinned up and coiled on my head. Jewels dripped from my ears and wrists, and a sharp-looking diamond tiara, like shards of ice, sat atop my head—nothing more than a pale imitation of the Frozen Crown of Seravesh. But for all the finery, for all the sumptuous fabrics and priceless gems, there was a tightness around my eyes that no amount of makeup could conceal.

I turned away from the reflection, trying to leave my worry behind. There was nothing more I could do. I would either escape tonight. Or I would die.

The skirts were full and heavy as I navigated the castle stairs with Qaden. I strained for grace, but every footfall only amplified the feeling of foreboding. If it was heavy now, when I was walking down a wide and clear staircase, how much heavier would it be when I made it outside?

My mind raced through all my carefully made plans again, and then again. If Zosha and the Nines had done their jobs, proper clothes would be waiting for us outside the city. It would simply be a matter of getting to them before hypothermia got me.

The swirling black waters of the River Tol flowed through my mind, both a taunt and a hope. It was our best chance at escape, that fierce river outside these castle walls. It ran so fast and strong that not even the killing Roveni cold could make it freeze. But as much as it could be our salvation, one misstep, one tiny slip, and it would be our doom.

I forced the thoughts away as we reached the bottom of the stairs. Radovan waited with two Voyniks and General Koloii. He turned as Qaden and I approached and bowed, his sickly eyes dancing over me, a smile deepening on his waxen face. "You look lovely, my dear," he said, brushing a kiss on the back of my hand. "As do you, Qadenzizeg."

Qaden and I gave identical wooden thank-yous, causing Qaden to shoot me a look of quiet laughter. It filled me with unexpected warmth. Bolstered by this tiny shred of camaraderie, I accepted Radovan's arm. Together, we swept into the Great Hall and found the party already in full swing. Nobles and high-ranking Voyniks packed the massive space. The swirling blue and white hall was filled with the echoing sounds of music and laughter. People milled about in small groups, talking and dancing and sampling food from the trays passed by discreet servants.

I trailed after Radovan, a dark shadow in his wake, and willed time to move. If the days leading up to the ball had slid past in gelatinous heaps, the hours leading to midnight seemed to stick, one yielding unwillingly to the next. Only the thought of Illya kept me going. If he could survive in that workshop of horrors, not knowing that rescue was coming, then I could manage a few hours of small talk and deception.

So I planted the mask on my face and clung to it with everything I was worth. I walked with Radovan among his simpering nobles and overconfident soldiers. And if it felt like being a planet orbited by many dizzying moons, then so be it.

With my eyes and ears wide open, I counted the number of Voyniks at the party. I thanked Lady Night when my count came in with far more soldiers indulging in food and drink than were currently on duty. It was a blessing I thought, then reevaluated when I heard someone talk about whole battalions being shipped out of the city.

They were heading for Raskis, one of the generals said, in a conversation I'd only been half listening to. Raskis, then on to Seravesh, and eventually Idun. It made something tear inside me, thinking of more Roveni soldiers heading into Seravesh, but that was a problem for tomorrow, for next week or next month. Tonight, it was something I had to be glad for.

My gaze went almost involuntarily to Zosha. After he'd made his hello to Radovan and me, he'd whiled the night away mingling with other Dorovnii, but now I found him near the workshop door smiling and talking with his dashing young Voynik friend.

"Who is Zosha speaking with?" Radovan asked, his lips brushing the tip of my ear.

"I believe his name is Dimitri," I replied, looking at Radovan through the sides of my eyes, gaging his reaction.

Radovan smiled. "Always did love a uniform, my Zosha."

"Who doesn't?" I said, almost managing a smile, before putting a hand to my stomach. I couldn't actually tell if I was hungry, too many stronger emotions whirled inside of me, but I knew I had to be, that I should eat with all that was coming next.

"Hungry dear?" Radovan asked, right on cue.

"I don't suppose you've seen a dessert tray?" was my careful reply. And just like that Radovan and I were heading off, away from Zosha and his guard. Away from the door. And if Lady Night was kind, Radovan wouldn't think of Zosha again, wouldn't watch him chatting up Dimitri. He wouldn't see Zosha passing the on-duty guard sugary sweets carefully dosed with just enough soporific to make him drowsy, to make him an easy target.

"Askia." Eliska appeared on my elbow. The force of her entrance was enough to make goose bumps rise on my skin. My hand stilled over a tray of chocolate truffles. I glanced toward her, and though it was only supposed to be fleeting, my gaze stuck.

Because Eliska, always composed and calm, was on the edge of tears. Her chest heaved with such undisguised panic. Her eyes were wide. Her mouth tight.

"What's wrong?" I asked, picking out a truffle with studied calm. I couldn't allow myself to feel her fear, not with Radovan's ever-present attention. *"Did something happen?"*

"No," she said, voice hitching on a sob. *"No, it's just . . . I did what you said I should. I went down to look them in the eye, and . . . and Lady Night save me, Askia—"*

A ragged cry tore out of Eliska's throat and I nearly reached for her hand, stopped myself just in time by taking a bite out of the truffle. *"Eliska, what is it? What did you see?"*

"My brother. Olexan."

I chewed slowly, hiding my confusion. *"What about him?"*

"He's down there."

My mouth filled with ash. It wasn't possible. The whole royal family of Raskis had died in the invasion. All four of her brothers had been killed . . . hadn't they? Now, though, she was telling me Olexan was not only alive, but here?

Eliska didn't wait for my confusion to clear. She seized my arm. Memories and sounds flooded into me, voices and faces and—

No. Not faces.

Just.

One.

Face.

My heart stopped dead in my chest, caught between one beat and the next. Lady Night, no. That face . . .

"Olexan—he's . . . he's down there, trussed up and chained and—"

"Are you all right, my dear?" Radovan touched my arm, and my awareness snapped back into my body so hard Eliska disappeared. The tether's cool touch fled and the sudden onset of warmth—and Radovan's scrutiny—brought an uncomfortable heat to my face.

I painted on a smile, nearly nodded—nearly lied through my teeth to change the subject. Nearly. But tonight was not the night to go back on my promise. If I lied now, it would all be over. His suspicion would ruin everything.

I let my eyes move over his shoulder, struggling to drown out the sound of my own internal scream. But Radovan didn't want my attention split. With the tip of a single finger he pulled my chin up. I had no choice but to look him in the eye.

Swallowing the mouthful of sludge-like chocolate, I exhaled hard through my nose. I strained for a truth—any truth—to of-

fer. "I'm finding myself feeling surprisingly nervous. About Goran. I know that he deserves this, that it must be done, but . . ." I
let my words trail off. Raised a shoulder. "Is that weak?"

I saw understanding—no, not that. Radovan wasn't capable
of true understanding, that required empathy, but a kind of aca-
demic curiosity grew in his eyes. "No, my dear. You are so very
young after all. No doubt you'll feel better when everything is
settled," Radovan said, patting my hand in an almost paternal
way. "Come. The time approaches."

The court parted before us, creating a path directly to our
empty thrones before Radovan so much as took a step toward
them. That was how attuned they were to his every movement. It
was almost magical. Like these people were nothing more than
puppets on strings. I suppressed a shudder as dread dragged its
long fingers down my spine.

Radovan handed me into my seat, and I made a show of ar-
ranging my long, cumbersome skirts to one side. Sweat slicked
my skin as the most dangerous part of the play began. I folded
my clammy hands together to keep from wiping them on my
dress. Instead, I pulled my back straight, shoulder blades skimming the seat.

Radovan raised an eyebrow.

I nodded.

He motioned, a flick of his pointer finger, and the Great
Hall's massive doors opened. Goran entered, flanked by two
Voyniks. He'd been cleaned up for the event. He was dressed
in head to toe white, the pristine sleeves of his immaculate coat
carefully hiding any lingering bruises. His face had been shaven,
and his hair combed tidily back. Somehow the effort only made
his face look gaunter, skeletal almost, like he was one foot in
death already.

If I didn't know better, I'd think Goran was no more than a
middling bureaucrat returning home after a long absence. But I

did know better. And though he walked sedately, I knew Goran was keenly aware of the clock ticking down to his demise. I saw it in the tightness of his spine, in the way his eyes darted around the room, in the way the guards escorted their unchained prisoner forward with their hands hovering above their blades.

Vitaly shifted at the corner of my sight, like he could feel the quiver of remorse worming through me and feared my resolve might falter. He needn't have worried. No matter my inner conflict, Goran's life was forfeit. Whether he died here by Radovan's hand, or in Seravesh by mine, his fate was sealed. At least this way, some good might come of it. If he distracted Radovan. If he pulled the Voyniks from the walls. If I escaped.

If. If. If . . .

All three men stopped at the foot of the dais. Their identical bows revealed a fourth member of the group. Freyda.

The ghost stepped quickly around the guards. *"The knife is up his left sleeve,"* she murmured in my ear before taking her post among the crowd of ghosts standing at my back.

I exhaled a half inch in height. Goran failing to secure the knife had been a very real possibility, one that I had planned for of course, but the chance of taking a shot at Radovan was too good to pass up.

My relief lasted all of two seconds. My heart leapt in my chest. The game began.

Qaden planted herself on the bottom step of the dais, one fist already closed around her sword. Her shiny new major bars glittered in the light. Zosha elbowed his way to the front of the crowd. I didn't dare look at him too long—didn't dare glance toward the workshop door.

The Aellium stone twitched against my breast, like it sensed my anxiety and hungered for more.

"Steady," Vitaly murmured.

"Lord Poritskii," Radovan said by way of greeting.

He leaned back in the throne, one ankle propped casually atop the other knee, hands folded in an attitude of prayer.

The pause stretched, until the wait for what was coming next became almost unbearable. Like a fish on a line, I felt drawn in, my whole body taut and tingling.

I clung to my mask and forced myself to think. For all its restlessness, the stone remained cold on my chest, and cold meant no magic. *Wait, Askia. Wait.*

"You've been brought before this court to answer for your actions in the Province of Seravesh," Radovan said at long last. "I hardly think it necessary to enumerate all your crimes."

"I disagree." Goran's voice was filled with so much venom it should have left blisters on his lips. "I haven't done anything wrong."

Gasps raced through the crowd as the watching men and women shifted. It was the first uneasy ripple in a wave of whispers that washed through the Great Hall. No one interrupted Radovan, and certainly not with such vehemence. Not even when they were already doomed.

The temperature dropped, and I felt the specter of past deaths rise from the too-clean floor and loom large over all of us. But Radovan had always been a man to glory in the fear of others.

"You claim to be innocent?" Radovan asked, head cocking to one side. "You stand here before the court of Roven, before your emperor, and claim you had no hand in the burning of Nadym and Kavondy?"

"That wasn't my fault," Goran said, face splotchy and red. "It was your men who did that. Your fire witch Branko and his gang of power-mad sorcerers committed those atrocities. Punish them."

"You do not punish a soldier for the commands of the general."

"General?" Goran said. The note of hysteria in his laughter

crashed off the tower walls and amplified into something else. Something tinged with madness. "I was never your general. I was your puppet. And when I so much as blinked wrong, you and yours took over. You want to blame someone for what happened to Nadym and Kavondy? Look in the mirror. But don't condemn me like any of this is my fault. You don't have that right."

If madness brushed the edges of Goran's voice, I saw a different kind of insanity flicker across Radovan's face. A darker mania for which I had no name.

"I have every right to punish my vassals. Especially when they use the authority I gave them to besmirch my name and befoul the reputation of the empire that I built with my own hands."

"Besmirch your name?" Goran exclaimed. "Look around your illustrious court. Go ahead. Use that fabled magic and find one man or woman here who actually believes your hands are clean. I dare you." Goran's arms flew wide and the Dorovnii closest to him recoiled. "What? No one willing to come forward. Of course not. Not when they know the true monster sits on the throne. Not when they see the beast lurking beneath your skin."

Qaden jumped down from the dais and for a terrible moment, I thought she was going to kill him. A cry welled up within me, catching beneath my ribs as I forced myself into stillness. Forced myself to watch. To wait. To pray.

Her fist barreled into his stomach in an odd answer to my prayer.

Goran doubled over, arms hugging his middle. He wheezed. Eyes bright with unshed tears, Goran looked up at Radovan, face filled with hate. "You style yourself ageless and immortal. Unchangeable. Look at you. Look at the woman next to you and tell me that sharing her bed hasn't changed your mind a time or two. No surprise really. Bastard get of a whorish mother—she's already seduced one emperor, why not two?"

"How *dare* you—" I shouted, pushing myself to my feet so hard my toes caught the inside of my gown. I stumbled, arms wheeling as one foot slipped off the top step. Radovan reached for me.

There was a great intake of breath. My body cut through the air. The eyes of the whole court followed me as I fell into Zosha's waiting arms.

Except Goran.

Goran straightened, the naked blade in his hand.

And threw it.

20

Radovan screamed.

Voyniks surged out of the crowd. Half went to Radovan, the other half fell on Goran. The court went mad. Men and women panicked, running for the doors. The stampede pushed more than one fleeing noble onto the Voyniks' drawn blades. Screams echoed through the hall, amplified by the tower, heightening the chaos.

I blocked it out. Zosha threw an arm around my shoulders and rushed to the side of the hall, protecting me. At least, that's what we wanted people to see.

We were through the workroom door so fast I nearly tripped over a set of legs at the top of the stairs. Righting myself, I spotted Dimitri lying unconscious on the steps. No time for pity, I snatched his sword, gathered my skirts, and ran.

The office below was empty—as Bora had arranged. Not even the unrelenting glow of my Aellium stone could dim my relief, as I pulled the keys from my bodice. I shouldered through the workroom doors, sprinted down the steps straight to Illya.

His gray eyes flew wide when he saw me. It was his only reaction, and I couldn't help but grin. A warning flashed across his face when Zosha ran to my side.

"Relax, he's with me," I said, my voice suddenly hoarse.

Illya nodded once, eyes flicking away from Zosha like the other man no longer existed. His gaze roved across my face, drinking me in, from the tip of my crowned head to the key shaking in my hand.

"I told you I'd be back," I whispered, my words as unsteady as my hands, as I fumbled with the lock.

The first key didn't fit. I cursed. Must be for the Aellium collars, I thought and rammed the second key home. Turned. The lock hit the floor with a thud. Somehow that little sound flooded my body with warmth. And hope.

Illya groaned, bursting free of the straps. I flung my arms around his neck, nearly knocking him back down. A low laugh huffed out of his lips as his arms came around me. He crushed me to his chest so hard I could feel his heart beating against my own.

"You shouldn't have come," he whispered into my hair. Still locked in his arms, I saw Eliska weeping over his shoulder.

I swallowed hard, felt my cheek twitch against his neck. "Do you honestly think I'd let you die before I got the chance to yell at you for not telling me who you really are?"

Illya froze. His breath hitched. Even his heartbeat stuttered. I felt his hands fall to my waist, pulling me back. We were face-to-face now, but the space between us was anything but empty. It hummed and crackled, filling with the edges of his true identity: Olexan Illyazhah Darkestii, Prince of Raskis.

His eyes were wide, worried I thought, and almost laughed because Illya was never worried. But he wasn't Illya, the stoic guard captain, now was he? He was the last living member of the Raskisi royal family. The man I'd been three days from marrying when Raskis fell.

I felt my cheeks grow warm, suddenly and keenly aware of his hands around my waist, of the heat of his palms radiating through the gown's thin lace. His throat bobbed, gaze locked on my lips.

One hand went to my neck, his calloused palm scraping deliciously up my cheek, and we were tipping into each other. Diving. Our lips met, a hot and cold clash of release that filled and emptied me all in the same instant. It was endless. It was—

"Uh, Askia," Zosha said, poking me in the shoulder hard enough to break the kiss, even if I couldn't yet take my eyes off Illya. "Hate to interrupt, but we gotta hurry."

"Yes, of course. You get the collars." I tossed the key to Zosha but couldn't quite pull away from Illya, who watched me as if I was life itself. I bit my lip, nodded to the sword I'd dropped in my haste to reach him. "Watch my back?"

A smile whispered across his lips. "Always."

Zosha and I worked in tandem, making quick work of the first row of prisoners and then the next. It was easier than it should have been—for only fifteen witches now remained. And yet felt impossibly slow. *Quicker*, I thought, guilt ripping through me.

"What's the escape plan?" Illya asked, as the prisoners gathered.

"Body hatch," I replied, nodding to the square metal door in the wall, same size as a large dumbwaiter, but fit with a slide rather than a tray and pullies.

"You want us to go down there?" an older man asked, face going green as he eyed the hatch.

"It's grim, I know," I said by way of apology, "but it's the quickest and safest way out of the city. There is a barge tethered beneath the hatch. Cut the line, and we can ride the river straight out of Tolograd."

"But . . . but look at us," the man said, gesturing to his tattered clothes with a shaking hand. "We'll freeze."

"I've arranged for winter supplies to be dropped outside the city," Zosha replied as we freed the final row of prisoners. "We only have to endure the cold long enough to make it there . . . Just stay out of the water."

"I don't know about this—"

"Quit your bellyaching," snapped the young Khezhari woman I'd just freed. "Not like we have a choice, unless you'd like to stay here and die in the warmth of Radovan's hospitality." There was something steely in her gaze, as she pushed herself to her feet and sneered the words in heavily accented Roveni. I liked her instantly.

"What's your name?"

"Nekhaia."

"All right, Nekhaia, you go down first. Help the others," I said, then looked at the hatch. No bodies piled up today, which meant they were all probably on the barge already. "Hope you're not afraid of the dead."

She scoffed. "Nothing a corpse can do to me that's worse than these Roven bastards."

"Good woman." I grinned and freed the final prisoner. Zosha and Nekhaia made a beeline to the hatch before I could even straighten. "Are any of you fire witches?"

"I am," the frightened man said, looking like he wanted to be sick.

"So am I," Illya murmured.

I blinked at that but pushed onward. "One of you needs to go down next, keep us warm enough so we don't freeze."

"I—"

"I'm staying with you," Illya said, in a voice that brooked no argument. He cast a baleful glare at the older man, and whatever passed between them made him wilt.

The older man went to the hatch, swallowed hard, and let

Zosha help him get a leg up. In a moment and with a half-cocked scream, he was gone. Gobbled up by the darkness.

None of the other prisoners shared his reticence. With help from Zosha and Illya, they went down one by one. Until there were only three left. They cowered away from us, clinging together in fear: man, woman, and child. A family.

The man licked his lips and issued a string of words I couldn't comprehend. I shook my head, glanced back at Illya and Zosha.

"It's Graznian, I think," Zosha said, shrugging. "I don't speak it though."

I cursed. Tried speaking in Switzkian, which was linguistically similar. *Not similar enough*, I thought when the family still looked lost. Lady Night help me, how much longer did we have before someone—before Radovan or Qaden—thought to look for us down here?

"Freyda," I called, not caring who heard me. "I need you."

"I'm here," the ghost said, appearing on my right. She held out her hand. *"Hurry. The Voyniks will be here soon."*

It was all the warning I needed. I grabbed her hand, felt my body go numb as her spirit filled me. If Katarzhina's soul was like a cold wine, Freyda's was an avalanche. It drove me to my knees, filled my mind with flashes of memory and snippets of words. Forests, caravans, cities, men, women, children. No. *Qaden.*

I gasped, falling onto my hands as Freyda's last memories filled me. She fought then, fought me, fought my mind. But there was nothing either of us could do to halt the transfer.

"Askia." Illya barked my name. "What is it? What's wrong?"

"I know." The words fell from my lips like unwilling drops of rain.

"Know what?" Zosha asked, kneeling on my other side.

"I know what Qaden's hiding."

Zosha's eyes widened. "Well, what is it?"

"No!" Freyda's voice echoed inside my head so hard it sent spasms through my muscles, filling my stomach with lead.

I shook my head, swallowing back fresh waves of nausea. "I can't" was all I managed, leaning on Illya to find my feet.

Feeling her panic wane, I ceded control of my voice, let Freyda speak through me. Let her order the frightened family about in her sharp, pointed Graznian.

Shaking with terror, they went to the hatch. Mother and child first. The father had barely climbed into the mouth of the hatch before a door above us banged open.

I whirled. Footsteps pounded against stone and echoed off walls. We were out of time.

"Zosha. Now."

He hurled himself through the hatch. And almost before I could think, Illya had me in his arms. "You couldn't have worn something more practical?" he asked, stuffing the long train of my gown into the hatch.

Adrenaline and relief and fear vied and swirled in my chest. "Well, it was my engagement party," I managed, far more dryly than I felt.

"What is it with you and weddings?"

"Don't be jealous." I laughed, too sharp, too frightened as the footsteps and shouts grew closer. Closer.

The workshop door slammed open. Soldiers poured through. Soldiers with crossbows.

"No!" I cried.

Too late.

Arrows flew. Illya curled over me, shielding me with his back. Leaving him open. A perfect target.

He pushed me forward, like I knew he would. Which was why I seized his collar, and dragged him into the hatch behind me.

We barreled together into the darkness. There was a moment

of free fall when the entire world was only that jet blackness. No up. No down.

Then the frigid night air stabbed through me. My stomach flew into my throat—every nerve in my body rose. I forced my eyes down. Screamed.

Because the barge wasn't there.

21

Hitting the water from that height and speed was like jumping off a roof and landing on cobblestone. White-hot pain shuddered through my body. But the heat didn't last. Not in that cold—no, *cold* was the wrong word. *Cold* implied that any tiny inch of my body could ever be warm ever again. There in the blue-black depths of the River Tol, heat was a distant memory, a dream of youth and folly.

Water pulled and tore at my hair and clothes. It pressed down on my chest, clawing with frigid fingers for the air trapped within. I lashed out, hands splayed, stretching toward the surface. But the river and my gown had other ideas.

Four yards of silk and lace and feathers slithered around my legs like malevolent seaweed, tangling my feet with each kick. The Aellium stone floated upward, a green beacon that seemed to laugh at my struggle. My heart pounded in my temples. The uncontrollable urge to gasp racked my body, as I fought for the surface.

But a cold, distant part of my mind watched my fight with utter detachment. Your heart is beating too slow, it said with infuriating calm. Can you even feel your hands? Your arms? That dizziness is from a lack of air. You won't last much longer. If you don't control the cold shock, you'll be dead in two minutes.

Heeding the voice, I willed my arms to move, my legs to kick. But here, submerged in the frozen river, my will wasn't enough. Blood retreated from my limbs, leaving them useless. And the ever-growing need for air was visceral. It was all I could do to resist it. But why? That was becoming fuzzy. Fuzzy like the edges of my vision.

Pretty, I thought. So pretty how the moonlight cut through the water. Dancing, shimmering white light fell through the waves. Like curtains blowing in a soft breeze. My eyes felt heavy. I blinked. Watched the light.

So . . .

Pretty . . .

Something harder than stone slammed into my back, and suddenly I was doubled over. Water gushed up my throat, as I wretched blindly. Coughed. Wheezed.

"Breathe, Askia. Just breathe."

It took my air-starved brain another minute to place the voice. Illya patted my back, wrapping me in his arms when no more water came out. We were both soaking. The air was cold enough to shatter glass. I had no doubt little icicles would soon form on our skin.

"Huh," I said, that detached corner of my mind taking control of my mouth. "I thought freezing to death would be more painful."

"You're not going to freeze to death," Illya replied, voice rough as he hitched me closer to his chest and wrapped my sodden train around my legs. "Fire witch, remember?"

I nodded in an agreeable sort of way, but it was another minute before comprehension followed. I wasn't cold, I realized, and not in a too-numb-to-feel sort of way. Steam rose off Illya in waves, joining a thick rolling fog all around us. Magical, I thought, conjured by one of the witches around me to shield our flight. I let Illya's magic seep into me, snuggling beneath my skin. It was cozy, I thought, closing my eyes.

"Hey, now. Eyes open," he said, giving me a little shake. "You have to stay awake."

I forced myself to obey, pried my eyes open, and let my vision expand. I saw Zosha this time, too, saw others: men and women huddling together for warmth. And . . . was that an arm? Gray flesh hard as stone was beneath me. I shook my head, closed my eyes, willed this strange terrible dream to go away.

"How is she?" Zosha asked, voice low.

"Confused and tired, but that will pass once I get her body heated up." Illya's voice rumbled through me like a cat's purr.

"Tired kitty." I sighed the words, but no one seemed to hear.

"Should you be using that much magic?" Zosha asked.

"I'm fine."

"But your shoulder—"

"Is there a healer on board?" Illya asked, voice hard like he was trying to make a point.

"One, but . . ." There was a long pause and the impression of significant looks being exchanged.

"Then I'm fine."

The talking stopped after that. The world went gray, misty, and quiet. It rocked me into a place of oblivion. Of peace.

Until I found myself with a face-full of furious queens. *Wake up. Now,* Ozura commanded, looking down her hawkish nose at me with white-lipped anger.

Am I not awake? The voice in my head was dreamy and light as my gaze caught my arm, snagging on the dancing design of ice crystalizing on my bluish skin. Funny, I'd never realized how beautiful my tether could be.

No, you're not. This time it was Eliska speaking, pacing in tight circles through the unrelenting gray fog. *You're just lying around on the corpse-barge while my brother is killing himself trying to warm you.*

Yes, do let's discuss that brother, Ozura said, her voice colder than the river's darkest depths. *"If you are determined to remain with us in the Marchlands, then you will have more than enough time to explain why you brought a Raskisi prince—and your fiancée—to Vishir dressed up as one of your guards."* Ozura smiled. It was all teeth. *"Well? I'm waiting."*

I gasped, coming back into reality with a fine crackle of ice on my skin. Zosha raised a frosted eyebrow. "All right?"

"Yeah," I muttered, giving my magic a hard shove, forcing it to sleep. "Just too many people in my head. What happened? Where the hell was the barge?"

Zosha shook his head, shooting a dark look over his shoulder at the huddled witches. "Someone got antsy and cut the line too soon. Luckily only you and Illya landed in the water."

"Yes, so lucky," I said wryly. "Everyone else is all right?"

"All things considered. The water witches are taking turns hurrying us along. We should be at the drop point in half an hour."

I nodded, and then blinked. "We made it out of the city," I said, wonder filling my voice. My eyes scoured the world around us. Though dawn was a few hours off, there was a slight graying of the darkness, which let me see to the river's banks.

We were gliding past a sleeping town bearing the well-ordered sameness that Radovan so favored. Like a child's impression of a town rather than reality. It made me shiver, and not just because I was cold.

I turned to Illya, who was hunched over me asleep. His skin looked wan, slightly green. Eliska's words came back to me. "What's wrong with him?" I asked, wriggling out of his arms to inspect him closer.

"Hit with a bolt," Zosha replied, grabbing on to my arm to slow me when the raft bobbed beneath us. "He let me pull it out once we got out of the city, but that seemed to sap the rest of his strength."

"Strength he shouldn't have wasted on me," I said, peeling back the ragged edge of his ripped shirt to peek at the injury. Shook my head, pressed the shirt back down. *Too dark to see anyway*, I thought, fear tingling through me. I laid the flat of my hand against the wound, pressing gently as I willed the barge onward.

By the time we reached the shore, dawn was minutes away and even the tiny village we'd passed was a distant memory. The supplies Zosha had arranged for were packed in several large crates and covered with a fine dusting of snow. That they weren't hidden spoke volumes as to how many people lived in this wilderness. No. Wilderness couldn't truly describe the world around us.

The forest that waited a few feet away was so deep and dense that night still reigned beneath its impenetrable boughs. It made me long for home—for the forests of Seravesh. *Soon*, I thought, jamming my feet into ill-fitting winter boots, military-issue like the winter coats and slacks packed in with food and supplies.

No weapons though. Illya had lost Dimitri's blade to the River and the Nines hadn't been able to secure any with the provisions—apparently the Voyniks guarded them too closely. I glared past the supplies, toward the surrounding trees. Better this than the great glacier desert north of Tolograd. At least the forest would provide some cover. Only the knowledge that those same trees would hide my pursuers tempered my optimism.

I sighed and looked back at the group. We'd decided to risk a small fire, breaking up one of the crates so that Maxus, the other fire witch, could set it alight. Our surplus of wind witches made it a matter of little effort to dissipate the smoke enough that it would look like nothing but a smudge on the horizon to anyone who was looking.

And people were surely looking.

Radovan was looking. I *knew* it. Felt his attention reaching through the stone—like entering a darkened room and knowing I wasn't alone.

Zosha met my gaze from the edge of the fire. He rose, joining me out of earshot of the others. "We can't stay here."

"I know," I said, but my attention went to Illya.

Our one healer, a wisp of a woman in her later seventies, had only enough energy to close the wound, warning Illya not to use the arm lest it reopen. Scouring out any infection or healing the torn muscle was beyond her powers. Little surprise his face was too gray, his expression tight with pain.

"Stop worrying," Illya said with a glare, catching me watching as he rose to his feet. "What's the plan?" he asked, joining Zosha and me.

"Zosha knows of a portal that can get us out of Roven."

"How far away is it?" Illya asked.

Zosha crouched down, sketching a little map into the snow. "We're about here," he said, poking a hole on the west side of the river. "The portal's here, on the edge of the Riven Cliffs." He added a second dot in the snow east of our current location. "It's a four-day hike from here, half that—or less—if we take the barge."

"You're talking about Kirskov," Illya said with a deep frown before shaking his head. "I came through the portal to Kirskov. It's heavily guarded. We'll never get in."

"We're not planning to knock on the door," I said with a dry smile. "The face of the cliffs are riddled with open tombs. Zosha's contacts have mapped out a path from those tombs to the lowest levels of the palace. It's risky, I know, but I'm guessing most of Radovan's forces will be pulled out of Kirskov to search for me, leaving only a handful of guards who won't be watching the cellars."

Illya chewed on the inside of his cheek, looking doubtful. "Well, it is one option."

I cocked him a look. "You got another one?"

"We head west. If we can get to the coast, we should be able to meet up with the witches who came with me in time to rendezvous with the *Fortune*."

"What's the *Fortune*?"

"The ship that is currently carrying General Arkady and your queen's guard," Illya replied.

I covered my mouth, momentarily speechless. "Arkady is here? With a ship?"

"You didn't really think the old bastard would leave you here to die, did you?" Illya asked, with a tired smile.

"Well, where's this ship of yours?"

"Outside a town called Croyshk. And Lady Night willing, that's where we'll meet up with the men I came to Roven with," Illya said, staring into the forest like he was already looking for them.

"Who came with you? Witches from the guild?" I asked, the eagerness in my voice compounded with the hope of seeing Nariko again.

Illya shook his head. "From the Wolves."

I blinked. "How? How is this all possible?"

"It's a long story, but Radovan has seeded not only the north, but Vishir with portals. I was able to use them to reach General Arkady. He sent me, as well as twenty other Seraveshi witches, ahead. We got separated in Kirskov," he said, voice faltering as a black look washed over his face. "If they made it out, they should be heading for the cove too."

"Other witches in the Black Wolves," I murmured. I'd always wondered if my grandfather and Arkady had hidden other witches in our army. Now that I had the answer, I wondered who else knew it. I'd have to wait to ask Vitaly. Although I was dry, it was far too cold to risk using my powers. Last thing I needed was my tether's ice when the air around me already raked frigid fingers across my face.

Still, with so many enemies behind, the urge to get off this shoreline and take refuge with old friends was physical. I looked to Zosha. "Where is Croyshk on your map?"

Zosha grimaced, looking back down. "Should be somewhere around there. It has to be five days from here, maybe four if we really pushed it. But we'd be journeying overland and on foot. It would be slow," he said, gaze darting toward Illya's pallid face. "Going to Croyshk would rearrange your priorities too."

An understatement if there ever was one.

Illya frowned. "Was there a specific reason you want to reach the portal in Kirskov?"

"It's too much to get into right now," I began. "But if we can get inside Kirskov, there is a way to strip Radovan—and all of his sorcerers—of their magic."

Illya swore, eyes staring hard at that map on the ground. I could feel the conflict boiling within him. It was within me too. Take the longer route to friends and allies? Or the shorter one, straight into the belly of the beast, in the hope of tearing Radovan down once and for all?

I knew my answer.

Illya looked at me, face grim. "You want to go to Kirskov, don't you?"

I nodded. "Radovan doesn't know that *I* know about Kirskov—about what's hidden there. This is our only chance to take his magic. We'll never make it this close again."

"This is insanely dangerous."

"It was always going to be, given the Aellium stone still chained to my neck." I shrugged. "Only Radovan can remove it. And he can use it to locate me."

Illya's attention cut to where the stone now lay wrapped in a cocoon of torn gown. "How accurate is it?"

"As long as I keep it covered, it's only a general sense of where

I am—but it will become clear quickly that we're traveling the river."

"And he can't control you through it?"

I shook my head. "No, he needs to be close to do that."

"Small mercies," Illya said, gaze darting back to the group of terrified people behind us, something unreadable in his eyes. "What we need is a distraction."

I followed his gaze, wishing I didn't understand his meaning. But I did. What had I become? What had my time in Tolograd made me?

I swallowed the guilt. "We have to give them a chance to come with us."

"They won't."

"Still. I have to try."

"What are you talking about?" Zosha asked, looking between us, confused.

I shook my head. "Just play along."

Both men nodded.

"Come, you should eat something," Illya said while Zosha kicked snow over the map.

We returned to the rest of the group, claiming an empty patch of snow and a hunk of frozen bread. I studied the people around me as I chewed. Sitting in exhausted clumps around the fire, I could practically see their adrenaline waning. They'd probably curl up right here and go to sleep if I let them. But then again they were witches, not soldiers, despite the well-used Voynik uniforms they wore.

The remorse that had shadowed me since Goran's death reared its head. But I didn't let it shake my resolve. I couldn't.

Because I was about to make them casualties of war.

22

Nekhaia plopped down in the snow beside me as I was trying to formulate what to say. "Whatever you're planning, I want in."

I turned to her, considering. "What makes you think I'm planning anything?"

The girl, a year or two younger than me, crossed her arms, jet eyes narrowing. "Please. You gonna tell me you just wanted to have a nice chat with your soldier and a Rovenese nobleman? You were making a plan. So tell me—will it hurt Radovan?"

"Yes."

"Then I'm in."

"It'll be dangerous." I didn't really expect it to change her mind, but the warning needed to be said.

The younger woman just shrugged. "I have nothing to go back to anyway. Radovan killed everyone I've ever known. Danger doesn't scare me."

I briefly wondered what did scare her but knew better than to ask. In truth I was glad she was coming with us—an earth witch would come in handy. And she reminded me of myself, in a way. Before I'd found purpose in Seravesh, when I was hardly more than an exposed nerve of heartache and mad for vengeance. I looked around at the witches gathered, innocents I was preparing to sacrifice in the hope of defeating Radovan, and wondered: Had I changed at all?

"We should all move as soon as we're done eating," I said, my voice carrying too loud in the dawn quiet.

"Must we?" one of the women said, a slight whine in her voice. "Can't we rest first?"

I was shaking my head no even as she spoke. "Radovan will be coming, and his soldiers won't waste any time resting. We have to go."

"She's right," Maxus said, even though no one had raised their voice to say otherwise. He looked me up and down, in a wary appraising sort of way. The kind of way that made my hackles rise.

I hadn't much cared for him last night, and the intervening hours hadn't changed my mind. There was something weak about him, the kind of weakness that demanded respect where none was deserved.

"Someone should begin taking the bodies off the barge," he continued, looking around like he expected the others to leap to work at his command.

When no one moved, I asked, "Who among you are earth witches?" My voice was soft in the echo of Maxus's bravado. Nekhaia raised her hand, as did Herrik—the Graznian father—when I'd repeated myself in his language. "Turn the bodies to stone and sink them into the river," I said. "Best not to leave any clues we were here," I explained when Maxus raised an eyebrow.

He stayed silent a moment longer, taking my measure. "You're her, aren't you? The last queen?" He asked the question like a challenge, so much so that both Zosha and Illya stiffened and Nekhaia paused in getting up, one hand resting suspiciously close to a large rock.

My lip twitched in a mirthless way, meeting his gaze with

a cold one of my own. "Askia Poritskaya e-Nimri ibn Vishri, at your service."

"An honor to meet you, my lady. And thank you for the rescue. Now I have family just over the border in Polzi. Way I see it, we just need to ride the river downstream—"

A very doubtful snort stopped him short. Red splotches appeared high on his cheeks as he turned slowly to Nekhaia.

"Genius plan. Too bad you'll kill yourselves going over the Riven Cliffs."

"We will carry the barge down the cliffs," Maxus said, sniffing away her words like she was nothing and turning back to me. "You and your men should rest. I'll see us all safely out of Roven."

The urge to sigh was almost overwhelming. Everywhere I went some fool man thought he could take over, and for what reason? The little brain dangling between his legs? I shook my head, swallowing my first response. "We won't be coming with you. Continue down the river if you wish, but it will be the first place Radovan will look."

"Perhaps," he said, eyes narrowing like he hadn't expected me to argue. "But it's fast. What's your idea? Go through the forest?"

My smile had teeth. "My plan is my own. You may join me if you wish, though there is more danger in it than even Maxus's plan to ride down the river. If you're hoping for a safer option, then yes, go over land."

I paused, trying to figure out how to drop a clue about the *Fortune* that wouldn't register with Radovan if any of these people got caught. "If you make it to the coast, look for merchant vessels bearing flags from Vishir or Idun. You may just find shelter with them. It's the harder path, for sure. But the wiser one usually is."

He crossed his arms at that. "I'm not dragging my old bones over land."

"I'm not asking you to. But everyone deserves to know their options—to make the choice for themselves. We'll divide the supplies fairly and part friends," I said, my voice firm, staring down Maxus and anyone else who might have other ideas.

I wasn't happy to send anyone off alone, but it was better to get this sorted now. Warm and with the prospect of plenty of food, I could be sure we'd reach an accord without violence. Friendliness, I could see, was clearly too much to ask. Whatever else he was, I was sure that after a few days of cold and hunger, Maxus would have taken all the supplies by force. Or tried, at least.

I stood, considering the matter closed. "Illya, Zosha—please portion out the supplies. Nekhaia, Herrik, let's go take care of the bodies."

I didn't relish grave duty, but I knew Maxus was too much of a coward to follow me. Indeed, he did hang back, and I could hear him squawking over the food distribution from the riverbank.

"*Ungrateful,*" Siv sneered.

"*He's scared. I don't blame him, especially what he went through.*"

"*I went through it too. He's alive.*"

With a shiver, I pushed the magic away before Vitaly or Ozura could appear and start arguing over my decision to continue to Kirskov.

The three of us made short work of the bodies. Nekhaia and Herrik had both managed to rest on the barge and were powerful earth witches besides, so powerful I wondered how they'd escaped Radovan's clutches for so long. In the space of a half hour, we'd sunk the corpses to the bottom of the river and returned to the others.

I supposed I wasn't really surprised that most of the group decided to go with Maxus. The river was the easier route, and nothing I said convinced them of the danger. Nothing I could do about that now.

Only Nekhaia decided to go with us. I was sad to lose Herrik and his family, but at least they had decided to head for the coast along with a water witch that knew enough Graznian to get by. We lined up on the bank saying good-bye to our short-time companions. Maxus loomed over me, puffing up his chest like he'd won something. He deflated when he spotted the look of pity on my face.

"Where will you go?" he asked, shifting from one foot to the other like he was suddenly afraid he'd made the wrong choice.

Illya put a hand on my shoulder, squeezing it before I could formulate a response. "South," he replied, tone so unmistakably hard not even Maxus was foolish enough to question further.

I almost said something then. *Wanted* to say something. But the woman I'd become these last few weeks, the woman who leveraged secrets and pain in a reckless gambit to escape this hellhole stopped me. I'd given these people their freedom. What they did with it now wasn't up to me. Even if it meant I was letting them throw it away. Yet I couldn't say nothing.

"Conserve your magic and your strength. The river will take you through the very shadow of Kirskov. Wait until night to try and pass it. You'll need to be quick and quiet if you have any hope of making it unnoticed. Good luck."

Maxus simply turned around, clearly intent on ignoring me out of spite. The others either followed directly or nodded at me before heading to the barge. The last one was barely on board before Maxus ordered the water witches to speed them away.

"Where are we really going?" Nekhaia asked, squinting up at Illya and me while the others floated out of sight.

I turned to her, bracing. "Kirskov."

"Well shit, if that's where we're going why not travel with the others?" she asked, voice incredulous.

Illya lifted his chin, though I saw shame writhe in his eyes before his expression shuttered. "The river is dangerous. It will be the first place Radovan looks. The less they know, the better."

"So you're sending them ahead as decoys. Giving good old Radovan someone to chase after so you can sneak in behind." Nekhaia whistled almost appreciatively. "Damn, you're coldhearted bastards. I knew I liked you two," she said, flashing us a feral smile. She shrugged when I frowned. "Don't feel bad. Who do you think cut the barge lines before you came down the hatch?"

"Maxus?" I asked, with little surprise.

She nodded. "Best to be well away from that old piece of shit when the going gets tough."

There wasn't much I could say to that. Even though my eyes scoured the river and my voice itched to shout, I knew it was too late. The barge was gone and most of the other witches with it. The ones on foot were already trekking west. I shook my head, swallowing an anger that I knew should have been hot and furious. Should have been.

But it wasn't. Not really. Because that calculating part of my mind knew they'd have just slowed us down. And if they distracted Radovan even a bit . . .

I supposed that indeed made me a coldhearted bastard.

"I'm guessing you need me to make a new raft?" Nekhaia asked.

"Please."

She grunted her assent, casting her gaze out toward the trees around us with a speculative glare. "Well, we're not short on good lumber. I can fell a few of these and grow some vines, but that will tap me out, so you lot will need to lash them together." She spit to one side. "Whatever's in Kirskov better be worth it."

"I'll fill you in on the way," I replied. "But it is."

Even with Nekhaia's magic aiding us, it still took two hours to build a new raft. We managed to push it out into the river, hopping on board before exhaustion overcame us. We lay or sat as room allowed, and let the forest rise up around us as the current carried us past.

The wind moaned a haunting melody, cutting across our bodies with clinging, skeletal fingers. I caught glimpses of bright sunlight through the canopy, but the trees snuffed it out with gnawing greed. I willed the river to move faster, trying not to wonder how far behind us Radovan was now.

The Aellium stone hung too heavily between my breasts, lambent and warm and thrumming with a heartbeat that wasn't my own. A reminder that Radovan hadn't been killed by Goran's knife. A reminder that while I was free now, that freedom might not last long. Not with Radovan coming.

And he was coming.

Had Goran even hit him? He must have, given Radovan's scream, and the panic that had exploded through the room. Yet I hadn't sensed Radovan's magic searing through the stone to kill Goran after the attack. And he would have, of that I was certain. A dull pang of sorrow echoed through my chest.

I sniffed the feeling away, knowing Goran deserved his fate. And if he was dead and gone, at least he'd injured Radovan along the way and given us this chance. It was the sweetest legacy Goran could have ever left to the world.

A sacrifice worth making, I thought, but my mind flickered traitorously to the witches I'd saved. The witches I'd let wander back into harm's way. Another worthwhile sacrifice. I hoped.

I lowered my head through the unyielding gloom and against the unrelenting wind, and we floated on.

And on.

Dusk came upon us not with the setting of the sun but with a howling wind carrying clouds so dark it swathed the forest in premature night. Snow hurtled out of the sky, pelting my face and plunging me in a cold I never imagined possible. There was a malevolence in this storm. A hunger that nature never intended. This was Radovan venting his rage. And while he might not know exactly where I was, he knew this storm would slow me. Stop me.

Because now the river rose and fell with each gigantic gust of wind. It was all we could do to hold fast. Water crested over the sides until we were all drenched. All shaking.

"We have to stop!" Illya shouted over the wind.

"No!" Zosha cried back. "Not yet! We should hit shelter if we manage a little further."

That hope of shelter—whatever it was—was enough. I clung fast to the raft, hands aching for the desperation of my grip. We continued on for what felt like hours, battered by the wind and the water and the ice until Zosha finally called out for us to stop—but that was its own kind of hell.

The current was hungry to keep us in its grasp. It took all four of us, wrestling the crude oars with all our strength, to make it toward the shore. But we made it, sodden and sore.

My boots cracked through the frozen snow, arms wrapped around my midsection like it could stop the shivers racking my body. I forged after Zosha into the tree line, the thick boughs of ancient evergreens just enough cover from the snow to allow me to see, squinting through the storm.

Shapes, giant shapes loomed out of the semi-darkness. Buildings. Nearly a dozen of them. Shutters closed, chimneys cold. A tiny village empty and waiting.

"What is this place?" I asked, hardly believing my eyes.

"One of the logging camps," Zosha replied, not bothering to look back at me as he trudged onward through the snow. "They're empty in the winter, but they should still be stocked with beds and blankets and firewood. Maybe even some food—pretty sure our supply got wet on the raft."

Considering how drenched we all were, I was pretty sure he was right.

We went to the largest building and wrestled the door open, hinges squealing in frozen outrage. The space we entered looked like some kind of communal space. Mess hall on the first level, with a staircase and balcony level above dotted with doors. While Illya started a fire in the giant hearth below, Nekhaia and I dragged ourselves up to the second floor, pirating as many blankets as we could find from the tiny bedrooms. They stank of stale sweat and were rather thin, but there were a lot of them. They'd do the job. While dinner cooked—a sad sludge-like mixture of presoaked porridge—the four of us huddled in blankets by the now-roaring fire, our discarded clothes drying over chairs and tables.

Zosha—thankfully—had the forethought to start fires in the bedroom stoves upstairs while we ate. Good thing, too, for as soon as she was done eating, Nekhaia stumbled up the stairs, heading straight to sleep. She wasn't the only one whose bones were lined with exhaustion. Illya was drowsing in his chair by the fire, and Zosha barely made it through his dinner before he went upstairs as well.

I longed to join them, but the specter of Radovan's rage rattled the cabin's shutters and for a dark moment I almost thought I heard his scream on the wind. I shook the thought away, scolding my foolishness. I had enough problems without adding fear to the list.

Or, more fear, I thought, my gaze snagging on Illya.

His skin looked sallow in the firelight. Summoning the fire after a long and frigid day of travel had drained him. He sat with one arm propped atop a scarred wooden table, eyes closed and his uneaten dinner in his hands.

Eliska knelt beside her brother, face tight with fear. It was the first ghost I'd seen in hours, for I'd stifled my magic to conserve energy. But here in the relative warmth of this cavernous mess hall, the power had slid out of me without my consent, proving just how exhausted I was.

I snuffed it out again, watching Eliska disappear in a puff of misty smoke, and dragged my chair beside his.

"Illya?" I murmured, placing a gentle hand on his arm.

His eyes opened, slightly glassy and unfocused. He blinked at the fire, looking like a bored wolf before his gaze finally found me. "What is it?"

"I need to look at your shoulder," I said, bracing for an argument.

He'd never been one to admit to weakness. If he'd ever felt tired or sore, sick or exhausted, he'd never let it on. Illya studied me for a long moment before grunting. He set his food to one side and let the blanket slide down his chest.

I cursed the heat flooding into my cheeks even as my eyes traveled unbidden down the length of his torso and back up. I pressed my lips together, suddenly and keenly aware that we were both naked beneath our rough woolen blankets.

But not even the desire pooling between us, nor the memory of that kiss burning beneath my ribs, was strong enough to make his shoulder look whole. The old healer's work hadn't been completely undone by our journey, but it hadn't been aided by it either. Though the wound remained closed, the skin was taut and puckered—not terribly surprising given the last few hours, but worrying all the same. Especially as it was hot to the touch, and that could not be good.

"Are you cold?" I asked, and tried not to wince when he shook his head no. Even this close to the fire and with his natural predilection for heat, he should have been chilled by now. Unless he had a fever. The specter of infection loomed large over me.

I shook my head, at a loss for what to do. "Try to be careful with it tomorrow—keep your arm as immobile as you can. I really don't think that wound will stay closed if you strain it too hard. I've boiled some bandages just in case," I said, gesturing toward the strips of cloth that lay dripping next to the hearth with all of our clothes, "but I'd rather not need them. You should try to eat something before you go to sleep."

He nodded, but his eyes were closed so I wasn't really sure how much he was hearing.

"Askia?" he murmured, voice rough. "How did you know who I was—who I *really* am?"

I sat back hard in my chair, as his eyes met mine. His gaze burned my face, so hot all my words dried up in my throat making speech impossible. I licked my lips, forced myself to reply, because really there wasn't ever going to be an easy way to tell him I was being haunted by his dead sister.

"Eliska told me." Pain lanced across his face, so sharp, so gruesome it was like seeing the arrow hit all over again. I bowed my head, hooked a finger beneath the chain, and dragged out the still-shrouded stone.

"You can see her?"

"Yes," I replied, glancing over my shoulder. "I mean, she's not here now, but I can see her along with the other wives."

"How?"

What did he mean? He knew I was a witch . . . I watched his eyes travel down to the chain around my neck, and a weight settled inside me. I really didn't want to have this conversation right now. It would do nothing to help Illya heal, but . . .

But how could I possibly deny him?

"The Aellium stones don't just capture a witch's magic. It traps their souls too."

Rage burned through Illya's eyes. "I'll kill him." The oath echoed through the hall, making the fire crackle bright for a moment.

"Get in line," I shot back, cool enough that his magic dissipated.

His mouth worked in the slightest of smiles. The expression faded too fast as he rubbed his eyes. "How are you able to use your magic, though? When the stone was around my neck, I couldn't do anything."

"But you would feel it?" I waited for him to nod before continuing. "It's the same with me. I can feel the magic, see the ghosts, but I can't *make* them do anything." The only time I'd successfully used my power was in commanding Ozura's full presence to form, fulfilling the vow that bound her soul to mine. And even that had been nearly beyond me.

"Then how did you manage to get us all free?"

Smug satisfaction warmed my cheeks. "Well, just because I can't compel the ghosts to obey me doesn't mean I couldn't convince them to spy."

"Spy for you? So what, you've been blackmailing Radovan's court?"

I peered up at him through my lashes. "Blackmail is such an ugly word."

Our laughter filled the night between us, and for a sparkling moment, the worry of Illya's wounded shoulder and the threat of Radovan faded.

Illya shook his head. "Princess, politician, soldier, and now spy? You never stop surprising me."

I tried for a smile. Considered making a joke about politicians, but I couldn't quite muster it. "Illya?" I began, then ran into a wall of muteness.

He sighed. "You want to know why I didn't tell you who I really am."

I nodded, remembering that cool spring day when my men and I had ridden up the mountain pass to meet the prince and his delegation in a small town that straddled the border of Raskis and Seravesh. It was supposed to be the day that changed my life. The day Goran left for Raskis and Olexan came to Seravesh. With me.

But Goran hadn't come with us, and in hindsight it was clear he'd already been planning his betrayal. And Raskis had already fallen, but I didn't find that out until the wind changed, sending smoke down the mountain.

The town was in flames when we arrived. Corpses littered the streets, the screams of dying men and women reverberating off the mountains. Roven had come, struck like lightning to ruin any hope of alliance and slipped away again. Of the four hundred people who lived there, we pulled eleven out of the rubble. Including Illya.

"Your grandfather told me not to," Illya said, looking away from me, eyes locked on the flames.

I was speechless again, but this time it wasn't from awkwardness. It was outrage. How could my grandfather take Illya in, only to treat him like nothing more than a guard? To hide both his status as a prince and his power as a witch? And if Grandfather knew, surely others must have known too? Maybe even Arkady.

Something in me went cold as I remembered Arkady's face when he sent Illya with me to Vishir in his place. "Why'd he keep it a secret, though?"

"In one sense, it was to protect me. My family had been butchered; my sister abducted. The world thought I was dead. It was safer this way. King Fredek said he would give me a place in his court, protect me. All he asked was that I keep my identity secret. Even from you."

"I wouldn't have told anyone."

"I know," he said, eyes meeting mine. Softening. "But he saved my life. And when he died, I—there just didn't seem to be a good time to tell you. And then we went to Vishir and you were already throwing everything you had into securing an alliance." He swallowed hard. "I didn't want to make it harder for you."

"It wouldn't have been a burden, Illya. I could have used your help, your voice."

"You didn't need it," he said, shaking his head. "And it wouldn't have helped. Imagine what the Vishiri court would have said about you, if you'd suddenly announced that the captain of your guard was the prince you were promised to. Imagine how it would have looked."

Unfortunately, I didn't need to. The memory of Ozura's ire was already burned into my brain. I pushed it away. Railed against it and wondered how he could have stood by and said nothing while I married Armaan.

He'd had chances. Like that night before the masquerade ball, when we'd stood alone in my garden and courted the edges between desire and duty. Or later, in the cemetery. Hadn't I asked him to . . . I swallowed the thought, but Illya seemed to read it on my face, for he nodded.

"Armaan wouldn't have married you if he'd known who I was. And you were already so conflicted." His face twisted with an emotion I couldn't quite identify. "I may have taken the coward's way out, letting your grandfather hide me, but so long as you were fighting, I felt like I was fighting too. And I didn't want to make it harder on you, by laying a claim to someone I don't deserve."

My heart thudded against my ribs, as I tried not to see the way his dark green tattoos wound over his shoulder and down his chest, down his abdomen, down . . .

I bit my cheek hard enough to taste blood and shoved my eyes to his. "Illya, you've crossed continents to save me. You are without a doubt the least cowardly person I've ever met."

He shook his head, gaze warm. "You would have done the same for me—for any of your men."

I wasn't sure that was true, but I hoped it was. And I hoped, as warmth wriggled through my core, that Illya was still one of my men. *Stupid thing to hope for now*, I thought, feeling my face fall. He was the lost prince of Raskis. We both knew where his loyalties must lie.

"Hey," he said, reaching out, tucking a lock of hair behind my ear. His fingertips skated across my skin, leaving a trail of warmth in its wake. "I meant what I said on your birthday. I will burn the world down if you command it."

The naked honesty in his voice, the heat in his gray eyes made my heart stutter. The inches that separated us shrank, and the air crackled. I felt like I was on the precipice of something I couldn't name but yearned for anyway.

"I know," I said, with a smile. "I didn't think you meant it so literally, but I know."

His lips twitched, but there was nothing soft in his face when his eyes dropped to my mouth. No, his expression was all wolf, edged in hunger and steeped in desire. His hand slid from my ear to the back of my neck, but I was already leaning forward.

This kiss was a free fall. It burned away thought and filled all the empty spaces I'd so carefully ignored all my life. It shattered me. Remade me.

And I wanted more.

One of Illya's arms snaked around my waist and in half a moment I was on top of him, straddling his lap. Somehow the kiss deepened and my hands ran across the smooth plane of his chest in desperate exploration. I ground my hips against his, shivering as he groaned against my lips.

"Askia, stop."

My eyes popped open, gaze dropping to Illya's face. He looked up at me, expression heavy and edged in regret. "We can't do this."

I drew back, clutching the blanket to my chest. "Why?" I asked, hearing the bite in my voice. "Back in Tolograd, and before that even . . . you wanted this. I want this. What changed?"

"Nothing's changed," he said, hands falling away from me. "That's the problem. The Wolves—your people, they don't know who I really am. And even if they did . . . Askia, I have nothing to offer."

Annoyance spiked through me. "Lady Night, do you really think so little of me? You think that I only see people for what they can get me?"

"No. But maybe you should."

"What the hell does that mean?"

"Askia, you're a queen—I'm just a guard."

"That's not all you are. But even if it were, so what?" I demanded, standing now.

"Your men—"

"Don't give a shit who I sleep with and they never have." I shook my head. "Don't hide behind them. I'm their queen, not their mother. They don't care who shares my bed."

"But they should," he said, getting frustrated now.

Good. He should be frustrated, the damned fool.

"Nothing's changed since Vishir. I still have nothing to offer you. You need to marry—"

"Who, Illya? Who do I need to marry?" I asked, throwing up a hand. "Some fairy-tale prince who will help me save my country? Because if that's what you're thinking, you might want to look in the goddamn mirror. Or are you thinking that I need to save myself for someone with an army? Well, let me tell you something, Illya, I've already married for Seravesh once. Nearly married you for it, too, if memory serves, and I'm done with it.

"The world in which the right marriage can save my people no longer exists. All we've got is this world, the one where we're crouched in some Roveni logging camp while Radovan chases us across the whole damned continent. I have no idea if we'll even survive the night, and no room to worry about who I marry and why. What I want is you, Illya. So tell me:

"What the hell do you want?"

The answer came before the question was fully spoken. His mouth was on mine once again, devouring, plundering in a way that made me burn for more. More of him. All of him.

My hands pressed into the hot plane of his chest, glorying in the corded muscle I found there. I pushed, laughing as he fell back onto the table, a sound I felt reverberate through his body as I straddled him.

His hands were in my hair then, and he groaned a prayer as I ground my hips into his. The hardness I felt there made the deepest parts of me ache for more. For everything.

As if he read the desire in my face, Illya pulled back, hesitating only for a moment. Long enough for me to nod, before tossing the blanket completely aside. The cursed necklace swung between us, still shrouded in the tattered remnants of my ballgown. For a second I wanted to rip the cloth away, let Radovan witness the affection he'd never have. But no, Radovan had no place here. Not tonight. I swung the stone behind my back and thought of him no more.

My hair fell loose and wild over my bare breasts. And what my tresses covered, Illya discovered with his hands. With his lips and tongue. In a surge of movement, he flipped us over, calloused hands scraping deliciously down my ribs, down my waist to my hips.

With a predatory gleam in his eyes and agonizing slowness, he eased back on the table, tracing his journey with feather soft kisses. Down my chest, my stomach. Lower. Lower.

"Lady Night save me," I whimpered into the gathering darkness.

Illya's answering laugh was laced with a promise that made my inner muscles clench. "No prayers for salvation tonight," he said, breath hot on already quivering flesh. "Tonight I'm going to spend a long, *long* time devouring you."

And his mouth was on me, teeth and lips and tongue until the world broke apart within me and time shuddered to a standstill. My chest heaved. Illya's unrelenting heat and the room's chill made my nipples harden and peak, aching for his touch. I was just coming back together again when I saw him. All of him. Every glorious inch. It was almost enough to make me come undone again.

Desire coursed through me on a surge of motion that had me pinning him down all over again. He closed his eyes as I eased down slightly, only enough for the tip of his manhood to part my flesh, letting my juices run down his shaft.

"Askia, please."

It was my turn to laugh, a throaty sound that barely sounded like my voice. "No prayers, remember?"

He growled at the taunt, hands driving my hips down as his pelvis thrust up, a driving that forced all thought from my head. I rode him, rode the ever-growing tide that ebbed between pleasure and pain. The promise of release built as we seized this moment. In spite of all the hardship and heartache—or perhaps because of it—we were here. Together.

Whatever the cause, when that release finally came it tore through me—through us, carrying our ecstasy to Lady Night Herself before crashing us back to reality.

Sometime later, when the fire in the hearth had banked to embers and thought had returned, I lay beside Illya. My leg was draped over his naked body, my long hair the only blanket we needed. He ran a hand languidly down my spine, across scar and skin alike, wonder in his eyes. I'd never felt as beautiful as I did in that moment. Never felt as safe. Or hopeful.

A hope that had crept between the cracks of my hardened heart like the green tips of snowdrops peeking through the frozen earth. Fragile, but oh so precious, this promise of peace and love. And cocooned in this warmth, I slept.

IN THE SWIRLING BLACK AND RED DARKNESS BEHIND MY EYES, Radovan waited. His eyes, normally the green of brackish water, burned with an ageless rage. That hate-filled gaze locked on to me. Pinned me. I could do nothing but watch, watch as he peeled back the collar of his tunic with long, crooked fingers.

My eyes widened, revulsion turning over my stomach at what I saw. Mangled crimson flesh. Twisted alabaster bone. And a green-black stone fused to an immortal man's sternum.

Radovan's face twisted into a rictus-like grin. He pressed a finger to the stone.

I screamed.

23

ROUGH HANDS FOUND my shoulders, shaking me. My eyes flew open. Illya's face was tight with fear and rimmed in red from the pain hazing my vision. Pain. Burning, burning pain. My mouth opened in a wordless cry. I pawed through the layers of cloth, ripping, tearing until I found it. The source of the agony.

The Aellium stone burned bright through its wrappings. Squinting, I could just make out Illya throwing up a hand to shield his face from the blazing emerald light. I grabbed the chain— knowing better than to touch the stone—and wrenched it away from me. Whimpered as a layer of skin snapped off my chest.

The light guttered. The only sound I could hear was the beating of my heart.

"What in the name of Lady Night was that?" Nekhaia broke the silence in a rough voice that echoed off the walls.

"Askia?"

That was Illya, I thought, eyes closed, riding out the last waves of pain.

"Askia, talk to me," he said, cupping my face.

I pried my eyes open. Blinked rapidly against the green aura of the Aellium stone's glare. Illya sat upright, grasping both my arms. Zosha and Nekhaia looked over his shoulder wearing identical frowns.

"What happened?" Illya asked, his voice low, ringing with a note of command I recognized from months of sparring practice.

"Radovan." Though I spoke the name softly, the fire flickered. A frigid wind slithered across the floor. "The stone," I tried again, still holding the chain away from my chest. The stone itself was smoldering hot enough that ominous black smoke rose off the cloth covering it. "It burned me." I looked down. My skin was blood-red and blistered where the stone had sat. The temptation to go outside and press a fistful of snow on my chest was overwhelming.

"I wouldn't. It will only make the pain worse," Katarzhina said from my right.

"How is that possible?" Zosha breathed, face waxen.

"Same way he can track me—our stones are connected," I replied, feeling sick as the memory of Radovan's twisted flesh rose in my mind. I swallowed hard, forcing down bile. "It always gets warm when he uses magic, but this was different." I looked at Illya, a fear I was afraid to name gnawing at my heart.

The same fear was in his eyes. "We need to go."

"Woah, now," Nekhaia said, holding up a hand. "You haven't even told me your big plan yet. I can still hear the storm going outside—and as long as it's going, neither us nor the Voyniks will be moving. So why don't we all get dressed, eat some more of those shitty rations, and figure out what we need to do next . . . aside from, you know, finding a different table to eat at."

She shot a pointed look at Illya and me and I smiled, realizing we were still naked. Nekhaia was right though, I thought as we took an hour to dress and cook and eat—Radovan's storm would work against him as much as it would us. We had time. For now.

"All right," Nekhaia said, leaning back in her chair, "what's so important about Kirskov?"

I opened my mouth only to pause a moment and wonder,

because Nekhaia was a Khezhari witch. And though she was younger than me—born after the theocracy fell—did she believe in the hate that they'd taught? Only one way to find out.

"Radovan has the Heart of Khezhar."

Nekhaia tipped forward, both hands slapping the table in disbelief. "He moved it?"

"He did," I replied. "Took it out of Khezhar two weeks ago and brought it to the Kirskov Summer Palace."

"What is it?" Illya asked, leaning forward.

"The heart of Lady Night," Nekhaia intoned, only to ruin the moment with a sardonic shrug. "It's what the priests always used to say. Probably bullshit. What it really is, is one giant fucking Aellium stone."

"The source from which all other Aellium stones grew," I said, trying to give Illya a better explanation. "The Heart has trapped the soul of every witch who ever died wearing an Aellium stone. If I can get to it, I could release the souls trapped there. If there are no souls in the Heart, there's no magic in the stones. Radovan and all his little sorcerers will be powerless."

Nekhaia whistled. "Damn, you weren't kidding about this being dangerous. The risk of failure here is high. Really high. One false move and the souls are lost. As is the death witch trying to free them."

Illya crossed his arms. "What if you can't release the souls?"

I wet my lips, thinking back to Tolograd, to that little workroom where Asyl first told me of the Heart. How her voice had cracked when she told me it couldn't be destroyed. When she lied.

"Then we destroy it."

Blood drained out of Nekhaia's face. "No. No, you don't understand. The magic trapped in the stone—it's not like smashing a rock. That much power could tear a hole in the world."

"Will it strip Radovan of his magic? Will it make his sorcerers powerless?"

"Yes, but—"

"Then it's worth it. It's the only way to beat him, Nekhaia," I replied, leaning toward her. "We're dead already. What do our souls matter if we're doomed to be eternally enslaved to the sorcerers who killed us in the first place? It's the only way."

"You're still alive," Nekhaia said, "so it's easy for you to say. What about the rest of the witches who have died chained to one of those stones? What about my parents? What about your other queens? I mean, you still see them right—how do they feel about you risking their souls?"

I opened my mouth, only to close it again. Because while I couldn't ask any other ghosts, I could ask the queens. Yet never had. Despite everything they'd done the past few days and weeks, I'd never even stopped to think about what might happen if I couldn't release their souls from the stone.

If the only option was to destroy the Heart.

"What exactly did you mean," Illya began, voice carefully controlled, "when you said their souls would be lost?"

Over his shoulder, Eliska appeared, face grave and filled with mourning. One by one, the others gathered. A line of women formed a wall between me and the door.

"The way I understand it," Nekhaia said, "their souls were never able to cross the Marchlands because they'd already been anchored in the Heart. The Heart is the only place they now exist. You destroy the Heart, that's it. They're gone. No afterlife. No eternal peace. Nothing."

Nothing.

As the word echoed, I looked to Asyl. The priestess. The one queen who had come to the workshop to stop me. Who'd declared that it was impossible to destroy the Heart.

She straightened her shoulders as tears fell down her face. *"Radovan has already taken everything from me. Now he gets my salvation too?"*

Katarzhina stepped forward, for once unveiled, and took Asyl's hand.

"*It isn't fair,*" the priestess said, but there was no fight in her voice.

Everything in me reached out, straining to find some words of comfort, anything to offer these fierce women. But what comfort could I give that wouldn't be a lie?

"*You're right,*" I said, opting simply for the truth. "*It's not fair—not to you or to the untold thousands whose souls are trapped in the Heart. I will do everything I can to free them—to free you. But if I can't . . .*

"*I'm sorry.*"

More than one of the queens closed their eyes against my words. Or looked away. Or simply wept in silent acceptance.

Only Katarzhina remained, standing tall. Unbent. Though perhaps this was the end she'd been waiting for all along.

"*Come now,*" she said, voice even and strong. "*After all the long years we've spent listening to Radovan, I think silence will be welcome.*"

Siv and Freyda both laughed, sharp broken things.

"*Aye. It'll be a relief to be done,*" Freyda said.

"*And if it'll take the old bastard down a peg?*" Siv shrugged, nudging Asyl good-naturedly. "*Worth it.*"

Asyl gave Siv a watery smile. Managed to nod but said no more.

All that remained now were Ragata and Eliska. But neither woman looked at me. Their eyes were on the men, surely lost to time.

"*If you have to destroy the Heart,*" Eliska said, gray eyes, which were so like Illya's, turning to me, "*you'll die. You'll all die.*"

"*I know,*" I replied, refusing to look away. "*So do they.*"

The words seemed to deflate something in Eliska. She took three long breaths, gathering herself, I thought. "*If he is willing to sacrifice his life, then I am willing to sacrifice my soul. I am with you.*"

My throat was too tight for words. I nodded.

"There are other portals in Kirskov," Ragata said, hugging her middle as if she feared she might fall apart. *"If you find that we can't be released from the Heart, get Zosha through one. Please."*

I wanted to promise her. Wanted to throw my arms about the broken woman and swear that everything would be fine. But I couldn't. All I could do was . . .

"I'll try."

A hand touched my arm then. Warm and calloused and shaking ever so slightly. "Askia?"

I turned away from the queens. Met the question in Illya's gaze.

"They understand what destroying the Heart will mean," I began, not allowing a single inch of emotion into my voice, clinging to strength for the two men beside me. "They are ready."

"But . . . but it might not come to that, right?" Zosha asked through white lips. "If we can get there before Radovan realizes our plan—we can still free them. We might not need to destroy the Heart."

He was holding on by a thread, a single fragile thread of strength and hope. Illya squeezed my hand.

And because of that, I was able to smile. "You're right. We just have to get there first."

Zosha swallowed hard, shying away from all thought of destruction, from the possibility of his own death and the idea of his mother's lost soul. "Then what are we waiting for?"

Nekhaia cursed, leapt up from the table and cursed some more. Only when her litany of swears had run dry, did she plop back down. "This is suicide and I hate it. But if it declaws Radovan, then I fucking love it. Tell me you have a good way into this Kirskov place."

I exchanged a careful look with Illya, trying not to laugh at this strange, wild girl. If we all got out of here, I was bringing her to Seravesh with me. I wanted her in my circle.

"Zosha has a map."

Nodding at my words, Zosha reached into an inner pocket, retrieving a slightly waterlogged square of sheepskin. "There are little pathways down from the top of the Riven Cliffs to the sky tombs below. Finding one of them will be the hard part, but once we reach a tomb, we just have to follow the cavern back into the earth. All the tombs connect to a central preparation chamber and from there to the palace itself."

"It sounds too easy," Illya murmured.

I tended to agree but withheld the thought to spare Nekhaia and Zosha. "It's doable. And if we can't find a path, perhaps Nekhaia here could make one?"

She grunted, but in a satisfied kind of way as if to say, of course she could and I was stupid for asking.

"In that case, we should get going. It sounds like the storm is letting up," Illya said, but I tugged on his hand to stop him from rising.

"Hang on, let me check with the queens. It'd be good to know where Radovan is before we head out."

"*Radovan is still in Tolograd,*" Freyda said, stepping forward, collected despite the emotion still rising from her fellow queens.

"*Really? I'd have thought he'd be out searching.*"

"*Make no mistake, he is doing everything he can to find you,*" Freyda replied, eyes lingering on Nekhaia's face. "*But his efforts are best spent tracking you from afar. Have no doubt that once he figures out where you're going, he will pounce.*"

I nodded, knowing all too well what would happen if he found me. "*How many Voyniks has he sent looking for me?*"

"*Hundreds—from both Tolograd and Kirskov.*"

"Shit." I rubbed my eyes. "*Is there any good news?*"

"*Perhaps. Radovan senses your presence in the forest, but the forest itself is vast. So far he has his soldiers placed heaviest to the west of the River Tol—a river that branches both east and west of Kirskov . . ."*

"*So if we can make it to the eastern branch of the river—*"

"*You'll avoid the majority of Radovan's troops.*"

I told the others what Freyda had said, and without any further words, we all rose and made for the door.

Dawn was barely more than a whisper above us when I stepped outside. Frozen snow shone bright in the weak light, gleaming blue and pink with the sky. It was beautiful, in a treacherous sort of way as each footfall slipped and slid beneath me.

Thankfully, despite the cold and the storm, the river hadn't frozen over. Our little raft, on the other hand, was covered in snow and ice. It took an agonizing number of minutes to haul it free, but the moment it was, we were off again.

Another silent day's journey lay ahead of us. But unlike yesterday's it wasn't exhaustion keeping us quiet. It was fear. My eyes clung to the shoreline, scrabbling the woods for any hint of life—the shifting of a shadow, the flash of an arrow in flight. I saw nothing, but the absence was no comfort—it only increased my anxiety. Like the forest around us was holding its breath, preparing to scream.

The stone felt almost restless on my chest, as if Radovan's very presence were trying to reach out from the pendant. The feeling of him searching, searching, *searching* wore me thin. Made me ragged. Like I was nothing more than a hare sprinting across a field, a hound hot on my heels. And though the river allowed us to travel quickly, I almost wished I was walking. Being able to do nothing but sit and wait—wait for the current, wait for Radovan—was driving me slowly mad.

Midday came and we were approaching the split in the river. It was as far as any of us dared come via the river. We hauled ourselves to the eastern shore, and Nekhaia buried the raft with a tendril of magic.

"Wait," I murmured before we headed too deep into the forest.

"Vitaly, Freyda," I called, reaching for the two ghosts best suited for this type of mission. *"I need you to scout ahead—the others too. Send a warning of any patrols."*

They nodded, dispersing in a swirl of gray cloud that only I could see. I leaned closer to Illya, trying to fend off my tether's cold hands by absorbing some of his heat as I looked out across the mist-shrouded forest.

"Are we going, or what?" Nekhaia asked from somewhere behind me.

"Not yet" was my clipped reply. "The ghosts are scouting ahead."

"But your tether will make you vulnerable to the weather," Nekhaia said, her tone guarded. "Is using your magic really a good idea?"

The answer was a resounding no. Drawing on my power now, in the middle of a Roven winter, was a colossally stupid risk. Even a sliver of magic would amplify the risk of hypothermia tenfold. But . . .

"Do we have another option? I'll use the magic in bursts—every ten minutes or so—to conserve energy, but I have to do it. How else will we know if we're about to run into any patrols?"

"Make sure you eat regularly," Illya murmured, his only word of warning.

It was Siv who appeared this time, barely more substantial than the fog blanketing the forest. *"It's all clear. Go now."*

I gave the order to move out and walked away, closing the discussion.

Despite only occasional dips into magic, my body temperature plunged. Not even the exertion of scrambling across the increasingly uneven ground could warm me. I pushed myself onward. I could take it. I could take the cold and the strain, take the tether. Because if my time training with Ozura taught me strength, my time under Radovan's thumb had taught me endurance.

But even that stamina began to falter after a few hours. A shiver that I couldn't stop coursed through my body making my breath come in shuddered gasps. My legs wove an unsteady path behind Nekhaia, whose body was outlined in a faint gray fuzz.

"Enough," Illya said, voice just loud enough to make us halt. His hands closed around my shoulders, drawing me tight into his chest. "Push it away. All of it. Let the magic go," he added, softer this time.

I couldn't stop the sigh of relief as I smothered my magic and Illya's flared. I closed my eyes, head tilted back on his chest, nearly losing myself to sleep as his heat sank into my bones.

"She can't keep this up, can she?" I heard Zosha murmur, drawing a sharp snort from Nekhaia.

"Not unless she wants to kill herself."

"Give me a better option," I replied, dragging my eyes open and pushing the desire to sleep as far down as possible. "We have to know if we're about to run into any Voyniks."

"Ten minutes obviously isn't enough time for you to recover from the tether. Not in this weather," Nekhaia said.

I felt Illya go still as he weighed our options. "Tell your queens to report back to you in an hour. You get one minute to speak with them, and then you draw back. Agreed?"

One minute would be next to useless if we got into any real trouble, and I opened my mouth to say as much, when Illya's cheek lowered against my ear. "What is the point in knowing about an oncoming patrol if you're too weak to fight them?"

Well, there was no arguing with that. "All right. Agreed," I said, bracing myself to move out of Illya's heavenly circle of heat. "Let's get moving."

We headed southeast, the terrain becoming ever rockier, the

forest denser the further we traveled. I knew from the many maps I'd seen that—so long as we gave the River Tol a wide berth— the forest's cover ran right to the edge of the Riven Cliffs. It was impossible to curse the cover, but it was rough ground for a pack of cold, exhausted witches.

As I thought it, Illya looked me up and down, took my hand with a heavy nod. I frowned, taking in the sheen of sweat along his brow. There was a flush of red along his cheeks that I didn't think had anything to do with exertion. I wasn't sure how much longer he could do this. Or how much longer I could.

I wrapped my hand tighter around Illya's. Closed my eyes and willed the tiniest trickle of magic into my heart—the barest edge that the cursed collar would let me reach. Enough to do nothing but see the queens. Enough to make my knees go weak.

Freyda and Asyl appeared, conjured out of thin air like rain drops on a clear day.

Asyl spoke first, much to Freyda's frowning dismay. *"There are Voyniks ahead."*

"How far?" I asked.

It was Asyl's turn to frown. She looked over her shoulder, spectral eyes traveling south as she tried to judge the distance. I stifled a curse. A real scout would have known how to gauge such things.

"A mile?" Asyl replied, her voice lilting upward. *"But they're moving north from the cliffs, searching slowly through the forest."*

"How many?"

"Five."

"I have twelve moving west on horseback," Freyda said, shouldering past Asyl with her own report.

Pain lanced through my skull like an ice pick. I shook my head, knowing better than to fight the tether as I forced my be-numbed mind to move. *"Are they coming this way?"*

"Not directly. They're on a southwesterly track, but if you don't

move, you'll be spotted. You have a half hour with how fast they're going."

I cursed and felt Illya's hands transfer to my shoulders, fingers digging into my arms. The others stumbled closer, waiting for the news, but Freyda wasn't done.

"There's more. Two sorcerers are with them, and I also saw—"

The world shifted beneath my feet, a hazy tilt toward snow-covered earth that I couldn't control. My knees hit the ground, not hard, for Illya still gripped my shoulders, but enough to make my joints croak in protest.

The magic was gone, and whatever Freyda was about to say was gone with it.

"Askia, talk to me," Illya said, the barest hint of panic giving his voice an edge.

"We're about to be caught between two bands of Voyniks," I said, shoving myself to my feet. "The smaller one, moving north, is five men strong. The larger group is twelve men, on horseback. Two sorcerers are with them."

"Well then, what are we waiting around for? We should hide," Nekhaia said, looking ready to run.

Illya was shaking his head before she finished speaking. The gray wash of his skin was increasing by the minute. "No, we can't risk getting caught between the two search parties."

"He's right," I said when Nekhaia looked ready to argue. "If the smaller group finds us while the second group is in the area, we're done for. No way we can fight that many Voyniks."

"But we can fight five?" Zosha asked, his voice cracking. "That's what you're thinking, right? Because in case you haven't noticed, there's only four of us, and one is injured and another is exhausted and hobbled," he said, pointing at me. "And we have no weapons."

"The odds only get worse if we stay and hide," I replied, bracingly. "And you've never seen Illya fight. Wounded or not, he's the best."

The warrior's mouth twitched in an almost-smile. "You're sure the smaller group doesn't have any sorcerers?"

I grimaced. "No. They could have Aellium stones beneath their clothes that Asyl couldn't see. And—"

"And?" Illya pressed.

"And I didn't get to hear the whole of Freyda's report. She said she saw something else when I gave out." I glared at the trees around us as if they were responsible for my weakness. "I could try to summon them again."

Illya rejected the idea with a sharp gesture. "No. We all need to preserve our strength. I say we keep moving, try to take them by surprise. If Nekhaia can use her magic to slow them down, you and I can take them out."

The confidence in Illya's voice made Zosha and Nekhaia stand a little straighter, walk a little faster as we headed south. But I'd heard that kind of confidence before. It came when the odds were stacked against you and the only move left was a desperate one. I bit down hard on my cheek, exchanging a knowing glance with Illya as we moved, looking for an ambush point. For something to use as weapons. For hope.

We walked less than ten minutes before Nekhaia's magic sensed the smaller group ahead. Pulse pounding in my ears, we drew back. The world around us, while still densely forested, was pocked with house-sized boulders and snow drifts as large as horses. It was good cover. Good enough that I should have felt calm. Confident even.

I leaned past Illya, unease threading through me as I looked across the narrow gully separating our hiding spot from Zosha and Nekhaia. They were crouched behind a huge gray boulder, whispering to one another. They looked as nervous as I felt, I thought. But then we were outnumbered. And for all Nekhaia's attitude and the limited military training Zosha had received as a Roveni noble, I didn't think either of them had ever been in a fight before. Had ever taken a life.

"You all right?" Illya asked, his voice low enough that it wouldn't carry.

One of my shoulders twitched. "We should have split them up. They're too green."

"Maybe," he allowed, lips setting into a thin line. "But I'm not letting you out of my sight."

"Don't be dramatic," I shot back, nerves wringing higher with every word. "Fifteen feet to your left is hardly out of sight."

"That's not the same and you know it." He leaned toward me, his fire-witch heat bringing a flush to my cheeks. He shifted further, until his bulk blocked my view of the others, and I had no choice but to look up at him. "You stay by my side, Askia. Stay where I can protect you."

"Enough of that," I said, matching fire for fire. "No more clinging to the oath you made to my grandfather. The only promises that matter are the ones we make now; we protect each other. Deal?"

The molten metal heat left his gray eyes, expression softening. I almost asked why, and then I realized that it must have been a long time since anyone had sworn to protect him. Another life. Another name.

He reached out, one calloused hand scraping across my cheek as he bent. Our lips met, too briefly for the heart pounding against my chest. "Deal."

The sound of twigs cracking beneath a booted foot echoed through the thin afternoon air, jolting me back to the business at hand.

"They're close," I whispered, my bottom lip catching between my teeth.

Illya watched me a moment longer, gaze scorching and hungry, like he was trying to memorize my face. He nodded once and pulled away, taking the heat with him.

I signaled the others and pressed my back to the boulder. My ears strained for the sound of footsteps. There. That telltale sound of crunching snow and murmured conversation. They were coming.

I slid slowly down, reaching my fingers as far as they would go, grabbing a rock from the frozen earth. Not the greatest weapon I'd ever wielded, but it would do. It would have to.

The footsteps came closer. Closer.

Nekhaia's gaze was glued to mine. Her face was twisted in fear and anticipation that turned her terra-cotta skin slightly green.

I held up my hand. Three fingers up.

Three. Two. One.

My hand fell. Nekhaia closed her eyes. The earth heaved.

I lost my footing as the ground gave way. The half-frozen snow slid beneath me, as the huge boulder at my back trembled with the urge to roll. Panic split the air, and I turned, only to find Illya surging forward alone.

I scrambled upright, hurling myself around the boulder. My eyes sprinted across the narrow gully, made narrower by Nekhaia's magic. Three Voyniks were sunken waist-deep in snow and dirt. Their swords lay discarded and forgotten beside them, as they clawed at the uncaring earth, struggling for freedom.

I dropped my rock and seized a sword, streaking past the trapped men to the two that had escaped the snare. The two who were fighting Illya with everything they had. Under normal circumstances, the fight would already be over, the two Voyniks dead in the snow. But nothing about this was normal. A cry lodged in my throat as I jumped into the fray and the smaller of the two men wheeled to meet me.

Smaller. Not small. A head taller than me and twice as broad, he leered as he brought his sword down again and again. Swiping right, stabbing left. Back and forth we fought, a dance I was unprepared to lead. Days of cold and exhaustion and weeks of little to no practice were taking their toll, but I couldn't give up now. Couldn't surrender. Wouldn't.

And if I hadn't had much practice, I'd sure as Lady Night's darkest dreams been watching. Studying how the Voyniks moved, analyzing the rhythms of their training. This man used all the movements drilled into him by an unrelenting teacher. But he was no Qaden.

Thank the Day Lord for that.

I let him ease into the pattern his muscle memory so desired. Let him pummel me down the slight hill. Let him think he was winning. It wasn't too hard.

My pulse pounded in my ears. Sweat dripped down my spine. My bones ached. Two more parries. One more strike. Feigned left. Rolled right.

Saying that my sword parted his flesh like butter was a lie—a lie warriors told themselves to make killing sound easy. It wasn't. It took every ounce of strength and weight in my body to shove the sword through his abdomen. The thrust brought us nose to nose, that poor Voynik and I. We shared a single breath before death took him, crumpling to the ground.

I almost went with him. Almost knelt in a prayer for peace and forgiveness.

But then Nekhaia gasped.

"Watch out," Zosha cried.

My neck snapped upward. I saw Illya. I saw his feet slipping beneath him. Saw his winter clothes covered in blood. Saw the triumph in his opponent's eyes.

I saw the boulder move.

I flung my body forward, sword forgotten in a dead man's

chest. I sprinted faster than I thought possible. My sight narrowed on Illya. On the fight he would not win.

The ravenous ground trembled beneath my feet.

I lunged.

My shoulder connected with Illya's side, as I tackled him. The edge of a blade rippled across my scalp, so close I heard its metal song ringing in my ears. Stone screeched against stone as Nekhaia's magic filled the air with the scent of sulfur and bone.

The stone we'd hidden behind—where we'd taken shelter— heaved and teetered.

And rolled.

I curled around Illya, felt his arms wrap around my middle as the shadow of the earth crashed over us.

But only the shadow.

My heartbeat hammered the walls of my chest so hard I thought it would bruise. A light dusting of displaced snow kissed my cheeks. I peeked up, and found we were, by some miracle, whole. The Voynik was gone. Crushed. And Illya, though pale and blood-soaked, was alive. He managed a slight, pained smile.

"Did he hit you? Or did the bolt wound reopen?" I asked, pressing down on Illya's shoulder, trying to stanch the bleeding.

"Bolt," he ground out.

"Zosha, I need the bandages from my pack," I said, but nothing met my words.

The sound of silence shrouded the gully, pulling my attention past the little world Illya's presence created. Nekhaia and Zosha stood a few yards away, both ashen-faced and shaken. But alive. Unhurt.

At least in body, I amended, looking at Zosha. At the blood-stained sword in his hand and the three dead Voyniks—still half-trapped in earth—behind him.

"Zosha," I said, my voice careful as I called him back into his body.

He looked at me, eyes watery and unmoored. Horror gathered in his face a second before he whirled. He made it a few unsteady steps before he doubled over, retching into the blood-stained snow.

I closed my eyes, grasping for something to say, but then stopped.

Because the forest had gone still. More than that even. It was as if the very fabric of the world had rippled and gone silent. Like the void after a child's scream. And then I heard it.

Horses.

The ghosts appeared in the echo of the hoofbeats. Their bodies bubbled out of the frozen earth like steam rising from a cauldron. Their faces were wrought with terror. But it was to Ozura that I looked. Ozura who I went to for courage . . . but there was none to be found there. Her liquid black eyes were set with fear.

"Run."

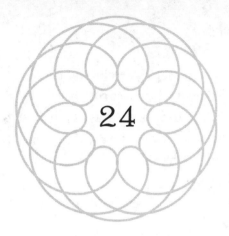

24

WE HAVE TO GO," I whispered, my voice hissing across the snow. "Nekhaia, cover our tracks. Zosha, help me."

Together, Zosha and I hauled Illya off the ground. With one of his arms draped over our shoulders, we half ran, half shambled our way across the snow-covered landscape. The slightest tremor of earth beneath my feet told me Nekhaia had sunk the bodies, and snow shivered at our heels as she erased our tracks. I ignored the urge to look back, knowing that if they saw us, we were well and truly done for.

"How much farther?" I demanded of the ghosts. Magic flooded into me, riming my joints in ice. I didn't fight the tether, but hugged it close, clinging to the magic that flowed through me.

"Less than a quarter of a mile," Vitaly replied, body streaking gray as he glided alongside. *"You'll need to angle slightly west to find a path down the cliff."*

A curse caught in my throat and became a growl. *"Show me!"*

Vitaly streaked ahead, dashing through trees as he went, leaving a faint phosphorescent trail for us to follow. We struggled through the always-grasping boughs of the evergreens. They grew so densely together that I couldn't see the way ahead. But we had to be close. A quarter mile, Vitaly said. We must nearly be upon it.

Lady Night, please let us be close.

As I thought it, we burst through a line of branches, and the world before us dropped away. I choked back a scream, throwing all my weight backward, dragging Illya and Zosha with me. We landed hard, skidding to a stop only a few feet from the drop-off.

"Day Lord save me," Nekhaia breathed. "*These* are the Riven Cliffs?"

I recognized the incredulity in her voice. Ragata had once told me of this place, of the fault lines that ran through the earth stretching and tearing the glacial plateau of Roven high above the rest of the continent. She'd told of massive plates pulling away from one another like lovers mid-quarrel. But never, *never* had I imagined this.

The sheer drop of the cliff ran as far as I could see to the east, and to the west the surge of the River Tol as it crashed over the side was nothing more than a distant echo on the breeze. But looking over the edge was like peering over the side of the world.

The cliffs stretched out, impossibly far, the ground beneath a mist-covered mystery. And the path Vitaly led us to was hardly deserving of the name. Carved out of the cliff face, it was barely more than a foot wide, rough-cut and slick. I wasn't normally afraid of heights, but this . . .

"How far down is that?" I asked, voice laden low by fear.

"Over two thousand feet in most spots," Zosha replied, pale face splotched with bright red patches as he looked over the edge.

"And that's the path?" Nekhaia asked, swallowing hard.

"We'll be fine," I replied, lifting my chin. "We just need to make it to the first tomb." I made sure to meet both of their eyes, refusing to allow even a hint of fear on my face, before turning to Illya.

He hadn't joined us in looking at the cliffs. Hadn't even

risen. Just sat in the snow, one arm resting on a bent knee, the other pressed tight against his chest. Pain lined his face, but he met my gaze.

"We can't tarry here. Just a little farther and we can take a rest. Fix up your arm."

He nodded, letting me pull him to his feet. Together, we slowly, *carefully* stepped onto the path. Nekhaia took the lead, her magic questing out ahead, searching for weak spots in the stone. But all she could do was strengthen the path where it flagged. She had no strength left for more. The rest was up to us.

The descent was agonizing. Hours—days—seemed to pass with every inch of hard-fought ground. And it was truly a fight. Wind tore my body, hungry fingers raking through my hair and tugging at my clothes. It was almost like a living thing, a malevolent presence that thirsted to throw me off the path and make me plummet to an inevitable death.

And always, the fear of Voyniks peering over the lip, finding us. Attacking us with rocks or arrows or magic. Dragging us back to Tolograd like lambs for slaughter . . .

I pressed myself to the rock face, feeling every jagged stone grind into my back as I inched forward. My hands burned raw, nails cracked and broken for how tight I clung to the cliff behind me. Inching further. Further.

Finally, after a descent that felt like miles but was only a distance of about forty feet, did we find one of the tombs. The opening was six feet square, but time and wind had eroded the edges so that the cave mouth was wickedly sharp as I scraped past it. It was empty but for a flat stone slab where a body had undoubtedly sat to decay and return to the world beyond. I could just make out worn etchings of writing on the side of the slab. The story of a life long forgotten.

Curiosity was a dull spark in the back of my mind, easily ignored by the need to escape the cutting wind. At the far back corner of the cave lay a gap in the wall. It was so narrow, Illya had to turn sideways to pass through it, hissing as his shoulder scraped against the rock. Beyond the gap was a hallway wandering both east and west along the cliff—exactly where Zosha said it would be.

There was barely any light in the corridor, just a slight graying of the dark where a tomb opened up to the cliff and sky. But it was more than we'd have deeper in, so I forced Illya to sit. I peeled back the layers of his coat and tunic, the fabric sticky with cold, congealing blood.

His flesh had parted into a jagged maw where the wound reopened. The skin was puffy and livid, but the worst of the bleeding had stopped. I shook my head in mute frustration, knowing there was little I could do for him but wrap it as tightly as possible. He needed a healer. Needed one soon—before infection could sink in.

"*Should I cauterize it?*" I asked as Katarzhina appeared out of the murk on a gust of frigid air, summoned by my fear. "*Illya is a fire witch—I could have him heat a blade . . .*"

My words petered out at the way Katarzhina was slowly shaking her head. "*I don't think that would be a good idea at this point. Whatever strength he has now would be utterly spent and would take him more than a day to regain. You'd be forced to leave him here to recover, or wait with him . . .*"

And risk Radovan finding us. She didn't need to say it. The words echoed down the long cave-like corridor.

Nothing to do but keep moving forward, I thought, but as I got him redressed my resolve faltered. His eyes were glassy with exhaustion, his body rag-doll limp as he tried to help me. And though we were close, *so close*, there was no way he'd be able to walk the few miles that now separated us from Kirskov. I pressed a hand to his chest, stilling him before looking to Nekhaia and Zosha.

"Let's rest here for an hour or two," I said, my voice carrying oddly through the caves. "Eat something. Sleep if you can."

The other two just nodded, because even if they wanted to argue, they were clearly too tired. I settled onto the floor beside Illya, resting my head against the wall, ready to keep watch while the others slept. But my body had other ideas. As the wind outside sang a crooning sort of lullaby, my eyes got heavy, and fell closed.

I wasn't sure exactly what woke me. The rough corner of an uneven stone wall was certainly not helping me sleep, I thought, stretching. Illya lay beside me, his bulk a barrier against the unrelenting darkness beyond us. One of his hands rested on the hilt of his stolen sword, and his face, even in sleep, was a silent threat to anyone who might move against us.

Against me.

I smiled and reached out, stroking the skin between his eyes until the small wrinkle there faded. His expression eased. He looked younger now, more at peace than I could ever recall seeing him.

I could have spent the rest of the night studying his face. Which was why I could do nothing but freeze when the edge of a blade pressed into his exposed neck.

"As pretty as the two of you are together, my dear, you should know that I do not like to share."

I followed the voice, gaze tripping up the sword's blade to the pale hand and the man who belonged to it. Radovan.

"Rada, stop."

"No." He growled the word, eyes flashing with a too-familiar hint of madness. It was the same look he'd had before he killed his own nobles in front of their children. "You turned my court against me. You turned my soldiers against me, Askia. For what? For *him*?"

He pressed the blade further into Illya's neck. An incoherent cry clawed up my throat. Blood brighter than any rose beaded on the edge of the blade. If Illya so much as twitched, he'd be dead.

But Illya didn't move. Didn't even open his eyes. No one did. Nekhaia, Zosha, all of them were completely still. Utterly asleep. Only Radovan and I were awake.

Or were we?

I blinked once. Twice. And sat upright, folding my arms. "This is a dream."

The corner of Radovan's lips twitched. "It is."

"What do you want?"

I willed his eyes to stay on mine, to ignore the way the shadows around us deepened under my command—it was *my* dream after all, why shouldn't I use it to obscure my location?

"Why, whatever do you mean?" he asked, sheathing his sword with a small flourish.

I let one of my eyebrows rise. "I mean that you took the effort to come here. You must want something. So what is it? To talk terms?"

"Is that what you're hoping for? That I might wish to discuss terms of surrender?" He shook his head with that little laugh I'd come to hate so, so deeply. "How funny that you aren't even entertaining the notion that you can escape me."

I winced at that, letting my face lie where my words could not. Let him think I was weakening toward despair. That the Voyniks crawling through the forest were dampening my hope. That Radovan invading my dreams was crushing my spirit. Let him think all of that and more. But never let him suspect the truth. Because I wasn't trying to escape. I was trying to win this war once and for all.

"What are the terms?"

Radovan surveyed me for a long moment. He stepped over Illya's prone form. Crouched, long legs bending like some kind of giant insect, until his face was even with mine. His pale green eyes peppered across my face.

"None."

"None?" For all my resolve, something in me trembled. "What do you mean?

"I will offer you nothing. Not. One. Thing. I don't want your surrender. I want to hunt you across the whole of Kinvara. Until I find you, and each and every one of your allies. And then I will kill all of you. Slowly. So, so slowly.

"And I am going to start with him." Radovan dragged one skeletal finger down Illya's face, a caress I would never unsee, intimate and terrifying. "This strong man you risked so much to rescue. And you will believe me when I tell you, that he will be a long time in dying."

He reached for me then, tucking a tendril of hair behind my ear as Illya had done so many times before. "You do believe me, don't you, Askia?"

Before I could reply, Radovan was in motion. He grabbed my face in both hands.

And snapped my neck.

I GASPED, HEAVING IN AIR AS I SURGED UPRIGHT. THE BREATH hitched in my lungs, as my body struggled to realign with a reality my mind couldn't quite believe. I ran a hand across my throat, sure I'd find it bent and broken.

Illya dragged himself upright, worry scrawled across his face. "Are you all right?"

I managed to nod. "Just a nightmare," I said, voice sounding raw to my own ears.

He looked at me a moment longer, like he didn't quite believe me.

"*Just* a nightmare?" Nekhaia's voice was loaded with all the doubt that Illya hadn't voiced. "Bullshit. What did Radovan say now?"

I squinted toward her face; the shadows deepening in the corridor made it hard to read her expression. But the one thing they did make clear was that we'd slept far too long.

"Only that he is going to hunt me to the ends of the earth and when he inevitably catches us, that he'll kill each and every one of you just to hurt me." I strained to sound calm, cavalier even. I knew I'd failed but was unspeakably grateful when Nekhaia rolled her eyes.

"So the usual then?"

"Pretty much."

"We should go," Illya said, lumbering to his feet.

I nodded. "Let me just check in with the queens first. See where Radovan is."

The cold caress of the tether on my face was a welcome balm to the phantom touch of Radovan's hands on my skin. It was Eliska who responded to my call this time, her eyes worriedly locked on Illya's face.

"Where is Radovan?"

"Still in Tolograd waiting for his men to find you," she replied, shaking her head as if to bring herself back to the business at hand. *"He knows you're close to Kirskov, though he still thinks you likely to be on the western side of the river. But with the number of people he has searching the forest . . . I don't think you have long before he figures out where you really are."*

We started walking as soon as I reported Eliska's words. What else was there to say? The only hope of our gambit succeeding was if we reached the Heart before Radovan realized our true intentions. So we set out at a hurried pace, our steps echoing back to us along the length of the rocky corridor.

With Illya too weak to light our path, the only illumination came from the tomb openings carved into the wall. They peppered the rock at uneven intervals, allowing ever-fainter traces of sunlight to filter through.

But for all my drive, something itched between my shoulders, a sense of eyes on my back. Like I could feel Radovan's attention turning this way, feel his hands stretching out, searching, reaching. The stone only amplified the feeling. Something inside it ticked against my skin, a clockwork heart coming to life to remind me that we were hunted. That *I* was hunted.

My unease grew as the tunnels began to slope inward, away from the meager light of the cliff face, into the earth itself. Soon even our shambling pace slowed to a crawl as we formed a human chain. I led, not because I could see the path—I couldn't. But darkness was no barrier to the ghosts, and I could see them.

Ragata floated in silence up ahead, taking us around twists and turns until eventually I realized we were going up a shallow incline. The darkness ahead lessened slightly, as if we were about to come to another room, this one lit not by sunlight, but candlelight. I saw the warm flicker of flame dance on the floor of the hallway—for it looked like a hallway now, the cave-like walls and floor had given way to pavers and brick while we walked in darkness. An open doorway lay to the right of the hall, beckoning.

By unspoken accord, we crept closer as silently as possible.

Closer.

Closer.

And that's when I heard it: the sound of a man's voice.

25

I HELD UP a hand for everyone to stop and flattened myself against the wall. My ears strained over the sound of my heart, trying to make out what the man was saying. Only it didn't sound like words. Not really. More an out-of-tune melody of some kind.

It clicked just as Katarzhina appeared at my side.

"It's Gethen," I whispered, looking back at my companions. "Radovan's son."

"What is he doing here?" Zosha asked.

I had no answer. I'd known Radovan had had Gethen moved from Tolograd weeks ago. But what was he doing here? Beneath the palace of Kirskov?

"*Is he alone?*" I asked the ghost at my side.

"*Of course he's alone,*" Katarzhina replied, her voice raw with a mother's anger. "*Radovan never hires enough minders for Gethen—and he loves to wander, explore really.*"

Explore, I thought, mind turning . . .

I looked to Zosha. "Do you think he might know where the Heart is?"

Zosha shrugged, his face thoughtful. "Gethen's a lot smarter than people give him credit for. He might not be able to tell us, but if he knows where it is, he might show us."

I peered around the corner, studying the space carefully before entering. It was a wide chamber—mostly empty. Directly across from where I stood was a staircase leading up into the darkness beyond my sight. Only a large stone table sat in the middle of the room, some kind of preparation slab I thought. Once used to ready bodies for entombment, it was now adorned with a single hand-lamp. A starburst pattern covered the floor in alternating red and white bricks. The design was mirrored in the ceiling and was what seemed to have captivated Gethen.

"Hello, Gethen," I called, voice light as I slid into the room.

He turned to look toward me and back at the ceiling again, as if my presence were no surprise at all.

"Are you looking at the pretty design?" I asked, feeling Illya, Zosha, and Nekhaia coming to my back.

Gethen just nodded, pointing upward to the center of the starburst.

"It's beautiful," I said, struggling to figure out what to say next. Finally, something came to me.

"Gethen, would you like to play a game with us?"

He nodded again, looking away from the ceiling now to study my friends.

"Good," I began slowly. "We are searching for something, a stone your father recently brought here. You may have heard it called the Heart." I smiled when he nodded again. "Well, the game is, we are trying to reach the stone, but we don't want any of your father's men to see us . . . do you think you can help?"

Gethen turned to the table, picking up his lamp by way of reply. When he left the room, it wasn't for the staircase, but for the hall where we'd just come. I exchanged a look with Illya, shrugged, and followed the prince.

Gethen turned left out the door, traveling deeper into the earth. Five minutes. Ten. Until at last the corridor ended in a narrow door that I would have taken for a closet until Gethen opened it. A tight spiral staircase lay beyond, narrow enough that even walking up one at a time, it felt like a squeeze.

The stairs let out of another closet-like doorway.

Right into a dungeon.

Nekhaia uttered a low curse as Gethen wandered down a hall pockmarked with cell doors. I understood her reaction. Her fear. Was this some kind of trap?

"Gethen isn't capable of cunning," Katarzhina said, in response to our unspoken worry. *"Please, trust him."*

And I did. I squared my shoulders and tiptoed down the hall, praying that whoever occupied these cells would say nothing. For if this was a dungeon, then there must surely be guards nearby.

We made it past the first three cells unnoticed but at the fourth, the prisoner stirred. And spoke. "My lady?"

I spun, nearly tripping over my feet in my haste. "Fyedik?"

Always a rangy man, Fyedik looked like he'd lost a good fifteen pounds in recent months, but the smile flashing beneath his grizzled beard was filled with joy and relief. "You're a sight for sore eyes, my lady. Cap."

"That's my good boy," Katarzhina said, eyes bright with pride at Gethen's cleverness in bringing us here. I beamed at him while Zosha patted his stepbrother's shoulder, murmuring praise.

"How long have you been here?" Illya asked, hurrying forward to clasp Fyedik's hand through the bars.

"Only one day," he replied. "Got caught in a freak storm and before we knew it, we were surrounded by nearly fifty Voyniks. I had no idea what they were all doing out in the middle of the forest—guessing it has something to do with you lot being here?"

I smiled. "Sorry for the inconvenience, but I decided I'd had enough of Radovan's hospitality and took an abrupt leave of Tolograd."

"To come here?"

"It's a long story," I whispered. "I can tell it as we work. Nekhaia, can you do something with the locks?"

She wasted little time, breaking the iron lock on the door with a burst of magic. But not even Nekhaia's power could break the all-too-familiar-looking chain around Fyedik's neck. Enchanted—just like the one around my neck—to keep the witches from accessing their magic. I filled Fyedik in on the details while we worked to free the other men.

Illya and three others went ahead, creeping through the twisting corridors to sort out the prison guards. We'd just reached Mav's cell—our jolly-faced camp cook—when a muffled shout echoed down the hall.

Followed by silence.

I took Gethen's hand, leading him back to Zosha and Nekhaia while we waited. And waited.

Footsteps clapped down the hall. Out of the gloom, Illya appeared, a triumphant shine in his eyes. "Got the key," he murmured and set to work unlocking the enchanted chains.

"Ah, that's the ticket." Mav sighed, stretching like the chain had been a physical weight crushing down on him. "You and your friends all right, my lady? I can help if you're hurt."

My face nearly cracked with relief. All this time, little old Mav was hiding healing magic behind his stew-stained aprons. "We're fine, but Illya could use your help."

"Just patch me up," Illya grunted, when Mav came over.

"Lady Night," the cook muttered as he looked at the wound.

"Pray later. We've got to hurry."

With twenty newly freed and battle-ready witches behind us, we made quick work of the guards dozing outside the dungeon. Pausing only to steal as many weapons as we could find, Gethen led us up another set of stairs and down another long hallway.

I knew I should be getting anxious as we crept closer and closer to the Heart. But the feeling of my friends, my countrymen at my back, buoyed me. I hadn't truly realized how much I missed it, being surrounded by my own people. Or how homesick I was beneath all my bravado.

We wandered a maze of corridors, following in Gethen's wake, never running into either soldier or servant. Either we were still far beneath the castle proper, or Kirskov had emptied in search of me. Perhaps both.

The sound of low-spoken Rovenese around the next bend made us all slow. I let Gethen go ahead, shuffling back to make space for my men.

"Eh now, Prince Gethen," a friendly sounding voice said. "You know your old pa doesn't want you wandering down here. Why don't you go to the kitchens and—"

Whatever was in the kitchens was lost as Fyedik and another earth witch pounced. Magic shot through the stone, swallowing the guard whole. Or guards, I amended as I came around the curve in time to see two long pikes fall clattering to the floor. Gethen paused to look at them, expression confused.

He was still frowning when he turned back to me.

And pointed at the door.

26

I EXPECTED TO walk into another dungeon-like room. Or a blank space, utterly white and sterile like the rooms of horror that lay beneath the castle in Tolograd.

Instead, I walked into a temple.

Yet it was unlike any temple I'd ever seen. Rough-hewn stone, cut from the earth by hand like the sky tombs below us, made up the walls and vaulted ceilings of this underground shrine. The floors were bare, but I could still make out the imprint from where a carpet had lain, marking the path between the pews all the way to the altar. Gold chandeliers hung dusty and unused from the ceiling. The space was lit instead by a series of perfunctory witchlight orbs hovering in the far reaches of the room. A stone altar, obsidian by its black sheen, sat atop three shallow steps across from me.

This place was old, I thought, entering the room past row after row of worn stone pews. As ancient as the sky tombs peppering the cliffs not far from here. It was evidence of a lineage that stretched back to time immemorial, a lineage Radovan had tossed aside in his unquenchable thirst for power.

A thirst evidenced by the green stone sitting across the room.

My steps echoed too loud as I walked up to the altar, beholding the source of the stones that had brought me nothing but heartache. I wasn't sure what I'd expected the Heart to look like. Something monolithic, certainly. What I saw instead was a melon-sized orb of stone. It sat in a metal pedestal, multifaceted edges shining in the low-light casting prisms of green and blue, purple and red onto the altar below.

It was beautiful and alluring and inviting and . . . incomprehensible. How could such a small thing contain so many souls? Or cause so much pain?

"So that's it," Illya said, coming to my right.

"I thought it'd be bigger," Nekhaia added to my left.

"So did I," I replied, feeling my lips twitch in an almost-smile. I looked back at them.

My men were taking up positions around the door, readying themselves in case of a fight. Gethen and Zosha had wandered to the wall on my left. They knelt on the floor, playing some kind of game with pegs and marbles. It was so natural, the camaraderie between them. Like the possibility of Radovan's sudden appearance wasn't hanging over them, suffocating them like a shroud. I tore my eyes away. Back to business.

"I don't suppose you know how to release the souls?"

Nekhaia snorted. "Fucked if I know."

"Fair enough." I cracked my neck, gaze darting to Illya. "Watch my back?"

He met my eyes, more unyielding than any stone. "Always."

I took one step up. Then the next.

"Asyl," I called, letting the tether slide around my body like cold rope around unguarded flesh. *"Will you help me?"*

The ghost appeared, not standing beside me, but kneeling prostrate before the stone. She straightened slowly as if willing her body to move bone by bone. *"This goes so far beyond sacrilege,"* she said, tears gliding down her spectral face. *"Can't you see that? Can't you see that what you now stand before is no mere stone, but a piece of Lady Night Herself?"*

I gave her a long look, because it wasn't that I didn't understand. I did. I knew what harming this stone would mean for
me—probable damnation. And if it had to be destroyed? The
deaths of everyone in this room—if not the castle beyond. People I cared for. Loved.

But it had to be done.

*"I don't want to destroy it, Asyl. But Radovan must be stopped.
The souls must be released. No one should have access to this power—
even Lady Night knows that. Help me."*

She was silent for a long moment. Finally, she took a deep
breath and said, *"Touch the stone."*

"That's it? Touch the stone?"

"It's a living thing, Askia," she replied sharply. *"Touch the stone,
commune with it, and learn what you need to know."*

I turned away from her, keeping my magic at the ready. But
as I took the final step up to the altar, the stone on my neck
moved. Not the phantom ticking sensation that warned me Radovan was searching, or the burning that happened when he
used magic. This was something else entirely. Almost like the
stone sensed the Heart and was eager to return home.

Repressing a shudder, I reached out.

And touched the Heart.

SENSATION FLOODED INTO ME, AN AVALANCHE OF SIGHTS AND
sounds, emotions and memories bore down on my mind. They
tore me open, searching, hunting, grasping, but for what I didn't
know. Couldn't even think. Couldn't fight. Or move. I was locked
in place, more thoroughly than Radovan's magic had ever held me
as the . . . the *sentience* within the Heart pillaged my mind.

And it was a sentience, I realized as the first wave of it
crashed over me and the next reared. One mind comprised of
thousands of souls. Formless and ancient and brimming with—

"*Love.*"

The word rose in my mind, but it didn't come from me. It came from the Heart itself.

"*Love?*" I asked, not understanding how something so painful could quantify as love.

"*You are young. There is pain in birth, pain in death, pain in life. But all these are labors of love. You know this to be true—how love can bring life-giving joy and how it can even be present in death,*" the Heart said, images of my mother and father, of Illya and Vitaly, Armaan and Ozura flashing through my skull. "*Perhaps one day you will learn how the pain of love can birth something new . . . but. You did not come to me to learn of love, did you?*"

"*No.*"

"*No. You, the darkest child of Lady Night, came here to kill me.*"

I flinched then. Not because the words were untrue, but because they were delivered with a voice I knew—my mother's voice. Plucked from my memory by the Heart and given life once more, if only for the space of this conversation—for Lady Night was a mother too. And what better choice could the Heart have made, but to commune with me in this way?

It was cruel and cunning and I wanted to scream. But it was right—*she*—was right. I had come to kill the Heart. If it could be considered alive.

"*You know better than most, that life doesn't require flesh.*"

"*I do,*" I replied, hating how the voice in my head wavered. Hating how, after so many years, I longed to hear my mother's voice speak to me in joy and pride. Not this recrimination. "*But I didn't come here to kill you, not necessarily. I came to release the souls trapped inside you.*"

"*You can't.*"

"*I have to!*" I cried, feeling like I was a child all over again, begging for my mother's help . . . but my mother never made me beg. Never. Not once. I closed my eyes for a moment. Reached for calm. *"If I can release the trapped souls, it will rob Radovan and all his sorcerers of their power. You have to help me."*

"If it's knowledge you wish for, then knowledge you will have," the Heart replied with infinite patience. *"But you cannot release the souls, because you don't. Have. Time."*

It took me a moment to understand—the knowledge dawning upon me like a black star rising overhead. The stone . . . the one on my chest . . . *it had moved.*

And if I felt it.

So did Radovan.

I whirled, dropping the connection with the Heart. Opened my mouth—

Pain!

Pain such as I'd never experienced. It tore through me, bombarding every cell in my body. My bones shook from it, my blood boiled. So blindingly hot, so filled with brilliant white heat, I thought I'd never see color again. I screamed. Tried not to. Tried to choke it back only to feel a tooth crack—such a small hurt compared to the agony contorting my muscles.

I heard Illya's voice. Felt Mav's healing magic zap through me. But it wasn't enough. Not against the full force of Radovan's fury.

And then it was gone.

I lay shaking on the floor, half-deaf in the echo of my own screams. Blood dripped from my mouth, coating my tongue in iron. Faces were all turned to me, Illya and Zosha, Nekhaia and Gethen watching me with fear in their eyes.

But not nearly enough fear.

Because there was only one way Radovan would have been able to bring down that much agony on me.

"He's here," I cried. "Seal the door!"

27

MY MEN TURNED instinctively to the door, but Nekhaia's magic got their first. Flinging her arms out, the rock wall around the doorway groaned and cracked as inch by inch the stone grew. Sealing us in.

And Radovan out.

Illya helped me to my feet, fingers digging into my arms before I could return to the stone. "You can do this," he murmured, and let me go.

I prayed he was right as I swallowed down my own blood and seized the stone with both hands.

"All right, I've bought some time. Tell me how to release the souls."

"It's not enough."

"It will have to be."

There was a pause, then, almost as if it pitied me, the Heart said, *"See. Know."*

The images came once more. Flashes of light, of song. Candles and ritual. And as I watched, my own heart fell. Broke. Because releasing the souls trapped was less like opening a box or snapping a chain. It was a birth. Arduous. Dangerous. And long.

The Heart hadn't lied. We didn't have time.

A thundering crash echoed against the stone door–turned–wall behind me. Emphasizing the point.

"What do I do?" my internal voice whispered.

"You do what you were made to do, darkest child of Lady Night. You kill."

"But how? How do I kill a stone? It's not as if I can just swing my sword and—"

"Are you not a death witch?" the voice demanded, as hard and unforgiving as the movement of the earth. *"Your province, indeed your very life, is death. So wield the magic you were given, and kill me."*

The stone said it so casually, but there was a problem: killing with my power was the one lesson I'd never been taught. Never wanted to learn. Because magic was meant to be a tool, one among many. But using it to maim, to kill, was so far beyond wrong, even considering it made me think of Radovan—of how he'd perverted magic itself, used it to kill twelve men and women, popping their heads off like a child does flowers.

A second earth-shaking boom reverberated across the room.

But that was why I had to do it. To stop Radovan.

So I had to learn.

"Show me. Show me how."

The Heart obliged.

And it was simple. So, so simple. For there was a thread in every living thing, a sort of anchor that tied together body and soul. It was fragile and priceless and made entirely of hopes and dreams. And if I could just see it, I could cut it. But in learning to see, *I would never unsee.*

It would be there, hovering just in the corner of my eye. Visible in everyone I loved and hated. In strangers . . . and in my own reflection. Wearing thinner and thinner as death slowly marched forward.

The sheer burden of it made my knees go weak. Because it meant I would always now know how close everyone was to death: Zosha and Nekhaia, Illya and myself. An accounting of time measured not in days or weeks, but in the slowly fading light of a thread that only I could see.

"That is not the true burden," the Heart intoned, phantom voice enveloping me in dread as the sound of a third thundering crash echoed into my back. *"I will not fight my death, but it will require sacrifice."*

I knew it was right. I'd known it for days. But there was a difference between knowing a thing and facing it. *"Show me."*

I saw myself then—a vision within my own head. Wearing the same clothes, the same scars. But my face did not bear looking at. Riven open with grief.

And resolve.

I couldn't look away.

I watched unmoving as my vision-self reached out, placing my palm to the stone. Saw my magic quest outward. A sinuous darkness wove through the Heart like poisonous blood through veins. The magic delved deeper. Deeper. To the tiny golden thread that lay at the Heart's center. Tears spilled down my cheeks. I pulled.

The universe pulled back.

Fire. Ash. Screams and death. Everything was destroyed. Not just the Heart, but the altar, the temple, and the palace beyond. All of it, wiped off the face of the earth, leaving nothing more than a crater in the ground. A crater soon filled by the raging black waters of the River Tol.

I wrenched my mind away. Tears poured down my face as denial—illogical and untamable denial—flooded out of me. *"Why? Why this? Take me. My death I accept. But everyone else? There is no need."* The force of this destruction . . . it wasn't fair.

I was prepared for my own death, but this? And now, with Radovan pounding on the door behind me, my promise to Ragata rang clear. A promise broken. Because I'd never get Zosha—or Gethen—out.

"No," the voice agreed, unfeeling in the face of my grief. *"There is no escape for any of them. You came here to kill me—to stop Radovan and the perversion he is spreading across these lands. This is the price.*

"You meddle in the realm of the Two-Faced God, my child. And the God cuts both ways. You may kill me, last physical remnant of Lady Night that remains on this plane. But a sacrifice must be made."

"There has to be another way. Another choice."

"There is always another choice," the Heart replied, softer now, its swirling center glimmering red and pink almost like it was trying to comfort me in its own alien way. *"Remember daughter, the stone you wear needs many days to take your magic. But it only takes seconds for you to give it. Remember this. And choose."*

My hand fell to my side. The Heart's last words echoed through my mind, but no matter how hard I scrabbled for them, I couldn't make them land—couldn't understand. Not with grief shuddering through me, unmaking me piece by piece.

A hand fell onto my shoulder. "Askia? What is it?"

I didn't want to look at Illya. Because if I did, I would have to explain. And if I explained, I'd have to ask—ask for permission . . .

To kill them all.

His rough hand found my chin, tilting it upward. Concern was written across his face, worry for the numb kind of horror that surely marred my expression. His eyes widened. And he understood. Nekhaia had warned us, after all. Destroying the Heart would have a cost. And the cost was all of us.

"It's bad, isn't it?" Nekhaia asked from somewhere behind me.

I grasped Illya's hand, squeezing it once for solace, and turned to the room. Nekhaia and Zosha were closest to me, now standing at the foot of the dais. They watched me, wide eyes beseeching, begging me to tell them otherwise. Tell them that everything would be all right. That we'd make it out of here alive.

But I couldn't lie to them. Not about this. And not when the battering ram of Radovan's magic punctuated my every heartbeat.

"It's bad," I said, forcing strength into my voice now, a strength that others could lean on. "I can destroy the Heart, with my death magic," I continued, loud enough for everyone to hear. "But the magic contained within it won't simply disappear. It will explode outward and take this whole palace with it—and everyone here will die."

A strangled cry came out of Zosha's lips, but he was the only one who made a sound. Nekhaia's shoulders dropped and my men—my soldiers—fell to stillness. They looked to me, and to Illya. To each other . . . and prepared.

"So now you're the one asking for permission?" Zosha asked, voice so, so bitter. But not bitter enough, not with his mother beside him, on her knees. Begging me to save him. "Permission to destroy my mother's soul? To kill me—kill all of us?"

I met his gaze and steeled myself.

And for one final time, made myself a queen.

"No. I'm not asking for your permission. I'm telling you what must be done. Day Lord forgive me. I am sorry."

"Tell that to my mother," he spat.

"I already am," I whispered, watching Ragata crumble. Watching Siv and Freyda hold on to her as if they could take on some of her grief. I watched Katarzhina standing mute and frozen, tears spilling down her face as she stood beside Gethen—who I prayed, *prayed* didn't understand what was coming.

And Eliska—watching her brother, watching me. Grim faced, but ready for what came next.

"You're still wearing the chain," Nekhaia said dully. "The enchantment on it will stop you."

I nodded, forcing myself to confront the pain ahead. "It will try. But we have a healer," I said, looking to Mav. "That is, if you're willing to help me by mitigating the worst of the punishment?"

Mav seemed to have sunk in on himself, and for a silent moment, he said nothing. But then he shook himself, all his long years etched onto his face as he looked up at me. And nodded. "I pledged myself to Seravesh. To you. I am with you, my lady. Until the end."

The other men—my men—nodded too. "Until the end." The words echoed through the chamber, an oath made in defiance of death, thrown at the feet of the Two-Faced God. To save the world. And die trying.

As Mav made his way forward, I turned to Illya, knowing his gaze had never left my face, not for one moment. His gray eyes betrayed no fear—not even an inch. But I knew it was within him. I could see it in the frenzied flicker of a gold thread dancing along his spine. It was the desperate desire for life—a life that had been robbed from him so many times and in so many ways. It was a feeling I recognized all too well, for I felt it too.

And seeing it made tears rise in my eyes.

We didn't speak then. Didn't need to, for leaving those three words unspoken didn't make them less true. He grasped my face in both hands and kissed me. It was the kind of kiss that made me—not whole, for I was already that—but new. It was a kiss that promised a future of hope and passion, joy and pain. A life that I knew we wouldn't have, but damn it I wanted it anyway.

I was breathless when it ended. Our heads tilted together,

foreheads touching. "I would have loved it," I whispered, voice breaking at the end, "that life we should have lived."

Tracing his face with my fingers one last time, I let him go and turned.

I reached for the Heart.

And the room exploded at my back.

28

THE CONCUSSING FORCE of the blast sent me careening forward. My body folded into the edge of the altar so hard it crushed my ribs and sternum to the breaking point. My knees folded beneath me. I shook my head, struggling to clear pain and disorientation from my eyes.

Through the tangled curtain of my hair, I watched Radovan stalk through the door with Qaden and fifty Voyniks at his back—no. Not just Voyniks. Sorcerers. My men, outnumbered two to one, could do nothing but watch while we were surrounded. As Radovan picked through the rubble, there was nothing human in his face. Nothing sane. There never had been, I realized. Just a carefully crafted mask.

The Aellium stone flashed on his chest—burning mine— and wind magic tumbled out of him. It caught Illya and Mav, lifting both men bodily off the floor—tossing them into the back wall like they were nothing more than trash. That same magic bore down on me, locking every joint, every muscle in place as if I'd been turned to stone.

I could do nothing but watch him come closer. Closer. His boots rapping against the floor like the first stones to fall in an avalanche.

"You went through all that effort to escape. And you come

here." He whispered the words, like his voice couldn't bare holding all the outrage he felt. "How did you even know about this place? Who told you? Who betrayed me?"

Radovan shouted the last words, spraying hot spittle into my face. His power punched down, not giving me time to respond or react. Invisible, clawed hands peeled open my mind, pulling out my memories of the Heart with ruthless precision. Faces were torn from my head: Tcheshin. Vitaly. Asyl. Roshko.

Everyone, living and dead, who had helped me get to this place—even Qaden, whose only crime was letting me flee the workshop that fateful day in Tolograd. But as angry as he was at her and the rest, I knew where his real rage lay. For their faces lingered longest in my mind.

Zosha.

And Gethen.

"Both of them," he said, almost as if he couldn't believe it. "You turned *both* of them against me."

There was no reply I could make of that. No reply Radovan would allow. For he had already made up his mind.

His head whipped around, attention arrowing straight to Zosha and Gethen as if he were a hound who'd just caught a scent.

Both Zosha and Gethen were on the edge of the room, crouched in the corner with Nekhaia. It looked almost like Zosha and Nekhaia had dragged Gethen off to one side of the dais when Radovan blasted into the room. But there was nothing to hide behind. The few stone pews covering the floor did nothing to guard them. Not when Radovan shoved them aside with a wave of his hand.

"*You,*" Radovan hissed, walking straight through Ragata, bearing down on Zosha with an ugly grin. "I should have known you'd eventually turn on me. I thought I had saved you from your mother's poisonous words, but no. After all I've done for you: fed you, clothed you, given you everything. Status. Power. And *this* is how you repay me?"

For a terrifying moment, I watched Zosha's hand twitch toward his pocket. Toward the vial of poison I knew he had hidden, given to him by the Nines for this very moment.

Instead, Zosha balled his fists. And stood tall, meeting Radovan's eye—not without fear. But in spite of it.

"What did you expect? You killed my real father, kidnapped my mother, and when she tried to save me, you had her tortured. No, not just that. You *broke* her, just to see if you could. And when she was no longer useful to you, you murdered her." I'd never heard Zosha speak so coldly, so righteously. "So yes. I'd say this is perfect recompense for the man who *took* everything from me."

"I gave you everything!" Radovan bellowed the words, as if volume alone could make Zosha's accusations untrue. "And you."

He whirled on Gethen then, grabbing his son by the collar and lifting Gethen bodily into the air. His toes scraped helplessly against the ground, eyes wild. Jagged cries croaked from Gethen's lips. But Radovan didn't see it. Or didn't care. Nothing was left of the man who so carefully played at humanity. All that was left now was the monster, and the ghost of Katarzhina prying vainly at his hands, begging him to stop.

"You unworthy defect of a man. I should have had you drowned the day you were born."

"Sire, stop." Qaden rushed forward, placing a staying hand on one of Radovan's arms. Her face was tight with fear, but I saw determination there too. The determination of a woman who didn't want to be ordered to kill any more innocent children. "Please, sire," she continued, voice low. "Prince Gethen doesn't know what's happening. None of this is his fault. He just—"

Whatever Qaden was about to say was lost when Radovan's fist connected with her face. The strike was so filled with magic and menace it sent Qaden to her knees with a sharp cry. Blood poured from a cut on her cheek and her nose hung awkwardly to one side.

"Silence! I will have order." Radovan dropped Gethen, bellowing the words so loud Qaden cowered further to the floor. Everyone did.

Except me.

Because in his madness to punish Zosha and Gethen and Qaden, Radovan's hold on me had slipped. I was free. But only as long as I kept him distracted. Interested. Engaged. As long as I made sure his curiosity kept the worst of his insanity at bay.

I rose, clapping my hands in a languid display of sardonic pleasure. "Well done, Radovan. Blaming your innocent son. Beating your most loyal servant. The true monster emerges at last."

He turned to me, back straightening as he slowly rearranged the lines of his face—pulling back the rage. But that insatiable bloodlust never quite left his eyes, and none of us could unsee what he truly was.

"Be very careful what you say next, my dear."

The threat was delivered softly, like the snick of a blade leaving its scabbard. But I would not cower before this man. Not now. Not ever.

"Funny. I was going to say the same to you. Your facade has cracked, *my dear*. What will your beloved countrymen say when they hear you accused Gethen, of all people, for collaborating with me? Especially after you murdered twelve of them for assaulting him?"

A vein in his temple leapt at that. For the man who desired nothing so much as to be loved, letting his people see the truth of him was certainly terrifying. "They will do as they always have and trust my word."

My answering smirk made him flinch. "They'll never believe you. They'll see the real truth."

"*I am the truth!*"

I couldn't help it—I laughed. Genuine, surprised laughter.

He truly believed this.

All attempts at self-control vanished from Radovan's face, power erupting from him. Throwing back both enemy and ally alike. Zosha, Gethen, six of my men, and a full ten Roven soldiers were blasted away, like Radovan was the center of an explosion. And he was.

The Voyniks on the edges of the room started shifting uneasily, swords and power ready. But the confusion in their faces told me all I needed to know—they weren't quite sure who they'd be fighting. Not anymore.

Good. I would need their help—need their magic if I had any hope of destroying the Heart.

I tutted. "You're giving your men quite the story to tell. Not even your prodigious powers will stop it from spreading. A plague of whispers spreading across Tolograd, telling the truth: Radovan isn't in control. Isn't strong. Isn't sane. Who will be left to love you then?"

Radovan's face darkened. His eyes darted around the room, glaring at his own men—his trusted Voyniks—as if he'd never seen them before. Like his favored servants, all of them wearing gleaming green pendants filled with stolen magic, were something to be feared. But Radovan didn't know what it meant to trust. For a moment he almost looked like a child lost in the wood, surrounded by wolves.

I could see the solution come to him, see it in the way his expression cleared. Every muscle in my body tensed. Ready for what would come next.

He smiled. "You underestimate me, Askia, if you think a single one of them will leave this room alive."

Radovan flicked his hand. A wall of fire erupted from his fingertips, instantly incinerating the three Voynik's closest to the door.

An attack instantly returned by Illya. By Fyedik. And by Radovan's own men. As I rushed for the altar, I saw General Koloii and the ancient Wenslaus—two of Radovan's closest aides—send matching attacks of wind and water. But not against me or mine. Against Radovan. The other Voyniks followed suit. The temple erupted in a cacophony of screams. Magic boiled in the air, like the metal tang of a lightning storm. The earth of freshly dug graves. The fire of funeral pyres. The sickly stench of lies.

I dove behind the altar, pressing my back up against the stone. Just as I ducked up to grab the Heart from its top, a hand pulled me down.

"What the hell are you doing?" Qaden cried over the din of battle and death. "You'll get your head blown off."

"I'm ending this," I replied, attention tripping over her battered face. "What are you doing?"

"Getting you out of here." She swallowed hard, and I knew what the words cost her. Knew how awful it must be to finally admit that the man she'd served and loved all these years was a monster. "You can get us through a portal. I'll get you back to Vishir. You can—"

"No, Qaden," I yelled over the sound of the battle. "I can't go. This has to end. Today. I have a way, but . . ." I paused, eyes darting to Freyda, watching with a pained look on her face, to Ragata and Katarzhina even now trying to shield their sons from attacks they couldn't stop. "Qaden, you have to go."

"The hell I do," she growled. "If you're staying, I'm staying. I'll guard your back while you do whatever it is you're doing but—"

"I know about Mai."

She fell back as if I'd struck her. Not just hit her as Radovan had. But truly struck the very center of her being. "What?"

"I know about Mai," I repeated, willing her to listen. "Someday I hope to tell you how, but . . . *I know*. And if I fail here. If

Radovan gets my magic, he'll know about her too. Somehow he'll find out and he will kill you both. So you have to go. Take Zosha and Gethen and run. As far as you can. Take the girl too. Nekhaia is an earth witch. She'll take you through any portal you choose.

"But go. Now."

Qaden closed her eyes for a moment. Swallowed hard. And drew a blade, the same blade I'd stolen from her on the night we'd met. She pressed the hilt into my hand. "Thank you," she whispered. And ran.

I watched her for half a moment. She darted for Zosha, Nekhaia, and Gethen, zigzagging through the battle, keeping close to the ground. Qaden exchanged a handful of words with Zosha before they each took one of Gethen's arms and started for the door. Nekhaia trailed behind them, power shooting from her hands, giving them cover.

"Thank you, Askia," Katarzhina said as she and Ragata appeared by my side, the rest of my ghost companions following a moment later.

I nodded, hoping it was enough. Hoping they got out in time. Because my time had come. I looked up at Vitaly. *"Tell me when."*

He stood, scanning the battle, eyes surely tracing Radovan's every move. *"Hold."*

I went to the balls of my feet. Muscles tense. Ready.

"Now."

As if his words were a spring releasing, I leapt up. I threw my arms across the altar, seizing the Heart in my fingertips. In that half second, I saw the battle raging. I saw Wenslaus and Fyedik dead on the floor. Saw Illya bloodied as he let out an ear-splitting roar. Saw Voyniks diving between pews as they fired attack after attack at Radovan.

Radovan who deflected them all.

I dragged the Heart back over the lip of the altar. Cradling it in my arms. It was time.

Closing my eyes, I summoned my magic. It pooled in my fingertips, a swirling force hungering to be unleashed. The oldest force in the world. Death.

It built and built within me, screaming, *demanding* release.

I obeyed.

But the chain responded first.

I'd felt its punishment before, felt how each metal link grew warm. Then hot. I knew it would burn my skin until my chest turned red and blistered. Thought I could fight it. Even without Mav there to heal me, I thought I could push through. But this . . .

The metal didn't get hot, no. Hot implied that there could ever be such a thing as cold. This heat was molten. The enchantment responded to my gathering magic by turning livid red. Then white.

It didn't burn, it seared *into* my flesh. A blister would have been welcome, but this burrowed into my skin. Blood poured down my chest, my clothes burned. Embers falling from ruined cloth peppered the floor around me.

The pain was all I knew.

And then it stopped. I stopped.

I couldn't go any further.

When I could see again, the ghosts were gathered around me, faces filled with despair and panic. But I didn't see any answers to the question on my lips.

"What do I do?"

Eliska was shaking her head, attention torn and helpless as she looked from me to Illya somewhere behind, and back again. *"I don't know. Asyl?"*

But the Khezhari witch was lost too. *"Only Radovan can remove the chain. And he'll only do that once he has all your magic."*

"It'll be days before he has it," I said, the voice in my mind grinding out the words. *"By then everyone here will be dead."*

"Then convince him to take it off."

Ozura. Of course it was Ozura who said such a thing. Who else would? Who else in the face of such overwhelming odds would simply refuse to give up and just will the world into submission?

I looked up at her, ready to spew all my hate and helplessness at her feet. Stopped.

Because Ozura wasn't the only one who'd lived every day of her life forcing the world to sit up and pay attention.

I was too.

"Convince him to take it off," I repeated, not to the ghosts but to the universe. To the Two-Faced God. To the Heart.

And the words came back to me: *Remember daughter, the stone you wear needs many days to take your magic. But it only takes seconds for you to give it. Remember this. And choose.*

A shaky, wild kind of smile twitched at my lips. *"I can sacrifice my magic to the Aellium stone, can't I?"*

"Yes," Asyl replied, aghast. *"But why would you want to?"*

"The moment you do, he'll force you to marry him," Freyda said.

Siv nodded. *"And then kill you."*

"But he'll remove the chain first," I replied slowly, forcefully.

"You'll have to be fast," Ozura said, eyes glimmering with that rare approval—catching on while the others scrabbled to understand.

"What are you thinking?" Eliska asked, brow furrowed. *"That you'll be able to use the magic in the stone?"*

"I suppose it's possible—the marriage vows strike both ways," Asyl said slowly, but I had a different plan in place.

And it was time to move.

I rose and placed the Heart back on the altar. The temple around me was a storm of chaos. Magic fired everywhere, ricocheting off the walls and morphing in uncanny ways as Radovan met each strike and returned it tenfold. Of the fifty Voynik sorcerers and twenty Seraveshi witches, only thirty now remained standing. It was an inarguable testament to Radovan's power.

His face was bright with madness. Elemental magic spewed out of him. Fire and ice and stone erupted from his hands, from the very earth itself. A torrent of hell raining down upon my allies. Upon Illya. Because even watching only a few seconds, I could see the whole of Radovan's rage was aimed at Illya.

I didn't have time to think or second-guess. Didn't have time to do more than fling a prayer to the Two-Faced God: protect them. All of them: Nariko and Iskander in faraway Vishir. Arkady and the Wolves. Zosha and Nekhaia. Illya.

I sucked in a breath.

"Radovan!"

The world went still. Faces turned toward me. Faces filled with pain and terror, with bloodlust and death.

I dragged Qaden's blade across my palm. And slammed it onto the Aellium stone.

Radovan and I screamed as the stone took, in one terrible soul-devouring bite, what it had been trying for nearly thirty days to steal. Before I knew what had happened, I was on my knees.

But I wasn't the only one.

Radovan looked up at me through a curtain of scraggily red-black hair. Blood dripped from his nose, painting the floor beneath him.

He smiled. "That, my dear, was *very* foolish."

29

PERHAPS," I ALLOWED, pulling myself upright by the altar's edge. "But this has to end, Radovan. And really, this fight was always meant to be between us."

I struggled not to look at Illya. Not to let anything like softness enter my face.

Radovan prowled forward like a wild animal on the hunt. I saw the thread in him then. Not gold and bright the way I knew it should be, no. All that anchored him to life was a thin cord, brown and mottled, like rotting fruit left out in the sun. But no matter how sickening it was to see, it didn't lessen his will to live. Nor the cunning edge to his face as he watched me.

"So that's it then? You're just going to stand there and say your vows like a good little woman? No, Askia. You're up to something. But what?"

Those pale green eyes, like so much scum in a swamp, looked back at the carnage and blood in the temple behind him. The men and women around him drew back in fear of what they saw. "Let's raise the stakes while I think, shall we?"

Our twin stones flashed green. I had a second to brace for the coming pain, but a second wasn't enough. It burned against the already ruined flesh of my chest as magic cascaded outward from the altar in an awful rush. I struggled to open my eyes as

I heard a baleful groaning scream of stone. Like teeth buckling against each other, the earth heaved.

I righted myself and saw.

"What have you done?" The words clawed from my throat raw and heavy with agony that had nothing to do with physical pain. Because Illya—

"You turned them to *stone?*"

"I *encased* them in stone," Radovan said, voice ragged from the same pain I'd felt. "Slight difference, but the marriage vows do have to be given freely, my dear. So while you cling to whatever plan is forming inside that head, you must also wonder— how long can they survive in there before they suffocate?"

"Hurry, Askia," Eliska begged, going to Illya even as I locked my knees in place to stop myself from doing the same. *"Hurry."*

"Let's finish this."

"Indeed." Radovan smirked. But he didn't move to cut his own hand. Nor to grab mine. Neither one of us spoke as I watched his mind turn. Thinking, thinking, thinking . . .

And as he did, I gathered my magic once more—not using it—not yet. The tether's cool touch felt wonderful, a balm against my battered flesh. I opened my arms to it, welcomed it into my chest. I'd need every ounce of cool resolve to pull this off.

More magic.

More.

Until I couldn't stand it anymore. Until I was certain it would burst out of every pore.

Radovan's eyes dropped to my chest, raking along the length of the chain where it had burned so hot it embedded in my skin. Something in his expression clicked.

"Now I see it," he murmured. "You think, because of the vows—that you'll be able to use the stone's magic against me."

One of my eyebrows cocked. "Why not. You expect me to say my vows, but you'll say none in return?"

"*Lady Night, no,*" Eliska moaned, face wild with fear now. "*No, no, no. He's guessed your plan. He knows—*"

"*He knows nothing. Be ready,*" I ordered, voice all steel now.

"*But he'll never let you keep the stone. You won't be able to use our magic,*" Asyl hurried to say, face grave and utterly without hope.

But hope was all that now sustained me. Hope, which Freyda had once said was Radovan's cruelest way to torture, was the only thing keeping me on my feet. Hope was what would topple this monster.

"*I don't need your magic to destroy Radovan. I just need my own,*" I said, slowly, willing them to understand. By the way they gasped, I knew they did. "*Be ready.*"

"*We are ready. For a long time, we've been ready,*" Ragata replied, nothing lost or dreamy in her voice now. The promise of vengeance had brought the true witch out of her madness.

"It's not a bad plan, my dear," Radovan said, leaning closer now, close enough that I could smell the blood on his tongue. "But you have to be touching the stone to use it."

Before I could so much as flinch, his hand snapped out, and ripped the necklace off.

I barely felt it, my half-melted skin ripping away as the chain broke and fell. Magic filled me. Demanding release.

I obeyed.

I shoved it open, the hidden door within me, and marveled at the dark power coiling there. I'd spent so many years afraid of it, this second shadow that haunted my steps. But no more. The Marchlands opened inside me, the veil between life and death nothing compared to my determination, my desperation to defeat this monster no matter the cost.

The Marchlands answered.

White light leaked out of my skin. It coalesced in the space between Radovan and me, a swirling void. Inescapable. Unstoppable. Brighter. Brighter.

And through it, they emerged.

The six wives of Radovan Kirkoskovich, the most powerful witches the north had ever known, stepped through the door. Resurrected. Alive. Whole. For one last time. One last battle.

"Kill him!" I commanded.

They were all too eager to obey.

The elemental witches took the fore. Fire raced down Freyda's arms, dripping from her fingertips in twin whips. They coiled around her, tongues of flame lashing out, striking Radovan faster than any snake.

As Freyda attacked with fire, so Eliska did with water. Javelins of ice burst from her hands, aimed at Radovan's head and chest. He parried them both, but Eliska wasn't finished. Twin swords, their blades bluer than steel, grew from her palms. She twirled them and launched forward. Body lithe and sinuous, she danced on her toes, swords spinning, demanding blood. Never had she looked more like Illya.

Illya! The thought punched through me, pulling my attention back to where it needed to be: on the Heart.

I turned away, trusting the wives to keep up their attack, and reached for the Heart. With so much magic in the air, my own powers felt restless—like a living thing: anxious and brimming with life. Or maybe it was my own will to live, asserting itself at last.

I reached, and with my left hand, I touched the stone and felt that same will to live swirling in its prismatic depths. And in those depths, I sensed him. Sensed Radovan. His magic was no more than an extension of the stone now. In my mind's eye, I could see them, too, the resurrected queens of Roven attacking Radovan with fire and ice, with wind and earth, hobbling his body with healing magic now perverted and tormenting his brain with mind magic.

But it wasn't enough—not against the man who was willing to burn whole cities to the ground. Not to the monster who would kill children simply to teach his own court a lesson. Even with the Aellium stone burning—literally burning—molten hot on his chest, his shirt in tatters of ash and blood, he fought. And fought.

And was slowly turning the tide.

So I marshaled my strength. And as I prepared to unleash it, I saw it. A back door. A way out.

I saw the path from the Heart to Radovan's stone, the stone containing the souls of those six women behind me. If I could just release their souls . . .

Radovan would be powerless, wouldn't he?

Just another man?

The idea glimmered so bright and shiny it made my heart leap. Hope filled my limbs and I reached for it. Reached for the way to cut his strings.

And stopped.

"*There can be no half measures,*" the Heart said, in a voice that was my own.

Because even powerless, Radovan wouldn't simply give up and surrender. He would fight. A fight I might win, yes, but Illya and all the stone men and women behind us? I was no earth witch. Without the power of Radovan's Aellium stone, they would still die. Could I live with that? Sacrificing their lives so that I *might* live?

And what of the rest of the north? It would still be crawling with the sorcerers Radovan had made. Those sorcerers wouldn't simply let Roven fall, no. Another would rise and continue his work.

No.

No. This had to end.

Now.

I let my magic go. A torrent of energy unleashed within me—

not darkness, for that isn't what death is—or it isn't *only* darkness, but also light. An end *and* a beginning. A border that we all must cross, into something new. And old.

The tether reared up in me then. The cold of it made my lungs heavy, my skin brittle. I'd felt the chain burn my neck with its heat, but the tether burned with cold. I gritted my teeth, refusing to look away as the tether clawed at my left hand—no, not simply the tether. Death itself came tunneling through me, pillaging and freezing.

A killing magic granted by a god with two faces could only mean a death that cut both ways.

My fingers went blue. Then black. Every nerve prickled, then itched, then burned. Screaming, *screaming* as they died. A death knell echoed a thousand times. A million, an eternity, as every living thing in my hand slowly perished.

I was screaming too.

Screaming my rage. My desperation.

My hope in the face of certain death—my hope that through it, Seravesh and the world just might live. And I held fast. Through an agony that defied description, I held on and refused to bend. Not even an inch.

A different scream smacked into the back of my head. I didn't even have time to turn before the sword took me through the chest.

I looked down at the blade, my own blood running rapid down its length, and couldn't quite comprehend. I tried to breathe, to scream, but only a slight gurgle escaped my lips. Still, I watched with rapt fascination as my chest expanded over the blade and back again.

Then, with an awful yank, the blade was pulled free.

It hurt. I *knew* it hurt. But with the shock of it, I couldn't quite feel it. There was only that cold, radiating up my limp, useless left hand. A numbness now echoed in twin points on my chest and back. And a rushing sound in my ears, like a song on the coming wind. My knees buckled, but I didn't fall. He was there to catch me.

"So, so close, my dear," Radovan crooned in my ear. "You fought well, as any woman worthy of me would. But now it's time to finish this."

I was dead. I *should* have been dead. Should have bled out by now. My shredded, broken heart should have given its final beat.

But then, Radovan still needed me, I realized. He was using his power to keep me alive long enough, just long enough to steal my magic.

"You still need me," I whispered, my voice a tired rasp.

"For now," he agreed, all solicitous and reason again, now that my strength—and magic—had finally given up and his other wives had disappeared into death once more. "Give me your magic, Askia. Say your vows. And perhaps I will free your friends."

Give him my magic? The fool. Didn't he see it? Didn't he see the black veins polluting the Heart, and know?

I looked up at him and smiled. "But I've already given my magic, Radovan.

"You're too late."

His whole body flinched at the sound of the first crack, like ice shattering underfoot. Comprehension dawned, contorting his face with panic and terror. He hurled me away, more with magic than might. My body flew across the room, crashing into the far wall. I fell limply to the floor, like a puppet with no strings. The crunch of the impact blinded me, but I had no breath left to scream, for blood now wet the back of my tongue.

Death was careening forward. But I resisted it. Not out of fear. Out of duty. To witness this final destruction.

And though I was far away, I could still see. For I was linked with the Heart now, tangling me up in a web I'd never live to break free from. Because my fight had ended. At long last, I could lay down my sword. Tears filmed my eyes as I counted down the last few beats of my heart.

And watched, my soul singing a prayer of peace to the Two-Faced God, as Radovan reached the Heart.

He marshaled all his powers. But I knew he was too late. The Heart began to collapse, a tiny pinprick hole swirled in its center. Swirling and growing, an eye of darkness no mortal should ever behold. It fell in on itself. Devoured itself. And wanted more.

It exploded—a dark star unchained.

Radovan unleashed all his stolen power.

Magic met magic in an all-consuming flash of white light. Light that stripped his flesh from sinew and his sinew from bone.

I was still smiling when the light crested over me. And the world went black.

30

I WAS FLOATING. Warm water rocked me back and forth. I could feel it rinsing blood and grime from my clothes and gently tugging the tangles from my long hair. Light shone on my face, warm and welcoming and peaceful. I opened my eyes, yearning for it—yearning to see that liminal line of light that defines the boundary between day and night.

Instead, I saw a crimson canopy overhead, yards and yards of plush Graznian velvet. I cried out in incoherent surprise as my body and soul struggled to come back to alignment. Arms encircled me then, strong arms and the smell of pine and snow.

Illya. Tears ran down my face as I clung to him, and he kissed them all away, rocking me gently until my heart and mind were ready for speech. For answers.

"How?" I managed to ask, as he helped me to sit up on the bed—my bed, I realized, from my room in Tolograd. All the finery the room once lacked had been restored. Not just the bed's canopy, but the curtains and tapestries too. It was the first sign that I was no longer a prisoner. I was free.

The first, but not the last, for I wasn't surrounded by enemies. Arkady and Zosha, Mav and Qaden were all there, too, as were Vitaly and Ozura, ghostly forms dappled by the light of a bright, merry sun.

Illya sighed, sitting beside me heavily. "It was Radovan, of all people. I could still see—I think he wanted me to see—even encased in stone. So that I would have to watch him kill you. Instead, I saw you trick him into unchaining you. Saw you . . . bring back Eliska, and the other queens." His voice hitched there, a pain that I knew would never quite ease darkening his expression. I reached out and squeezed his hand.

And realized with some dread that my left hand—and only my left hand—was swathed in a dark-colored glove. And completely numb.

I swallowed, forcing my mind away from it—from a truth I wasn't yet ready to acknowledge. "You saw them fight Radovan?"

"I did," he agreed, clearly marking the path of my gaze. "And I saw you kill the Heart. I saw Radovan . . . saw him stab you.

"After he threw you across the room, the Heart . . . *imploded* I guess is the best word? Radovan met the blast might for might—not enough to save his life, mind you. But enough to save us. That whole half of the temple collapsed, as well as the catacombs below. The impact of the magic cracked the stone encasing about a third of the witches. We were able to free the rest."

I swallowed the sadness at those losses. "And the Voyniks?" I asked, eyes darting to Qaden and back.

"Free as well," Illya replied.

"And already sworn in service to you," Qaden added, with a small, tired smile. "All hail Askia Poritskaya e-Nimri ibn Vishri Kirkoskovich, Empress of Roven and Vishir."

Zosha grimaced. "You're really going to have to find a way to shorten that."

The others laughed, but their words made me go still. From the corner of my eye Vitaly shifted uneasily.

And Ozura watched hungrily.

"Radovan and I never married," I said, careful to keep the fear of such a title out of my voice.

"We decided not to expose that particular fact to the court," Arkady said, striding to my side now, face beaming with pride.

But I didn't feel pride. "And you were both all right with that?" I asked, looking to Zosha and Qaden.

"Between Qaden and the Voyniks you saved in the temple, you have the overwhelming support of the army. And the Dorovnii are behind you too—especially those on the Council of Nine," Zosha said, shrugging like he knew the news wouldn't please me. "We can't simply leave the throne empty. Not even for a few hours."

Qaden crossed her arms and nodded. "Better the Red Widow on the throne than some vengeance-mad Dorovnii or power-hungry Voynik," she said, shaking her head. "Radovan made sure there were deep scars between us all here. It's going to take a lot of time to heal them."

"Red Widow? Is that supposed to be me?" I asked, not sure I wanted an answer.

"Got it in one," Qaden replied, cocking an eyebrow. "What? You don't think you've earned it? Your husbands do have a tendency to die rather spectacularly."

"Something the young prince of Raskis might want to keep in mind," Arkady added. He was smiling as he spoke, but something hard passed between the two men that had me bristling. There was a story there, I was sure. But I couldn't pick at its threads—not yet. Not when it was undoubtedly rooted in questions of loyalty. Of duty.

"It seems like an incredible amount of work has already been done. How long was I out for?"

"Three days," Illya began, rubbing his eyes. "We found you in the rubble, barely alive. Mav was able to get you stabilized, and he's been working to heal you nonstop."

I smiled at the older man as he rose rather stiffly from his chair and circled around the bed by Arkady. There was a tightness to

Mav's expression, I noticed. And worry. "I've done my best, my lady, but I'm afraid it's not all good news."

I nodded, mouth suddenly too dry to form words.

"When Radovan stabbed you, he injured part of your heart. I was able to repair much of the damage, but I don't think it will ever function as fully as it once did."

"Ah. I see," I managed to say, although I wasn't quite sure I could truly parse his words. Not fully. I'd been so preoccupied by being alive, by seeing my friends and by the political ramifications unspooling around me even now, that I hadn't spared a thought to the injury I took at Radovan's hands.

And for the injury I did to myself . . . "And my hand?"

"That is more of an enigma, my lady. The muscles and tendons, the bones are all individually whole. They're just . . . no longer working together. The nerves themselves are all dead—an aftereffect of wielding your magic, I believe. If you look," he said, reaching for the glove until I caught him.

Stopped him.

"I know what it looks like," I murmured, remembering the way that dark blue-blackness of hypothermia and death had crept up my hand, my forearm . . . I didn't need to see it. Didn't want to see it. Though I'd come to love everyone in this room, some things were best done alone.

Mav's gaze was filled with understanding. "Well. One never can tell with magical injuries. Perhaps in time you will recover feeling."

I managed a small nod, but in truth I knew I'd never regain the use of the hand. I knew it was such a small, small price to pay for destroying the Heart, but . . . but so much of my identity was wrapped up in the physical strength of my body. And now to hear that not only was my hand useless, but my heart injured too?

"Hey now," Illya said, nudging me as if he could sense how

deeply this blow was felt. "There are plenty of fighting styles that only require one hand. And your heart . . . well, you'll just have to take things slowly for once."

The words were balm enough that I was able to truly smile. The thought that Illya would be there with me, every step of the way, curbed some of the pain. If only for a moment.

But the moment couldn't last. There was work that needed doing. A way forward that I still needed to forge. Decisions needed to be made. Decisions about the future. About the north and Vishir. Decisions about my place in the world.

They'd been a long time coming.

I looked up at Vitaly and Ozura. They were my two guiding stars. But so often of late, they had been pulling me in opposite directions.

So. Which way to go?

I didn't really need to ask.

Because the thing was, I already knew the answer.

I turned to Arkady and Zosha. "I need you to summon whatever leadership remains of the conquered kingdoms. Day Lord willing, they will agree to use the portals to come here."

"Already done, my lady," Arkady said, shocking me into momentary silence.

"News of Radovan's death traveled fast," Zosha added with a smug smile. "The Council of Nine made sure of that."

"Now they're all crowded in the Great Hall, ready to bite at anything that moves," Qaden grumbled. "The sooner you talk to them, the better."

"All right." I nodded, wishing nothing more than to throw the covers over my head and stay where I was. "I'll need to bathe and dress—can you send in a servant?"

She mumbled her assent and turned to go but halted when I called her back. "Make sure that you, as well as whatever remains of the Voynik leadership, are present when I come to speak.

Zosha, if you could do the same for the Dorovnii—whether or not they were part of the Council of Nine, I want them there. And if you would also go into Radovan's study—he told me he kept copies of letters he's sent to the Shazir. Please bring them to me."

The men and women around me all wore identical looks of confusion, but I didn't elaborate, turning instead to Illya. "If you would please inform our guests that I will be down to speak in two hours," I said, my throat almost too tight to speak.

But now wasn't the time for weakness.

"Consider it your final command as captain of my guard," I said and let go of his hand.

He recoiled as if struck, face uncomprehending.

I glanced at the others. "Give us a moment, please," I murmured, banishing living and dead alike.

Only Arkady tried to linger.

"No," I told him, standing my ground with a firm look. "Leave us."

I knew there were a hundred things my old general wished to say to me, and I would listen when there was time. But I didn't need his advice on how to move forward. Especially not when it came to this.

To Illya.

Olexan.

I took a deep breath, cursing my eyes as they began to water, and looked up at Illya. "I want you to know that what I said in the temple . . . I meant every word of it. I would have loved that life."

"But we can still have it. Askia—"

I reached for his cheek, pulled his face close to mine. "I hope so," I whispered. "Lady Night have mercy, I hope so. But everything that led us here, that brought us together—casting off your name, serving as my guard, protecting me—you did for love of

Raskis. I *understand* that. I understand what it is to love your country, to sacrifice everything for it.

"I need you, Illya. But Raskis needs you more. And I think you need it," I whispered, eyes filming with tears. "If there is any hope of a future for us, we both must look to home now first."

There were no words then, but tears and long kisses, heartfelt embraces. And a single promise for a not-too-distant spring, where we might finally meet in that little mountain town. Meet and claim a future. Together.

He left when the maid arrived, taking my already wounded heart with him.

The tub was nearly full by the time I drew my attention and found a familiar face folding the covers back on my bed.

"Your bath is ready, Your Majesty," the old woman said, her voice husky from many long years of disuse. Husky, yet beautiful all the same.

"What is your name?" I asked, smiling in wonder.

"Mila."

"It's nice to meet you, Mila."

"And you, my lady."

"I don't suppose you've seen Prince Gethen?"

"I have. He is doing well and has taken quite a shine to your young Khezhari witch—Nekhaia I believe she called herself." Mila shook her head, with a soft smile. "She is a fearsome young thing, but I think Gethen will be far less lonely for knowing her. Come, let's get you washed while the water is warm."

She spoke to me then, a steady stream of words and stories, as she helped me bathe and dress. At first I thought she was so filled with unspoken words she simply couldn't keep them in. Then I wondered if it was meant as a kindness to distract me from the necklace of scars that matched those on my neck and back, marring my chest where a chain once sat, or the mottled flesh of my lifeless hand.

But no. As I listened, I realized her stories weren't of herself necessarily. They were of Roven. Of all the many men and women who lived, faceless in the city below. People who toiled and laughed, lost and mourned the way everyone did. Her words weren't chatter, I realized. They were testimony.

"Why are you telling me all this?" I asked, watching her, my gaze steady.

She set down the hairbrush and gave me a long assessing look. "I know that what Roven has done in the north is . . . well, it's nigh unforgivable. And I know that the people here—the ordinary people—aren't blameless. But we aren't victimless either.

"I pray you remember it, my lady, when talk comes of what to do next. I'm not saying we don't deserve to be punished. But we'll never find peace, true peace, if we keep on harming each other."

While she'd started speaking with such surety, her voice shook now. It was a terror that echoed to the very center of her being, where a tiny golden strand of light wavered in fear of me. In fear of my reaction. The fear that she might have gone a step too far.

Ozura, glaring in white-lipped anger, certainly thought so. She'd appeared while Mila spoke, as if afraid I might now be swayed in a direction contrary to her liking.

"Asking for mercy? After all the devastation her people have caused?"

"You'd really punish a peasant for the work of an emperor?"

Ozura's face only hardened. *"I will forgive none of it. Not a single inch. And neither should you."*

I patted Mila's hand, but said nothing. Not when she finished setting my hair. Nor when she lay a fur capelet about my shoulders—its fabric marred with a hastily stitched coat of arms: the Roveni falcon, the Vishiri lion, the Seraveshi wolf.

"Fitting," Ozura mused, looking at the crest, her whole body

humming with pent-up energy, *"if premature. There won't be a Vishir to return to if you don't get there soon. You have the might of Roven behind you now, Askia. I hope you see that. There will be nothing Enver can do to stop you from the Lion Throne. You and Iskander. You can finally take the Shazir down too. The power is yours."*

I didn't reply. Simply rose and went to the door. Arkady was waiting for me with a ready arm, helping to steady me. I hated that I needed the support. But my left arm felt unnaturally heavy, ready to pull me over with every limp swing.

Or maybe the feeling was more to do with the added weight of duty piling upon me. Heavier and heavier with each step. For while Ozura continued her litany on my responsibility to Vishir, Arkady had taken up the same song—but not only for Seravesh. For the whole of the north.

And there was Vitaly beside me, wondering in silence. I could feel it, read it on his face. Was my staying in power a foregone conclusion? Empress of the world?

And what did that mean for Seravesh?

These thoughts filled me as we descended the stairs and crossed the short corridor into the Great Hall. The cavernous space seemed smaller somehow, as if Radovan's mere presence had elevated it into something vast and unassailable.

Now it just looked like a slightly gaudy tower, echoing with the fission of distrust and decades-long anger. Men and women hailing from across the north stood in clumps throughout the space. Separate. They eyed each other, gazes filled with contempt and suspicion. Gazes they all transferred to me as I walked in.

I let go of Arkady's arm, raised my chin slightly and cut a path through the center of the room. A whisper of sound chased me down the length of the hall, and the soft murmur of *Red Widow* bounced off the rounded walls peppering my face. As if the nickname had become a curse. Perhaps it was.

I ascended the dais and sat in Radovan's throne. As Arkady

took his place at my right, and my Seraveshi close guard arrayed themselves at my back—intermingled with Qaden and her Voyniks—I looked out on the gathered crowd and felt a moment of despair.

Everything I had long labored for was in reach. Seravesh was so, so close to freedom I could taste it.

But even now, Radovan remained. Not physically present, and I prayed that Lady Night kept his ghost locked firmly away—but in spirit he lingered. A shadow that no one gathered could quite shake. I could see it. The fault lines running through the crowd. See how grasping for power and for vengeance would slowly tear the north apart. Cast us all into chaos—a chaos from which we might never reemerge.

In that despair, I finally understood. Understood the urge to close my fist on the power this throne represented. For in my hands that power wouldn't be evil. I could use it for good. Set the north to rights. I could be the impartial eye that commanded peace and ensured justice. I could . . .

I could . . .

I could become Radovan.

Vitaly appeared, barely visible beside Arkady and Ozura. His gaze was filled with empathy. With understanding. Because he knew. He always knew the avenues my mind struggled down. Knew how hard it was to trust, and to let others go their own way.

He'd been trying to warn me all along. From the moment Ozura had come to me and placed the responsibility of Vishir's future at my feet. Just because I *could* claim the world as my own, didn't mean that I *should*. For no one was incorruptible.

Not even me.

The crowd had begun to shift nervously as these thoughts raced through my mind. The feeling of their impatience, their fear, had even Ozura looking worried. I didn't have the luxury of showing my concern. Not to so many strangers. Not even to my friends, I thought.

I let my eyes shift to Illya. He stood tall in the crowd, surrounded by a knot of his own countrymen. He met my gaze, the one lone spot of calm in a sea of fear. He nodded slightly, a vote of confidence that lifted me up.

Over his shoulder I spotted Nekhaia and Gethen slide into the room. The young witch shot me a sardonic salute before leading Gethen to an empty table. Zosha came in behind her, a case clenched in his hands. He gave me a questioning look, and I shook my head—a silent command to wait.

I crossed my legs, leaning back in my chair. The picture of certainty that the people around me so needed.

"For those of you who don't know me, my name is Askia Poritskaya e-Nimri. Wife of the late emperor Armaan ibn Vishri . . . and of Radovan Kirkoskovich." That last untruth left my tongue unwillingly, but exposing the lie Qaden and Arkady had told in grasping for stability would only undo everything we could now attain. Still, it was bitter, knowing that my first act as Empress of Roven was to lie.

"Thank you all for coming and witnessing the start of a new day—a new future for all of the north. There is much that this council will need to discuss over the coming days and weeks, but before we wade into the murky waters of politics, there are a few things I must address."

I turned now to the Voyniks standing on the edges of the room. To Qaden on my left and to General Koloii—looking battle scarred and exhausted from fighting his onetime friend.

"For my first act, as Empress of Roven, I am ordering the immediate withdrawal of all Roveni soldiers and personnel from the territories conquered by the late emperor Radovan Kirkoskovich.

"In doing so, you will relinquish control of any portals to

the local authorities. I am trusting you both, General Koloii and Major Qaden Zima, to see it done efficiently and orderly, and I am trusting *all of you*," I said, pausing to look about the room, marking the faces of those representing the conquered nations of the north, "to see it done peacefully."

Voices erupted all around me, rising quickly with anger and hatred. But I refused to let it spill over. Refused to cede control of the room.

I held up a hand, and silence fell—unwillingly, perhaps even grudgingly—but it fell all the same. The aura of power this throne contained made even the most hate-filled people in the room quail. Perhaps not just that, I thought, as the name *Red Widow* fell like a mantle upon my shoulders. The legacy of a woman who'd been drenched in blood and secrets. My legacy.

It already chafed.

"As for the Voyniks currently stationed in Seravesh and Raskis: have them loaded on ships and sent to Bet Naqar. An emissary of my choosing will deliver—into Prince Iskander's hands alone—documents proving that Radovan was colluding with the Shazir to destabilize the Empire of Vishir."

"Askia, what are you doing?" Ozura demanded. *"You cannot expose the Shazir. Iskander won't have anyone left to support him!"*

"Should Prince Iskander act on that information, the soldiers will remain in Bet Naqar at his discretion, to use in his bid for the crown," I said aloud for everyone present, though my eyes were on Ozura. "If Prince Iskander decides not to act, the soldiers will withdraw and return to Tolograd immediately."

"You can't do this. You can't leave him there to fight alone."

"I'm not leaving him to fight alone. I'm giving him the tools he needs." I paused a moment, willing Ozura to understand. *"He has lived comfortable and secure in your shadow his entire life, Ozura. It kept him safe, yes, but it also stunted him. If he is ever going to grow up and earn his seat on the throne, he must stand alone. And he can't*

do that by cowering behind me. And he definitely can't do that with the Shazir."

"So you're just going to forsake him? Forsake your duty to Vishir?"

"Whatever duty I might have had to Vishir died with Armaan."

"Vishir is your home."

I shook my head, knowing that the living crowd around me must be wondering what ghost was currently in their midst. *"Vishir is the land that birthed me. But it is not my home. Its future is not my responsibility, and it deserves a ruler who lives and breathes for it in a way that I do not.*

"And I'm not forsaking Iskander. I'm aiding him the best I can. It's up to him now, to accept that aid—and act on it."

"You can't do this," she said, tears actually swimming in her eyes. *"You can't just stay here—make me stay here—while Iskander fights for his life."*

"I can, Ozura," I said, imbuing my voice with all the power of command my magic contained. *"But I won't."*

Magic roiled within me, a tidal wave of power. And pain. It echoed up my left arm, stabbing through me so viciously, I'd have cried if I were alone.

But I wasn't.

So I endured.

Endured as ice crystals crackled up my left hand and wrist, drawing startled gasps from the crowd around me. As my vision narrowed, I saw several people draw back, felt fear build in the room. It was the deep rumble of Illya's voice that stopped them. Stalled the panic. It was a gift—him giving me the space to focus, not on the crowd.

On Ozura—and the rest she'd forsaken. I didn't know if it was allowed. Didn't care. Because for all that I'd suffered, the Two-Faced God damn well *owed* me this.

"You swore your soul in service to mine, to help me defeat Radovan. And now your service is ended. Go now in peace and with my thanks.

"Cross the Marchlands if you wish or return to Vishir where Tarek and Iskander are waiting. The choice is yours, Ozura."

Both hands covered her mouth as the edges of her ghostly body began to shimmer, casting prisms of light that only I could see. A constellation of emotion swirled in her eyes, too many and too vast to identify.

"Thank you," she whispered.

"Good-bye," I replied.

But she was already gone.

I gave myself one heartbeat. One single moment of silence and grief and hope.

And then I continued.

"My second order of business is to name an heir for this throne. Should this seat become empty, the crown will pass not to Prince Gethen"—I paused here, my eyes darting to the edge of the room, where Gethen sat at a table playing some kind of game with the ever-watching Nekhaia—"but to Princess Mai Kirkoskovich, full-blooded daughter of Emperor Radovan Kirkoskovich and Major Qadenzizeg Zima."

Qaden whirled on me, face bloodless. "No."

I wanted to apologize then. To beg forgiveness for the terrible weight I was laying upon a child I'd never even met. But I couldn't. Not here. Not now. "Yes, Qaden. It is Mai's right."

"But—but what about Prince Gethen?" Zosha asked quietly. He stood, I noticed, stranded in the empty space between the Roven Dorovnii and the delegation from Polzi, his mother's home. It made something twist inside me, seeing him alone, accepted by no one.

"We all know that Prince Gethen is not fit to rule. He would be made into a tool, nothing more than a proxy for those wishing for power. To ensure this does not occur, Gethen will become a ward of Seravesh. He will live out his days in peace and comfort under my care.

"Princess Mai, meanwhile, will have two regents to guide her. Lord Zosha, Major Qaden, this will be your responsibility." I paused then, willing them both to understand the full burden of what I was laying on their shoulders. "Zosha, you teach her everything she needs to know to be a fair and just ruler. And Qaden . . . you make sure she's strong enough to bear the weight."

"You've recalled the Voyniks. Named an heir," a stocky man beside Illya said, eyeing me closely. Suspiciously. "Does this mean you *don't* intend to take Roven as your own?"

I allowed the smallest, bitterest of smiles. "That's what you all came here fearing, isn't it? That I would take this throne, and all the lands it conquered. Stake my claim on Vishir. Instead of a mad emperor, you'd have the Red Widow, rising to take the whole world and rule it from this frozen keep."

I shook my head. "I understand why you would fear it. It's what many of you would do—whether or not you're brave enough to admit it to yourself," I said, shooting a knowing look at many of the finely dressed noblemen and -women throughout the room. "And you're right to fear it. You don't know me. But perhaps you know my story.

"You know I have traveled the length and breadth of this world. You know what I have sacrificed, you know the unspeakable losses I have endured to bring Radovan down. And I swear to you, I will not now become that which I spent so long killing."

More than one member of the crowd scoffed, still unconvinced. But I managed a smile, understanding how hard it was, after all the darkness we'd faced, to believe that a better tomorrow might actually rise.

"Queen Freyda of Graznia once told me that hope was Radovan's cruelest form of torture. She was right. And because she was right, I urge each and every one of you to join me in defying Radovan one last time.

"Hope doesn't have to be a weapon. Let it be the light that will guide us to a new and peaceful future.

"And in the name of that future, hear now, my last act as Empress of Roven: I hereby dissolve the empire, and relinquish all claim on this throne."

I rose in the echoing crash of my words and tossed down the cloak, letting the intertwined crest of Vishir, Roven, and Seravesh fall to the floor. "I join you now, an equal.

"I am Askia Poritskaya e-Nimri. And I am the Queen of Seravesh."

PEOPLE OF THE WARRIOR WITCH DUOLOGY

SERAVESH

Princess Askia Poritskaya e-Nimri

King Fredek Poritskii, Askia's grandfather (deceased)

Tasiya Poritskaya e-Nimri, Askia's mother (deceased)

Sevilen e-Nimri, Askia's father (deceased)

Goran Poritskii, Askia's cousin

General Arkady

Lieutenant Vitaly (deceased)

Captain Illya

Misha, a guard

Ivin, a guard

Fyedik, a scout and earth witch

Mav, camp cook and healer

EMPIRE OF VISHIR

Emperor Armaan ibn Vishri (deceased)

Queen Ozura, Armaan's principal wife (deceased)

Prince Enver ibn Vishri, son of Armaan and Na'him

Prince Iskander ibn Vishri, son of Armaan and Ozura

Prince Tarek ibn Vishri, son of Armaan and Ozura (deceased)

Queen Marya, wife of Armaan

Queen Hiriku, wife of Armaan

Queen Na'him, wife of Armaan

Lord Vizier Ishaq

Lord Marr of Tamett Province

Lord Gianno Trantini of Serrala Province

Lady Nariko Tatame of Kizuoka Province

Soma Lot-Na, a servant

General Ochan

Captain Nazir

ROVEN EMPIRE

Emperor Radovan Kirkoskovich

Count Dobor, Roven Emissary to Vishir

Branko, a fire witch in Radovan's service

Prince Gethen, Radovan's son

Qadenzizeg (Qaden) Zima, captain of Radovan's close guard

Jai Zima, Qaden's sister (deceased)

Lord Pjeder Tcheshin

General Kostya Koloii

Wenslaus, Radovan's adviser

Lieutenant Bora Roshko

Private Dimitri

Lord Zosha

THE SIX DEAD QUEENS OF ROVEN

Katarzhina of Nivlaand

Ragata of Polzi

Asyl of Khezhar

Freyda of Graznia

Siv of Switzkia

Eliska of Raskis

ACKNOWLEDGMENTS

THIS BOOK STARTED off as nothing more than a dream of a woman on a hill riding to war. It's almost impossible to believe that that dream has become my reality, not only because of an image that wouldn't fade but the many wonderful people I've met along the way.

Thank you, first and foremost, to my agent, Stephanie Kim. Debuting a novel—especially in a pandemic—is a wonderful and terrifying undertaking. Your undimmed optimism and ready advice not only made me feel like I was in the best of hands, but that I had a partner along for the ride.

Thank you also to David Pomerico and Mireya Chiriboga, who helped transform this story (and duology) into the wild ride it became. Askia's story would never have finished as beautifully without all your wisdom and support.

A huge thanks to Holly Rice, Angela Craft, and the entire Harper Voyager team for putting so much time and love and enthusiasm into these books. Your support means more than I could ever say.

A huge and heartfelt thanks to my beta readers and critique partners: Dan Scott and Claudia Berry. To my brother, Karl, and my dad for reading this book on a trip to Florida and being excited about it (even though it was a bit of a mess). To my dear friend Rachael Butterfield, who believes I can do anything. To Steve Berry and the whole of my D&D and Seventh Sea crew, for showing me that stories can live and breathe in crazy and unexpected ways—even when we have to take them online.

Love and gratitude to my parents and siblings and family and friends, who supported me through this strange and winding process and who didn't laugh me out of the room when I finally admitted I wanted to be a writer.

To my daughters, Lorelei and Nadia, to whom this book is dedicated. It never ceases to amaze me just how much you have both impacted and changed my life. I love you more than words can ever describe. And I can't wait to see the wonderful people you will grow to be.

To my husband, EJ. I will never be able to thank you enough for your support, your love, and your unending belief in me. You are my best friend and my guiding star, and I feel so privileged to be your partner in crime.

Finally, to Rain, who is not forgotten.

ABOUT THE AUTHOR

GRETA K. KELLY is (probably) not a witch, death or otherwise, but she can still be summoned with offerings of too-beautiful-to-use journals and Butterfinger candy. She currently lives in Wisconsin with her husband, EJ, and their daughters, Lorelei and Nadia, who are doing their level best to take over the world.